KISS ME NO MORE

Margaret Thomson Davis has lived in Glasgow from the age of three, except when evacuated during the war. She is the author of sixteen previous novels, an autobiography and over two hundred short stories.

KISS ME
NO MORE

Margaret Thomson Davis

ARROW

Published by Arrow Books in 1996

1 3 5 7 9 10 8 6 4 2

© Margaret Thomson Davis 1995

The right of Margaret Thomson Davis to be identified as the author
of this work has been asserted by her in accordance
with the Copyright, Designs and Patents Act, 1988

First published in the United Kingdom by Century in 1995

Arrow Books Limited
Random House UK Ltd, 20 Vauxhall Bridge Road, London SW1V 2SA

Random House Australia (Pty) Limited
20 Alfred Street, Milsons Point, Sydney,
New South Wales 2061, Australia

Random House New Zealand Limited
18 Poland Road, Glenfield
Auckland 10, New Zealand

Random House South Africa (Pty) Limited
PO Box 337, Bergvlei, South Africa

Random House UK Limited Reg. No. 954009

A CIP catalogue record for this book
is available from the British Library

Papers used by Random House UK Limited
are natural, recyclable products made from wood grown in
sustainable forests. The manufacturing processes conform to
the environmental regulations of the country of origin.

ISBN 0 09 935351 2

Printed and bound in Germany by
Elsnerdruck, Berlin

This book is dedicated to Mark Hamilton of Rock Steady Security Ltd with admiration. And to an undervalued profession – the teachers.

KISS ME NO MORE

kiss me no more, nor let
flesh fusion mar that other bliss,
wherein a firmer compact's set
to outlive far the transient kiss:
or if we kiss, then let it be
a seal of deeper harmony —
whose tremulous note, lingering still,
abjures the trumpet's blatant shrill.

red roses deep in shadows lie,
conceal an all-consuming fire,
who quickly plucked as quickly die
to yield too soon a petalled pyre:
white roses fair in sunshine shake —
no rabid hands those petals break,
but constant still breathe sweeter breath,
and live with life, and know no death . . .

— James Muir

I would like to thank all the people who helped with my research, especially Mark Hamilton of Rock Steady Security Ltd. for giving me so much of his time. Also John Milligan BSc, Murdo Mackay MA. Hon., and all the other teachers who spoke to me. Then there is Morag Ottley, BSc. MCSP who gave me the information I needed about stroke patients. The people who meet in the Knightswood Community Centre in Glasgow to share their experiences of living with a stroke victim and to help and support each other were also very kind. They invited me to sit in at their group meetings. All the people I have mentioned have a special brand of courage and dedication which I greatly admire.

Chapter One

'For better or for worse.' That's what Laura had promised. Now it was for worse. She had to keep reminding herself that she'd once been in love with Derek. As far as she was concerned, the man she'd loved and married twenty years ago no longer existed. He used to call her his little china doll because he towered head and shoulders above her. And her complexion was so fair compared to his tanned skin. Sometimes she'd gaze at his photograph and feel sad. Sometimes she'd smile and shake her head at how devil-may-care he'd looked in his RAF pilot's uniform. He'd been so proud of that uniform and his luxurious handlebar moustache.

Like so many wartime fighter pilots he'd faced incredible danger and seen many of his friends and their Spitfire planes blown from the sky. He'd had courage. There had been a recklessness too and a living for the moment. He had swept her into marriage. She remembered the breathless excitement of it all. Also the agony of never knowing, each time she kissed him goodbye, if he'd return from his next mission. She'd watched the dogfights on newsreels and trembled in case he was at the controls of one of the British planes swooping and snarling across the sky.

It had been difficult for him to settle into civvy life. It had taken him a long time to find a job and her teacher's salary had to support them both. His eventual post behind a desk in the office of a building society hadn't suited his personality.

'A monotonous dead end' he'd called it. Although in fact he'd been promoted more than once. To him it only meant being chained to a bigger desk. Nevertheless he kept on pushing himself, determined to make a success of his job, not to be defeated by it. And they'd continued to enjoy happy times together.

She could understand his frustration now. She had to fight to control her own negative emotions. There was a constant danger of her taking her irritation out on him and she knew she'd never forgive herself if she allowed that to happen.

Derek had had a stroke – a cerebral vascular accident, they'd called it at the hospital – a year ago, in August 1967. A year ago to the very month. And from that month he'd not only changed physically; his whole personality was different. She marvelled at how she'd put up with him like this for a whole year. Immediately she felt ashamed. She banished the thought from her mind.

It had been Derek who'd suffered, and in so many ways. Derek was the one who'd had to give up his work. He was trapped in the house all the time. She was able to escape to work each day, thank God.

She struggled to be kind, patient, supportive. Especially now that she'd been unfaithful to him. Not in body but in mind and heart and spirit.

She was in love with Robert Anderson, a colleague at school. Not that he reciprocated her feelings. At least not at first. He too was married, although he seldom mentioned his wife. If he spoke of anyone in his personal life, it was his daughter, Jennifer. He obviously adored the child. Laura had come to the conclusion that Robert Anderson would never leave his wife because it would mean deserting his daughter. Jennifer was his Derek. They both knew this. They didn't need to talk about it. Many a good talk they'd had about other things, though.

Not only at break-time. Often they snatched a few minutes in her classroom or his while the children were busy. The classrooms were divided by a glass-topped partition and often she and Robert would catch each other's eye and exchange secret smiles. Or they'd have companionable talks walking to her car after school. They both had a love of the ballet and the opera. Unfortunately Robert's wife didn't share his enthusiasm for the arts. Laura could just imagine Andrina Anderson's taste being more Mills & Boon than Mozart. Laura had got into the habit of giving Robert a lift home despite his protests that his flat in Monteith Row facing Glasgow Green was in the opposite direction from her bungalow in Bearsden.

2

He knew Bearsden well of course. His in-laws lived in Drymen Road just five minutes along from her place. She regularly saw his mother-in-law, Sophie McPherson, at the Drymen Road shops, often with Jennifer in tow. Sometimes Laura was tempted to introduce herself as a colleague of her son-in-law. She resisted the temptation. Sophie McPherson looked so severe with her tightly pinned back hair, steel-rimmed glasses and dark, restless eyes. Yet she was an extremely well-thought-of woman in the area. Mainly, Laura supposed, because of her energetic work for the local Church of Jesus and all the innumerable committees she served on. There would be no doubt that Sophie McPherson did a lot of good work. It was said of her: 'That woman never spares herself and she's had such a heavy cross to bear all her life, poor soul.'

Sophie McPherson's parents had committed suicide not long ago. Laura remembered what a stir it had caused. All Bearsden had been talking about the tragedy. The old couple – they must have been in their eighties – had saved up their sleeping tablets and taken them all at once one night. The home help had found them in the morning, with a note. 'Sophie, we're sorry' was all it said.

Apparently they'd neglected Sophie when she was a child, she'd been taken into care and they'd lost touch after that. They'd only met up again when Sophie and her husband, Andrew McPherson, came to live in Bearsdon. McPherson was a senior bailie of the City of Glasgow and a most influential man.

Robert never said much about his mother-in-law, except that she was too obsessive and hard-working for her own good. 'I wish she'd slow down and relax a bit more,' he'd confided. 'Her constant anxiety doesn't do Andrina any good either.'

Andrina was the McPhersons' only child and Sophie treated Andrina as if she was still a child. She was always worrying about where Andrina was and what she was doing – always phoning up or landing on the doorstep to check on her.

Laura didn't feel in the least sorry for Andrina Anderson. She'd seen her along Drymen Road often enough to form an opinion of her: tall, long-legged, auburn-haired, and with unusual, aquamarine-coloured eyes. Not a man passed but she'd slide him a pseudo-shy, sidelong look brimming with sexual promise. Despite Andrina's obvious beauty and elegance, Laura thought of her as a tart. It was Robert she felt sorry for. What with a mother-in-law like Sophie and a wife like Andrina . . . Even his father-in-law could cause problems. Robert said McPherson was always getting on at him about 'bettering' himself, moving to another school, getting promotion. Or even leaving teaching altogether. McPherson never gave up reassuring Robert that he could get him 'a really good job. A worthwhile job'.

As if Robert wasn't doing a worthwhile job already. He was a dedicated teacher. He was wonderful with pupils that some of the other members of staff had (after stressful years of trying their best) given up on. Many a time she'd gone with him to visit the home of some troublesome pupil in a last-ditch effort to contact equally troublesome parents. The parents would consistently have failed to turn up at the school to discuss their son or daughter's behaviour and had, one way or another, to be tracked down. The most common reason of the failures to respond to the school's invitations, pleas and – finally – demands, was that the parents just didn't care enough to bother.

Robert cared. That was one of the things she loved about him. No matter how hopeless either the children or the parents seemed, he refused to accept defeat. Most of the youngsters, and the parents for that matter, viewed art as a 'poncy' subject and it took a lot of guts and perseverance to awaken interest in it. Often she couldn't. Chaos would reign as she completely lost control of thirty or forty pupils in her charge. Most of them were bigger than her, which didn't help.

Then Robert would explode into her classroom and with one roar would silence them. Often his presence alone and that dagger of a stare with which he could strafe the room was enough to quell the riot. They knew that Robert was not a man to take risks with. They admired him. Many of the boys were in his karate club, which he ran in his spare time in order to keep as many of the children as possible off the streets and

4

out of trouble. For the same reason he organised outings to the country during weekends and summer holidays. Other teachers did this too, of course. Robert's outings were supposed to be for sketching and painting but the youngsters usually ran wild among the Campsie Hills or wherever they'd decided to go. The Campsies were a favourite place because they weren't very far from Glasgow and a bus went right from the centre of town to the Glen. Many a lovely memory she treasured of walking through the Glen with Robert, talking or laughing at the antics of the children.

Robert always said, 'It's better and safer for them to express their energies and aggression in the glens or the hills than on the streets of Blackhill.'

Blackhill was where most of the children lived and it was considered by many outsiders to be a 'no-go area'. Taxi drivers had been known to refuse to take fares there, or if they did venture into the area, they kept their head down.

As often as possible, Laura went on these outings with him – even though most of them were out of school hours, or at weekends. She had tried to persuade Derek to go away with her for a weekend or a holiday in the summer but he always refused. At one time he had been recklessly impulsive and adventurous. But that was for more sophisticated, rather than sporty adventures. He'd come in and suddenly announce, 'Right, get the glad rags on. We're flying off for a dirty weekend in Paris.'

She'd laugh and say, 'I know you – any excuse to get up in a plane!'

They'd fling a few things into a case and off they'd go. It would be a mad scramble to make the flight in time but they'd laugh and she'd be happy to see Derek happy. And on summer holidays they'd flown to some wonderful exotic places. Sometimes she was secretly tired of the long flights. Even nervous: they had experienced a few hair-raising near disasters in aeroplanes. It was then Derek really came to life. Danger seemed such an exhilaration to him.

Since his stroke he'd been literally grounded by a heavy iron calliper and the walking stick he had to use to steady him. It was painful to see his efforts to move around the house with the calliper swinging awkwardly out in a half-circle at every step. But even worse was the humiliation and frustration he suffered. Especially when he tried to eat. One side of his face had no feeling and often pockets of food would remain there unknown to him and later dribble out with excess saliva. Because of this he now refused to set foot in a hotel or restaurant or even to invite friends for a meal. Eating out was something he'd always enjoyed and he'd been quite a connoisseur of wines. Now it was a big enough ordeal and humiliation for him to struggle to eat a meal or drink a cup of tea in front of her. She was desperately sorry for him. She tried very hard not to feel disgusted.

Robert had been such a support to her in the first few months after Derek's stroke. It had been a devastating event and it had taken her nearly three months to come to any realisation of what had actually happened. She continued working as if in a daze. It had been her grieving time. After work she hurried to the hospital every day to see Derek, to sit holding his hand and telling him all her news of the daily happenings in the school. Derek, usually an irrepressible talker and raconteur, was silent. She felt forced to fill these terrible vacuums. It was during this time that she became aware that the silent figure propped up in the hospital bed was not Derek. She had lost the man she knew, the man she had loved and married.

Robert had covered for her at work, taken her classes when she hadn't been able to cope. He'd stayed after school with her to help with the work for the next day; sometimes he came home with her to help with the preparation. After Derek returned from hospital, Robert still did this.

She had to cope with so many changes. She was still overwhelmed. Derek had become emotional. Frequently and unexpectedly he burst into tears, and found this as difficult – probably even more difficult – to cope with than she did. It was a source of deep embarrassment and difficulty for friends as well. A grown man bursting into tears was not socially acceptable. Their friends would shuffle and clear their throats and look away. If it happened in Robert's company, Robert would say in his strong, confident voice, 'It's just a symptom of your illness, Derek. Don't worry about it.' Sometimes they'd even end up laughing together.

Once, driving Robert home from work, she had over-flowed with tears and had had to stop the car. Robert had put his arm around her and she'd said, 'It's just the thought of going home. Sometimes I feel I can't face it. You don't know how he was before.'

'Yes, I do. He used to call for you, remember. And there was that time at the school dance. Half the sixth-year girls fell madly in love with him.'

She smiled through her tears. 'I forgot about that. But it's not just his looks.'

'I know.'

'He tries so hard to retain some dignity and independence. He was always such a proud man.'

'He's still the same man inside.'

'No.' She shook her head and a fresh gush of tears forced her to make a quick search for a handkerchief. 'No, he's not. He's not the same man at all.'

She drove on, unable to talk any more, and Robert didn't pursue the subject. On arrival at Monteith Row, he put a hand over hers on the wheel and held it there for a long, silent minute before getting out of the car and watching her drive swiftly away. The time they spent together in her car had become very precious and her heart faltered when one day Robert had called at the bungalow to tell her of a last-minute change in a school plan. Instead of their usual run to the Campsies or Loch Lomond, he was hiring a minibus and taking the kids down to Newcastle to a karate display and contest.

'There's a Japanese master coming over,' Robert told Derek. 'Should be worth seeing. Why don't you come along?'

Derek made an attempt at laughter.

'Not my scene, old boy. All those super-fit guys doing their high kicks. And me with my gammy leg . . .'

'God, I'm sorry, Derek. I forgot . . .'

'It's OK. I'd much rather have somebody like you who forgets about my disabilities and treats me like a normal human being.'

7

'I could take you in the car,' Laura said. 'It would do you good to get away for a break. You're stuck in the house far too much on your own.'

Derek sighed.

'What I hate most of all is being so dependent . . . especially on my wife.'

'I'm getting a bit too dependent on her myself,' Robert said. 'It's time I had a car.'

Laura immediately felt apprehensive, but so far no car had materialised and they continued to enjoy their outings together. She had become increasingly worried about him, though. Often there was a sad, faraway look about his eyes and his face was so gaunt. Worriedly she'd remarked on this and he'd just laughed and said, 'I've always had these lantern jaws. It doesn't mean I'm going into a decline. Maybe you should come along to the karate club some time and watch me in action.'

Later, he'd unexpectedly touched her arm and said, 'It's good of you to care about me.'

Then one day, in the car on the way to his house, he'd asked if she could stop at a café, so that they could talk. They'd never had any difficulty talking in the car before.

She was curious, excited, apprehensive, hopeful. She didn't dare think what there could be to hope for, or to get excited about.

In an ice-cream shop with grey and black marble-topped tables with ornate iron legs, they'd ordered coffee and sat opposite each other in silence until the steaming cups were set in front of them.

'I'm leaving St Francis,' Robert said.

'Leaving?' Laura was incredulous. 'Giving up teaching?'

'No. I've got a promoted post. Head of department.'

Laura felt ill. The marble table was sending an icy chill from her hand along her arm. Her ribcage, even her skull, was freezing.

'Where?'

'Not far. Sinnieglen. I can still keep the karate club going – and include the same crowd if they want to come to the Sinnieglen drill hall after school hours.'

'St Francis boys going into a Protestant school?'

'Sinnieglen is – to use the latest jargon – non-denominational. There's some Catholic pupils on the roll, as well as a few Jews and even Muslims, I'm told. There's a wide catchment area too. Not only Riddrie and Blackhill but Ruchazie, Cranhill, Provan.'

'All you need in that lot is Possilpark and the Gorbals.' She sounded bitter and she felt bitter, but it wasn't because of the toughness of these particular areas of Glasgow. It was because of life in general – the unfairness of it.

'We can still keep in touch,' Robert said.

'Can we? How?'

He was silent for a moment.

'This is one hell of a situation.'

'I know.'

'If it had only happened before Derek's stroke . . .'

'Don't you talk about Derek to me.'

She gave way to shivering, allowing her whole body to be possessed by the terrible chilling cold.

'Just you get on with your new life – your great promotion. It'll mean more money of course. You'll be able to buy a car.'

Laura rose, almost knocking over her coffee cup.

'Darling, sit down. Wait, please . . .'

She couldn't bear him calling her darling. It was too much.

Chapter Two

The 25th of August 1968 would be special. That's what Andrina had thought. It would herald a new era of freedom. She looked forward to it. She had woven passionate dreams around it. It meant she would have more wonderful hours to enjoy with her lover.

It was her daughter Jennifer's first day at school.

'Don't want to go.' Jennifer's face clamped hard. Everything about her small body took on a stubbornness that rooted her to the ground.

Andrina had not reckoned on this. Jennifer had only played a small part in her dreams, floating off gladly to school where she immediately made lots of nice little friends and was perfectly happy.

'Darling, you'll love it.' Andrina's eyes were more childish in shape than the little girl's. 'There'll be lots of other children to play with and the teacher will give you Plasticine and show you how to make things. And if you're a very good girl and try very hard to please her, she'll maybe tell you a story.'

Suddenly Andrina had a disturbing feeling of *déjà vu*. She remembered how her mother used to say to her, 'If you're a very good girl and try to please Mummy, Mummy will maybe come and tell you a bedtime story.'

She'd tried to please her mother, was still trying, and with little more success than she'd ever had. But she *wasn't* her mother. God forbid that she'd ever be like Sophie.

Andrina hunkered down in front of the child, making her skirt ruck up and reveal a shapely expanse of thigh. (That certainly wouldn't have pleased Sophie.) Her heart melted with love for her daughter. Already Jennifer was losing her baby plumpness. It looked as if she was going to be tall like her mother and father. She had Robert's almond-shaped grey eyes instead of Andrina's round turquoise ones, and Jennifer's hair, caught severely back in two ponytails, was brown like

Robert's. There wasn't a hint of her mother's warm auburn tints. Only time would tell if she'd inherit Andrina's sexy curves, as her lover, Bernard O'Maley, called them.

At the moment, despite her stubbornness, Jennifer looked helpless and vulnerable in her bulky blazer, too-long gym slip and clumpy new shoes. A stiff leather schoolbag was strapped to her back.

'I liked school when I was your age.'

'You don't want me any more,' Jennifer said unexpectedly.

'Oh darling, that's not true.' Andrina snatched her daughter into her arms. 'What a terrible thing to say. You're Mummy's little girl. I'll always want you and love you.'

Jennifer's words had shaken Andrina so much she barely had the strength to get to her feet again. Had the child sensed the real reason she had been left so much with other people over her five short years? Not with friends. Andrina had long since lost touch with friends she'd had before her marriage to Robert. But with Sophie? With neighbours? With Robert? Every moment of her time, any time she could beg, borrow or steal, had been spent with Bernard. She felt a thrill at the mere thought of him.

It was impossible that the child had any idea of the truth, she assured herself. Even though she knew Uncle Bernard – as she called him. Even Robert didn't suspect anything. He and Bernard had been friends for years. Bernard had once been a pupil of Robert's at St Francis. Then he helped Robert in the karate club that Robert ran, and he still 'worked out' and helped as often as he could when he was in Glasgow. But Bernard's security and protection business was growing and when he wasn't working nights in Glasgow, he was travelling around the country.

'Now, no more of this silly talk, Jennifer. Take Mummy's hand and we'll go and see the nice school, and meet Miss Chisolm and all the other little girls and boys.'

Jennifer refused to budge. Her brows lowered. Her lips pressed tightly together. There was a desperation about her that was both pathetic and infuriating.

'Please, darling, try to understand.' Andrina gave a tug at

the small hand. 'It's the law. Whether I like it or not, whether I want to or not, I've got to take you.'

'Don't want to go,' Jennifer repeated, stiffening her legs and digging in her heels.

'Stop saying that, Jennifer!' Andrina didn't mean to sharpen her voice but she was getting harassed. 'You're going and that's all there is to it.'

Jennifer capitulated quietly. Too quietly. Andrina couldn't help remembering her own childish fears of being taken to school for the first time. No, her emotions had been stronger than that. Terror would be a more accurate word. Terror and panic that she'd never see her mother again. But there could be no comparison between her childhood and Jennifer's. Jennifer had never been neglected as a baby, left alone for cold, dark hours without food and adequate clothing, or as a toddler, fearfully aware of gathering darkness and the pit of total abandonment. Jennifer could have no idea of such things. All right, she'd been left alone once, just for an hour or two, but that was different. She'd been warmly tucked up in her cot. She'd also been put in a day nursery for a couple of hours twice a week, and hadn't liked it. Indeed, if Robert had seen his daughter dragged there screaming in protest, he would have been furious and forbidden her to take Jennifer again. But Robert had been safely away in Blackhill. It had been easier to persuade him that nursery would be good for Jennifer than to convince her mother. Robert, being a teacher, could appreciate the idea that Jennifer would benefit from mixing with other children and from the educational type of games and toys he imagined she would enjoy.

Sophie had always been the difficult one about everything. Often Andrina felt bitter about the high standards her mother set for her and the neurotic and constant way she checked to make sure that there was no hint of backsliding. Who was Sophie to insist on such perfection? She had been far from perfect herself, and in more ways than one. In the early days, Andrina had heard her father accuse her mother of 'going with every Tom, Dick and Harry while I was away at the war . . .' And 'I was never so horrified and ashamed in all my life when I found out how you'd been neglecting that child. You'd actually been reported to the RSPCC!'

Of course everything changed when her mother had joined Father's church, the Church of Jesus, and been 'saved' and 'born again'. Andrina was nine or ten years of age but by then abandonment and the panic had burrowed into her very soul. Even yet, at thirty-one, she was totally unable to rid herself of these emotions. She could pretend she had. She could live and laugh and love and seem to be coping perfectly. But it only took a suspicious look from her mother, a sharp criticism, the threatened withdrawal of imagined affection – for Andrina doubted if any affection had ever been there – to pull the panic switch.

Emotionally, she pitched back into the terror of being abandoned in icy darkness. Her common sense kept telling her that this was nonsense: she was safely married with a husband and a child of her own. Common sense, however, had nothing to do with it.

Both she and her mother had always spoken about Andrina's being 'safely' married to Robert, but for different reasons. Sophie thought she was saving her daughter from the wicked lusts of the flesh. Robert, like his mother, was a member of the Church of Jesus the church for which Sophie worked with such energy and zeal. Robert was a decent Christian man, Sophie insisted, not like 'that disgusting Pape' – meaning Bernard. Her mother had hated Bernard from the moment she'd first set her flinty eyes on him. She'd forbidden Andrina to go out with him because of his religion, but it was obvious that the more compelling reason for her hatred was that – to use her own word – he was too 'physical'.

Her father had tried to say that he thought Bernard seemed 'a nice enough lad, polite-spoken and ambitious to do well'. He'd been won round to Sophie's way in the end by the indisputable fact that Andrina was far too young. She'd been only fifteen when she'd first met nineteen-year-old Bernard, and even more intimidated by her mother than she was now. She'd been a very well-developed and sexually aware fifteen, however. It seemed as if she had been eagerly awaiting someone like Bernard to arouse all the passion that her curvaceous body contained. He had lit the flame, and even though they had often been parted for days, weeks, months, and sometimes even for years, the flame continued to burn. It consumed her still.

She kissed Jennifer goodbye in the noisy bedlam of the 'baby class' and left her in Miss Chisolm's care. Some of the other mothers loitered about anxiously watching, until Miss Chisolm firmly shooed them away. Andrina too felt the tug of love and at the last minute was reluctant to part with her daughter. It was distressing to look at the child's white, tense face. She assured herself, however, that she had every confidence in the teacher. Jennifer would soon settle in and be perfectly happy. The thought helped Andrina escape from the classroom and out to the echoing well of the corridor. It was strange how schools were such hollow, echoing places. Even when they were busy and noisy, they had a ghostly clangour.

She shivered. Not because of the atmosphere in the school, but at the thought of the danger and the excitement of what she was about to do. It had been decided long ago that she and Bernard shouldn't meet alone in her flat (although they sometimes did). For one thing, Robert often came home earlier than expected. Or his mother, despite her arthritis, came shuffling round. Mrs Anderson senior only lived across Glasgow Green in Adelphi Street. Worse still, her own mother might suddenly appear. Andrina broke out in a sweat at the mere idea of Sophie finding Bernard in the house alone with her. Neither she nor Robert mentioned to her mother the occasions when Bernard and his wife Jane came on perfectly respectable visits.

Robert often said, 'I know your mother's a bit of an extremist, Andrina, but I've never understood her hatred of Bernard O'Maley. And don't tell me it's just because he's a Catholic. It's more than that.'

A bit of an extremist? The understatement of the year, Andrina thought bitterly. Her mother was so extreme about everything, Andrina sometimes wondered if she was mad.

It had been decided that Andrina and Bernard would meet whenever possible in the home he now shared with Jane. It belonged to Jane and was a big villa in the prosperous district of Pollokshields. If she went there at night during the winter months she took a taxi. There was so much talk about the unsolved murders that had been taking place in Glasgow, people said it wasn't safe to be out after dark any more. Bernard would have preferred to drive her there and back but she wouldn't allow him to in case anyone saw them together. They had once used Bernard's flat in Sauchiehall Mansions but there had been no plausible excuse to keep the flat after Bernard got married.

'After all, you've got an office in town,' Jane said, 'and Pollokshields is only fifteen minutes or so in the car from Sauchiehall Street. Why would you want a flat there as well as a house here?'

Jane didn't often get her own way nowadays. At one time she'd been spoiled by her rich daddy and had sailed through life with perfect self-confidence, knowing she could get whatever she wanted. But the rich daddy was dead now, and all she wanted was Bernard.

It was a pity about Jane. She and Andrina had become friends and Andrina even liked her. Bernard had married her on the rebound after a terrible quarrel with Andrina: she'd told him she was finished with him and proved it in no uncertain terms by destroying his flat and everything in it in a jealous rage. Looking back, she realised it had been an unreasonable thing to do – especially when she'd told Bernard to lead a normal life. After all, she had Robert and Jennifer. She agreed with him that he couldn't be expected to live like a monk. Sometimes they didn't see each other for ages.

He kept asking her to leave Robert and live with him – marry him as soon as possible. He'd been divorced from his first wife for a long time by then. (Poor Doris! Andrina had liked her too; still saw her occasionally.)

The mere mention of marriage to Bernard never failed to panic her. Her mother would never forgive her.

'Have a girlfriend,' she'd told him. 'Lead a normal life. We'll still be happy being with each other like this as often as we can.'

But then she'd found out about Jane – beautiful, wealthy, self-confident Jane – and how he'd taken Jane to Paris one weekend. She'd flown into that terrible rage.

'Welcome home you bastard!' she smeared the walls of his flat with her lipstick after destroying the place. 'I hope she was worth it.'

Jane wasn't so self-confident now. Her original self-confident nature had shrunk into uncertainty, almost timidity. Once Andrina and Bernard started making love again, he couldn't make love to his wife. It had been the same with poor Doris. Andrina had never dared to tell either woman the truth, of course. But she had tried to comfort them (was still trying with Jane), and assure them that Bernard's neglect wasn't their fault. Jane especially was a beautiful, desirable woman. She kept telling her that.

'He's proud of you. He takes you out, doesn't he? He treats you well in lots of ways.'

'He refuses to take me to night clubs when I ask him.'

'But that's because of his job. He's explained the danger of that. I've heard him. He has the same attitude towards his family. He won't allow his brother near any of these places. It's because he cares about them and you . . .'

Jane had given a sad half-laugh then. She was never bitter like Doris.

'If only I could believe that, Andrina. Oh yes, he cares about his brother but as far as I can make out, he's completely indifferent to me.'

'Nonsense,' Andrina comforted. 'It's just his way. He doesn't show his feelings. Scotsmen are notorious for that. And in Bernard's job, that kind of hard-man image isn't just important – it's essential.'

Jane made a brave effort to brighten. She lit another cigarette.

'You're probably right. Now, enough of my troubles. How are you, darling?'

'I'm fine.'

It was such an understatement. She blushed as she said it. Bernard wasn't indifferent to her. Far from it. She felt adored and adorable. She felt saturated with sex.

'Just fine,' she repeated.

Chapter Three

It wasn't often the O'Maley brothers got together. Their mother was dead and their father Patrick still lived in the notoriously tough district of Blackhill. Frank lived in the 'arty farty West End', as his father called it, and was becoming successful as a poet and playwright. Tony still did gigs playing his drums but at thirty-six it was a bit late for success in that field. The competition was so young these days. Anyway, he'd never been that good. He had resigned himself to banging away in his spare time and had settled back into his old job in Herraty's butcher shop. He hadn't yet grown out of his Teddy Boy clothes and his ridiculous cockscomb of hair on top of his head.

Michael, Bernard's twin, had been forced to give up the boxing after losing an eye. But his alcoholism had been the real reason for his downfall. For some time he'd been on the wagon, thanks to Alcoholics Anonymous.

The reason for the get-together was to discuss Tony's wedding to local girl, Theresa MacGowan. Theresa's brother, Roderick, worked in Bernard's security business. The parents of Theresa and Rod were dead and they had no other relatives, so the O'Maley family had taken over.

Bernard had agreed to chip in a fair amount to the expenses. So had Rod. Frank had been very generous, but Tony, despite his regular job in Herraty's, never had a penny to his name. It was hoped that Theresa would have a good influence on him and would knock some sense into the man. But that was, they all knew, expecting too much.

It was a mystery to everyone what Theresa saw in Tony. All right, she was no raving beauty herself with her untidy frizz of hair and weight problem. But it wasn't just Tony's looks (or lack of them) that were enough to put anyone off. He was, as many people had said to his big buck-toothed face, 'a right bampot'. How would Theresa put up with the noise of him for

17

a start? Everything he did was at maximum decibels. Cough, laugh, talk, sneeze, snore, fart – he held the world record. Everyone agreed on this – even Theresa. So she wasn't going into the marriage ignorant of the facts.

Worse than all that though was his loud-mouth Republicanism even though he'd never been to Ireland or actively involved with the IRA.

'Aye, OK,' he said now. 'Whatever you like. As long as there's no Proddies at the wedding.' He cast a meaningful glance at Michael, who'd disgraced the family, in Tony's opinion, by marrying Caroline Stoddart who was from a Proddie family, if ever there was one. Her father, an Orangeman, had actually dropped dead a few weeks ago while on an Orange parade. 'Served him right,' Tony had said at the time.

Tony had, on occasion (when the family had been unable to restrain him), actually made his way through the ranks of an Orange walk. That had been one of the times he'd ended up in hospital. Tony was so anti-Orange he even refused to eat an orange jelly.

'Shut up.' Bernard impatiently dismissed his brother's attempts to be included in the conversation. Tony accepted this dismissal with good grace. For one thing, it was never any use arguing with Big Bernard. For another, despite his noisy reckless ways, Tony was 'a good-natured lump', as Theresa often loyally referred to him.

'That's settled, then,' Bernard addressed the assembled family, and prospective family.

There was a general murmur of assent. The wedding was to be a white affair. There had been some ribald remarks about this but only from Tony, who had been the one to announce that Theresa had 'a bun in the oven'. The union was to be blessed by Father Riley. Afterwards there would be a slap-up feed in the Co-op hall in Springburn. So far the Co-op, or indeed any other shop, had not ventured into the dangerous depths of Blackhill. One mobile van selling groceries and odds and ends occasionally nosed its way in but even though the van was reinforced with iron bars and wire netting and the driver kept at the ready to beat a hasty retreat, he had been held up at gunpoint and robbed.

The wedding date was to be sooner than originally intended –
right away in fact – because of Theresa's 'bun'.

'Right, I'm off.' Bernard rose. Michael spoke up.

'If Caroline can't come, you won't see me at the wedding.'
His father groaned.

'Since when have you listened, knuckle-head. Of course
Caroline can come. As long as you don't bring her old
mother.'

'Can you imagine it? Big Martha at a wedding in St
Stephen? She's a worse bigot than he is.' A jerk of Michael's
head towards Tony was unnecessary. Everyone inside the
family and far beyond it knew what Tony was like. Everyone
also knew the peculiarities of Big Martha Stoddart, and none
more than Michael. Caroline and their three children had
given up their nice wee room and kitchen in the Gorbals to go
out to the wilds of the Castlemilk housing scheme to live with
Big Martha.

As Caroline said, 'She needs help now that she hasn't got
Da. She's crippled with her phlebitis and arthritis.'

Everyone was sorry for Michael. The old woman had
always hated him. 'Ugly-looking Green Grape,' she'd spat at
him more than once.

If Tony was a stupid Catholic bigot, he certainly had his
match in Big Martha.

Of course nobody could deny that Michael was ugly, with
his broken nose and one eye. He kept the other – or rather the
lack of the other – eye covered by a black patch held on by a
piece of elastic stretched over his cropped head. It never ceased
to amaze Michael that anyone as beautiful as Caroline had
married him, had remained loyal to him through the hell of his
drinking, and loved him still. Never a day passed but he
thanked God for Caroline and the children. She was quite a big
armful now and her hair was as much grey as blonde, but he
still thought of her as his little Shirley Temple. They had been
so happy since he'd managed to beat the booze. If only Big
Martha would stay in the Co-op convalescent home in Largs
for ever and ever, Amen. She went there for a few weeks every
year and that's where she'd just gone now. He prayed for that
too. He lit candles.

'We want everything to be organised and settled for her coming home,' Caroline said. He wanted nothing of the kind, although he didn't wish her any harm. He wasn't a vicious man. Before they'd come to Castlemilk, he'd told Caroline that he'd be perfectly willing to look after the old woman and do his best for her if only she'd be a bit more reasonable. Caroline had just kissed him and said, 'I know you, Michael O'Maley. You'll do your best for her anyway.'

At least they'd be able to enjoy Tony's wedding without Big Martha breathing down their necks.

He said cheerio to Bernard and not long after that he too left. He could have got a lift home in Bernard's car but, not feeling the best of company, he preferred to get the bus. Caroline would be better pleased at that. She never said much against Bernard but if Michael said something good about him, she clammed up in tight-mouthed disapproval. She had never forgiven Bernard for refusing to help him when he was drunk.

'Called you a drunken bum. Wouldn't touch you with a bargepole,' Caroline kept reminding him.

It was true that Bernard had never given him any hand-outs, which was just as well. He would only have squandered the money on drink. Bernard had been quite right to refuse him. It was just the callous way he did it . . .

Michael thought that now Bernard could see he was off the drink, it might be worth asking him for a job in his security company. Caroline had put an immediate damper on that idea. She preferred him to stay as a brickie.

'I couldn't stand the strain of you working in Bernard's line of business. It was bad enough when you were in boxing. I'd never have a minute free of worry.'

She argued too that working on the building site meant he'd be out in the fresh air, which was healthier.

'Working with Bernard's firm you'd have to hang about in pubs and clubs and dance halls till all hours.'

He supposed she was right. Anyway, brother or not, there was no certainly that Bernard would give him a job. One thing was certain: Bernard was as hard as the gun he often carried.

'And of course,' Michael reminded himself, 'I need to keep fit to be able to deal with Big Martha.'

The thought of Big Martha and Castlemilk depressed him again. He hadn't really felt light-hearted since the removal. When it came to the bit there wasn't much to remove . The scrubbed kitchen table and spar-backed chairs, the room wardrobe. They had left the mattresses in the set-in-the-wall beds. Bit Martha had a four-room and kitchenette flat five stairs up.

'Mammy says we can have the big front room all to ourselves, and the children can share one of the bedrooms. It's very good of her.'

'Oh great,' he'd agreed without enthusiasm.

'It won't be so bad, dear, and it's nice fresh air out there. It'll be good for the children.' He knew it would be anything but good for him and Caroline, though.

Quite apart from the problem with Martha, Castlemilk itself wasn't a cheery prospect. The housing scheme was a great wilderness. It consisted of a few multi-storey blocks and almost everything else was three-apartment or four-apartment flats in grey featureless stone. Thousands of homes had been thrown up in no time at all and with an apparent lack of caring, or thought for the quality of life of the prospective tenants. Over 10,000 people had been crowded into the area. But only those people who were least able to get a house anywhere else and were desperate for anything took a house in Castlemilk now. Just to look at it weighed Michael down with depression. It was a giant-sized Blackhill. A wasteland without end.

He had spent the last night in the Gorbals house just appreciating it, and his wife and children. It was as if it was his last night on earth. Oh, the cosiness of it, the privacy of it, the happiness. He remembered watching Caroline strolling about the kitchen from the black range to the sink at the window singing softly to herself, plump flesh rocking like a lullaby. It always soothed him to watch her.

The children were playing on the linoleum. The twins, seven-year old Sean and Sally, were sticking scraps in a scrapbook, colourful bits of paper in the shape of angels and cherubs, and four-year old Maureen (called after his mother, God rest her soul) was on her knees tucking her dolly into the cradle he'd made for it. The doll had a stuffed stocking body and woolly curls. Caroline had made the doll and stitched on a mouth and eyes. She'd made the dress and knickers out of an old nightdress belonging to Martha. He'd remarked at the time that there was enough flannelette left over to make a parachute. Caroline had just laughed and made a pair of doll's pyjamas instead.

Maureen loved that doll. She was always fussing over it and kissing it and cuddling it. She would make a great wee wife and mother one day. Just like Caroline.

Sean had got bored with the scraps.

'Scraps are a bit sissy for me, Daddy,' he announced. 'Can I go out and have a game of football?'

'If it's OK with your mammy, son.'

Caroline, still singing, smiled her agreement.

'Can you come out and play with me, Daddy?'

'Sure, son, where's the ball?'

Sean's sturdy body was suddenly galvanised with energy and delight. 'I'll get it, Daddy,' he shouted, already half-way through to the front room, his tackety boots clanging on the linoleum like a miniature Clydesdale. Just about everything had been stuffed into the front-room cupboard.

'Look at my new scraps, Daddy.' Sally barred his path. 'Which do you like best?' She held up the book, its coloured-card pages rainbowed with shapes and figures she'd stuck on.

'These two cherubs,' he said, 'because they're the dead spit of you and Sean.'

Sally rolled her eyes.

'Don't be daft.'

'You calling me daft?' He stuck up his balled fists. 'I'll daft you. Come on, put up your dukes.'

His daughter giggled.

'Stop acting silly.'

Just then her brother came clumping back into the kitchen clutching a football.

'Are you ready, Daddy?'

Michael twitched his shoulders, winked his good eye, and rubbed his hands together.

'Fit and ready for anything, son.'

He only wished it had been true.

After they'd moved there had been so much time taken up travelling back and forward to work and the children travelling to and from school, they hardly ever saw each other. At least, not to relax together, or do things like kick a ball about. He was always hoping to devise ways of lightening Caroline's burden.

Big Martha weighed a ton and Caroline quickly became worn out with helping her in and out of bed and chairs. Martha was literally pushing Caroline into the ground. He took over as often as he could. Every time he was at home, in fact, it became his job to heave her up and down and stagger about the house supporting her. The doctor said her weight was causing most of the problem, but she was a bit old to go on a diet. Greedy, more like. She ate like a piranha. Really enjoyed her food. Any kind of food. Always had done. He began to feel as if he was slaving away on building sites just to keep up with paying for the food she consumed. And never managing to keep up with her. Sometimes he felt she was pushing him into the ground too.

Still, as Caroline said, she was an old woman. Allowances had to be made. With a sigh he got off the bus and trudged through the dismal streets of Castlemilk towards the grey building in which he now lived. Caroline hadn't come to the family conference about Tony's wedding because wee Maureen had been complaining of a sore throat.

Instead of taking the lift he ran up the stairs, the thought of being alone with Caroline and the family bringing a sudden rush of gratitude and pleasure.

Inside the house Caroline greeted him warmly. The children seemed pleased to see him too.

There was a different atmosphere. A lightness. No crushing weight, no disapproving shadow of the big Buddha tonight.

'Hip, hip hooray!' he shouted for no apparent reason. He flung his arms heavenwards and danced a Highland fling. Caroline and the children laughed.

It seemed a very long time since they'd all been so happy together.

Chapter Four

'Don't touch that!' Frank hadn't meant to sound aggressive but that's how the words came out. What he felt was more like panic. He couldn't bear his wife anywhere near his desk.

'I only wanted to help.' Bridie stiffened defensively. 'You used to let me read everything you'd written.'

That was true. He remembered how close they'd been during his early struggles. Right from the start, Bridie had been the only person who'd believed in him. They'd been happy in their wee room and kitchen in the Gorbals, the one Michael and Caroline had moved into after they'd left. Now Michael and Caroline had gone out to Castlemilk, he wouldn't be a bit surprised if Bridie, given half a chance, would return to the Gorbals. She didn't seem to realise that it was impossible to move the clock back. Life went on. Things changed. People changed. Bridie had changed.

Once she'd shared his dreams of getting a home with all mod cons. They used to lie in the cosy bed-recess with the fire sending shadows flickering all around, and talk wistfully about one day having a bathroom, and a bedroom so that they didn't need to sleep in the kitchen. They dared to dream of a guest bedroom, and a sitting-room, and carpets from one end of the house to the other, and washing machines and hoovers. Now they had all of these things and instead of being happy and fulfilled, Bridie seemed to be withdrawing from him, closing into herself. Often he detected a twist of bitterness on her mouth. Sometimes even a shadow of hatred passed over her face. He kept telling himself that it was his imagination. Imagination was his stock in trade, after all. Yet he knew that the kind of imagination a writer really needed was tied up with observation, instinct and intuition. It was the ability to get into another person's skin and understand what made them tick. He had made a lot of money doing that. At least, a lot more than he'd ever done as a clerk in the office of Goldmayers.

He tried to understand what made Bridie tick. After all, he'd got it right with his play about the priest, and the one about the bent bailie. Not to mention all his short stories and poems and articles. Apart from the rave reviews of his plays, he received stacks of fan letters. Practically everybody in the country, it seemed, knew a priest exactly like his priest, and a bailie exactly like his bailie.

He'd come to the sad conclusion that Bridie was jealous of his success. She was floundering. She couldn't cope. He'd written a play about that too, or at least the first rough draft of a play; he felt it was the best thing he'd ever done. It was the manuscript lying on his desk now.

'It's not nearly finished,' he said. 'It needs a lot of tightening up and polishing.'

'The idea used to be that I helped you to do that. I gave you constructive criticism.'

But it had become more destructive than constructive over the years. That was the problem. He didn't believe she planned it that way. It was unconscious, he kept telling himself. But it hurt nevertheless, and it played havoc with his still vulnerable self-confidence. Or at least his artistic self-confidence. He enjoyed company too much, and was too intensely interested in other people, to be shy or lacking in any kind of social self-confidence.

He'd been immediately fascinated by the new world of television opening up to him: the technicians, producers, directors, actors, actresses, affected him like continuous shots of adrenalin. He tried to share his enthusiasm and excitement with Bridie. At first they had lots of parties in their new luxurious flat in the West End (so handy for both the BBC and the BBC Club), and he introduced everybody to Bridie. But soon it became obvious that she hated the whole scene. He'd leave a roomful of guests to come for another bottle of wine from the fridge, and find Bridie at the kitchen table hunched over a book, her straight hair drooping forward over her face. She'd jerk guiltily to her feet, blinking and fidgeting with her spectacles, and she'd say, 'I just came through for a drink of water, Frank, and I noticed this book and somehow I got caught up in it . . .'

The truth was she always slipped away as quickly and as often as she could from these gatherings. He'd cut down on the parties and the visits to the BBC Club. This was really painful to him because he was an intensely social person. Or at least one part of him was. This part of him alternated with the lonely, private writing part, when he shut himself away to work on a new play or story.

He became hyper-sensitive. One sarcastic stare at his work from Bridie, one dismissive word, one burst of laughter where no humour was intended, could completely disintegrate – at least temporarily – his faith in himself and his writing. It was then that the black shadow passed over his soul and he hated her. But it was only a very temporary aberration.

He had loved Bridie from the moment they'd got together at her twenty-first birthday party. It was the same party that Bernard had first made a date with Bridie's sister, Doris. Poor Doris still hadn't got over the break-up of her marriage to Bernard, even though he'd since married someone else, a wealthy woman, which seemed more in Bernard's line. He'd always been ambitious, but not like Frank. Bernard had never been a dreamer. Frank had been surprised when Bernard picked Doris as his wife. She'd been pregnant, of course, and his mother had pleaded with him to do the decent thing. Even so . . .

Frank wondered if things would change for the better if he and Bridie had a family. They'd tried, but so far without any luck.

'Reading my work just worries you,' Frank said.

'Oh God.' Bridie closed her eyes. 'Does that mean it's another controversial one? Who is it you're attacking this time? You've already angered the Church and turned them against us. And the Glasgow Corporation.'

'You're exaggerating, Bridie. Nobody's turned against us. Especially not against you.'

'Is this the one you were talking about setting in Blackhill? Don't tell me you've been giving your da and his neighbours and friends a showing up.' She visibly paled. 'Or is it one about the Gorbals? I'll never forgive you if you've rubbished our old friends and good neighbours in the Gorbals. The salt of the earth, they were. They were good to us and don't you forget it.'

He had been going to write about Blackhill but was diverted by the story of a subtle disintegration of a marriage, the growing lack of understanding and communication that was being illustrated now. He was hurt to think that Bridie had such a low opinion of him and his work. He despaired at her lack of understanding. She'd read all the praise the critics and reviewers had heaped upon him. Why couldn't she be proud of him and share his happiness and success?

'I don't "rubbish" anything. I tell the truth as I see it.'

'You use people to your advantage.'

'I don't think in terms of my advantage. I've never thought like that, Bridie, and you know it. If anything, I try to create bridges of understanding between people. The result of writing about Blackhill for instance would, I'd hope, help people in more affluent situations to understand the predicament of people living in a place like Blackhill. Although of course when I'm writing, I don't consciously think along those lines. I just try to tell a good story.'

'You use people.'

He couldn't help feeling a stab of guilt. There was a certain degree of truth in this – inasmuch as he got his ideas and triggers from real life and real people. But he didn't use them in the detrimental sense that Bridie was meaning. Rubbishing was such an ignorant simplification.

'For God's sake.' He turned away, hiding behind anger. 'Why don't you stop talking about things you know nothing about.'

'Oh, I'm ignorant now, am I?'

He wanted to shout back at her, Yes, damn it, you are! He faced her again, eyes bulging, tongue at the ready. Then he saw his Bridie, pale and trembling. The Bridie he'd waited for many a night at the second-hand bookshop where she'd once worked. His plain, straight-haired, bespectacled, intelligent Bridie, who loved books and was proud of him trying to be a writer. The Bridie who had been the first person in his life who had taken him seriously and hadn't called him a poof because he wrote poetry.

He shook his head.

'No, pet, you're not ignorant. You're a well-read, intelligent woman and I love you.'

She was still trembling as he pulled her into his arms and just held her, not knowing what else to do or say.

'I love you too, Frank.'

'Well, what do we keep fighting about? We never used to.'

'I know. But you've changed.'

'*I've* changed?' He let her go. 'How can you say that, Bridie?'

'Because it's true.'

'How have I changed?'

The bitter twist returned to her mouth and her eyes shadowed over.

'Oh, you've changed all right.'

He felt angry again but managed to control it – outwardly at least.

'It's your attitude that's changed, Bridie. You used to be proud of my writing. Now it seems to have become the root of all the trouble between us.'

'That's your fault, not mine.'

He rushed his fingers through his hair in frustration.

'How do you mean? Why should my writing cause trouble between us? My writing's *me*. And you say you love me. I don't understand.'

But of course, deep inside himself, he did. But what could he do? he kept asking himself. Go on writing simple love poems for the rest of his life? For one thing he couldn't make a living at that. More importantly, it meant mental, spiritual and emotional stagnation, never getting out of the one groove, never developing, never being totally honest.

Her shoulders sagged.

'It doesn't matter.'

'Bridie, it does. It does. Maybe it's because you don't understand the way writers work. Maybe you take things too personally. The play about the priest, for instance, that upset you so much. The priest in the play wasn't Father Riley. He was my Father Maloney, a fictional vehicle for a wider truth I felt compelled to investigate.'

'Pull the other one! It wasn't only me who thought you were attacking Father Riley. Dozens of folk thought the same.'

Frank leaned over his desk and flicked through a pile of his favourite quotes. 'Lawrence explained this . . .'

'You and your precious Lawrence,' Bridie interrupted in a low voice that sounded as if it had barely struggled through her teeth.

'He's not a particular favourite of mine, as you should know, Bridie. We've discussed our favourite authors often enough in the past and the reasons we feel an affinity or admiration for certain writers. Nevertheless, Lawrence – '

'I don't care a damn about Lawrence or any of your stupid writers. I'm sick and tired of hearing about writers. Writers and writing. It's all you care about, self-opinionated, big-headed, boring writers.' She was really getting worked up. It was all coming out. He felt sick and sad. 'Not forgetting all your "darlings" in the BBC. Your darling producer, darling director, and oh darling, all your darling actors and actresses. Vehicles of truth, did you say? What vehicles of truth are they? I've never met such a bunch of shallow, hypocritical, in-sincere, conceited posers in all my life.'

She rushed out of the room, banging the door behind her. He was left standing beside his desk, a tall gangly man with thin features, long, lank hair and dark, unhappy eyes. He wanted to run after her, to snatch her into his arms again, but felt paralysed by hopelessness and despair. What was the use?

He didn't believe this was happening to him and Bridie. Not Frank and Bridie – they'd always been such a happy couple, so well suited. Everybody said so. A perfect match. Her with her nose never out of a book and him always scribbling away at something. Friends and relations in the old Garngad, and Blackhill and the Gorbals, smiled and shook their heads at them. What a pair. A right odd couple.

'It just goes to show,' his father once said, 'there's a right mate for everybody – even the likes of our Frank.'

His father, who slaved as a brickie all his life, regarded anyone who didn't work with his hands as either 'poofie', 'lazy' or 'useless'. To Patrick O'Maley, his son Frank was all three.

Tonight in bed, he would take Bridie into his arms and tell her once again how much he loved her. Once again, she would tell him how much she loved him. The making up, as usual, would be desperately loving and tender. They would cling to each other and assure each other that everything was all right. They would promise fervently to forgive and forget.

But all the time, behind his emotional outpourings, his anguish at the though of losing Bridie, there was the detached interest, the cool voice saying, 'I must remember everything about her and this disintegrating relationship, and use it.'

Chapter Five

A tinny piano and a fiddle fought to be heard above the battle of voices and the screeches of laughter at the wedding reception in the Co-op hall. Tony, resplendent (or so he thought) in black drapes, shoelace tie, drainpipe trousers and brothel-creeper shoes, was banging away at his drums. He had to be hauled off them by Bernard, who threatened that if he didn't dance with Theresa, he, Bernard, would bounce Tony's empty head off the floor.

Theresa's frizzy hair had been dampened down with sugar and water, kirby-gripped back and held in check by a coronet of white heather, topped by a froth of veil. The white heather was unusual for a bride's head-dress but it meant good luck and Theresa need all the luck she could get.

Her dress had been made by one of the Co-op dressmakers, cleverly draped in front so as to hide the extra guest at the feast. And a feast it certainly was. Before the dancing started, long trestle tables groaned with generous helpings of the traditional steak pie, peas and potatoes. There were also plates of bread (both plain and pan), slabs of butter, saucers of jam, bottles of tomato and HP brown sauce, and bowls of trifle made with strawberry-flavoured jelly, not orange. Tony had warned the Co-op waitresses well. Second helpings were on offer for anyone who wanted them, encouraged by Tony's bellows of 'Dig in, folks. Don't be shy.' A quite unnecessary piece of advice.

The speeches were, for the most part, hilarious, owing to the fast-flowing whisky.

Afterwards Tony, accompanied by the piano and fiddle, gave a rendering of 'The Merry Ploughboy', an IRA song. Then, before he was pulled down by Bernard, he roared out another song that ended, '. . . So don't wear a green scarf in Bridgeton, or a blue one in Cumberland Street, unless you're a heavyweight champion. Or you're helluva quick on your feet.'

If anyone enjoyed the wedding, Tony certainly did. He galloped around like a Clydesdale horse showing every tooth in his head and threw some of the dances like the Strip the Willow into total chaos and confusion. But nobody seemed to care. Except perhaps a couple of old maids, the sisters McInly. They were sitting on the benches against the wall, tutting at the uninhibited carry-on and confiding in each other how 'real sorry' they were for 'that poor wee lassie', meaning the bride. They had nearly stayed away from the wedding. Since reading about the awful murderer who was still on the loose in Glasgow, they seldom went over the door unless they were accompanied by a male relative. Most of their messages were delivered, including their meat, sausages and Scotch pies from Herraty's, where Tony worked.

Theresa was enjoying herself so much that she became red-faced and out of puff. Eventually she collapsed on a chair and left Tony to continue his gallop with somebody else. In the end, Bernard had to drive both her and Tony back to Blackhill, where they were continuing to live with Patrick until they got a place of their own.

He'd promised to go back to the Co-op and have the last dance with Jane before they both went home to Pollokshields. But somehow he couldn't face her. The wedding had disturbed and saddened him. Not because of any feelings towards Tony or Theresa, but just because of the ceremony itself and the occasion for rejoicing.

He'd been with Andrina earlier that day and he wished with every fibre of his being that she had been the bride and he the groom. But of course their wedding – and it would come one day – their wedding would not be a ramshackle affair in any Co-op hall. It would be in some romantic place, probably in the country. Luss for instance, that lovely village on Loch Lomond-side where they'd had so many romantic rendezvous in the past. He'd have one of the local hotels overlooking the loch bedecked with red roses. They'd be married in a rose-scented bower.

He decided to send a taxi for Jane with a message that he'd been called to an emergency at work. But as it turned out, there *was* an emergency. When he radioed in to check with some of his men how things were he was told by Jack McArthur at the Clyde Club that he'd had a tip-off that a guy there had a sawn-off shotgun hidden under his coat. Now that he was on the job, he banished all thoughts of Andrina from his mind. The Clyde Club was always busy on a Saturday night. He surveyed the situation when he arrived and guessed that there must be a few hundred people packed into the place. It was difficult to see, of course, with the practically non-existent lighting and the blue smoke rising up like a ghostly veil. He had a word with two of his bouncers at the door before shouldering his way to the bar, where MacArthur was waiting. McArthur indicated two men who were standing on a raised area in the club.

'What do you reckon?'

'Let's just go up there now and deal with them,' Bernard said, already striding forward, immediately followed by McArthur.

As soon as one of the men saw the two aggressive-looking security guys, he knew he'd been rumbled. He put his hand into his coat pocket; it was a raincoat-type thing that obviously had an opening right through to his jacket.

Bernard and McArthur closed in and Bernard said, 'Don't even move your arm. Just start walking.'

The man hesitated, sizing Bernard up. Then both he and his companion allowed themselves to be walked towards the door. At the door, Bernard said, 'Beat it and don't come back.'

'Right, fair enough,' the man with the gun said. 'I've got no argument with you. I don't want to start trouble with you guys.'

Bernard and McArthur knew he was lying. He'd be back if not tonight, some other night with his team to back him up. He was what Bernard called a paper gangster: someone who thought he was a gangster but was just a small-time villain. Paper gangsters had a little team and they went around in suits and did things in a gangsterish sort of way, making people buy them drinks. They exerted terror but didn't have the power and influence of the real gangsters.

Back at the bar, he bought McArthur a beer. He knew McArthur would have been drinking very little, if anything, all night. Bernard hadn't had much either, even at the wedding. He liked to keep all his wits about him. It had become a habit. He loosened up occasionally in the shadowy recesses of the Arches Club under the railway bridge, but only when he had a good crowd of his men around him and they reckoned it was a quiet enough night for them all to relax. It was a good place for them to meet and talk over a couple of drinks. The Arches had always been a quiet club, apart from the occasional deep, hollow rumble of a train.

'He'll be back,' McArthur said.

'Too late tonight.' Bernard shook his head. 'By the time he's rounded up his team, this place'll be shut. He's not that daft.'

'I thought you were taking the night off,' McArthur said, remembering. 'Your brother's wedding, wasn't it?'

He had to raise his voice to be heard above the sea of talk and laughter and parting shouts. The punters had had a good time and were now roaring home on a tide of song.

No trouble. That's how Bernard liked it. It spelled success in his book.

'Tony was pissed out of his mind. I had to take him and the bride home. He'll be no use to her tonight.'

It was the opposite with him. Stone cold sober he was no use to Jane. Even after a few drinks at home, he seldom managed to get it up. Occasionally, he fantasised that he was having sex with Andrina, but even that was succeeding less and less often. His fantasies withered against Jane's lean body. To make love to Jane was to bump against bone. With Andrina, he was enveloped, lost in soft cushions of sensuous flesh, in full, uptilted breasts, in soft abdomen, in rounded hips. She was his darling, lovable, sensual, sexual passion of his life. No way could there be any comparison.

'Isn't Theresa's brother one of our lot?'

'Yeah. Rod MacGowan. I passed him snogging with one of the bridesmaids in the Co-op corridor on my way out. Really enjoying himself. He was lucky I didn't order him to take his sister and the groom home.'

'You're all heart.'

'I know.'

The place was emptying. Sound was seeping away, leaving a quiet devastation like the aftermath of a bomb-blast. Lights were switched on, harshly revealing the seediness of the club. Ashtrays overflowed on beer-puddled tables. Grubby paint was peeling from walls. Floors were littered with empty crisp and cigarette packets. Bar staff began gathering up dirty glasses. Bernard's men were checking lavatories and corridors to make sure no bodies were left lying about.

'Are you going on to the Arches?'

'No. The wedding's finished me off. See these Scottish reels and all that galloping about and heughing. They can export it all to England, as far as I'm concerned.'

McArthur laughed. 'Och, I don't know. I've enjoyed a few Highland flings in my time.'

'I'll bet.' Bernard grinned, then downed the last dregs of his drink before leaving.

He changed from inside to outside of the club with automatic caution. He never blundered about. The guy with the sawn-off shotgun would already have vowed to 'get him'. He could live with that. But he was a professional. He always took sensible precautions. His intuition for danger had sharpened over the years.

The real gangsters preferred to keep trying to manipulate him onto their side. He walked a tightrope. He stood at bars talking to them. They dealt in extortion and drugs, but thought of themselves as businessmen so he spoke to them as if he was another businessman. Talk was OK. They insisted on buying him drinks. Sometimes he shrugged and acquiesced, but he never bought them a drink in return. He had no quarrel with them – unless they started trouble in a club in which he was being paid to stop trouble.

The police would see him standing at a bar talking to gangsters and they'd be convinced he was 'in' with them. They'd say to him, 'You've got something going, alongside your security line. One of these days, we're going to find out what it is and nail you.'

It was the most difficult line for him to walk in his life. Managing to mix with hoodlums without getting into trouble with the police was one of the cornerstones of his strength.

All the time it was taking things to the limit. It was convincing the gangsters that you were a lot stronger, more powerful, than them. He used props. He had a Ford Granada, one of the old box style, that looked like a strong car. He kept himself fit. His well-developed muscular body told of regular weight-lifting sessions, as well as karate. The gangsters didn't know what discipline was, but they'd look at him and think, this guy's got his act together. They believed because he had a good car, and was clean-shaven and wearing a Chester Barrie suit and Crombie coat, and a gold sovereign ring he was powerful, a guy to be respected.

The club in the Broomielaw faced on to the Clyde. Tugging up the collar of his coat, Bernard walked alongside the pewter-coloured river that was darkly shivering in moonlight laced with rain. Ignoring the rain, he reached his car, his thoughts already turning to Andrina.

He had always been obsessed with the idea of possessing her in marriage but never more than tonight. His shoulders hunched forward in misery as he started the engine. He tried to understand why, at the mention of marriage, she literally jumped away from him like a startled fawn. There was no mistaking her fear. It wasn't fear of him. He'd established that. It wasn't even fear of what Robert might do if she left the family home. No, it was her mad old witch of a mother.

But even so. 'What could she do to you?' he kept asking. 'For God's sake, Andrina, you're thirty-one years of age. It's your life. You can do what you like with it. Tell your mother to go to hell.'

This kind of talk almost sent Andrina into hysterics. It only served to chase her further away from him. He thought her attitude was ridiculous but he wasn't angry with her. He couldn't be angry at Andrina. He was determined to understand. There was the religious thing, of course. Her mother wasn't just a maniac, she was a religious maniac. She'd probably threatened Andrina with the wrath of God all her life. And hell and damnation. If there were such things, he fervently wished them on Sophie McPherson.

It had stopped raining, except for melancholy drips from trees and roofs and he found that, without thinking where he was going, he'd made for Monteith Row where Andrina lived and which hugged close to Glasgow Green. He stopped opposite one of the black gaping closes and sat, big hands locked on to the wheel, shoulders tense. The windows of the building darkly glittered. Behind one of them lay his only love. He concentrated on her as if by the sheer power of his will he could draw her to him, lock her for ever in his arms.

The trees of the Green whispered and sighed into silence. So quiet was it, and so still was Bernard, he could have been a lone statue in the Necropolis, the city of the dead, entombed in the darkness of his car, staring at Andrina's window.

Chapter Six

Sinnieglen School looked not unlike the prison that was situated immediately over the wall from it: dark brown and sprawling, with thick walls and high windows. Except the school windows were unbarred. Robert Anderson had heard that some teachers, before they started lessons, told their pupils to 'wave to your daddies over the wall'. It was probably a joke – although he soon found that many of the pupils did indeed have a daddy incarcerated in Barlinnie prison, the Bar L as it was known locally. Of those fathers who were not in prison, the majority were unemployed.

On his first day, the headmaster shook his hand and, with a booming funereal voice, wished him well. It was as if he was being sent on some long and dangerous journey. Samuel McDowall was tall, about the same height as Robert, but looked as if he weighed in at about twenty stone, and stately with it. McDowell had a black felt homburg hat jammed on his head, even at his desk, and he wore either an overcoat or a giant-size black academic gown over his pinstriped suit. He had an extremely polite, although still recognisably Glasow, voice and his manner of delivery was more suited to a thespian. Altogether he was a dramatic kind of man and despite his eccentricities and his penchant for sarcastic wit, much admired by the staff. Robert discovered that McDowall kept a high profile. While the headmaster at St Francis tried to lead a quiet life and was rarely seen, in Sinnieglen the headmaster was always billowing about in windy corridors like an Elizabethan warship in full sail. He would unexpectedly burst into classrooms, subduing even the rowdiest and toughest of the pupils into shocked silence.

In the staffroom, which was the usual bleak slum of a place, Robert met the other teachers, including the art teachers. He already knew Lachlan McKenzie, or more accurately, he knew his work. He'd been impressed by several exhibitions in the past of McKenzie's paintings and he wondered now why McKenzie hadn't been offered the post of head of department. Could be, of course, that he didn't want it.

'Welcome to the Sin Bin.' McKenzie extended a hand.

Robert laughed.

'I'd heard that's what they called it.'

'Gavin Stuart.' Another man stepped forward. 'Maths.' He bore an uncanny resemblance to Hitler and Robert could imagine what mileage the pupils would get out of this, behind his back, if not to his face. He was small too, another disadvantage.

A man introduced himself as Kirk Hunter, 'one of the brave souls from the Sinnieglen art department'. Hunter added, 'Of course, you'll be prepared for our lot if you've come from down the road. Only, be warned – this place is even worse than St Francis. I came here straight from Kelvinside Academy. Can you imagine?'

'You've obviously survived,' Robert said.

'I've a wife and family to keep.'

The mention of family made Robert think of Jennifer. At least the Green Street School wasn't a jungle like this. He had enough experience of teaching in the district and had sufficient knowledge of Sinnieglen's reputation to have no illusions about it.

'I found in St Francis, and I expect it will be the same here, that inactivity is your biggest enemy. You have to know exactly what you're going to do. If you're not prepared and start footering around, they're likely to assume you don't know what you're doing and really take advantage.'

'Too true,' Sholto Bryce growled. He had been masking a pot of tea in a brown delft teapot with a chipped spout. 'And if you're having an off day, the wee devils'll spot it.'

'Not so wee, some of them,' Stuart sighed, and Robert could imagine him having a serious problem trying to discipline teenagers. All the same, he'd known tall teachers who'd ranted and yelled and got absolutely nowhere, and small teachers who only needed to glare at a pupil to successfully quash bad behaviour. It wasn't anything to do with height. It was acquiring an air of authority, staying calm, being disciplined oneself. This was his theory but he was the first to admit that it wasn't easy to keep calm in schools like this.

Other teachers, women as well as men, smiled their greeting but they were somewhat absent smiles. It was Monday and another week of war was about to begin.

Walking up the stairs and along the corridor with Kirk Hunter *en route* to their repective classes, with noise rioting and clattering and reverberating around them, Hunter said wistfully, 'When I think of Kelvinside and the kids all sitting there quietly waiting for me in their clean shirts, all the same colour, and blue uniform, and badges, and all so *clean*. And all ready and willing to be *taught* . . .'

Robert laughed.

'See you later.'

He was used to the sweaty, sour and other sickly smells that could thicken the air in classrooms. It was just another difficulty. There was nothing one could do to improve the situation. Laura had tried once. There had been a girl in her class – twelve-year-old Sadie McGhie – who really stank to high heavens. Every teacher knew Sadie. She was a nice enough, harmless kind of girl and Laura had felt sorry for her. Even her classmates, no fragrant flowers themselves, kept their distance and would have nothing to do with her.

Laura had taken her aside one day and gently tried to tell her about the importance of hygiene. Laura's problem was her gentleness. The next morning, Mrs McGhie came rampaging up to the school and burst into Laura's class. When Robert had gone through to rescue Laura, Mrs McGhie was purple in the facing and bawling,

'Ah sent my wain tae school to learn how tae dae sums, no how tae smell like a fuckin' geranium.'

Now he entered his first new class of the day and strode over to his desk. He ignored the bedlam of bawls, hoots of laughter as boys flicked a variety of messy missiles at girls, scraping and squeaking of seats, banging of desks, got his papers organised, then suddenly riveted his attention on the children and roared, 'Quiet!'

He had lungs like drums and an exceptionally powerful

voice. He had trained it, not only to deal with classes but to bark out karate instructions, many in deep-throated Japanese. The authority and the resonance of his voice took everyone by surprise. There was silence.

'Right. I'm going to explain what we're going to do in this class. I'll also tell you about the karate club I run. But first the register. Put up your hand and say "Here, sir" when I call your name.

'Crichton.'

'Here, sir.'

'McGill.'

'Here, sir.'

'Quinn.'

'Here, sir.'

By the end of the day he'd more or less got each class's measure – as tough a bunch of fourteen- and fifteen-year-olds as he'd ever come across. And, as he'd told Andrina later, that was just the girls. She'd laughed but in fact it wasn't much of a joke. Some of the girls *were* tough, many were troublemakers but most of them, troublemakers included, were just poor souls, neglected or abused at home. Much the same as the boys, really. And much the same mix as at St Francis.

By the time he returned home he was exhausted. He tried to keep himself fit. He *was* fit but he needed all his energies to cope with his work. The extra strain of his private life was making everything so much more difficult, was drowning him. He hadn't wanted a promoted post, but he'd been in a quandary about his deepening relationship with Laura Cairns. Working beside her all day and every day, talking with her at coffee and tea breaks, lunching with her, sitting close to her in her car, being with her on the outings to Loch Lomond and the Campsies was too much. It couldn't go on. But he wanted it to – he was always at his happiest and most relaxed when he was in her company. There were so many other considerations and complications. There was her husband, for a start. He felt sorry for Derek. It was tragic what had happened to the man. How could he take advantage of Derek's misfortune – and his trust – by cuckolding him? He wasn't that kind of louse. Although at times he'd come very near to it.

To a lesser degree he worried about betraying Andrina's trust too. Not that he believed she had any deep feelings for him but there had always been a kind of naivety and innocence about her, despite her sexy-looking body. She had the wide eyes of a child, sometimes twinkling with naughtiness, sometimes confused and frightened, but always quick to revert to a blank innocent look.

Looking back, he realised with sadness that she'd never loved him, although probably she had thought she did. In truth, it had been the novelty of having a home of her own and getting away – or so she'd believed at the time – from her mother. That novelty, that belief, had intrigued her and kept her comparatively happy for a while. She had been like a child playing with a doll's house, pretending she was a grown-up lady. Right from the start, however, she'd turned away from having sex with him. Oh, occasionally she'd suffer him in silence while he made love to her. Until his pride prevented him from trying any more. She was obviously relieved and happy with this development and it had even made her more affectionate for a time. She'd give him an impulsive kiss on the cheek or a quick hug.

Sometimes – although not for a long time now – she'd even say, 'I love you.' But he knew that it was only a sign of gratitude to him for no longer touching her in any intimate way. This had hurt him. His pride had helped harden him against the love he'd once had for her and which had made him so vulnerable. He was glad of the extra time he gave to his pupils in and out of the classroom and at the karate club. Once he'd felt guilty, worried in case he was neglecting her, not spending enough time with her. Now he realised that she didn't care. She wasn't interested in him or anything about him. He had tried to share his enthusiasms: he'd taken her to the theatre and to concerts but it became obvious that they bored her. She'd started making excuses. She told him, 'You go on your own. I don't mind.' She was glad to be rid of him, happy to be free as a bird, to fly away to her choir practices and keep-fit evenings, and cookery classes and mannequin shows. All her own interests. This hurt him too. But it was mostly hurt pride. And sadness. In a way he loved her still. He loved her as the silly immature child that she was. He was firm but patient, always willing to help her. He struggled to keep a secure background for her and protect her, much in the same way as he'd try to do for any child in his care.

He tried his best. And, he believed, in her own way, she did too. The house was always spotless. She laundered his clothes. She saw that Jennifer was well turned out. She was an excellent cook. Why she still needed to go to cookery classes, he didn't know. She was unfailingly charming and attentive in public. To all appearances, he was a lucky man. People had often said, 'A beautiful wife, who can cook as well! By God, Anderson, you're a lucky man!'

Once he'd thought so. She was such a beautiful, desirable woman. But as well as freezing away from him in bed, there were the innumerable blank and faraway looks, the forgotten birthdays, the lack of interest in wedding anniversaries, the unconscious insensitive remarks, the subtle, barely disguised impatience, as if he was a bit of a nuisance for being in the house at all. All of these things made him draw away from her, isolate himself in a cold vacuum of pride and unhappiness.

He might have made some attempt to have it out with Andrina, try to make her see that this was not how a marriage should be. He wanted to tell her that it would be more sensible for them to pack it in and seek a divorce. He knew, however, that she would panic. She would be terrified at the mere idea of a scandal because of the repercussions from her mother. Had it not been for this he might have thought she was having an affair. She certainly had plenty of opportunities to meet a lover. But her terror of her mother and of any scandal was far too strong he felt sure.

Another thing that kept him back from seeking a divorce was the thought of abandoning Jennifer.

It wasn't her fault that the marriage had failed. He felt an immense tenderness and sense of protection towards his child. She seemed so vulnerable, so quiet and introverted, at times so intense. He worried about her. He had come to the conclusion that being so much with his mother-in-law wasn't doing Jennifer any good. He'd told Andrina this but she'd pooh-poohed the idea.

'Mummy adores Jennifer. Nobody could be more conscientious with her.'

'In the first place,' he'd said, 'I don't know why you need to be always running over to your mother's with Jennifer. And especially why you need to leave Jennifer with her so much.'

Her reply had poured out in a breathless rush.

'Mummy loves to see her. So does Daddy, and letting them babysit makes it easier for me to do shopping or visit friends, or invite them round for coffee or lunch. Or go to my keep-fit class. Or choir practice. Or even just to get on with some housework.'

'Your mother is very neurotic, to say the least, Andrina. You're a bundle of nerves in her company, even when she phones you. God knows what effect she's having on Jennifer.'

'Nonsense. Jennifer loves going to visit her nanna.' She always cut the conversation short by turning away to make a fuss of Jennifer, or to clatter dishes about in the sink, or to fiddle with the wireless in an impatient effort to change the programme from the Mahler he had been listening to to some pop programme or other. It wasn't that he didn't like pop music, but his taste was not confined to the pop scene.

He looked after Jennifer as often as he could. He didn't mind Andrina going out in the evening to whatever class or meeting she wanted. After all, he spent quite a lot of his spare time with all sorts of projects and diversions to try to keep his pupils out of trouble.

He could do nothing about Andrina's activities during the day. He could not stop her going to visit her parents, especially considering how good both Sophie and Andrew McPherson had been to them. They were too good. That was part of the problem. He didn't want to take anything from them and more than once had refused the offer of a car from McPherson, who seemed to be able to get God knows what at incredible (indeed suspiciously) knock-down prices. He preferred to buy his own car when he could afford it.

He couldn't stop them giving presents to Andrina and Jennifer, however. Sophie insisted on buying all of Jennifer's clothes, or making them. She'd even presented Jennifer with a leather schoolbag. She showered the child with everything.

Sophie was a woman of such extremes. He couldn't help feeling sorry for her. He suspected she'd had a pretty rotten childhood. No doubt that was one of the reasons she was so keen to make sure that Jennifer had everything she needed to make her happy and perfectly well cared for. Or everything Sophie *thought* Jennifer needed to make her happy and perfectly well cared for.

It was much the same with Sophie's attitude to Andrina. Although not quite. She gave Andrina presents certainly, and would do anything for her. But there was an unnatural anxiety to check up on Andrina to make sure that everything Andrina did was not only perfection but 'holier than thou'.

Nobody could be that perfect. OK, both Sophie and her daughter kept an immaculate house. Sometimes he felt he was committing a crime by denting a cushion in either the McPherson's house or his own.

They also kept themselves immaculate. Andrina did her best to keep his clothes looking as smart as possible, despite her disgust at the shoulders or the back of his jacket. Schoolboys had a habit of aiming spittle down over banisters at any teacher walking below, and if Robert noticed it on his jacket, he always made an attempt to clean it off. But never to Andrina's satisfaction.

She and her mother said their prayers every night. Andrina knelt on the floor beside the bed and he was sure Sophie did too. They went to church three times on Sundays and as many times as possible during the week. Andrina sang in the choir of their Rose Street church and, as often as not, in her mother's choir in Bearsden as well.

His own mother, a good Christian woman, had never been given to such extremes; she put her Christianity into practice quietly and unobtrusively in her daily life. Not that she could do much of anything now, crippled as she was with arthritis. She still struggled to get out and around and never complained, but her life was very difficult and restricted. He visited her once a week and did odd jobs for her about the house. Neighbours were very kind and did most of her shopping.

Andrina never went to see his mother or did anything to

45

help her, even though she lived within walking distance across the other side of the park. If his mother wanted to see Jennifer – and of course, she did – he had to take the child over to Adelphi Street. On one occasion he discovered that his mother had hobbled across to Monteith Row and somehow managed to climb the stairs. Andrina had been out. Josie, their next-door neighbour, had found the old lady sitting helpless and exhausted on the stairs. She'd taken her in and given her a cup of tea and looked after her until he'd arrived home from school.

Robert had been furious.

'Where the hell were you this time?' he'd bawled at Andrina when she eventually turned up.

She'd looked innocent and hurt.

'Over at a church meeting in Bearsden. How was I to know your mother would arrive like this?'

His mother had hushed him, assured him that she was all right. And right enough, she said, she should have phoned. But often when she did phone, she went on to explain, it clicked off and she thought he should see the Post Office about getting it sorted.

'It's my own fault, dear, for coming out and not letting anyone know. I should have written a note. I'm sorry. You shouldn't be angry with Andrina. It wasn't her fault.'

For his mother's sake, he controlled his fury.

He'd stared at Andrina in bitter silence and thought, You and your bloody church meetings. You bloody hypocrite. He had stopped going to the church for some time now. This saddened his mother but he couldn't help it. Over the years he'd gradually become more embittered.

Although recently he'd often thanked God for Laura, who'd brought back some warmth to his life. She wasn't beautiful like Andrina but she was a genuinely caring person and she loved him, as he loved her. He longed to take her in his arms, and loosen the long nut-brown hair that she always had pinned back at the nape of her neck, and stroke it, and kiss it, and kiss her soft cheek and tell her that everything was going to be all right.

But everything wasn't all right. Every time he saw Derek

Cairns hirpling along in his iron calliper or with food dribbling helplessly from his mouth, he knew how impossible it was to make love to the poor sod's wife.

But still he longed to. God help me, he thought. Don't let me do it.

Chapter Seven

Folk in Castlemilk could recall the days when they lived in single-ends, or one room and kitchens, in old districts like Garngad and the Gorbals. They remembered waiting anxiously every day for the postman to bring them a letter telling them they'd been allocated a new house in one of the new housing schemes – Castlemilk, Drumchapel, Easterhouse or Barlanark. Big Martha Stoddart had believed that the postman was keeping back her letter just to be spiteful. He was a Catholic and as far as Martha was concerned, that meant he was capable of any foul deed. At one point she had threatened him that if he didn't bring her letter the very next day, he would get his bag and its contents round his ears. Fortunately for the postman, her letter did arrive the next day with many others, and so the way of life of the tenants of the old districts was changed.

At first they didn't realise exactly how much, or in what way. They were perfectly content, indeed deliriously happy, to follow Moses (the housing officer) out of the wilderness of tenement houses that had no hot water and outside lavatories, and into the promised land of back boilers and bathrooms.

It wasn't until much later that some people began to say, 'We were happier where we were.'

The first problem was how to furnish a house with two or three bedrooms, a sitting-room, a living-room and kitchen-ette, when all you've got is maybe just a kitchen table, a few chairs and a wardrobe. Even the recessed beds had been a fixture in the old tenements.

Club men or tick men or Provident men descended on Castlemilk and quickly ensnared people in never-ending debt. They came with vans stacked with everything anybody might need. Women queued up and men came home from work and no dinner ready for them because their wives had been afraid to lose their place in the queue. As one van emptied, a phone call made sure another would take its place. The usual sales line from the club men and the one that always worked with Big Martha, was, 'Your neighbour's brought such and such, you don't want her to get one up on you, do you?'

A grocer's van ventured into Castlemilk thinking he'd make a fortune with there being no competition. But too many people pleaded, 'Can you give me my messages and I'll pay you next week?' and the van man was too soft-hearted. He had to give up the van eventually. He was owed hundreds of pounds that he couldn't reclaim.

In the old tenements everyone had been related and lived only doors away from each other. If there was a problem, well your ma or your sister or your aunty or your granny was there to help. If you were short of money, there was always the corner shop and of course a pawnshop nearby. If a man was staying too long in the local pub and spending too much money, his mother-in-law could come to her daughter's rescue and haul the man out. Big Martha had done this to Michael in his drinking days. She'd given him a right hammering. He remembered it well.

Now money, or the lack of it, was a nightmare. The rents were three times what they'd been before and the new tick man had to be paid each week. There wasn't enough money to squander in pubs. There were no pubs, for a start. Money had to be spent on the fare to get to work back in the Gorbals or anywhere in the city. Previously work had been within walking distance. Higher fares were needed to reach schools or shops, or any form of entertainment. But most serious of all, it was too costly to travel across the city to visit relatives.

People became isolated with their problems and in hostile situations that would never have arisen before. A family from the Bridgeton would never, in the old days, have moved willingly to the Gorbals. Or people from Garngad wouldn't have settled in the Calton. It just wasn't done. Now the Glasgow Corporation had mixed everybody up, and in too many cases it didn't work. There was always someone like Big Martha and her late husband singing 'The Sash' and somebody next door or across the street retaliating with 'The Merry Ploughboy'.

Martha, now unable to dash out and grab anybody by the throat, settled each day at her front room window, filling it like a martyred mountain and bitterly criticising all who passed down below in the street.

'This house had been unlucky for me,' she kept repeating. 'It's an unlucky place, this.'

But that did not stop her from urging her daughter to join her there.

She blamed everything on Glasgow Corporation. The whole trouble was, she insisted, that the Corporation was a bunch of Papes. Green Grapes were getting into everything these days, she never tired of telling Caroline. Ruining everything. She usually glared at Michael when she said this. If it wasn't the Corporation, it was him that caused all the city's, if not all the world's, problems. He suspected she even believed he was to blame for the weather.

'Tell the silly old cow to shut up,' Bernard said, when Michael told his brother what was going on. No doubt that's what Bernard would have done and never turned a hair. But he wasn't Bernard. For one thing, he cared about his wife, and Caroline cared about her mother.

Tony and Patrick had helped with the flitting. The coalman hired them his horse and cart for the day, the cart brushed and scrubbed clean of coal dust. The journey went all right. The trick was getting everything in the lift on the way to Martha's high-rise flat. At the time it hadn't seemed much consolation that her flat was only five flights up, not fifteen. After every difficult manoeuvre had been successfully completed and his brother and father had been given a thank-you dram, they left, wishing him luck.

Martha couldn't get out to the hairdresser's, even if there had been one, and Michael had been given the job of cutting her spiky grey hair. He dreaded the thought that she might command him to shave her next. An unmistakable moustache and even suspicions of a grey beard were visible on her big leathery face. He cut Caroline and the children's hair too. It was one of his jobs in the house, like washing the windows. Caroline was nervous of heights and seldom looked out if she could avoid it. There were times she was forced to, to keep her eye on the children, but even if she'd seen them getting into any trouble or danger she could never have got to them in time. This was another worry and one which caused a lot of friction. Caroline became too frightened to let the children out to play.

'The twins are only seven,' she reminded him, 'and Maureen's barely five. Just babies.'

'You can't keep them in the house all day and every day,' he argued. 'It's not good for them.'

'They go to school. They can play there. And I'll take them out afterwards as often as I can.'

'For one thing there's school holidays. For another, in the Gorbals they played in the streets from the time they were barely able to walk.'

'I know. But it was different there. Either me or one of the neighbours could get to them right away if they fell or anything. I don't know anybody here and sometimes I think I'll go mad waiting for that lift.'

It was something Caroline and the children would have to get used to. Sometimes he lost his temper and snapped, 'I told you we shouldn't have come. I told you there would be difficulties. I told you it wouldn't work but you didn't listen, did you?'

'Yes I did,' Caroline wailed tearfully. 'But what could I do? She's my mammy.'

They'd had another quarrel when he'd seen Caroline's new sewing-machine and candlewick bedspreads. He had a dread of them getting dragged down with debt as so many of their neighbours had been. One poor woman had gassed herself because of it.

'No, no,' Caroline protested. 'I didn't have anything to do with the club men or any kind of tick. It was Mrs Bain. She'd bought the machine and the bedspreads off the club men but she got herself into debt with the grocery van as well. She's a decent wee woman and wanted to pay the van man. She knew that poor man is all but ruined with customers not paying up. So she went back to the Gorbals and pawned the stuff. Then she sold me the pawn tickets and I redeemed it.'

'That's still not right, Caroline. Mrs Bain will still be paying the club man.'

'I know,' Caroline said. 'Poor soul.'

She looked so happy with her new acquisitions, especially the sewing-machine, he hadn't the heart to spoil things for her. It gave her one of the few lifts of happiness she'd had since they'd come to Castlemilk. Anyway, what could he do?

What maddened him more than anything was that he was becoming more and more sure that Martha wasn't nearly as helpless as she tried to make out. She certainly rested enough. But he'd heard her shuffling through to the bathroom in the middle of the night, or to make herself a cup of tea. Probably she put a good slug of whisky in it. And no doubt she'd be stuffing herself with all the food she could lay her hands on. During the day she'd make out to Caroline that 'a wee drop scrambled egg is all I'll be able to manage. Lightly done, remember. None of your dry lumpy stuff.' Or, 'I fancy a nice wee bit of fish. The doctor said I needed to eat a fillet of fish two or three times a week to keep my strength up.'

He was sure the doctor (who no longer came now anyway) never said any such thing. Nor did the doctor advise a nice poke of chips each time to go along with the fish. Martha Stoddart was a lying, selfish, ignorant old bigot, always was and always would be. He hoped she'd choke on the fish that his hard-earned wages bought her. The worst of it was he'd to carry the fish suppers from the Gorbals each time on his way home from work. She would touch no other than from the shop she'd patronised for years. He was sorely tempted to tell her that the Bennitos, who ran the fish and chip shop, were Catholics but Caroline said she'd never forgive him if he did.

'Mammy's an old woman and there's very few pleasures left in her life. She loves Bennitos' fish suppers. Don't you dare upset her and spoil her only wee bit of enjoyment.'

Her *only* wee bit of enjoyment? That was a laugh. She enjoyed nagging at him and putting him down at every turn, for a start. Or she'd do it through Caroline in his presence.

'I don't know what you see in him. He's certainly no oil painting. What on earth does he look like with that black eye patch? Some boxer he must have been to lose his eye *and* get his nose flattened. And I've said it before, and I'll say it again – you could have done a lot better than a brickie and a Papish one at that . . .'

'Mother,' Caroline always protested, 'you know you don't mean all that . . .'

But he knew she did. Evil old arsehole. Yet he also knew he didn't mean that. Ignorant, yes, bigoted, yes. But not evil. She was good to the children. She'd even supported him against Caroline on the question of them playing outside.

'He's right,' she'd chipped in. 'It's not good for the weans being cooped up here all the time. They'll have to learn to fend for themselves for one thing. You're doing them no good babying them. They've got to learn to be tough.'

'Tough!' Caroline had dismissed such an idea as ridiculous. 'They're only babies.'

'I'm telling you they'll need to learn. This is Glasgow, no' bloody Bermuda.'

He'd had to laugh at that. He'd asked her later, 'How were you brought up, Ma?'

'On the streets. My father was killed in the steelworks. He fell into the furnace, and my mother was left to bring ten of us up on her own. We were in the workhouse for a while. What a disgrace that was for us all. Even as a wee lassie, I felt the shame of it. A Pape ran the place. Or at least the bit we were in. I'll never forget that bloody sadist. I'm telling you, if you weren't tough in that place, you didn't survive. And I survived.'

He detected a ripple of a tremble in her mountainous body and he understood her a little better. He felt sad. He couldn't really work up a hatred of her; he wasn't a hating kind of man. He was even fool enough to buy her a second-hand wheelchair he'd seen in the Barras.

This meant in the end that he had to help her into it, which was no mean feat. Moses moving the mountain, he'd told his da. Then he had to negotiate the chair into the lift and outside, where he pushed her around the streets, cursing under his breath. She was a helluva weight. And Castlemilk was built on a hill.

Caroline tried to console him by saying that as well as doing her mother so much good to get a breath of fresh air, the exercise was keeping him fit. Him that was running up and down ladders all day carrying hods of bricks! That was all he needed. And Martha talked all the time. She got her beady eye on an old man who used to work beside her husband in the Gorbals.

'Look at that lazy old sod,' she announced. 'Never done a stroke of work since he retired.'

'Would you look at that,' she commanded further on. 'Another inch off that and you'd see her arse, bloomin' disgrace. When I was young . . .' And then she'd be off on a journey down memory lane telling him all about her youth and what Glasgow was like in those days. 'You could walk the streets without needing to worry about murderers prowling about like you do now. There were gang fights but they just fought among themselves. They'd stop fighting and break ranks to let an old woman pass.'

'When my father was a boy,' Martha told him, 'he loved horses and when he left school at twelve, he became a trace boy. He worked with big Clydesdales. Powerful animals they were. They would pull carts loaded with heavy goods and barrels of beer. My granny told me he had the best turned-out horses. Their brasses were always shining and their manes pleated and ribbons at each side of their bridles and often a flower tucked behind their ears. But because of lack of money, he'd to leave and go to the steelworks. He always hated it, my mother said.'

Michael had to admit (but only to himself) that this quite interested him. He could see in his mind's eye the carriages rattling along cobbled streets in the West End. The white aproned and mob-capped servants scrubbing front steps. The men in tail-coats and gold watch-chains and top hats. The ships crowding the river, the cranes crushing for space, jutting up to the clouds. The big heart of the Gorbals full to bursting with immigrants: the Poles, the Irish, the Highlanders, the Jews.

'Here,' Martha would say eventually, spying an ice-cream van (by this time they would have left Castlemilk and reached Croftfoot), 'take this shilling and get us both a pokey hat.'

At least these walks gave Caroline a break. After all, she was the one imprisoned in the house with her mother all day and every day and he could see the strain was beginning to tell on her. Sometimes she was quite snappy with the children. Even with her mother. This wasn't like Caroline. Not like her at all. She was the kindest, most loving, most good-natured of women. Sometimes after coping with the three children and Big Martha, she just collapsed into bed and was too drained even to make love. He held her in his arms until she fell asleep.

At times she wept with exhaustion. She'd maybe walked a mile or more carrying heavy shopping over and above everything else, and of course she delivered the children to school and collected them afterwards. Michael tried his best to be of help to her but he had his work to go to and what with the extra travelling time to and from Castlemilk, he was away from home for extra-long hours.

It was strange how claustrophobic the house in Castlemilk became when it was so much larger than the one in the Gorbals. At least in the number of apartments. But of course the ceilings in the new house were lower and the rooms smaller. And with being higher up and often the lift breaking down, it was easy to feel trapped. Seldom seeing any of the neighbours and never getting to know them didn't help. The dampness and the fungi that had developed in the walls and the fusty smell that came with it was another thing. He tried to deal with it. He'd also complained to the factor. All to no avail. Caroline said it was unhealthy, and she was right. He was sure it was the reason wee Maureen had developed asthma. Caroline was up to high doh about the child and he didn't blame her. He was finding it hard to contain his own panic. It was frightening to see the poor wee thing choking for breath. They'd been glad of Martha's help with her. Martha had run the bath with hot water and told Caroline to bring a kettle of boiling water into the bathroom as well, and then go out and shut the door.

'Steaming,' Martha had said, sitting on the lavatory pan holding the distraught child firmly on her splayed tree trunks of knees. 'That's what the wean needs. Steaming.'

Sure enough it had helped. Nevertheless, things were going wrong in their lives, just as he'd feared. He's always known that the moment they left the Gorbals and went to Castlemilk, everything would begin to change for the worse.

Perhaps things were developing in a slightly different way than he'd expected. But it was for the worse all the same.

Chapter Eight

'Where were you last night?' Sophie's hair was pinned back so tightly it wrenched at the skin round her eyes, giving her a warped look. 'You didn't say you'd be out.'

Andrina sighed.

'Mummy, why should I say? It wasn't as if you needed to get in touch with me. You'd already phoned in the morning.'

'You've not answered my question. Have you been up to something?'

'For goodness sake, Mummy, I was just visiting Granny McPherson. What's wrong with that?'

Saturdays and Sundays were always difficult because those were the times Andrina had to depend on her mother. Robert was off school but had marking and other paperwork to concentrate on when he was at home in the evenings. During the day he'd outings with his pupils or he'd sometimes go to a matinée at the Theatre Royal. The problem was that Jennifer was off school too.

Sophie said, 'Every time you say you've been to see Granny McPherson, she says you haven't. She swears she hasn't seen hide nor hair of you for months.'

'Surely you don't need me to tell you that poor Granny's senile. She forgets what day it is, where she's put her purse or her keys, even her false teeth.'

'She remembers when I've been to see her. Or your daddy. Although God forgive him, he doesn't go to see his mother as often as he should.'

'She tells me quite the opposite, Mummy. She tells me you never visit her.'

Andrina tried to control the increase of her heartbeats. She hated the way one simple lie could become a complicated cluster. The important thing was to allay her mother's suspicions, direct the river of her attention. She widened her eyes.

'Was that Jennifer crying?'

Jennifer had gone out to play in the Bearsden back garden. Immediately Sophie hurried away to check that her granddaughter was all right. Of course, she was: Jennifer would always be perfectly all right here, despite what Robert said. Her mother and father being such loyal members of the Evangelical Church of Jesus, better-living people could not be found anywhere. Who better to look after Jennifer? Anyway, Robert exaggerated. It wasn't true that she was always running over to her mother's and leaving Jennifer with her.

It was just occasionally during the week and at weekends. Sometimes weeks passed and she didn't ask either her mother or Robert to babysit. It all depended on Bernard. If he was working in Glasgow, or if he was away on his travels.

Oh, what a joy it was to see him after he'd been away for a time! He was due back from London today. Robert was off with a crowd of pupils from his new school to Stirling Castle. He'd be away for most of the day. Everything was going to be perfect.

Even the sun was shining. Beautiful Saturday. Beautiful Glasgow. Beautiful world.

She came to life with Bernard. She'd never known what living was before they'd come together in passionate love. Bernard had awakened her to all the lusts of the flesh. Since knowing him she'd become deliciously conscious of her own sensuality, the way she could dress to accentuate her curves, the sexy way she delighted in walking, or crossing her long legs. His auburn-haired Marilyn Monroe, Bernard called her.

Today he was coming to the flat in Monteith Row because Jane would be at home in Pollokshields most of the time. There would be no need to hurry, no danger at the flat. Once Robert was out with his precious pupils, he forgot the time. And Stirling Castle was a safe enough distance away.

Excited anticipation was already pulsating through her, swelling and moistening her secret places. She struggled to appear calm and normal when her mother returned to the room.

'I'd better rush if I've to get any shopping done today. And then I'm meeting a friend for lunch.'

'What friend?'

'Now be a good girl for Nanna, Jennifer. Remember she doesn't agree with nuts, Mummy. I think she's got a bit of an allergy to them.'

'I know that. I've always been very careful with her food. A lot more careful than you, I'll warrant.'

'Bye, Mummy. Bye, Jennifer.'

Andrina escaped from the house. It was as much as she could do to prevent herself running along Drymen Road to the bus stop at Bearsden Cross.

Freedom – a whole day of wonderful erotic pleasure. Bernard was an artist in making love. He took his time caressing and fondling and kissing every inch of her body from the tips of her toes to the top of her head. For such a hefty hard-boiled-looking man, he could be incredibly tender and self-controlled. Very gradually he allowed his passions to quicken. Often she would be so aroused she would be begging and pleading with him to plunge inside her. And then . . . And then . . . Oh, the abandoned, animal-like ecstasy.

She arrived back at Monteith Row and ran breathlessly up the stairs. Josie was just coming out of the flat next door. Sophie had warned Andrina to have nothing to do with her. Josie's main crime in Sophie's eyes was that she worked as a barmaid in a Castle Street pub that was frequented by many people from the Garngad and Blackhill areas, 'of all places'. To compound the evil of selling the demon drink to the dregs of society, Josie had a well-developed bust and a cleavage which she showed off to advantage with low-cut tight-fitting sweaters or blouses. Often she wore short tight skirts and sported dangly earrings. And she smoked.

When Sophie had discovered Josie in Andrina's house having a cup of tea she had frozen Josie out. Later she'd said to Andrina in disgust, 'How could you allow your settee to be dirtied by that slut's disgusting thighs?'

And for nearly three weeks after this incident Sophie hadn't spoken to her. Andrina had been ill with anxiety. She'd kept phoning, only to have the phone at the other end hung up. She'd felt so shaken that she hadn't been able to go out to Bearsden at first. At last she'd taken a taxi out at a ridiculous price she couldn't afford and promised her mother faithfully that she'd never even speak to Josie again, far less allow her over her door. Gradually, her mother had thawed out. Andrina's relief was indescribable. She wept with it. Her relationship with her mother was one thing that Bernard couldn't understand. Once when he'd been trying to persuade her to leave Robert and live with him, he'd said, 'Don't worry about your mother. I'll deal with her. I'll speak to her.'

She'd nearly fainted with terror at the thought.

To Bernard it didn't make sense. She knew it didn't. It was nothing to do with sense. It was blind panic. She didn't want to talk about it, even think about it.

She hadn't stopped speaking to Josie, of course. How could she? Josie was a very kind and good neighbour who often babysat for her. They were good friends. Then the friendship went sour, and it had nothing to do with Sophie.

Josie had been going on a day trip to Dunoon with some of her mates from work and Andrina had seen this as a chance to spend a day with Bernard. It was Saturday, so Robert would be at home. She'd told him in plenty of time that she needed him to look after Jennifer for the day because Josie had asked her to join the trip to Dunoon. So he didn't plan outings for his pupils, and she persuaded Josie to go along with the lie.

'I'll explain why later, Josie,' she'd told her neighbour, who had been a bit mystified but had reluctantly agreed. She was reluctant, because she liked and admired Robert and felt guilty at deceiving him.

'It's all right,' Andrina gave another hastily whispered assurance. 'I'll explain later.'

Andrina remembered how special that day had been. Bernard made every day special. Often he phoned her up and told her how to dress for him, what preparation to make or what he wanted her to do.

That day, he'd given rather stranger than usual instructions. She had a key to his flat in Sauchiehall Mansions and she was to bring over everything she'd worn on her wedding day. He told her to be wearing her dress and veil, everything, when he arrived. This she did, down to her white satin bra and suspender belt, and French knickers, white stockings and high-heeled satin shoes. She heard him arrive but she waited for him in the bedroom as instructed. Eventually he entered the bedroom immaculately dressed in a grey tailored suit and winged collar. In front of the long mirror they went through a ceremony: he flung the ring Robert had given her aside and placed on her finger another gold band – the Russian-type ring she'd always wanted. Then he lifted her crinoline skirt and plunged inside her again and again.

She could hardly wait to tell Josie. She'd thought it would be all right: Josie had been hoping she'd meet an American sailor at Dunoon. Josie was a woman of the world.

To Andrina's astonishment, Josie had been horrified.

'That's bloody obscene,' she'd cried out. 'You get me to lie to your good man. And you get him to look after your wean while you go off and dress up in the white dress you married him in, and you let another man fuck you. That's bloody obscene!'

That had been the last time Josie had obliged her by babysitting. Josie hadn't understood how beautiful it had been. And how romantic.

She said hello to Josie now. And Josie gave a brief hello back, passed her and clipped away down the stairs on her high heels.

Bernard liked Andrina to wear high heels, and as soon as she was safely in the flat she kicked off the sensible flatties that her mother liked, and her long skirt and high-necked blouse and petticoat. She donned a sexy, lace-edged basque, stockings and very high-heeled sandals. On top she wore a black fitted dress, which flowed wide over a stiff taffeta skirt. She put on a diamanté necklace and earrings and pinned up her long thick hair, leaving loose curly strands hanging provocatively down.

It was a crazy way to dress in a forenoon but her and Bernard's world had always been crazy. Private and perfect for them alone. She drew down the blinds and shut all the curtains. They were going to pretend it was the evening and instead of lunch she would have a candlelight dinner. Bernard arrived, dressed in a dinner suit, and she'd never seen him look so handsome. His eyes mirrored his smooth coal-black hair. She'd heard people say, Jane for instance, that it was his eyes that frightened people, and he often did have a hard, watchful look. She supposed he needed to be hard and forever watchful in his business. She'd told Jane that. What she refrained from saying to Jane was, 'He never looks at me like that. When he looks at me, his eyes are filled with love and tenderness. Or passion.'

Admittedly, a silent kind of watchfulness was part of the pattern of his behaviour towards her. He liked her to parade about in front of him or sit in provocative positions. Or just lie back in bed while he stood above her, not doing or saying anything, just observing her. At first this had made her embarrassed and self-conscious. But she'd become used to it, blossomed under his stare and become wicked. Enjoyed it.

There was another kind of watchfulness, though that she didn't enjoy; that made her feel insecure and uneasy. She never knew when his unwavering stare was fixed on her outside. And following her. His memory of these occasions seemed uncanny. He could tell her what she had been wearing down to the last detail at functions she'd attended with Robert years ago. Or when and how often and what she'd been wearing each time she'd visited her mother. He could even list each outfit she'd worn and where she'd gone while she was pregnant with Jennifer.

She didn't like him to do things like that. It frightened her. He'd taken her in his arms, and said, 'What could you possibly have to fear from me? I love you.'

Still the unease of unknown shadows remained . . . But oh, how handsome he looked in his dinner suit.

He had brought boxes, including a big one marked *Harrods*. It wasn't her birthday and she couldn't imagine what any of the boxes contained. You never could tell with Bernard. He was always exciting and delighting her with surprises. How foolish both his wives had been to try, as he put it, 'to make me into a pipe and slippers man'.

Jane was still trying. She never tired of pleading with him to work nine-to-five hours and be at home more often, be more settled, more of a family man. Jane wanted a family. Poor, foolish Jane.

'What on earth have you got there?' she laughed.

'Come on through to the bedroom and I'll show you.'

He opened the Harrods box. Andrina gasped and giggled and said, 'You're crazy.'

'Well, you were always going on about the lovely big stiff Egyptian cotton sheets you get in posh hotels. So here you are. Help me put them on the bed.'

Laughing together they stripped the bed and spread out the pristine sheets. Then he told her to go through to the kitchen until he called her. When she returned, he opened the curtains and raised the blind. A watery sun was streaming in through the window and on to the virgin white bed with its snowy pillows stacked high. He'd scattered long-stemmed red roses all over the bed. She stood in the doorway, stunned with the beauty of it, until he came across and swept her up into his arms and carried her over to the bed and laid her gently on top of it.

And it became their bed, in their special world. Jane and Robert were forgotten.

Chapter Nine

Frank decided to make a big change to his play. It was still about the disintegration of marriage and how one partner couldn't cope with the success of the other, but instead of having the floundering character the woman, he made it the man. It entailed a lot of extra work, but the more he thought about it, the better he liked the idea. After all, as he'd often told Bridie, creative writers didn't just report on what actually happened in real life. A creative writer didn't just copy, he made an arrangement to suit his own purpose. So Frank arranged that the wife in the play became successful and the husband couldn't cope with it.

Yes, he liked the idea and not only because there might, just might, be less chance of Bridie recognising herself as the trigger for the play. It began to dawn on him that he had touched on something here that was going to be one of the big social problems of the future. He was sure it had already taken root but it was bound to grow as women gained more freedom, opportunities and power.

Men would have a lot to learn, a lot of readjusting to do. From time immemorial, the man had been the breadwinner, the head of the house. It was on this role that so much of maleness and pride depended. Especially in Scotland.

The more he thought of this reversal of the status quo and its potential for conflict and drama, the more exited he became. He noted Bridie's dour looks and sarcastic glances. He had come to expect them and usually became depressed and felt insecure and vulnerable. But now he was using them to good effect and every nuance secretly interested him. She was jealous. That was obvious by the sudden darkness that came down and burned away the normally gentle expression in her eyes. He made his man – Sol, he called him – have moments when he seethed with the same dark hatred. He grafted on to Sol's mouth Bridie's bitter twist. He took inspiration from the subtle, and sometimes not so subtle tricks Bridie had of undermining his self-confidence and made them part of Sol's behaviour towards his wife, Amy.

Amy was climbing the ladder of success in the fashion world. She had to look good and that was one of the areas where Sol chipped away at her. There was always something wrong with the way Amy looked, as far as Sol was concerned. He became expert in deflating her every happy moment. Not to mention putting difficulties in her way.

Frank felt heart-sorry for them both. Underneath all the aggro they still loved one another. Just like him and Bridie. The play worked out well until near the end when he took writer's block. It gave him a tension headache. An iron cap was screwing tighter and tighter over his skull.

He locked the play in his desk drawer and tried to forget it. Forget all about writing. Get his priorities right, for God's sake. He had a good wife: it was time he put her first, paid more attention to her, made her feel special, not just second best to his writing. He'd never meant her to feel that way but that's how she did feel. She'd told him.

'Your writing comes first with you. I'm a poor second, Frank.'

Another time she'd said, 'If this house went on fire, Frank, the first thing you'd think of saving would be your manuscript.'

He'd thought at the time – well, it wouldn't take a minute to grab his manuscript. After all, it represented days, weeks – months of work. And it was the kind of thing that couldn't be thought of again. Once the excitement of writing about a subject had gone, been worked out, it couldn't be repeated.

Now he remonstrated with himself, told himself he must pull himself together. So he concentrated his full attention on Bridie. They talked over morning coffee. He took her out to lunch. They did some shopping in the afternoon and in the evening they visited Bridie's mother and father in Garngad.

Carragh and Scobie welcomed him with open arms. They didn't see nearly enough of him, they said. He refrained from saying that this wasn't entirely his fault. They seldom came to visit his house either these days. It had been a lot different when he and Bridie had lived in the Gorbals. Before that, of course, he and Bridie had lived in Carragh and Scobie's front room. Bridie looked wistfully back at that part of their lives now. In fact, living in a room and kitchen with Carragh and Scobie, and Doris as well after her marriage to Bernard had broken up, had been sheer hell. Scobie, who was an alcoholic, had still been drinking then and battering Carragh about. Frank shuddered every time he remembered the time he'd nearly killed a drunken Scobie in an attempt to stop him battering the poor woman. Barely five feet she was, and bandy-legged with it. Scobie wasn't much more than five feet himself, but as strong and as dangerous as a Rottweiler in a fight. Frank could hardly credit the nostalgic way Bridie could talk about their stay at her mother and father's place. He'd tried to put her straight.

'Bridie, the only peace we got there was when your da was in Barlinnie and he was in and out as if he was attached to the place with elastic. Each time, as soon as he got out, he was on the booze again and creating absolute hell. You couldn't get away from there quick enough.'

'That was just at first,' Bridie protested. 'He gave up the drink. A nicer man and better husband and father than my da, you couldn't meet.'

When Frank thought of all the bother he had had in getting Scobie to Alcoholics Anonymous . . . It was Frank O'Maley that Scobie Gallacher had to thank for giving up the drink. He felt like telling Bridie that. But what was the use: she didn't want to know.

There could be no doubt of Carragh and Scobie's delight at seeing him. They had always been fond of him, and indeed he had always been fond of them. He wouldn't have tried so hard to help Scobie, for one thing, if he hadn't cared about him.

Carragh made a pot of tea. 'How've you been, son? Still scribbling away?'

'You know me,' Frank said.

'Aye, you were always a funny one. I mind you used to shut yourself through in the room, and Bridie and me kept the wireless down low so's not to disturb you. Not that Bridie bothered about listenin' to the wireless like me. She always had her nose buried in some book or other.'

It hurt him to remember that. No black looks, no bitter twisting mouth, no jealousy, no belittling jokes then. Why couldn't they still be the same with each other? He felt the same person as he'd always been, despite his success.

'How's the family?' he asked.

'Tam and Billy and Eamon are doing real well with their group.'

'Right enough,' Frank agreed. 'There's been quite a lot of publicity about their latest gig. Or tour, was it?' He tried to remember. He wasn't a fan of the Who Dun Its.

'And Charlie's a petty officer now in the Navy. Imagine! Our wee Charlie.'

Frank couldn't. But he said, 'Great. That's just great, Carragh. And Geordie and Haggis?' he prompted, while at the same time it was occurring to him that Bridie never told him any news about her family any more. Or did she? Maybe he'd just never paid any attention.

'They're still going the rounds with the Fair folk. Still as happy as larks.'

'Great,' Frank repeated. 'That's just great, Carragh.'

'Have another cookie, son.'

'Thanks.'

Bridie asked, 'Where's Doris, Ma? Is she going with anybody yet? She always clams up when I talk to her about getting a boyfriend.'

'A nice-lookin' lassie,' Scobie said. 'I keep telling her she'll make a rare wee wife to some lucky fella.'

Carragh sighed. 'She's still pining after that big brother of yours, Frank.'

'I don't know why,' Bridie said. 'He was never that good to her. A downright bastard, in fact.' The bitter twist had come back and the hatred. It was as if she was talking about him, Frank thought.

'Now, now, hen,' Carragh chided. 'There's always two sides to every story. And if our Doris had been a good Catholic, she would never have divorced Bernard O'Maley. I told her that at the time. He was her man and she'd vowed to stand by him through thick and thin, for better or for worse. I

told her I'd gone through far worse with this wee bastard.'
Laughing, she jerked her head in Scobie's direction.

'See her,' Scobie said, giving Carragh's waist a squeeze,
'she's daft about me. Always was.'

'I admire the pair of you,' Frank said, really meaning it. 'The
way you've stuck together, kept your feelings for each other.'

There's a story there somewhere, he told himself, filing the
idea away in his mind, hoarding it. Then he felt guilty. Here I
go again. Pull yourself together.

'The last I saw of Bernard was at Tony's wedding. We're
not on visiting terms. I mean we couldn't, with Bridie being
Doris's sister,' he said.

'Oh, that's right, blame me,' Bridie cried out. 'I stop you
seeing your brother as well as all your fancy friends.'

'Bridie!' Carragh sounded shocked. 'There's no call to be
like that. Frank was only trying to be loyal to you.'

'I know I could see Bernard if I wanted to,' Frank explained.
'As I said, I saw him at the wedding and sometimes I bump
into him in Blackhill when I go to see my da. The truth is I'm
not too keen to see him. To be honest, Bernard and I have
never had all that much in common. I'd far rather that Doris
visits us. I'm very fond of Doris and I honestly wish she could
find someone else.'

'I know, son,' Carragh sighed. 'So do we.'

Scobie said, 'She's a wee smasher as well. She'd have no
bother if she'd just have a bit of sense.'

'Yes,' Frank agreed. 'She's a nice-looking girl. I wonder . . .' he added thoughtfully, 'if I could fix her up with
someone. At least, introduce her to a few nice guys from the
BBC. You never know, it might help. I know some good-
looking guys. How about an actor?'

Scobie laughed. 'Here, that might tickle her fancy. Trust
you, son. You've always been the clever one.'

'Oh, hasn't he just,' Bridie said.

Carragh eyed her.

'What's up with your face?'

'Nothing.'

'Well, keep a civil tongue in your head. At least Frank's
trying to help.'

'Frank doesn't know his arse from his elbow. He couldn't help anybody if he tried. Doris wouldn't fit in with his crowd any more than I do. Frank just opens his mouth and dreams come out. He's always been the same.'

Frank could have wept. Once she'd shared his dreams.

'At least Frank's trying to help,' Carragh repeated. 'I don't know what's got into you, Bridie. Talking like that about your good man. He's too good to you, if you ask me. You're a right spoiled wee bisom, so you are.'

'Nobody's asking you, Ma.'

Scobie bristled. 'You watch your tongue to your ma.'

Frank could see Bridie struggling with herself. At last she managed, 'Sorry, Ma. I don't know what's the matter with me today.'

'Have another cup of tea, hen. Would you like a wee aspirin?'

'No thanks, I'll be OK with the tea.'

'I was talking to Patrick the other day,' Scobie said. 'He was telling me your Michael's awful good to that auld harridan he's got for a mother-in-law. And it's not only your da that's said. One of the lads on the site told me they'd seen him trundling her along in a wheelchair and gabbin' away nineteen to the dozen. At the weekend it was, as well. When he could have been at the match.'

Frank was afraid to say he'd never seen much of Michael either.

'He was a good boxer in his day,' he said instead.

'The best,' Scobie agreed.

'Pity about the drink.'

'Aye.'

'He's got you to thank for getting him off that, Scobie.'

'No, son. He'd just reached the stage when he knew himself he needed and wanted help. I just pointed him in the right direction.'

A thought occurred to Frank, 'Here, I hope Big Martha doesn't push him too far . . .'

'You mean, he might be tempted to go back on the booze?'

'Yes.'

'I'm sure he's tempted every day, son. Once an alcoholic, always an alcoholic. And I should know.'

'A terrible addiction,' Frank sighed. And then another thought occurred to him. Maybe writing was an addiction too. And, as far as personal relationships were concerned, just as destructive.

Chapter Ten

'Earl Grey or Lapsang Souchong, Mrs McPherson?' Mrs Pemberton's plump bejewelled hands hovered over the silver tea-tray.

Sophie flickered a smile at her neighbour.

'Earl Grey, thank you.'

'My preference too. Such a delicate flavour.'

Mrs Dinwoodie, the minister's wife, agreed. Mrs Dinwoodie and her Reverend husband lived in one of the large villas looking on to the St Germaine loch. The other two ladies enjoying afternoon tea in Mrs Pemberton's elegant house were Mrs Hawthorn, the bank manager's wife, and Mrs Jones, who both lived at the other end of the terrace.

Mrs Jones said, 'You're still looking very pale and drawn, Mrs McPherson. I know they say time heals but I don't believe anyone could fully recover from such a tragedy as you suffered. Losing not just one parent, but two. And after such a terribly sad background. I mean even before – '

Mrs Dinwoodie interrupted. 'I don't think it's an appropriate time to remind any of us, especially poor Mrs McPherson, of her tragic loss, Mrs Jones. We're having afternoon tea.'

Mrs Jones was a member of the dramatic society and tended to make a drama out of everything and cast herself as the leading light whenever she could.

The other ladies murmured their agreement and Mrs Jones was suitably, if temporarily, subdued. In no time at all, however, she'd bounced back with the latest newspaper headlines about another unsolved murder of a Glasgow woman. That brought the total to three. They had all been middle-aged to elderly, and perfectly respectable housewives. 'Not prostitutes or anything like that.'

'But of course – ' all the ladies agreed with Mrs Jones in this – 'nothing like that could ever happen in Bearsden.' The city of

Glasgow was a most dangerous and violent place. Not to mention downright common.

Sophie had lowered her eyes. She was thinking, Loss? Loss? I lost my parents a lifetime ago when they first used and abused me. The filth that they were. I hope they're burning in hell.

For years, she'd hoped and prayed they were dead. Then just when she believed she had at last put the past behind her, and had found a respectable, safe and happy niche in the lovely district of Bearsden, they turned up. Agnes and Duncan Noble. Noble, of all names! Noble they certainly were not and never had been. Everybody, including McPherson, had thought her parents were dead. That's what she'd told them. Then she'd been forced to confess how she'd been taken into care when she'd been very young and had lost touch with her parents. She didn't tell what her parents had done that had caused the authorities to take her into care. That was another ironic word. Care! Care she had never got. When she thought of the institution she'd been incarcerated in and what she'd suffered there, she shuddered even now. She didn't tell her new-found Bearsden friends and neighbours about that either. Their comfortable little apple-carts wouldn't have been able to cope with such sordidness. No, the enjoyable (to them) scenario was of a frail and elderly couple who regretted any peccadillo of their foolish youth and now just wanted to be reunited with their long-lost daughter and end their days as a happy family.

The suicide and the suicide note had been a genuine shock to everyone. Except Sophie, who secretly wept with relief and felt free of the danger of losing her respectable place in Bearsden society, and the church. Especially the church. She had been in a state of collapse, fearing that the Nobles might confess the filthy perverted truth and make lepers of her as well as themselves. After their death, she'd thought all would be well. She'd be a changed person. Her previous apprehensions and anxieties would evaporate for ever. She would be able to relax – only it didn't work out that way.

Andrina reminded her so much of her mother. How she remembered her mother when she'd been a younger woman. That same red hair. That same voluptuous body, so shamelessly flaunted. Andrina had become the focus of all her anxieties. She didn't trust the girl. Never had. Oh, she sang in the choir like an angel and she was very careful in dressing modestly when she came to visit Bearsden. On those occasions she wore very little make-up and no jewellery except her wedding ring. But Sophie had caught her on more than one occasion in Monteith Row dressed in disgustingly provocative clothes, earrings and jangly bracelets, and her face like a painted doll.

McPherson accused her of being neurotic: Andrina was a lovely-looking girl and he was sure anything she wore would look attractive on her. Anyway, she was a married woman in her thirties. What she wore, he insisted, was surely her own business. Her own business, was it? Did he want Andrina to get involved in some scandal? How would that not be their business, she asked him. Andrina was their only child. She was well-known and often sang in their Bearsden branch of the Church of Jesus, as well as the one in the city centre. His fellow councillors in the City Chambers had met her. The Reverend Dinwoodie and his wife and all the respectable influential people of Bearsden had met her.

Her own business, would it be? 'Listen to me,' Sophie had warned him. 'If she gets involved in any scandal, it could bring us down, ruin our reputation just as easily as the Nobles could have. That was a near thing. You know damn well now the Nobles could have ruined us. We'd have had to move . . .'

'But Andrina hasn't done anything,' McPherson gasped in exasperation. 'I'm telling you, Sophie, if you don't get a grip of yourself, you'll be driving yourself completely mad. You're unbalanced enough as it is.'

What did he know? How lucky he was. Always able to withdraw behind a fragrant screen of pipe smoke and switch off, shut her out. She envied his calmness, his ability to relax, to ease on the slippers she always had ready and waiting for him and lean his portly body back in his chair. He had no reason to criticise or complain about her. She kept his home immaculate. She cooked delicious meals which he obviously enjoyed. She was a good hostess. They entertained a lot, carefully and conscientiously nurturing friendships with all the best people.

Doing all the right things. She was an active member of the Women's Guild and various other societies. He was a member of the expensive local golf club. They both were learning to play bridge and had been accepted by the bridge club.

'I don't know what you're nagging on about,' McPherson said. 'We've come from a wee room and kitchen via a Corporation house in Drumchapel to this big terrace house in Bearsden. What more do you want?'

She wanted nothing more. Not a thing. This was her paradise. To have a home to be proud of. To have a place in decent society. And no one, not her father, not her mother, not Andrina, no one would ever be allowed to take these things away from her. She'd kill to keep them.

She kept trying to relax, to believe what McPherson said about having nothing to worry about. But anxiety and apprehension had become such an integral part of her that she couldn't shake them off. On the surface, she could chat quite normally with all her lady friends at their coffee mornings and afternoon teas or soirées. She worked tirelessly for the church. She and McPherson got on very well on the whole. They went to most functions together, and were always well dressed, walking a little apart, he portly and dignified clutching his bible, and she lean and rigid-backed, handbag clamped under armpit. They never touched, especially in public. She was not a touching kind of person.

It was Andrina who constantly threatened this hard-fought-for pattern of life. In some subtle, undefined, unproven way. Sophie struggled to keep her suspicions at bay, firmly back in the darker recesses of her mind. She could bask in the warmth of compliments about her daughter, especially in the church.

'What a lovely girl, Mrs McPherson. Really lovely. You must be very proud of her.'

'She sings like an angel, Mrs McPherson. It's a real treat for us all to listen to her. Quite an inspiring and uplifting experience.'

The more people spoke with such glowing admiration for Andrina, the more they complimented Sophie on having produced such a paragon of virtue, the more Sophie hugged herself with satisfaction. Andrina was a valuable addition to her standing in the community. Just as McPherson was, with him being a senior bailie of the City of Glasgow. Andrina was even more so, however. Andrina was her own flesh and blood. But as well as being a feather in her cap, Andrina was the Achilles heel to both her and McPherson. He never could see this.

'You're just being neurotic,' he kept accusing. Then in a more concerned tone, 'Sophie, I wish you'd stop working so hard. You get like an overwound spring. You're going to snap one of these days. Be good to yourself. Take time off. Treat yourself to something nice to wear. Have a good meal in a first-class restaurant in town. We can afford it.'

He didn't understand. She had to keep busy every waking hour to stop herself from thinking, from remembering. But it didn't matter now, she tried to assure herself. She was safe. Her parents were dead.

'They're dead. They're dead,' she kept repeating over and over like a mantra.

'*They're dead.*'

McPherson was right. It was time she pulled herself together. The house was spotless; it looked unused like a glossy picture from a *Good Housekeeping* magazine.

There were no meetings today. It wasn't her turn for a coffee morning or an afternoon tea until next week. McPherson had to meet a business associate and wasn't coming home for lunch. Time panicked in her hands. She decided to take the bus into town and do some shopping. Then she'd treat herself to a nice lunch. She bustled about getting ready then hurried along to the bus stop, bent tensely forward as if against a blustery wind.

Perhaps after lunch she could drop in to see Andrina and Jennifer. Of course, they were coming to Bearsden later that night for dinner. But still it would do no harm to drop in for a few minutes while she was in town. Andrina had said Jennifer loved school and was getting on splendidly but Sophie felt uneasy about this. She'd get the child on her own this afternoon while Andrina was making a cup of tea. Andrina would never bring Jennifer to the phone. Always some excuse: Jennifer was in the bath. Jennifer was having a nap.

Jennifer was out with her daddy. She'd quite a few questions to ask Jennifer.

Sophie bought herself a lavender twinset. Mrs Pemberton had weaned her off dark browns and blacks.

'They're too severe for you, dear. I'm afraid they just drain you. You simply don't suit them. You need something softer, dear. Much more flattering.' But Sophie still hung on to her black coat, hat, gloves and shoes.

'So handy for funerals, don't you think?' she pleaded to Mrs Pemberton, who was a recognised architect of good taste in Bearsden. Mrs Pemberton had to agree. Sophie hoped Mrs Pemberton would approve of the Pringle lavender twinset in pure cashmere. It was frighteningly expensive but McPherson wasn't mean. He grudged her nothing. In fact, he always said, 'Always make sure you get the best, Sophie. We owe it to our image and our good standing in the community.'

She was really very lucky in having a husband like McPherson. Nothing but the best. He applied the same rule to himself and she was glad. It made her proud to see him dressed in well-cut expensive suits and shirts and overcoats. She took great pains in brushing his shoes until she saw her thin, sweating face in them. She always pressed his clothes, including his ties and wouldn't allow him outside the door each morning until she'd flicked a clothes brush over his shoulders and carefully brushed every inch of his trilby.

They never kissed but after he left she'd dash to the front-room window and wave to him and he'd turn to wave back. They had a good marriage. They suited each other. But far more important, she could trust him.

She wondered where she'd go for lunch. There was the Palm Court restaurant in Copland and Lye's where the orchestra competed with the chinkle of china and cutlery. In the La Scala you watch a film while you had a cup of tea and something to eat. There was the Rogano if you fancied seafood. Or Miss Cranston's with its elegant Rennie Mackintosh interior design. Indeed, there were so many good restaurants and tea-rooms in Glasgow that Sophie dithered for a time, turning this way and that, trying to make up her mind.

Eventually she found herself in Gordon Street, near the

Central Station and her eye was caught by the Corn Exchange restaurant across the road. She'd often heard McPherson talk about this place. He liked the Corn Exchange and had remarked on how good the food was there. It was getting late and she was beginning to feel tired as well as hungry. She wasn't used to all this traipsing about the town, so she decided not to look any further. She was crossing the road when it occurred to her that McPherson might be having lunch there with his client or associate, or whoever it was he was meeting. Somebody important, anyway. So would it be proper for her to suddenly appear? Would he mind? Would her appearance interrupt some deal or other that might spoil it for McPherson? She didn't want to cause him any trouble or inconvenience. She'd always kept in the background as far as his work was concerned, respecting his position, his ability. She had deferred to him in this area, given him every support. And McPherson had always supported her, through thick and thin. He had been the saving of her by introducing her to the church. He was her lifeline.

Reaching the door of the restaurant she hesitated, still not sure what to do. Of course it was late. Probably McPherson, if he had been in this restaurant today, would be long gone by now. She pushed the door open and entered the cool brown interior. The change from the bright sunlight outside confused her for a moment. Her eyes strained to find a free table.

Suddenly she stopped in her tracks. Over by the wall she saw McPherson and he saw her. His companion's sleek ebony hair and dark satanic eyes were unmistakable. The blood drained from Sophie's head, making her feel faint. The filthy Papish scum who had wicked designs on Andrina. Her mind peppered with fearful suspicions. She saw McPherson rise and beckon her over. O'Maley, noticing her, rose too.

Blindly, in silent hysteria, Sophie turned and hastened back outside.

Chapter Eleven

'Oh God!' McPherson groaned. 'Do you think I should go after her?'

Bernard laughed.

'I wouldn't advise it. Not after a meal like that, a bottle of claret and two brandies. What with your girth and your wife as lean and fast as a greyhound, you wouldn't stand a chance.'

'You're right. She'll be half-way back to Bearsden by now. Oh God!' he repeated. 'I think I'll have another drink.'

Bernard signalled to the waiter.

'Beats me,' he said, 'what she's got against me that always sends her into such a state. She looked as if she was going to take a fit there.'

'I don't know either, Bernard, and that's a fact. And she's as bad now about you as she ever was. I daren't even mention your name. Although I'm sure I've told her that you did a bit of work now and again for the council.' (In fact he was not sure at all.)

'Well, I'm sorry if I upset her so much.'

'Don't worry about it. It's not as if you've ever done anything. Other than having been born a Roman Catholic, of course.'

'I don't think I've been to Mass since my mother died.'

'Sophie's a good woman in her own way. I couldn't get a better wife. She keeps my house like a palace and there isn't a chef in Glasgow can cook any better than her. But nobody's perfect. She had a hard life, you know, before she met me. It's affected her. Then that awful business with her parents killing themselves. Did I tell you?'

Bernard nodded.

'Her nerves are shot to pieces. I don't think she'll ever get over it. The damnable thing is, it was me who egged her on to have a day in town and treat herself to a meal. Of course, I didn't know she'd decide to come today. Or come here. Oh God!'

'If you tell her we do business together, what can she find wrong with that?'

'As I say, the mention of your name is enough.'

McPherson quailed at the mere idea of Sophie knowing how many long brown envelopes he'd received from Bernard. Their contents had paid for many comforts and luxuries that Sophie had innocently enjoyed. He and Bernard had a very happy and profitable relationship. If the Glasgow Corporation was entertaining foreign dignatories or industrialists and security arrangements were needed, he made sure that Bernard's firm got the job. He'd never asked Bernard for any commission. Everything had been Bernard's idea right from the start. Bernard was a good businessman as well as a tough character. Another thing – there could be no doubt about it, Bernard and everyone who worked for Bernard did an excellent job. Whether it was bodyguarding important visitors to the city, or crowd control at pop concerts, or keeping order at any events big or small, Bernard made sure that he and his men were in control. He was splendid value for the city's money, was big Bernard O'Maley.

He was an appreciative and generous man too. The contents of the envelopes that Bernard regularly and discreetly passed to McPherson never diminished. He was a man after his own heart, was Bernard. Many a good lunch Bernard had treated him to as well.

'What do you propose to do?' Bernard asked, leaning back in that relaxed yet hard-eyed way of his.

McPherson shrugged.

'I don't suppose I've any choice. I'll have to tell her you're doing security work for the council, I suppose. Then just try to calm her down. As I told you, her nerves are shot to pieces. I've been trying to get her to go to see a doctor. It's not natural, the way she carries on.'

'Well, I wish you luck, McPherson – ' Bernard raised his glass – 'and continuing success.'

'Continuing success,' McPherson echoed.

He decided to go straight home instead of returning to the City Chambers. There was nothing urgent to attend to this afternoon. And Bernard was right. Sophie did look in a state.

But by the time he had completed the drive from the city centre to the leafy suburb of Bearsden he was feeling irritated. It was such a ridiculous situation. He would have to be firm with Sophie for a change. For her own good.

As soon as he entered the kitchen where he normally found her, he announced, 'Now look here, Sophie, I've had enough of your ridiculous attitude to Bernard O'Maley. I have to do business with him. He's responsible for all the security work for the Corporation. Bernard and I have to sit down and discuss things. You gave me a right showing up today. What was the meaning of it? What's he ever done to warrant you snubbing him like that? And worse, dashing off as if he'd leprosy. It just doesn't make sense.'

She'd had time to calm down but there was still a grey tinge to her skin and her mouth was a twisted thread of bitterness.

'I don't trust him.'

'Why not, for God's sake?'

'You know why not.'

'No, I do not know why not, Sophie.'

'He went on seeing Andrina after I'd forbidden him.'

'For pity's sake, Sophie, that was years ago, when Andrina was just a schoolgirl. Anyway, if I remember correctly, it was Andrina you spoke to, not him. If anybody disobeyed you, it was Andrina.'

'Oh, I know she's not to be trusted either.'

'Sophie, you'll have to pull yourself together.'

'So you keep telling me.'

'I mean it. You're getting paranoiac.'

'It's not just a matter of disobedience.'

'If it's his religion you're on about now, he's never been to Mass since his mother died. But even if he had, it's really none of our business. Live and let live, that's my motto.'

'Oh, I know you always take the easy way out.'

'Out of what?'

She was becoming agitated again, hunching her shoulders, twisting her fingers, avoiding his eyes.

'It's not just his religion either.'

'What then?'

'There's something . . . something obscene about him. He's so . . . physical.'

He'd forgotten about that. Being too physical was one of the things she'd said about Bernard years ago. He had some idea what she meant, or how she felt, knowing Sophie and the way she shrank from even an affectionate touch on the arm. The only physical contact they ever had was in bed in the darkness of their bedroom. There she would have a desperate, furtive coupling with him before turning away again into her own tormented isolation.

Bernard had an aura of power about him that had strong sexual overtones. He could imagine Sophie sensing and fearing that. For the first time it occurred to him that perhaps Sophie had been sexually abused as a child. It would explain why she had been so bitter about her parents and why the discovery of them living in Bearsden had distressed her so much. It would certainly explain why she'd been taken into care as a child.

Suddenly all his anger and exasperation dissolved into pity and compassion. He loved his wife and it upset him to think of her suffering.

'Oh Sophie.'

He didn't know what to say or do. He wanted to take her into his arms and comfort her but knew that she would only tense up and shrink away from him. 'Oh Sophie,' he repeated helplessly.

Her eyes darted up to his face then flicked away again.

'I'll make a pot of tea. You go through to the room and sit down. I've got some of that fruit cake you like. I baked it yesterday.'

He sighed.

'I'm a lucky man, Sophie. You're a good wife. I appreciate you. I hope you know that.'

'Go away through. I'll bring the tray.'

He flopped heavily into his favourite chair and lay back, motionless for a few minutes before bending forward, grunting with the effort to reach over his paunch, to untie his shoelaces. He was thinking. Should he say something like, 'You've nothing to fear from Bernard, Sophie. Put him out of your mind,' Or 'Perhaps Bernard is awakening fears and triggering off distressing memories from your past, Sophie. But you must try to realise anything you suffered in the past has nothing to do with Bernard.' Or perhaps, 'It's not only the business with Bernard. So much of your behaviour is extreme and obsessive, Sophie. Perhaps you need to discuss everything with a psychiatrist.'

He felt he needed to talk to a psychiatrist about her behaviour himself. There was still so much that he didn't understand. Before she'd been 'saved', she had been with other men while he was away at the war. Or so people had told him. If that was true, how did it fit in with his child abuse theory? And then there was the way she'd neglected Andrina when she was a baby. The cruelty inspector had actually been after her. It had been a terrible shock to him when he got out of the army. His return home and his good character (probably assisted by his well-publicised VC) and his immediate action to put things right had saved Andrina from being taken into care. God knows what and for how long the child had suffered before ever the cruelty man had found out. But eventually Sophie had joined the church and, true to character, had gone right to the opposite extreme.

Now her whole *raison d'être* seemed to be to protect her good reputation. If she worked any harder for the church, they'd be giving her a sainthood.

'Here you are.' She put the tray on a small table beside the arm of his chair.

'Sit down and have a cup yourself,' McPherson said.

'I've still the potatoes to peel for the dinner. Andrina and Robert and Jennifer are coming tonight, remember.'

'You've time for a cup of tea. Have you heard how Robert's getting on at his new school?'

Sophie gave a jerk of her bony shoulders.

'Andrina hasn't said much. Just a vague, "Oh all right". You know what she's like.'

McPherson took a mouthful of tea and the heat of it darkened the port wine hue of his skin.

'Could you beat it? We succeed in persuading him to make a move at last, get a bit of promotion, and where does he go? Sinnieglen!'

Sophie leaned worriedly forward.

'It's not as bad as St Francis, surely. It's a Protestant school, isn't it?'

'It's what's now called non-denominational. That means anybody and everybody can go there, and they do. From not just one tough area, but several. It's common knowledge that the so-called Glasgow Godfather, Joseph McNally, was a product of that school. I wouldn't be a bit surprised if this murderer the papers are full of graduated from the same place.'

'Why does Robert do things like that?' Sophie gasped. 'Surely he could get a job in a good school.'

'I've told him often enough. I could easily use my influence. He doesn't even need to stay in teaching. He'll never make decent money in that profession.'

'I don't understand people like that. There's that woman along the road who works at St Francis.'

'What woman?'

'Mrs Cairns. Across in the bungalows. I've often seen her along at the shops but I didn't know who she was. Mrs Pemberton told me. Her husband was an officer in the RAF. Fancy her working in a place like St Francis when she could be nearer home in a nice respectable school like Bearsden. He's a poor soul now, Mrs Pemberton said.'

'Who?'

'Mr Cairns. He had a stroke. They aren't members of the Church of Jesus. But at least they're Protestants, although Mrs Pemberton said Mr Cairns hasn't been seen in the church since his illness. Mrs Cairns was never a good attender at the best of times. Mrs Pemberton's friendly with one of her neighbours, and the neighbours told Mrs Pemberton that Mrs Cairns sometimes goes on these school outings that Robert organises. A shabby van filled with these awful rough children draws up at her door. Mr Pemberton's friend said it really lowers the tone of the place.'

'Surely, as head of department now, he won't still be doing that,' McPherson said. 'Surely he'll at least acquire a bit of dignity.'

Sophie took an absent-minded sip of tea. 'I hope he'll stay at home more at weekends. It's not good to leave Andrina alone so much. There's no telling what she could get up to.'

'Sophie, you must learn to relax and trust people.'

'What do you know or care about trust?' she said with sudden venom.

'What on earth do you mean by that?' he asked.

But of course he knew. Her thoughts had returned to Bernard O'Maley.

Chapter Twelve

They had been invited over to Bernard and Jane's house for supper. Robert had not been keen on going. He was tired, he said. Would she never be satisfied with a quiet night in their own home? he said. Part of the trouble was, Andrina decided, that Robert was getting old. He was forty-two and, despite his wiry physique, looked fifty-two. Acted like it as well. When she thought about it, Robert had never been any fun with his serious music, and love of the ballet, and the way he could wander about boring art galleries and exhibitions. He had never excited her in any way whatsoever. Now his brown hair was thinning on top. It had also acquired a peppering of grey at his temples. He didn't care about the grey so much but he was self-conscious about losing his hair and kept trying special shampoos and lotions to rub into his scalp. Bernard's hair was thick and smooth and as black as sin. Bernard never got tired despite working long unsocial hours in a very dangerous job. Bernard's stamina was amazing.

When she'd asked Robert why he was tired (after all he did work comparatively short hours), he'd claimed that teaching was a stressful job.

Stress? Robert didn't know the meaning of the word. It was Bernard who had the stressful job. Anyway, it was Robert's own fault for working in teaching.

'Oh, all right, I'll go but only because it's Bernard,' Robert said eventually.

Andrina wore an emerald green crossover dress with a tulip-shaped skirt and high-heeled shoes of the same colour. Her dress was topped with a dark green coat with a high fur collar. Outside, a November wind stung their faces and squalls of rain flurried at their clothes. They ran for one of the buses that were pushing grimly along the inadequately lit street. Or perhaps the mist from the river made the area so muffled and shadowy. Robert wore a zipped-up anorak. He was always so casually dressed. He had no sense of style. Tonight, for instance, he had put on a polo-neck sweater.

'For goodness sake, Robert,' she'd gasped in exasperation. 'If a collar and tie is good enough for your work, surely it's good enough to go out with me.'

He sighed.

'Andrina, I've had one hell of a day. Friday is always *the* worst day of the week. All the kids are interested in is getting shot of the school for the weekend. I just want to relax tonight. It's not as if we're going to a swanky hotel or even that there's to be other guests. There's only going to be Bernard and Jane.'

'Oh, please yourself.' She'd given in without any more argument. After all, what did she care? Bernard would look like a million dollars and he was the only one who mattered.

'I hope Jennifer will be all right,' Robert said, after they'd settled in the bus.

Andrina tutted impatiently. 'Of course she'll be all right. Why shouldn't she be all right? She loves staying overnight at her nanna's.'

'Has she ever actually told you that?'

'Oh, for goodness sake, Robert! And another thing. She keeps Mummy off my back.'

'Oh, I can believe that.'

'Well, you know how Mummy keeps going on. Talk about the Spanish Inquisition! You've said yourself how neurotic her behaviour is towards me.'

'Yes, that's true, but the point is I don't want her to be behaving like that to Jennifer.'

'She doesn't. Honestly.'

They both lapsed into silence after that. They never spoke very much to each other. Usually when Robert was at home, he had his nose in a book. He had to wear reading glasses now, and they accentuated his seriousness. Andrina thought they made him look so schoolteacherish.

Bernard had not only perfect sight, but dark, disturbing, wickedly exciting eyes. Some people might have considered his burly physique to be the most attractive thing about him. But to her it was his eyes. She could have an orgasm just with him staring at her.

They had a bit of a walk after they got off the bus to reach the imposing villa where Bernard and Jane lived.

'This is just ridiculous,' Andrina gasped, as they hurried along.

'What is?'

'Not having a car.' She felt angry to the point of almost hating him. Her hair was in danger of being ruined with the wind and rain. 'I'm thoroughly sick of your selfish attitude. There's no excuse for not buying a car. Especially now that you're head of a department. What will the other teachers think?'

'I don't care what the other teachers think. But as a matter of fact, I have decided to acquire one. But *I'll* buy it,' he added hastily, 'I will *not* have your father giving me expensive presents. I told him I'd get a car when I could afford it. And that's what I'm going to do.'

'The trouble with you, Robert, is your pride.'

'There's nothing wrong with having some pride.'

'There is if other people suffer as a result of it.'

'Andrina, I have always tried to do the best I could for you and Jennifer.'

She longed to say, 'Well, your best's not good enough', but managed to hold her tongue.

Inside the villa was as familiar to her as her home in Monteith Row. Not only had she been invited here on many occasions by Jane but she'd been here often when Jane was out at the hairdresser's or the beauty parlour or the yoga classes she attended over in the West End. Jane was not a happy woman. Her nerves were a bit run down, she explained, and yoga helped her. So soothing and calming, Jane said.

While Jane was being calmed, Andrina was in Jane's bed being excited. Sometimes Bernard almost went too far, drove her wild, nearly sent her over the top into hysteria. Making love almost under Jane and Robert's noses really terrified her but it was a terror hardly distinguished from the wildest of passions.

Bernard always lived on the edge. He pushed everything to its limits. He seemed to thrive on danger.

'I think that's why you chose the kind of job you're in,'

she'd told him. She understood him far better than any other woman ever had. Especially his wives. Poor Jane. She was about as helpless and hopeless as Doris had been.

Jane welcomed both her and Robert with a kiss while Bernard fixed the drinks. Whisky for Robert and himself, and a dry Martini for Jane and Andrina. At least Robert hadn't asked for a beer. He often drank beer at home. She hated even the smell of it.

'Remember to get some decent wine,' she would remind him when Jane and Bernard came to visit them. This never failed to annoy Robert, of course.

'I do know something about wines. I can also appreciate more sophisticated food than you appear to give me credit for.' She supposed this remark referred to the plain fare she normally served up. Only when cooking for Bernard had she any incentive to produce something different or exotic.

Sometimes Bernard brought a bottle of champagne but only on very special occasions. He knew how touchy Robert's pride could be. Anyway, Bernard preferred to keep the champagne for the occasions when he and Andrina were celebrating on their own.

'How's the new job, Robert?' Bernard asked once they'd all settled around the big log fire.

'You know what St Francis is like,' Robert said.

'Sure do.' Bernard grinned.

'Well, Sinnieglen is ten times worse.'

'You're kidding!'

'I only wish I was. If I could just get more of them interested in the karate club. As it is, I've lost some of the St Francis boys in moving to Sinnieglen.'

'Tough, are they?'

'You could say that.'

'You'll have heard of Joseph McNally, Glasgow's Godfather?'

'I've seen him around.'

'I'm supposed to teach art to his son, Benny.'

Bernard laughed and Jane said, 'Is that really true, Robert?'

'I'm beginning to think I've got all his cohorts' sons – and daughters as well. It's no joke, I can tell you.'

'If it's so awful,' Andrina said a little more dismissively than she meant to, 'why do you do it?'

Robert gave her one of his serious looks.

'Because I'm a teacher.'

Bernard cut in, 'And a very good one too. I remember what a tearaway I was and you soon managed to get me sorted out. You'll do the same for Joe McNally's son.'

Robert looked worried.

'He has this fascination with guns. He knows a lot more than me about them. Which wouldn't be difficult, right enough. But he's always talking about them. Every chance he gets. Like this afternoon, for instance. Remember how all the kids used to be so restless on Friday afternoons? I've long ago given up making any attempt to teach them.'

Bernard nodded.

'Yes, you used to let us gather round and just talk to you about anything, give you all our news and opinions. I remember.'

'Well, I was doing that this afternoon, and Benny kept going on about guns. There's something about that boy, something that's going to be very difficult to deal with. No wonder, of course. Can you imagine the kind of background and example the boy must be having at home? This is what depresses me. It's being unable to do enough about the social problems. It's not so much the actual teaching.'

'Oh, for pity's sake, Robert,' Andrina burst out, 'you'll have us all depressed if you keep on like this.'

'Sorry,' Robert said. 'Am I being a bore?'

Jane rose and said good-humouredly, 'Not at all, Robert. Not to me anyway. Come on through and help me to do some last-minute things in the kitchen. Bring your glass. You can talk to your heart's content and then trundle the hostess trolley through to the dining-room for me. 'Darling,' she said to Bernard, 'did you see to the wine?'

'Everything in that department's under control.'

'Come on, Robert,' she repeated, linking arms with him. Andrina caught her saying, 'What age is this Benny McNally?' before the voices faded away across the hall.

Immediately Bernard came over to her and pushed up her

dress. She was wearing nothing underneath except a flimsy suspender belt. Bernard always told her to wear 'something accessible'. He entered her over and over again, making her crazy with the danger of being so outrageous. Jane or Robert could return at any moment. The thought of such a terrifying discovery nearly drove her mad. His timing was perfect as usual. At the very last moment he withdrew, allowing her to scrabble her dress respectably down. When Jane and Robert returned to announce that dinner was served, it was to find Bernard lounging back in his chair just staring at Andrina with what seemed a hard, aggressive expression. Andrina knew that it was not aggression. It was concentration. She gazed back at him softly and dreamily.

Then she turned her head slightly to smile her shy, sideways smile at Jane and Robert.

Chapter Thirteen

'Why can't you come, you stubborn ould woman?' Michael said.

Big Martha jutted out her bristly chin. 'Because I'm not going into any house that's full of Papish ornaments and pictures, that's why. And don't you tell me there isn't any in your da's place, because Caroline's told me there is.'

'I only said how pretty they were,' Caroline hastily explained, 'after she asked me, Michael. I thought that coloured picture of Jesus and the wee children and the lambs was really nice. I told her how nice it was.'

'Look, Ma, it's Christmas. We can't leave you here in bloody Castlemilk all on your own. I'll get Da to hide all his holy pictures and ornaments if it'll please you. Everybody in the family's going to be there, and lots of friends from old Garngad. Tony and Theresa have done a lot of work decorating the house with streamers and balloons. The kids'll love it. And you should see their wee Bobby. He's a right stoater. Frank and Bridie will be there too. Remember how you enjoyed Frank's play on television?'

'Theresa O'Maley,' Martha said, 'a Papish name if ever I heard one.'

Michael rolled his eyes.

'Christ, I'm a Catholic. I'm an O'Maley. What harm have I ever done you? What harm has any of the O'Maleys ever done you?' Or any fuckin' Catholic, he thought, but for Caroline's sake, he swallowed the words.

'Ma, for the sake of the weens,' he gentled his voice. 'Da's got a tree. And Bernard sent money. Remember the presents the children asked Santa Claus for? Well, he's sent them. Santa, I mean – a whole lot of smashing toys are piled up at the foot of the tree, ready and waiting.'

That was enough to stir the children into action.

'Aw, Granny, please come. Och, please, *please*!' They hopped and danced around the old woman.

Martha fussed where she sat, agitating herself about like a dog giving itself a good shake.

'Oh, all right then. All right.'

Her mutters of 'Little did I think I'd be socialising with a bunch of Green Grapes' were drowned out by the squeals of delight from Sean, Sally and Maureen.

'Well, thank God that's settled at last,' Michael said. Then to Caroline, 'Scobie and Carragh are coming. Carragh's going to bring along one of her famous cloutie dumplings.'

Caroline laughed.

'Remember how she used to bring big slices of it upstairs to us, all steamy and spicy and that moist with all the fruit she'd put in it.' Then more seriously, 'I'll never be able to thank Scobie enough for getting you off the drink, Michael. I know he says it was just you wanting to come off that did it. But it was him, wasn't it?'

'Him and a few others at the AA.'

'I've thanked God many a time as well for curing you.'

'I'm not cured, hen. I've told you, and Scobie's told you. Once an alcoholic, always an alcoholic.'

'Please don't frighten me, Michael.'

He put his arm around her.

'God forbid. Here, cheer up. It's Christmas.'

She laughed again. 'Well, almost.' She called over to Martha, 'What are you going to wear for the party, Ma?'

'My blue dress or my orange blouse,' Martha said, making both Michael and Caroline laugh.

Secretly, however, Michael was more than a little apprehensive. Not for his own sake, but for Caroline and the children. He determined to have a word in Tony's ear and first thing after work next day he took the bus to Blackhill. Theresa was delighted to see him.

'Come away in, Michael. Your da and Tony's not home yet, but they won't be long.'

She looked pregnant again.

'Where's wee Bobby?'

'Through in the room, out for the count. I wish he'd sleep so well through the night. Of course, Tony's always dead to the world. He never hears a thing. I think Bobbie's cutting teeth. Is he the right age for that, do you think?'

'Haven't a clue, hen.'

Theresa shook her head.

'What about your Sean and Sally and Maureen?'

'You'd better ask Caroline. Or her ma. The old harridan's coming to the party. I couldn't very well leave her behind. I wanted to warn Tony to watch his big mouth. You know what he's like. He wouldn't take a blue ticket in a tramcar. He'd rather get a dearer, green ticket to a further stop and walk back. He's a bigoted bampot, and she's a bigoted old faggot. She says she's going to turn up in a blue dress. Or worse, an orange blouse. I can just imagine Tony's face. But it's what he'll say or do that's worrying me, Theresa. She's an old woman. Allowances have got to be made for that.'

'Do you want me to speak to him as well?'

'Would you, hen?'

'I'll do my best, but you'd better be on the safe side and get your oar in as well.'

'Aye, OK.' Then a cheerful thought struck him. 'Here, maybe we could hide Martha's blue and orange stuff.'

Theresa laughed.

'A good idea.'

That's what happened in the end. Martha was fuming and tried her best to find the clothes, but Caroline had put the blouse and the dress in a carrier bag and stuffed it behind some suitcases on top of the wardrobe in their bedroom.

'You're far nicer in your brown dress,' Caroline told her mother. 'With the fawn modesty vest and your good cameo brooch.'

Caroline helped her put it on, not without some difficulty because now Martha was sulking and being as uncooperative as she could. Caroline was pink-faced and sweating profusely when she emerged from Martha's room.

'Honestly,' she told Michael, 'she's worse than the kids.'

The children were shiny clean and dressed in their best. They were each clutching a present. One for their Grandad O'Maley. One for their Uncle Tony, one for Aunty Theresa.

They didn't expect their cousin Bobby would be old enough to understand about Christmas and presents. Nevertheless, a teddy bear had been wrapped and stuffed into Caroline's shopping bag along with the Christmas cake she'd baked as her contribution to the meal. There were also the presents from all of them for Granny Stoddart.

It was a tradition that the children got a few presents from Santa in their stockings on Christmas morning. Any other present wasn't received or opened until after lunch when the whole family was gathered together.

Michael had pushed Martha in her chair to the shops in Croftfoot so that she could buy something for the children.

'You don't need to get anything for Caroline or me,' he told her. 'We know you can't afford it when you've just got your pension.'

But she'd just narked back at him. 'Shut up, ya one-eyed monster. You're always bossing me about. Who do you think you are?'

She'd bought Caroline a box of peppermint creams. Peppermint creams were Martha's favourites, not Caroline's. Greedy ould sod, Michael thought.

But she'd bought him a really smart shirt.

'I'm fed up being seen with you looking like a bloody tramp. There's down-and-outs smarter turned out than you.'

He would have liked to wear the shirt to the party because, true enough, he didn't have anything else decent. Bernard would be there in all his new expensive gear. Frank always looked smart nowadays too. Even Tony could put on a good show. Michael hadn't had anything new for years – since the kids were born, now that he thought about it. Not that he begrudged them anything. But he would have felt good wearing that new shirt at the party. Martha refused to part with it, however, until after the Christmas lunch. He could have throttled her. She could be as stubborn as a mule, that woman.

He said to Caroline, 'Sometimes I wonder if she really is your mother. Are you sure you weren't adopted or found on her doorstep or anything? I've known you both for years now and I've yet to see one scrap of resemblance.' Thank God, he added silently to himself.

'Maybe I'm like my granny,' Caroline said. 'I vaguely remember her. Daddy's mother, I mean. She seemed a nice, gentle wee soul.'

'That's it then. You to a tee.'

Caroline kissed him.

'Go and get her into the chair, love. That's us all ready.'

It was a terrible hassle to get to Blackhill with Big Martha, even with the taxi they'd saved up to take. The chair was a folding one so they had no difficulty in getting it into the car. But there was more of a problem with Big Martha.

'We should have hired a crane from one of the yards, ould yin,' he told her as he and the taxi driver struggled and grappled and heaved to deposit her on one of the seats.

'Shut your ugly face,' she told Michael, 'or I'll poke yer other eye out with ma umbrella.'

They had assured her that an umbrella would be unnecessary. It was neither rainy or snowy and anyway the taxi was taking them from door to door. But when she went out dressed in her good brown dress, the musquash coat she was so proud of and that reeked of mothballs, and brown felt hat with the shiny petersham binding, she felt she must take her umbrella. Always had. She was also very attached to her outsized scuffed but good leather handbag. She'd had that bag for donkey's years, Caroline said.

Martha spread over the whole seat of the taxi so Caroline and Michael had to balance on the drop-down seats facing her, with their backs to the driver. The children were perched on their knees. It was a very cramped and uncomfortable journey.

It was even more difficult to prise Martha out of the taxi than it had been to lever her in. They were the first arrivals and so there was only Tony and his da there to help. Tony was in his green suit and shirt and tie. Fortunately, Martha was so harassed she didn't notice. His da wasn't of much help. Since Patrick became a foreman, he'd got into the habit of just standing by and issuing orders.

'No, turn her round,' he called out. 'Tony, get your shoulder under her arm. Michael, go round and in the door at the other side and give her a shove from the back.'

'Da, if you don't shut up, I'll shove your teeth down your throat,' Michael warned, through a nose and mouth full of musquash fur.

'See you.' Patrick had started drinking early and was ready for a challenge. 'Think you're a fighter. Well, yer no. I can flatten yer ugly mug right now. Come on. Let go of that woman, and put up yer dukes.'

Martha suddenly succeeded in exploding through the taxi door.

'See you,' she bawled at Patrick, 'I'll flatten your ugly mug if you don't do what that boy says.'

'OK. OK.' Patrick put up his hands and suddenly became polite. 'Far be it from me to pick a fight with a lady.'

Tony was hee-hawing fit to burst. Martha cocked a head in his direction and said to Michael, 'Has he got a screw loose, or what?'

'You could say that, Ma.'

'Well, where's this Christmas dinner I'm supposed to get? My belly thinks my throat's cut.'

He wheeled her through the draughty, graffitied close. Then there was the breathless struggle between Patrick, Tony and Michael to lift Martha and the chair upstairs and into the house. All the children were dancing with excitement round the tree and the women were laughing and greeting one another and shedding coats.

'I had a hell of a job with these fairy lights,' Tony gasped, still winded. 'I had to get Da to help me. Between us we managed them but it took us half the night.'

'And a bottle of whisky between you as well, I'll bet.'

'Are you still off it?'

'Yes.'

His father came swaying towards him. 'Holy Mother of God, you can't refuse a drink today, Michael. Not at Christmas. Be a man. Enjoy yourself.'

Michael, still harassed and sweating, kept spitting out musquash hairs.

'See that ould woman,' he managed. 'She'd drive any decent man to drink.'

Chapter Fourteen

Laura lost her will to teach in St Francis School after Robert left. She found she couldn't cope. She realised more than ever before how Robert had helped and supported her. The knowledge that he was on hand to discipline them kept the children's behaviour within bounds. Now, for the most part, chaos reigned. She had a perpetual headache and hoarse throat with her efforts to control the rabble. Morning and afternoon breaks held no relief or pleasure any more. There was nothing to look forward to. She dreaded going home.

A new neighbour had moved into the bungalow next door. Mr Pritchett, a bachelor in his late fifties and with five cats, had lived with his mother (a woman well known locally as an absolute tyrant) and the cats in one of the big villas by Kilmardinny Loch until his mother died. He'd told Laura in his soft, quiet voice that the villa was far too big for him to manage on his own.

On several occasions Laura had been forced to ask for his help. Despite Mr Pritchett's small stature, he had surprising strength and it seemed no trouble at all for him to lift Derek. She tried to manage and wished with all her heart that she could do it on her own; more and more, Mr Pritchett was insinuating himself into the house. She felt ashamed for disliking him so much. The man had never said a wrong word to either her or Derek and he was always so willing to help. There was just something she couldn't take to about his thin sandy hair and amber eyes (the same colour as one of his cats), and the way he was always nursing one or other of these animals while the rest purred around his legs. She had to be firm with Mr Pritchett about not bringing any of the cats with him when he visited Derek.

'They bother my husband,' she told him. 'He feels so helpless when they jump on him.'

Mr Pritchett had apologised and assured her quietly that she had no need to worry. He would come alone next time.

She wanted to tell Robert about Mr Pritchett. Ask his advice. Normally she confided everything to Robert. Now, however, Robert was teaching in another school and there were no more cosy, intimate chats while she drove him home to Monteith Row every day.

He had been to visit her and Derek two or three times. 'Just to keep in touch,' he'd said.

Derek had been pleased to see him and to hear all his news about the new school. But his visits had been a torment to her – never being alone with him, never being able to say what she wanted to say.

Then one day he'd phoned her at the school. After wishing her a Happy New Year (although it was now the end of January) and all the best for 1969, he told her he'd be waiting for her in his car after four o'clock. She palpitated with happiness, but then was beset with worries. Her hair didn't look its best and she was wearing her old heather-mixture tweed suit and fawn raincoat. His wife always looked as if she'd just stepped out of a beauty salon. And how she could afford such elegant clothes on Robert's salary, Laura couldn't imagine.

He said he wanted to take her for afternoon tea, somewhere out in the country. Just so that they could talk. He said he missed her. With shaking hands she struggled to comb out her long hair, then loop it back into a chignon before going outside to meet him.

She abandoned her car so that she wouldn't waste a moment's opportunity to be near him. 'I can collect it later,' she told him, 'if you don't mind bringing me back for it.'

'Let's hope it won't be vandalised.'

Laura didn't care. She relaxed into his car beside him, savouring the warmth she could feel emanating from his body.

The car moved off.

'Oh, Robert.'

He hushed her. Then after a few minutes, he asked, 'How is Derek?'

She sighed.

'You saw what he was like before Christmas. Just the same.

We had a pretty miserable time over the so-called festive season. At least, it was miserable for me. Our new neighbour came in. You haven't met him. He's helpful with Derek but he's beginning to haunt the place and I don't like him. Nor his cats, for that matter. At the last count he'd five. I wouldn't be surprised if he's got double that number now. We can smell his house from our place. Although, when I told him to keep them away from us, he didn't argue or anything. In fact he's never actually done anything, or said anything I could object to.'

She stared out of the window.

'Maybe it's just me. I get so tired with one thing and another. Derek gets depressed, and I don't blame him. He was such an active man before and I can understand his frustration . . .' Her voice trailed off.

There was silence for a long time after that but it was a loving bond of understanding and compassion between them: there was no need for words.

They found a small hotel in a village near the Campsies where they ordered tea in a lounge with a crackling log fire in an open stone fireplace. A low ceiling heavy with oak beams darkened the room. They were the only people there. Even the village outside the latticed windows seemed deserted. It was dark and a January wind was funnelling rain along the street.

'I love you,' Robert said, making tears immediately well up in her eyes, blurring the outlines of his face. 'I wanted to say it. I wanted to make absolutely sure that you knew. Never a day passes that I don't think of you and long to be with you. You were angry with me for moving away from St Francis . . .'

She shook her head, making the tears spill over but she couldn't bring herself to speak.

'And for me buying a car. I wanted to make sure you understand, Laura, that I didn't want us to be separated in any way. It was because I wanted exactly the opposite that I felt I had to do something – because of our circumstances, I mean. Because of Derek, because of Andrina, because of Jennifer. We both have responsibilities and neither of us is the type that can ignore that fact. It doesn't come easily to us to behave irresponsibly.'

'All I know is that I love you,' she managed at last. 'Perhaps I'm not as responsible as you think. I long to leave Derek and live with you.'

'But could you?' Robert asked. 'Would you actually be able to walk out on him tomorrow?'

Her head rolled about in miserable confusion, as if trying to escape from painful unwanted thoughts.

'You couldn't, could you?' Robert insisted.

'Is this why you met me today, just to make me miserable?'

'Oh darling,' he caught her hands and held them. 'It's the last thing in the world I want to do.'

'What then?'

He shook his head.

'I don't know. I wanted to talk things through. Could we, for instance, have an affair? It's the same problem really. *Could* you? Think it through, Laura. How would we feel? To be honest, I believe I *could* cheat on Andrina. I'd feel guilty. I wouldn't feel proud of myslf. Cheating is cheating, and betrayal is betrayal. In her own way she's been a good wife to me and there's such a childish kind of innocence about her. Oh, I'd feel guilty all right, but I could do it.'

A wave of bitterness hardened away Laura's tears. It was wicked the way a woman like that could hoodwink a decent man. Andrina Anderson was no innocent. Laura felt she could stake her life on the fact.

'But, let's face it, Laura,' Robert went on. 'Derek is a different matter. Both to you and to me.'

Laura closed her eyes.

She was visualising lying in bed in Robert's arms. She was becoming one with him, joining him in the closest and most intimate act of love, and Andrina, Derek, everyone else in the world, was completely shut out, forgotten.

'What are you thinking?' Robert asked.

A moment's shyness made her hesitate, but almost at the same time came an urgent awareness that time was precious between them and there was no place for coyness or false modesty. Anyway, coyness was anathema to her. She told him the exact truth.

'Oh darling, I've felt like that, I've thought like that a

thousand times. I long to book a room here and go upstairs and make love to you right now. But the point is – and my whole reason for talking to you like this – afterwards, could you look at Derek – '

'I don't want to hear about Derek, or think about Derek, when I'm with you,' she interrupted, jerking her hands away from him and covering her ears.

'I know. I know. But avoiding the issue doesn't solve it or make it go away. I could face Andrina afterwards. But remember, you've to cope with Derek every day. I don't want you to end up in a situation that causes you even more stress that you're in now. All I'm asking is that you go home today, and you look at Derek and you think this through. I'll meet you again next week – '

'I'll feel the same next week and every week . . .'

'Try to put our feelings aside and instead give the situation a few days' serious thought, Laura. You see, there's bound to be emotional complications develop, as well as practical ones. I want you to be sure you can cope with them. You've so much to cope with already.'

She could hardly believe it when, half an hour or so later, they left the hotel. She kept thinking how it could have been. They could so easily have booked a room and gone upstairs and lain in each other's arms, belonged to each other. Robert held her for only a moment. She felt a physical wrench as she stepped from the warm hallway and out into the cold blustery street. Suddenly everything was hopeless and frightening again. It was as if she was already alone and not knowing what to do without him.

Once back in her own car and driving home, she wept stormily, railing against life, anything and everything that prevented her from being with Robert. She had come to hate her own home, to dread returning to it every day, especially now that there was the added stress of the Pritchett man. Once she had to call for his help at night and he'd come round in striped pyjamas, a grubby fawn dressing-gown and checked carpet slippers. She detected a hot stale smell about him, as well as the usual odour of cats. It was as if he'd had sex but never washed afterwards. She had an unpleasant vision of him masturbating.

He was the first person she saw when she stopped the car in front of the house. He was inside watching for her at the window. Before she had time to insert her key, he opened the door.

'There you are.' He had a gentle voice but even his mild manner repelled her. She felt guilty about this and blamed it on her nerves and the stress she was under. 'We were getting worried. But then I said to Derek, I said, "Our Laura will be all right. I feel it in my water." '

Laura walked past him, barely able to choke down the words, 'I'm not *your* Laura.' In the sitting-room she went over and kissed Derek, avoiding the dribble of saliva spilling from his mouth. He was sitting in front of the television set.

'Sorry I'm late, dear. I should have phoned. But I bumped into Robert and we went for a cup of tea and a chat. Have you had anything to eat yet?'

'Yes, thanks. Mr Pritchett scrambled some eggs and I made the toast and we had it in here on a tray while we watched the news.'

'Oh good. Are you sure you don't want anything else? There's chocolate mousse in the fridge.'

'No, I'm OK. You go and make something for yourself. Mr Pritchett and I want to watch this programme.' Before she reached the door, but still with his eyes on the television set, he asked, 'How's Robert? Still liking his new job?'

'Well, I don't know if "liking" is quite the right word. Remember we read about that gangster Godfather the other day?'

'Uh-huh.'

'Well, his son is in Robert's class. Robert says the boy is fascinated with guns. Apparently, he knows a lot about them. Too much for his own good, Robert thinks.'

Mr Pritchett settled himself on the chair she usually sat on.

'I know what I'd do with scum like that,' he said, without deviating from his normal mild tone. He even managed to keep smiling. 'The belt's too good for them. I'd birch them, then hang them. Get rid of the animals.'

She felt a headache developing.

'I'm afraid you wouldn't make a very good teacher,

Mr Pritchett,' she said, marvelling at her self-control. She even dredged up a ghost of a smile before leaving the room.

In the kitchen the sink was piled with dirty dishes. Eggshells and other debris cluttered every working surface. Crumbs and sugar grains and God knows what else crunched under her feet. She felt indescribably tired. She could have sunk down on to the floor and wept hopelessly among it all.

Instead she took off her raincoat and jacket, hung them away in the hall cupboard, tied on her apron and splashed hot water into the sink.

She comforted herself by clinging to thoughts of Robert. But Robert seemed miles away now. In another world. On another planet.

Chapter Fifteen

'Here one day an' gone the next,' Scobie said. 'Christ, I'll miss Patrick.'

'I never knew his liver was bad, did you, Scobie?' Carragh asked.

'Tough as an old boot, that's what I always thought.'

Patrick had been in hospital several weeks before he died and his four sons had been at his bedside. Now they and their wives and families and a few close friends were sitting down to a funeral tea in the Elgin Hotel.

'A man in his prime as well. Same age as me.'

'Prime my arse,' Tony said. 'He was sixty-seven. Ach well, at least we'll have the house to ourselves now that he's gone.'

'You're as sensitive a soul as ever, I see, Tony,' Frank said.

A heavily pregnant Theresa rolled her eyes.

'Could you beat it!'

'What's up?' Tony looked aggrieved. 'We'll need an extra room when the next one arrives. You said yourself.'

'That was when your da was alive and well. God rest his soul.'

'When's the new baby due, Theresa?' Bridie asked.

'The end of June.'

'You haven't long to go then?'

'A couple of months. Maybe less. You know how I was with wee Bobby.'

Bridie had no idea how she was with wee Bobby. Nor did she regard Bobby as 'wee'. The child was big and solid looking and excruciatingly energetic, bouncing in his high chair and banging away with his spoon. He obviously took after his daddy. At least Tony was dressed a bit more respectably than usual. He'd long ago abandoned his flashy Ted gear. He was wearing a green suit but it was toned down by a black armband and tie.

Bridie hadn't seen Theresa for some time and she noticed

that there was a difference in her, apart from her pregnancy. She looked neglected. She had never been all that attractive but she had kept herself clean and neat and tidy. Admittedly, it couldn't be easy trying to maintain a neat appearance when you looked as if you had an elephant stuck up your smock. Nevertheless, it would have helped if the smock hadn't been stained. And her stockings hadn't been laddered. Poor Theresa was acquiring a defeated look and Bridie didn't blame her. Not with Theresa being married to an O'Maley. Bernard's wife didn't look a picture of joy and contentment either. Not that she looked neglected. She was perfectly groomed. Her make-up, sleek hairdo and black velvet trouser suit must have cost a fortune. Her eyes, however, were a dead giveaway – dead being the operative word. There was no life in her eyes, even when she talked and smiled, and she talked and smiled quite a lot.

Frank noticed too. Of course he would. The great writer. The keen observer. The know-all about everybody. 'The trouble probably is,' he said after they returned home (her mouth always gave a sarcastic twist when she referred to the West End flat as 'home') 'that Bernard is away so much. Even when he's at home, he's not, if you know what I mean. He's out most nights working in all these clubs and pubs.'

She knew what he meant all right. At home. Yet not at home. That was Frank to a tee. Recently he'd been taking spurts of keeping away from his desk, taking her out, looking at her, listening to her with desperate concentration. It was worse than when he was away in a dream with one of his stories and living with his story characters. She knew that his attention on her was false. He was in agony all the time, his writing room forever beckoning him back.

He never mentioned the play he was supposed to be writing. Instinctively she felt there was something suspicious about this. One awful thought shocked her. He couldn't be writing a dreadful play about Blackhill and his da and all his friends there? Not now that his da was dead. Surely he couldn't sully his da's memory? Of course she knew all the time that he could. As far as his writing was concerned, Frank could stoop to anything, stop at nothing. She could just imagine what he would do with the way his da and Tony used to raid the goods trains in Blackhill. Probably Tony still did. Frank would think nothing of blackening the character of his own father and brother. Or making them a laughing stock.

Or was it Garngad and *her* da he was writing about? She quailed at the thought. He could get a lot of mileage out of that subject all right. Make a pile of money. There was the drink, and all the awful things Scobie used to do when he was drunk, all the fights, all the batterings he'd given her ma, all the stretches in Barlinnie. She shook inside so much her legs gave way underneath her. She thumped down on to a chair. What a showing up Frank could give them all. Her da didn't deserve that. He'd been off the drink for years, did good work for the AA, and was the best of husbands and fathers. It was enough to put da back on the drink.

Frank was making a cup of tea and when he turned to fill her cup, he noticed her shocked face.

'What's wrong, pet?' he asked worriedly. 'Don't you feel well?'

She took a few comforting mouthfuls of tea before speaking.

'Tell me one thing, Frank. What are you writing about just now?'

His eyes became evasive. He made an important job of putting milk in his tea and settling on his chair and sipping at his cup. She knew it! He was hiding something. He was ashamed of something he was doing. But of course, that wouldn't stop him doing it.

'Well?' she persisted.

He shrugged.

'This and that.'

'What this, and what that, Frank? I want to know.'

'Why?'

'Why are you not telling me?'

'Look, Bridie, you ought to know by now – if I talk too much about what I'm writing, while I'm writing it, I talk out all the excitement. Then it's no use. So just leave it, will you?'

'No, I won't leave it. You shut me out of everything now. First it was your social life, your friends, now it's your work.'

'I shut *you* out?' Frank sounded incredulous. 'Right from the start you never wanted anything to do with my friends and what you call *my* social life. It wasn't supposed to be like that.'

'Oh?' She raised a brow. 'And what was it supposed to be like, Frank?'

'I thought the people I met and introduced you to would be your friends too. It wasn't for the want of them trying. It was you, Bridie. You froze them out. Ignored them. Hid away through here with a book rather than even try to be friendly.'

'What was I supposed to do? Be like them? You fancied doing a bit of cloning, did you? Have me gush about dearing and darlinging and Dear Hearting and pouncing on everybody and kissing their cheeks?'

'There's no use talking to you. We've been through all this before. I don't know why you've brought it all up again. I thought we'd put that phase behind us. I thought you didn't want me to bring friends to the house so I stopped bringing them. Now you accuse me of shutting you out. And they're not all that you always make them out to be, by the way. Just because some of them don't speak with a broad Glasgow accent and come from Garngad or the Gorbals, doesn't mean that they're no use.'

'You're the expert on people and character, of course.'

'Bridie, why are we quarrelling? I've just come back from burying my father. I could do without this.'

She had forgotten about the funeral, despite the fact that she was still in her black dress and Frank looked totally different from normal. Instead of his tight denims and open-necked shirt, his lanky body was lost in a loose-fitting black suit, starched white shirt and black tie. A suit never hung right on Frank's long bones. She felt ashamed, yet angry at Frank for making her feel ashamed. She controlled her anger, even managing to say, in between mouthfuls of tea, 'I'm sorry, Frank. Forget it.'

There was silence for a few minutes, then Frank said, 'Doris decided not to come then? Not that I blame her,' he added hastily. 'Not with Jane being there. Even just Bernard would have been bad enough.'

'Bernard looked prosperous as usual.' She tried to keep the

bitterness from her voice. Bernard had never done her any harm. But when she thought of her poor sister . . .

'So did Jane. But did you notice her eyes? They had quite a sad expression, didn't you think?'

'Yes, and there was a kind of false brittleness about her when she talked and laughed.' A bit like some of your so-called friends, she could have added, but didn't.

Frank looked thoughtful. Probably wondering how he could use Jane in one of his plays.

'Yet she's still fond of Bernard, to put it mildly. Her expression lit up every time she looked at him. Did you notice that?'

She hadn't but she could believe it. Doris had been crazy about Bernard too. Still wasn't completely over her feelings for him.

'Bernard's too caught up with his work to have any real time for a wife,' she said. Like you, she thought. 'He should never have got married.' *Nor should you.*

Frank sighed.

'Probably you're right.'

Another silence.

'One of these days, I'll write about his twilight world.'
She knew it.

Frank absently topped up both of their cups.

'That's what he calls it. His twilight world.' His face brightened a little. 'Not a bad title for a story that – "The Twilight World".'

Oh God! Would they never have a conversation in all their lives without his writing coming into it. Even back in the old days, come to think of it, that's what had mattered most to him. That's what had never failed to switch on that light in his eyes. Everything he ever said, or saw, or heard, or did, he connected with his writing. She remembered him sitting at their front room window in the Gorbals house, face cupped in his hands, staring down at the rich panorama of life, as he called it, passing by underneath. He couldn't just enjoy looking out a window like anyone else. He had to be 'observing', 'storing everything away for future use'. Even sitting in a restaurant when he was supposed to be taking her for a night out to give her a treat, he'd say things like, 'Look at that couple over there. See the body language and the looks passing between them . . .' And she'd know he wasn't taking any time off at all.

Often she longed to say, 'Frank, for pity's sake, will you shut up about your bloody writing! I'm bored out of my skull with it.'

Once she actually had, and she immediately regretted it. He'd looked so shocked, so taken aback, so hurt. She could have bitten her tongue off. She didn't want to hurt him. He was her husband and always would be. She believed in the sanctity of marriage. She wasn't going to make the same mistake as Doris. Her Ma had been right: Doris shouldn't have gone against her faith and divorced Bernard, no matter what he was like. She should somehow have coped with him, changed him. After all, look how Ma stuck to Da through thick and thin and look how he changed. Happy as larks they were now. A right old Darby and Joan.

Somehow she had to change Frank. Yet she couldn't – for the moment at least – see how. Part of the problem was that writing was the way Frank earned a living. But there had been a time when he'd been perfectly happy working in the office of Messrs Goldmayer Wholesale Warehousemen. It had been a decent collar and tie job: not a thing wrong with it. She had been happy then too.

Suddenly, out of the blue, Frank said, 'That's me lost both of them now. It's hard to believe somehow. I still often think of Ma and wish . . . and wish I could see her again, and talk to her.'

'Oh Frank.' Bridie was overcome with love and compassion. She went over and put her arm around his shoulders and pressed her cheek against his. 'I'm so sorry,' she said helplessly.

And salty rivulets of their tears met, and flowed together.

Chapter Sixteen

Andrina loved the summer because of the outdoor sex she and Bernard could enjoy. There was a terrific 'at one with nature' feeling about making love in the open air. First they'd have a picnic, and their picnics were always sumptuous affairs with smoked salmon, half-chickens, strawberries, Belgian chocolates and a bottle of champagne. She always took care to pack a starched white damask cloth to lay out on some grassy spot and two fine crystal glasses. They would feed each other erotically, then laze and chat before taking a walk entwined in each other's arms. They'd stop to lean against a tree. He'd lift her up into his arms and, supported by the tree trunk at her back, she'd wrap her legs around his waist. Each time he came, he'd call out louder and louder how he loved her, adored her. She'd never forget those moments: the feel of the cool air on her bare legs and bottom, the sounds of the birds calling overhead, the pungent aroma of pine.

As usual it was proving more difficult to get away. The problem was Jennifer, and of course Robert. Both were on holiday from school and too often in the house. Robert still had commitments to the children at his school, however, and he took them on day outings. Then he announced that he and some of the other teachers were taking their pupils up north for a weekend. Andrina prayed that there would be more weekends like that. Meantime she determined to make the most of this one. Her mother took charge of Jennifer. She'd pretended that she wanted to be free to give the house a good cleaning, and Bernard told Jane some story about going away on business for the weekend. He was often away overnight so that was no problem. He came and stayed with her at Monteith Row. He offered to take her to a picturesque hotel out in the country but she had to remain in the house most of the time in case her mother phoned.

'She always does,' Andrina sighed. 'To check up on me.'

Bernard told her over the phone what to be wearing when he arrived. He always orchestrated their times together. This never failed to excite her. She thrived on it, looked forward to each new instruction. This time he said he'd been fantasising about her in high heels, and a wide-brimmed hat she'd previously bought for a wedding. It was always such an erotic pleasure getting ready for Bernard. First she showered and powdered and perfumed her body. She carefully applied her make-up, then dressed in a lacy bra, a ribbon of a suspender belt, and lace-topped stockings, before wriggling into the dress and stepping into the high-heeled shoes. A last touch to her hair before she placed the hat on top of it. There could be no mistaking the fact that she looked stunningly beautiful and, because she knew her appearance would give Bernard pleasure, it gave her pleasure too.

She left the outside door a little ajar so that he could come straight into the bedroom and find her sitting on the edge of the bed, long legs crossed and thighs provocatively revealed through the slit in her dress. The long black gloves had been a last-minute touch. As usual he scrutinised her in silence for a time, walking leisurely to and fro, savouring her from all angles. His obvious pleasure spurred her on to desire him with even greater longing. She rose and began parading around, thrilling at his dark eyes boring holes in her legs, ankles, hands, breasts.

Then suddenly the sexual tension was shattered by the harsh jangle of the doorbell.

'My God.' Andrina's self-confidence immediately crumbled. She seemed to shrink in size. She hugged herself in terror.

'It could be my mother.'

'So what?' Bernard said. 'Ignore her. Or better still, invite her in and face her with the truth.'

'Are you crazy?' Andrina hissed. 'Can't you see how afraid I am?'

'I'm not. We can face her together. Or if you prefer, I'll face her alone.'

The bell jangled again. Andrina flung off the hat, kicked off the shoes, fumbled frantically with the zip of her dress, before managing to step out of it. She grabbed her dressing-gown.

'Stay here. If you love me, Bernard, please, *please*, stay here.'

She ran through to the hall and opened the door. As she'd feared, it was her mother and Jennifer, whom she'd delivered to Bearsden the night before.

'Mummy! For goodness sake, what brings you here this morning? I thought you were going to have fun with Jennifer – take her for all sorts of treats. She was looking forward to it. Weren't you, darling?'

She fluttered after Sophie and Jennifer into the kitchen.

'We're on our way to visit a children's museum in Edinburgh. Jennifer wanted to collect a doll that she'd forgotten to bring with her last night. Why are you still in your dressing-gown at this time of day, Andrina?'

'Mummy, can't I treat myself, just this once, while I'm on my own, to a nice long lie in bed without being questioned about it by you or anyone else? I've a weekend's cleaning ahead of me, don't forget.'

Andrina kept a grip of the edge of the table. She needed its support. Any moment now she was going to collapse. She felt sure of it. The situation was more than she could cope with. A nightmare scenario. While she was talking, Jennifer had run through to her room to fetch the doll. What if she decided for some reason, any reason, to look into the main bedroom. Or what if Sophie did?

By some miracle, Andrina managed to ask in a perfectly calm voice, 'Can you stay for a cup of coffee, Mummy?'

'No, we've a train to catch. Jennifer, come on. Nanna's leaving.' Then to Andrina: 'You'll be turning into a right slut. It's high time you were decently dressed and getting on with some work.'

'I'm just going to, Mummy.'

They met Jennifer in the hall, hugging the doll Robert had bought her for Christmas.

'I'm ready, Nanna.'

Andrina thought Jennifer a strange child, not a bit like her: thin, with mousy pigtails and freckles across her nose.

'Aren't you going to give Mummy a kiss before you go?' Andrina bent down and the child suddenly gave her such an intense embrace she dropped the doll. Andrina laughed.

'My goodness, poor Maisie! She'll think you don't want her, tossing her away like that.'

Her words brought unexpected tears to Jennifer's eyes.

'Darling, I'm sorry.' She hastily picked up the doll and pushed it into Jennifer's arms. 'I didn't mean to upset you. I was only joking. Dolls can't think.'

'Children can, though,' Sophie said. 'Come on, Jennifer. You and Nanna are going to have a lovely day seeing all the toys.'

After the door shut behind them, Andrina leaned against it, violently shivering. She was still standing like that when Bernard came through to the hall. He put his arms round her.

'No,' she said. 'No, not now. I couldn't.'

'I'm only going to make you a cup of coffee.'

He led her into the kitchen and sat her down in one of the chairs at the table.

'You know, Andrina,' he said after he'd poured out the steaming liquid and Andrina was cupping her hands around the heat, trying to gain comfort from it, 'this can't go on.'

'Oh I know all right,' she managed. 'Oh now I know, all right.'

'I mean we've got to come out in the open once and for all. It's got to be faced some time. As far as I'm concerned, your mother can go to hell. It's none of her business. I don't care about her any more than I care about my wife. Oh, I don't want any harm to come to Jane, whereas I'd put up a cheer if your mother was run over by a bus. But I don't love my wife and she's got to be told. I want at least to be straight with Jane. I want to tell her that it's you and you alone I love and want to have as my wife. She'll be better off without me, and she'll be all right for money, so there's no problem there.'

'No problem?' Andrina half laughed, half cried. 'My God!'

Ignoring what she'd said, Bernard went on.

'Then there's Robert. I know your feelings for him are much the same as my feelings – or lack of them – for Jane. I have more regard for Robert than you do.'

'Oh, sure.' She gave another tearful laugh.

'It's true. I feel terrible about two-timing him. He's been a good friend to me since I was a boy. He saved me from the gutter and worse. My mother thought the world of him for that.'

The word mother triggered off Andrina's shaking again.

'You don't understand how I feel about my mother, Bernard.'

'No, I don't. But if I can face Robert with the truth, then you can face your mother.'

'I couldn't. I couldn't. It would destroy her.'

'Well, let it.'

'How can you say that? The guilt would destroy me too.'

'Nonsense. You'd get over it. It's time you did. You know it yourself. There's a mad, bad bit about your mother. Always has been. Once rid of her you'd be a new person, we'd be free to be happy together.'

'If only it were that simple.'

'Do you love me, Andrina?'

'You know I do.'

'All right, it *is* that simple. You've nothing to worry about as long as you've got me. I've told you a dozen times. Now this time, you've got to make a real effort to let it sink in. *I can deal with your mother.* Do you hear me? *I can deal with your mother.*'

'Bernard,' she pleaded. 'Do me a favour and go now. I feel so shaken and I've got such a headache, all I want to do is rest. I'll phone you. Please, darling.'

'I mean what I said, Andrina. I'm going to bring all this out in the open. All you need to do is come away with me. You could do that right now. Why don't you?'

She felt so threatened that she passionately hated him. Avoiding his eyes, she murmured, 'I just want to rest and be on my own for a bit. I'll phone you at the office this afternoon.'

'Promise me you'll think seriously about all that I've said.'

'Yes, I promise.'

'All right. We'll have dinner this evening. I could either book a table somewhere or bring everything here. Let me know.'

She nodded, then turned away from his kiss so that his lips only brushed her cheek.

114

'I'll be all right after I get a rest and time to think,' she said, still without looking up at him. 'Could you see yourself out, darling?'

'See you later then.'

'Yes.' Anything to get him out. Safely away.

What if her mother was still waiting at the bus stop outside? She would have to get a bus into town in order to catch the Edinburgh train.

She heard the outside door shut. With rubbery legs she stumbled through to the room, plucked at the curtains and peered from the window at the deserted street below. In a couple of minutes, Bernard's tall figure emerged from the close and strode across to his car. He glanced up at the window and she raised her hand and gave him a faint smile. She felt sad, yet immeasurably relieved. She prayed she'd never see Bernard again as long as she lived. Or, perhaps more accurately, as long as her mother lived.

She hardly gave Bernard time to reach his office before she phoned him. It was impossible to wait until the afternoon.

'I don't care what you say,' she told him. 'I can't see you again. Not without Jane and Robert being there. Not on your own. No way. Not for any reason. Not anywhere.'

'This is all because of your mother?'

It was a question that didn't need an answer.

'I mean it,' she told him. 'I don't want you ever to come near me again.'

'You don't mean that, Andrina.'

'I do. I do. Please, Bernard. For my sake. Please try to understand.'

Then she hung up.

Chapter Seventeen

It was a very odd situation. Laura had remarked on this to Robert more than once and he'd agreed with her. She had thought long and hard about everything and so had he, and they'd come to the conclusion that neither of them could live with cheating on Derek. Yet they couldn't say goodbye. They'd decided that they'd settle down to being affectionate friends and that affection, that friendship, would include Derek. Robert visited the house every week without fail, and the three of them would play cards or catch up on all the news. Both she and Robert would make Derek laugh, and sometimes shock him with tales about their respective schools and pupils. Robert's wife, his mother-in-law, his father-in-law – everybody – knew about their friendship and how good Robert was with Derek.

Robert quite often came when Andrina and Jennifer were spending Saturday or Sunday at Robert's mother-in-law's place. He'd have lunch with the McPhersons then he'd say, 'I'm away along the road to keep Derek company for an hour or two.'

Sometimes he came straight from school and spent the evening with them. The three of them would have a meal together and then have a cosy few hours.

Nobody minded. It was such a relief. She and Robert relaxed into this new pattern of life like an old married couple. They had each other as loving friends. It was a good compromise: it was better than nothing. And it was making Derek happy. He too looked forward to Robert's visits and he had lost all self-consciousness about eating or drinking in front of him.

Laura could look Sophie McPherson – or Andrina, for that matter – straight in the eye and with a clear conscience. Sometimes she felt sorry for the older woman. There was such a terrible tension about her. She definitely wasn't a happy person.

On the other hand, Laura hated the sight of Andrina. Sophie usually stopped for a minute or two to chat to her now if they met along at the shops. Once Andrina had been with her and Sophie had introduced her daughter. There had been a lift to Sophie's head as she'd done so and a gleam of pride in her eyes. Again Laura felt sorry for Sophie, although she had to admit that she had nothing concrete against Andrina. She tried to be fair. She chided herself that she was only jealous of Andrina because Andrina was Robert's wife.

It was certainly true she was jealous. It was a black emotion that she'd never experienced in her life before. So unaccustomed to it was she that she had a terrible struggle to prevent a shadow of hatred from darkening her face every time she was with Andrina. Fortunately, she was never in the woman's company for more than a few minutes.

Derek became much more cheerful and optimistic. He began to believe that with a bit of determination and will-power he could get better.

'Always been a bit of a fighter, you know,' he'd boast. He certainly seemed to be recovering from the depression he'd suffered from at first, not to mention the worst of his frustrations. A couple of times during the summer, Robert had taken her and Derek for a run in his old banger. It was wonderful to have Robert's strong arms to help Derek in and out of the car. He could always make Derek laugh, instead of allowing him to feel helpless or foolish. They could all laugh together. It was a kind of happiness, a closeness that they all felt and treasured.

They'd take a picnic so that Derek wouldn't need to face the ordeal of eating in a hotel or restaurant. On the way home they'd have a sing-song as they bowled along. Robert's driving was very laid back. They were all relaxed and happy as they sang, oblivious of other cars shooting past them like arrows.

Robert even got Mr Pritchett sorted out in a firm but tactful way. Mr Pritchett had tried to make a foursome when Robert came to visit. Derek didn't mind him too much, indeed he was grateful for the man's company, especially during the winter months while Laura was out working all day. There were also the occasions, even when Laura was at home, when she needed his help with Derek. This embarrassed and upset Derek in a way that he'd never felt when Robert helped him. Perhaps because Mr Pritchett treated Derek more like a child.

'Not that he means any harm,' Derek said. 'And I'd rather not need any help but . . .' he shrugged, 'what can I do?'

Robert had explained to Mr Pritchett that it would be of most help to Derek if he came when there was no one else there. The idea was to spread the help needed, so to speak, and, he said 'He'll look forward to me visiting him one day, you see. Then he'll have you to look forward to another day. That'll keep him going, keep his spirits up.'

Mr Pritchett had gently offered to come on both occasions – when Robert was there and when he was not.

'No, there's the danger of making Derek feel he's a burden. We mustn't overdo things. Keep a sensible balance. Act as normally as possible. Make Derek feel as normal as possible. That's what Derek wants.'

Robert's voice had such a ring of conviction and authority that Mr Pritchett conceded with good grace, smiling as he said maybe it was the best idea. All he wanted was the best for Derek. Laura thanked him for being so understanding.

She felt relieved. Nothing would intrude into or spoil the happy and private relationship she, Derek and Robert had built up.

Then one morning she woke up and looked across at the other single bed and immediately knew something was wrong.

'Derek?'

She flung aside the blankets and clambered out of bed.

'Derek, darling, what's wrong?'

He was lying unnaturally still, on his back, staring at the ceiling. She agitated him from side to side.

'Derek, please, speak to me.'

Eventually, shaking with distress, she phoned for an ambulance.

While waiting for it to arrive, she dressed quickly and flung a few toilet goods and a change of pyjamas into a holdall for Derek. Then she went with him, sitting beside his stretcher, holding tightly on to his hand.

'You'll be all right, darling,' she told him once they'd arrived and she had to let him go. 'I'll wait and see you after the doctors have made their examination, and given you something to make you feel better.'

The doctors told her that Derek had taken another stroke. This time a more severe one: a bigger area of the brain had been damaged.

They kept him in hospital for nearly two months. During that time Laura's life disintegrated into dust. Confused emotion blew her this way and that. At first, Derek couldn't speak. It was horrendous to sit watching a silent Derek with one side of his face twisted and ugly. One hand and arm was so spastic that it curled up like a grotesque claw. But it was the fact that he knew what had happened, it was the tragic awareness in his eyes, that was the hardest to bear.

She refused to allow Robert to come with her on these visits to the hospital. Somehow to have the spotlight of strangers' eyes on their harmless *ménage à trois* would have tainted it, spoiled it – especially now.

It was spoiled anyway. With Derek helpless in hospital, it was no longer a *ménage à trois*. Or anything at all. So she went alone to visit Derek. And Robert went alone on the few occasions when she couldn't manage. She and Robert only met once – for a cup of tea in a café in Castle Street. She told him that it wouldn't be right for them to be together again, not while Derek was in such an awful state. He had got a limited amount of speech back, which was so torturous it sometimes made him angry; and his ineffectual struggle to form coherent words made him weak. He'd never be able to walk again, and when he came home it would be in a wheelchair. He wouldn't be able to eat unless she cut food up for him, because he only had the use of one hand. There were so many humiliations for him now she didn't think he could bear anyone to see him. Not even Robert. This had been obvious to Robert himself on the visits he'd made so far to the hospital. Derek had never uttered a word, had turned his head away as if he didn't even want to look at him. It had caused Robert considerable distress.

'It's because he feels so humiliated having people –

especially people he loves – see him look so pathetic and helpless, Robert. It's not that you've done anything wrong.'

'I know. I'm just so sorry for him. It's hellish. I wish there was something I could do to help.'

'I've told him that I'd speak to you. For the moment at least, he doesn't want anybody to see him. Even my being there upsets him. I have to speak to Mr Pritchett as well. He was turning up at visiting times. Derek doesn't know how to cope yet. I told him you'd understand.'

'Poor sod. Why should this happen to him? Why should something like this happen to anybody?'

'They're letting him out in time for Christmas. To be honest, I'm dreading it. I don't know how I'll be able to cope.'

'Oh Laura . . .'

'There's nothing you can do.'

'Maybe he'll feel better about me visiting him at home. Maybe in time we'll get back to how we were.'

A black cloud of hopelessness descended on her but she managed to say, 'Let's just take it one day at a time, one step at a time. I'll see how he is once I've got him home.'

So it was agreed that Robert didn't go back to the hospital to see Derek. They both knew without needing to say anything that they wouldn't see each other either. Laura wouldn't have much, if any, opportunity in the first place, with working all day and visiting the hospital every night. Then there was the afternoon and evening visits on Saturdays and Sundays. Apart from the time element, they both knew that it just wouldn't be right.

Before she left, he covered her hand with his and held it there for a minute. Instead of saying goodbye, he gently echoed her words: 'one day at a time, one step at a time'. She nodded, then gathered up her gloves and bag and walked away.

By the time Derek was allowed home the schools were closed for the Christmas break. She hadn't thought about what she'd do afterwards – whether she'd be able to keep on her job or not. She prayed that she would. Meantime, she did her best with the Christmas preparations. There wasn't time to bake and make her own Christmas pudding so she bought one in the supermarket. It was there that she bumped into Sophie McPherson.

'I heard you're getting your husband home for Christmas, Mrs Cairns.'

'Yes.'

'How is he?'

'Not so good, I'm afraid. He can't walk any more but we've got a wheelchair organised.'

'Are you having any friends or family over for Christmas Day?'

'No, there's just the two of us.'

'You must come to us then. I've cooked more than we'll need. Robert and Andrina and Jennifer will be there.'

'Oh, I couldn't put you to any more bother.'

'Bother? There's no bother as far as I'm concerned. I enjoy cooking and having people in. And I consider it my Christian duty to help when and where I can.'

Laura sighed. She would dearly have loved to accept the invitation if for no other reason but to be in Robert's company for a few hours. It would be sheer purgatory being alone with Derek as he was now. It was worse than the worst loneliness. Indeed she would have settled for any company, even Sophie McPherson's, without Robert being there. She believed she would have gone as far as welcoming Mr Pritchett, but Mr Pritchett was going up north to spend Christmas and New Year with an elderly cousin. His tribe of cats were 'having a nice little holiday', as he put it, in a Glasgow cattery.

'The truth is I'd love to accept your invitation, Mrs McPherson, but my husband wouldn't come. He's very disabled now and it's terribly humiliating for him to have people see him the way he is – especially when he's trying to eat. He's really very depressed at the moment and doesn't want anything to do with anyone. But thank you. Thank you very much. I really appreciate the thought.'

'Maybe there will be something I can do later on to help.'

Laura couldn't trust herself to speak and Sophie manoeuvred her shopping trolley away round another alleyway of high shelves. Later, after Derek had arrived home in the ambulance and the ambulanceman had trundled the wheelchair into the house, Laura thanked him and shut the door. Then she turned in the silent hallway to look at the grotesque and silent stranger who was imprisoned with her for the rest of his life.

Chapter Eighteen

'What the hell's up now?' Robert groaned to himself. It was the beginning of another day and before he'd even opened the door of his classroom, he heard the silence. It was total. Something instantly suspicious. Earsplitting bedlam was far more natural in most classes in Sinnieglen. Each morning it was the first problem that had to be dealt with. The first struggle. The first pitting of wills.

Something was seriously wrong today. He entered the classroom and felt the silence muffle around him like a heavy cloak. Thirty-eight pairs of eyes were fixed on him. It was as if they were waiting in breathless anticipation for him to react to something. He strode over to his desk and it was then, as he was organising some papers, that his eye fell on Benny McNally who always sat in the front row. Benny, son of Godfather McNally.

Robert had once mentioned to Bernard that Benny was in his class and how, apart from the boy's unusual interest in and knowledge about guns, he never gave him too much trouble. The father had been up a couple of times at the school of parent–teacher meetings and had seemed a perfect gentleman, well dressed, civil spoken . . .

He'd said to Bernard, 'Are you sure it's true what they say about him?'

Bernard had replied, 'I'm quite sure.'

'He seemed to me just like a well-to-do businessman.'

'Big business,' Bernard said. 'Drugs, extortion, the protection racket. Torture. Murder.'

'I find that so hard to believe.'

'Believe it!' Bernard said.

Benny McNally was leaning forward in the front row with a hard glitter in his eyes. He was holding a gun, pointing it straight at Robert. Robert forced himself to breathe evenly and calmly while he tried to figure out how to deal with the situation.

He could, of course, walk right out of the class and go to the headmaster's office and the headmaster would call the police. Robert immediately discarded that option. For one thing, he couldn't abandon the other children. He had a duty to all the pupils in his charge and for all he knew, Benny could turn the gun on them. The boy was emotionally unstable. He'd come to that conclusion long ago.

For another thing, Robert Anderson was not a coward. Nor was he in the habit of walking away from responsibilities.

While he was still thinking, he walked through the silence to the back of the class and collected some art materials from a cupboard. Benny turned round in his seat and kept the gun aimed at him. All the way to the cupboard and back to his desk again.

Eventually Robert looked calmly across at the boy and said, 'What kind of gun is that, Benny?'

Interest immediately brought Benny's face to life. The hard glimmer was forgotten.

'A Luger automatic pistol, sir.'

'Really? Quite an impressive-looking piece. Luger. Sounds German. Is it?'

'Aye.'

'Can I have a closer look at it?'

Without hesitation, Benny came across and handed the gun to him for inspection. Robert held it, turned it admiringly this way and that. Then he released the magazine and saw that it was empty. Well, thank God for that, he thought.

But knowing Benny, it could just as easily have been loaded. He could just as easily have pulled the trigger; sprayed teacher and class with bullets just for a laugh. He felt himself sweat and hoped it didn't show.

'Right now, Benny, do you not think it would be a good idea for me to keep this gun here in my desk until after school? Then you can take it home and give it back to your father.'

'Aye, OK,' Benny said cheerfully, before swaggering back to his seat.

Somehow, Robert managed to turn his thoughts back to the lesson he'd prepared for that day. It was never easy to concentrate these children's interest on art. Today it would be doubly difficult.

When he'd joined the staff at first, and met his first classful of children, he'd tried to find what their interests were so that he could base his teaching plans on whatever these interests might be. If the boys liked football, he could work out all sorts of ideas to develop and further this interest through art projects. If the girls were interested in fashion, he could cope with that too.

What his questioning had initially been met with, however, was total lethargy, or vagueness, or shrugs. Don't knows. Even to the question, 'How about football?' (and surely at least *one* of the boys was *bound* to be interested in football), the response was a sneery 'Naw.' Or a dull-eyed uninterest. Or a silent couldn't-care-less kind of shrug. It was the same with the girls. And with every class that came to him. Over and over again he had the same struggle to get through to the children. To battle with the hopelessness that was such an integral part of their lives. It was a big enough struggle to cope with his own hopelessness. Especially now when he'd no contact with Laura. Sophie had mentioned that she'd been speaking to her along at the shops in Bearsden just before Christmas. She'd even invited Laura and Derek to join them but of course he understood how that would be out of the question. He'd explained to Sophie and she understood. For all her faults and her neurotic personality, Sophie did her best to act in a Christian way. He warmed to his mother-in-law for trying to help Laura.

The class were getting restless. Sound was building. Anarchy, always a danger, was beginning to rear its ugly head. Instinctively Robert knew that his original project of still life in the form of a jug and a couple of apples didn't stand a chance after the drama of the gun. The thought occurred to him that he could – for a future project – bone up on weapons through the ages and have them draw pictures of Stone Age axes onwards. That would catch and hold their interest all right. Rivet them, even. It also occurred to him that to teach such a subject in a place like Sinnieglen might have some disadvantages – to put it mildly.

He'd worry about future lessons later that evening. The problem was what to do now. He decided to have a period of informal discussion. He'd already established this successfully in the last periods of Friday afternoon. It was too Herculean a task to teach on Friday afternoons, even for him.

'Right,' he barked out. 'All gather round. This morning we'll have an informal discussion.'

There was a gasp of surprise, then a whoop of delight and a thunderous clatter of seats and boots, and squeals of girls being knocked aside in the rush. The idea was that he sat on a stool and they all squatted cross-legged in a semicircle in front of him on the floor. First of all he went around hauling boys up by their collars (ignoring the protesting cries of fuck! and shit!) and rearranged them so that the girls would have some places near the front.

Boys and girls alike loved to be listened to, to be paid attention to. Nothing excited them, or made them happier, or interested them more. Robert knew it was a sad reflection on their home life. Most of them were at best ignored, never told when to come in, never asked where they'd been. As long as they kept out of their parents' way, that was the main thing. It didn't matter if they were stuck in front of a television set in a corner, or roaming the streets. Nobody cared. If any attention was levelled at them, it was all too often in the form of physical or sexual abuse.

'Right then,' Robert said. 'First of all, tell me all your news.'

There was a delighted babble, with everybody shouting at once.

'Look,' he bawled above the racket, 'I'm really looking forward to hearing what you've got to say but I can't make anything out if you all speak at once. It's got to be one at a time. How about you to start off, Malcy?' Malcolm Jedburgh was an undersized lad with cropped hair and a nervous tic. It was generally agreed among the staff that Malcolm would end up beside his brothers in Barlinnie. 'OK, Malcy?' Robert encouraged.

'Ah, wis wonderin' about the date, sir.'

'It's February the 10th, 1970. Why?'

'Aye, I thought it might be that. It would have been my dad's birthday today.'

'Is your dad dead, Malcy?'

'Aye, he was killed in a gang fight. Then after my mammy's boyfriend moved in, I run away to ma granny's. That's where I am now.'

'I see. I'm sorry about your dad, son. Is it all right at your granny's?'

Malcolm shrugged.

'She takes a bucket but even when she's drunk she doesnae hit me. No' like that shite at ma mammy's place. Granny's OK.'

'Well, at least that's something.'

Robert didn't know what else to say. He was no psychologist.

'A girl now. Kitty?'

Kitty was a waif, extremely malnourished. He was often sorely tempted to take her to a café and treat her to a decent meal, but this was out of the question. Teachers had to be very careful with girls. Professions could be and had been ruined by some nasty tongue. The nasty tongue usually belonged to an abusive parent, misrepresenting a situation and making scandalous accusations. Or, even more difficult to deal with, the girls themselves might try to 'come on' to a teacher or, being rebuffed at that, make scandalous accusations. Robert, like all male teachers, had to be constantly vigilant in making sure he was never left alone in a classroom (or anywhere) with a girl pupil. Not every girl of course behaved, or rather misbehaved, in this way but one could never be sure which was which.

Poor wee Kitty had been battered when she was a baby and was slightly uncoordinated as if she had a mild form of cerebral palsy.

'Speak up, dear,' Robert encouraged.

Kitty flushed with pleasure, probably at the 'dear'.

'I live in St George's House and Sister Adeline is going to take us all to the pictures on Saturday.'

He wondered if this was perhaps a case of wishful thinking on Kitty's part. However, he said, 'Great! What picture are you going to see?'

Kitty looked confused.

'I don't know.'

There followed a general discussion of what film was on where and each film's critical rating by those who'd seen it.

After that several of the boys told tales of how and what they'd nicked from shops in town and their near squeaks dodging security guards. Benny gave a detailed description of his dad's collection of knives and guns (a disclosure Robert suspected Mr McNally would not have appreciated).

At long last the buzzer could be heard echoing down the corridor, signalling a change of class. The whole school reverberated with noise and movement again.

Robert tried to snatch a few moments to reorganise the papers that contained all his plans and blueprints for the day's activities. He had got off to a bad start. He must pull himself together and get on with what he'd intended to teach today. But as another crowd of shabbily dressed, grubby-looking children trooped in, his heart sank. Oh, how he longed to be in Bearsden with Laura – anything but here. He kept worrying himself sick about how Laura was getting on. But he was unable to do anything in case it would add to her worries, make Derek more difficult. Anyway, he'd promised her to keep away for a few months – at least until she got in touch and let him know if Derek had settled down at all. If he'd learned to accept what had happened. So far there had been nothing.

As casually and discreetly as he could, he had begun asking Sophie if she'd seen Laura or heard anything about how Derek was keeping.

She said no. It was as if Laura had disappeared off the face of the earth.

'I've never even bumped into her at the shops,' Sophie said. 'And I used to see her there quite often. I wonder if I should just go along there and brazen it out. Knock on her door and say I was wondering what had happened to her.'

Robert was about to eagerly say, 'Yes, I think you should,' but McPherson got in first.

'Fot pity's sake, Sophie. Have you not enough on your plate? You work like a slave in this house. You serve on far too many committees, helping this and that cause. When you're not doing all that you're entertaining our friends and neighbours, or you're looking after Jennifer. You don't want to get involved where you're not wanted. The woman doesn't want you ferreting over there, poking your nose in, interfering. And her poor man will want it even less.'

Robert suddenly became aware of the chaos and the screeches of laughter in his class. Some of the boys were pelting the girls with pencils. Others were splattering them with paint.

Immediately he banished everything from his mind. He needed all his energies, physical and mental, for the job. He couldn't afford to start losing his grip. He was tempted to have another discussion group but resisted the temptation. At any other time than Friday it meant admitting defeat. It was the first step down the slippery slope to disaster.

Chapter Nineteen

'But *why* not?' Jane asked. 'Please, Andrina, tell me the truth. Is it anything I've said or done?'

'No, no.'

'Well, why do you keep refusing our invitations? We used to have some wonderful nights – just the four of us. I'm sure Bernard is worried too. We were such good friends. Bernard and Robert. You and me. What's gone wrong? I don't understand. You never even invite us to your place any more.'

They'd met by accident in town and Jane had persuaded Andrina to accompany her to the nearest restaurant for a cup of tea and a talk. Andrina couldn't very well say 'I don't mind you coming to visit on your own, but don't bring Bernard.' Jane would obviously want to know what she had against Bernard.

Andrina shrugged.

'Oh, I don't know. I've been so busy and Robert's so busy. We've just never had any time for socialising.'

'Bernard works long hours. I hardly ever see him but I'm sure he'd stay at home for you. It's the spring break now,' Jane reminded her. 'Robert won't be at work. Oh please, Andrina, I've missed you – please come to dinner tonight.'

'Oh, I couldn't possibly. I'd have to check with Robert and we'd have to take Jennifer out to my mother . . .'

'Well, tomorrow then?'

She couldn't think of any other excuse.

'Yes, all right.'

Jane pounced on her and kissed her.

'I really have missed you. And Bernard will be so delighted.'

Now Andrina found herself floating in a fairyland of delight. She had only existed these past few months. She mechanically moved about, dusting, hoovering, cooking, laundering clothes, ironing. Everything was such a *bore*. The light had gone out of her life. Even Jennifer, despite her fondness for the child, could do nothing to bring it flickering back. Anyway, most of each long, boring day, Jennifer was at school.

The only consolation was that Andrina was no longer plagued with the anxiety and fear of her mother catching her with Bernard. She was safe. But oh, what a bore that was too. Her life was flat, monotonous. She had no interest in it. Or in Robert. Especially in Robert. He was duller than ever. He looked so gaunt and worn. She had no sympathy for him. He knew, he had always known, that he had only to say the word and her father would get him a cushy job with a good salary. Perhaps even a consultancy. Anything would be better than where he was. But no. He was such an unimaginative man. Absolutely no get-up and go in him.

Her father had offered to buy Robert a house in Bearsden. To *buy* him one. Give him a *present* of it. How could Robert be so stupid as to turn such a generous offer down? She dismissed him from her mind. All her secret thoughts, dreams and longings were as concentrated on Bernard as they had always been.

Oh, how she'd ached for him these past months. But the terror she'd felt when her mother had nearly caught them together took a long time in fading away. Each time she was tempted to contact Bernard, the sight of her mother's knife-blade eyes was enough to trigger the memory into life again and she'd be glad she was safe. At the same time she'd never really believed that she and Bernard had separated for ever. Not in her heart and soul. Sometimes she even felt that somehow they hadn't separated at all. She'd be walking from the close with Robert and Jennifer to their car, to go for their usual Sunday visit to Bearsden for lunch with her mother and father and in that short walk she'd suddenly have the feeling that Bernard was near. She experienced the concentrated scrutiny that had been so often and so erotically directed at her in the past. It brought a *frisson* of fear but a swift arousal as well.

At other times, she'd gaze out of the front-room window at the trees and shrubbery of the Green and sense his watching presence, even imagine the shadow of him blending with the shadows of the trees.

Now she was so excited about being close to him in reality that all fear, all caution, was thrown to the winds.

'It's been a long time,' Robert remarked when she told him about the invitation. 'It's sad when one loses touch with friends.'

Robert looked depressed all the time, Andrina thought. It had nothing to do with losing touch with friends. He had just got himself on to a treadmill. Her happiness made her feel more kindly disposed to the whole world and everyone in it, including Robert.

'You need a bit of social life and relaxation, Robert. You work too hard.'

He shrugged.

'Somebody's got to do it.'

'Then let somebody else do it for a change.'

She saw his eyes drain of expression. He knew she always started on about what her father could do for him, and her and Jennifer. They would all reap the benefit, she kept telling him. He seldom argued now. He just acquired that closed, distant look. This time she didn't say any more. Why waste her breath? She turned her attention to more positive, more important, happier things.

She had her hair done. She bathed and perfumed her body and admired its seductive nakedness in the bathroom mirror, turning this way and that, stretching up her arms, pushing up her long hair. She took her time choosing what outfit she'd wear. Jane had said it would be 'just a little informal evening for the four of us', so she didn't want to be too dressed up. It was a warm evening and so she settled on a cream lace petal blouse and long straight cream skirt. The pale cream was a wonderful contrast to her deep auburn hair. Round her neck she tossed a long turquoise chiffon scarf the exact shade of her eyes, and draped it over her shoulder. She looked stunning. Even Robert noticed.

'You're a beautiful woman, Andrina,' he told her. 'And you've never looked lovelier than you do tonight.'

She was so happy she impulsively kissed his cheek.

'Thank you, dear.'

Robert looked somewhat more presentable than usual. At least he had made the effort and was wearing a decent suit and crisp, fresh shirt. Recently he hadn't even been bothering to change out of the clothes he'd been wearing all day at the school. Ignoring how crumpled they were, he'd sit about the kitchen, his reading glasses on, immersed in a book. As often as not, he was in her way and the cause of much irritation. He'd commandeer the kitchen table to work on the plans of some lesson or other for the next day, or he'd be bent over notes he was laboriously writing for a lecture.

But now there was no hate in her heart, only happiness. She was as excited as a child being taken to her first Christmas party.

At last, there Bernard was, rising from his chair in the luxurious lounge in Pollokshields, coming towards her with welcoming arms outstretched. Jane had already given both her and Robert a welcoming hug. Oh, the thrill of Bernard's touch! Even in such a brief and carefully controlled embrace, electric currents of passion darted along her nerves, caught at her breath, made her feel light-headed. And where else on earth had she ever seen such eyes? Unfathomable. Sometimes moody and menacing, sometimes glimmering with humour. Sometimes smouldering with passion. She wanted to go to bed with him right now. Go anywhere with him. Have sex anywhere with him. It seemed a miracle that they were able to behave normally in Jane and Robert's company. They joked and laughed and talked. The evening was a huge success. Even Robert managed to be entertaining for a change. Instead of his depressing stories about the poverty and distress of his pupils' lives, he had them howling with hilarity at some of his Friday afternoon 'News and discussion' sessions.

'Of course,' he explained at one point, 'everybody knew that Miss McNiven was having an affair with Mr Bothwell from Science. We often used to watch old Bothwell's bald head bobbing up the stairs *en route* to a rendezvous with Miss McNiven.' He laughed to himself and shook his head. 'This liaison was confirmed for all time by Lachlan McKenzie from my department going into the photographic darkroom for some stuff he'd to collect, and discovering Miss McNiven and Mr Bothwell in double exposure.' For a few minutes, Robert couldn't go on because of the laughter of the others. Eventually, he managed, 'Then one day old Bothwell got transferred up to Aberdeen and that was the end of their nonsense. Shortly after that, I had to deal with an incident involving some of Miss McNiven's pupils. Some silly girls were skipping along the corridors chanting at the tops of their voices, "We want sex! We want sex!" I ordered them to shut up and behave themselves, marched them along to Miss McNiven and reported the incident to her. Later, I learned that she gave them five of the belt each and shouted at them, "You'll just have to learn to do without like the rest of us!" '

Jane and Andrina had to get their hankies out to dab away tears of hilarity. It just went to show that Robert didn't need to be a dreary old bore; he could be quite passable company if he tried. The trouble was that nowadays he seldom bothered to make the effort.

Later, when they were leaving, Jane said, 'We mustn't lose touch again. I've enjoyed your company so much this evening.'

'Come to us next time,' Robert said. 'As far as I'm concerned, you're always welcome. I'm sure that goes for Andrina too.'

'Yes, of course,' Andrina said and right there and then a date was agreed.

She chattered excitedly to Robert all the way home about how wonderful the house looked: 'I'd forgotten about those gorgeous chandeliers. Did you see the way they sparkled?'

About how wonderful the food and drink was: 'Did you ever taste such a delicious starter? That chicken-liver pâté laced with brandy was just perfect.'

'Yes, that was good,' Robert agreed.

'Oh, and that rainbow trout.' Andrina was lost in a dream of pleasure and sensuality. To her and Bernard, the appreciation of good food had always been part of the sexual experience.

'I've never tasted it with cashew nuts and orange fritters before.'

'OK, OK,' Robert laughed.

'And oh, that wicked chocolate mousse . . . mmm, mmm!'

'I bet you've put on a few pounds tonight.'

Trust Robert to spoil the mood. She swung back to her previous irritation – but only until Bernard returned to her mind with his dark eyes full of promise.

Chapter Twenty

Michael had heard the phrase often enough: 'Once an alcoholic, always an alcoholic.' He knew it to be true. Now, he'd made up a saying of his own: 'Once a fighter, always a fighter.' As he said to Big Martha, 'What's the use of greetin' and growsin' about everything and not doing anything to try to put things right?'

Martha agreed with him. There could be no denying the fact that she was a fighter as well. She brandished a fist in the air as if to prove it.

'We should join the Tenants' Association. Fight for our rights.'

Caroline smiled indulgently, shook her head and started clearing the table.

'Aye. I was thinking about that myself,' Michael said. 'The church is quite supportive to the Association, I hear. *All* the churches,' he added hastily, in case Martha thought he was giving special credit to the Catholic Church. 'It's the Councillors who aren't so co-operative. They always think they know best. Know everything, in fact. Some folk just encourage them by being in awe of them. Frightened of them even. Well, I'm not.'

'Nor me.' Martha stuck out her bristly chin and folded her arms in aggressive pose. 'I'm ready to tell them a thing or two if I get my tongue on them. About the dampness in this house for a start. Bloody disgrace.'

'Mammy!' Caroline took quiet offence. She didn't like bad language, especially in front of the children. Sean and Sally and Maureen were waiting, ready to do their homework on the table. They stole giggly glances at one another. Caroline had been really upset the other day when Sally had stamped her foot on one of the motors that Sean was crawling round playing with. She had shouted angrily at her brother, 'You're an ould sod, so you are!'

'She's heard you saying that word, Michael,' Caroline accused. (Michael often referred to Martha as an ould sod.) 'What'll her teachers at school think of her if they hear her using foul language like that?'

'I'm sorry, hen,' he said, but his one eye had given Sally a wink behind Caroline's back.

Now he agreed with his mother-in-law.

'I blame wee Maureen's asthma on the dampness. And she's not the only wean who's wheezing and coughing in this street.'

'It's what's given me my arthritis.' Martha's mouth was set with anger. 'I never had arthritis – or phlebitis for that matter – before I came to Castlemilk.'

'There's a meeting tonight,' Michael said. 'Caroline, are you coming with me?'

'Och, just take Mammy, dear. I've an ironing to do. And I like to see that the weans get to bed at a decent hour.'

Caroline had got into the habit of foisting Big Martha on him. He understood why. It was the only time she got a bit of peace and freedom to do what she liked without her mammy criticising or narking on at her. Or having Caroline run about after her like a slave. He didn't mind. As long as it was making Caroline happy. He'd come home from work and he'd barely have finished his tea, when Caroline would say things like,

'How about taking Mammy out for a wee hurl? She's been cooped up here all day. It's time she had a wee breath of fresh air.' Or,

'Mammy was just saying, Michael, how she'd love to drop into the Old Folks' Club for half an hour one night. I said I was sure you wouldn't mind taking her.' If they were alone, she'd add, 'You're that good with her, Michael. You really are. I just love you for being so good to my mammy.'

At weekends it was:

'Michael, if you take Mammy for the messages I could take the weans to their Saturday gym club. They enjoy it so much and all that exercise is awful good for them.'

He knew that after she delivered them to the club and before it was time to collect them again, she enjoyed a cup of tea and a blether with some of the other mothers. So he said, 'Aye OK, hen.'

But honest to God, he sometimes thought that he and Big Martha were getting like Siamese twins. He was developing muscles like tree trunks with pushing and pulling her elephant weight about. It had become his job to get her in and out of her coat as well, and to tie on her shoes. He always thanked God for the lift. He'd warned her, 'If that lift ever breaks down' –and it was a fuckin' miracle it hadn't with her weight – 'I'm not bumping you down those stairs.' For one thing, if he ever did get her down like that, he'd never manage to get her back up.

She'd called him an ugly, one-eyed, flat-nosed Pape. (She never allowed him to forget how ugly he was.) Then she'd gone into a sulk. It was as if the lift had already broken down and he had already denied her an outing.

He sighed. It seemed he never got out anywhere with Caroline these days. But he said his usual, 'OK hen.' Then 'Right, ould yin. Are you game?'

'Of course I'm game,' she said. 'Well, don't just sit there, bullit-head. Fetch my coat and hat.'

'I'll bullit-head ye,' he replied, getting up. 'One of these days, ould yin, you're going to take a short cut out that window.'

'By God,' she said, 'you'll come with me if I do.'

He believed her. To hell and back it seemed, he was struck with her. He went to get her coat. Then came the momentous sweaty wrestle to get her into it. Eventually victorious, he squashed her maroon velour hat over her wiry bristle of hair. God, her hair looked as if it needed cut again. What a life!

'Here, you.' She gave him a punch in the solar plexus that genuinely winded him. 'You watch what you're doing with my good hat!'

'Mammy!' Caroline gently remonstrated. 'Michael's only trying to help.'

'I'll help him,' Martha growled. 'Flat-faced Green Grape.'

'See you,' he told her once he'd wheeled her chair from the house. 'One of these days I'm going to stuff a bunch of green grapes down your throat and fuckin' choke you with them.' (He never used the 'f' word in front of Caroline but being with his mother-in-law was as tough as being with the lads on the site.)

'You and who else,' she scoffed.

He had to give credit where credit was due. For an old crippled woman, she had loads of bottle.

They had picked a good night to attend the Tenants' Association, as it turned out. One of the Glasgow councillors was present to give a talk. He was a portly, dignified man and it was his first visit to Castlemilk. He'd rashly agreed to answer questions. He had not known of course that Big Martha would turn up. Had he known anything at all about Big Martha, the chances were he would not have taken the risk of being there at all.

She didn't even wait for question time. Her foghorn voice heckled the councillor so much and in such an abusive way that Michael became sorry for him. The poor guy was struggling on as best he could but he was clearly out of his depth.

'Will you shut your face,' he hissed at Martha. 'At least give the man a fair hearing.'

'Fair? Fair? What's bloody fair about your wean choking with asthma and me suffering agonies night and day with bloody arthritis?'

There was no arguing with that.

'OK. OK. But there's other folk wanting to get a word in as well.'

It had to be admitted that no one put across their point as forcibly as Martha. But she had ignited the fuse of anger and fired the others with the courage to speak up, even if it was just to agree with her.

Now, at least, the council had been made aware that there *was* anger here and that something had better be done about it. Some of the old members told them that in the earlier days of the scheme they'd got gutters cleared regularly, for instance, but Castlemilk had become so huge they couldn't keep up with that sort of programme.

Michael said, 'If inspectors were sent round regularly they'd see that some of the grouting between the bricks had come out and needed replaced.'

'I know,' a man called Bill Brady agreed. 'We'll have to keep fighting for that.'

Both Martha and Michael had, if truth be told, enjoyed the meeting. They felt energised, fired up with enthusiasm for the challenge. They spoke heatedly about it all the way home. Back in the house it was almost a let-down to find peace and quiet. The children were in bed and sound asleep. Caroline had the ironing-board out in front of the fire and she was softly singing as she slid the iron back and forth. There wasn't even the raucous noise of the television. Their small black-and-white set didn't work very well at times and Caroline seldom could be bothered with it.

She smiled a welcome.

'Hello you two. Are you ready for a wee cup of tea? I'll just put the kettle on.'

'No, it's OK, hen,' Michael said. 'I'll do it.'

He still felt good and he whistled while he awaited for the kettle to boil, then masked the tea.

'Any biscuits, hen?' he shouted through.

'Aye, in the round blue tin on the shelf,' Caroline called back.

While he was setting the tray he could hear Martha's booming tones still relating, blow by blow, everything that had happened at the meeting. Every now and then Caroline's voice, a feather in comparison, would murmur, 'You didn't, Mammy!' Or, 'Oh, in the name of the wee man!' Or, 'Heavens, I'm glad I wasn't there!'

Caroline had never liked confrontation. Many a time before they got married, she'd wept with distress in the face of her parents' opposition to the match. But she'd married him nevertheless. In her own quiet way, she usually got what she wanted. Michael loved her for loving him, and for sticking by him through thick and thin. He still had nightmares about the despicable way he'd treated her when he was on the booze. Time after time he vowed he'd do anything to make it up to her. If it took him the rest of his life, he'd make it up to her.

She always hushed him when he spoke like that. As far as she was concerned, he was and always had been the truest and kindest of men, and the best husband in the world.

Over his cup of tea, he said, 'Did I tell you I saw Bernard today?'

Caroline selected a biscuit.

'No! Whereabouts? At your da's place?'

They hadn't yet got out of the habit of calling the house in Blackhill Da's place.

'No. I was working on a site away out past Drymen. And I noticed his car stop at a temporary set of lights we'd set up.'

'Did you get a chance to speak to him?'

Michael shook his head.

'He might not have wanted me to anyway.'

'Huh! A snob now, is he? Him with his big house and posh car and rich wife. Well, he's not half the man you are, Michael. You're worth two of him any day. You're a good hard-working – '

'OK. OK, hen,' he laughed. 'Hold your horses. I didn't mean he'd be looking down his nose at me. Bernard's not like that.'

'I'll never forget how when you needed a helping hand, Michael, he sent you packing and called you a drunken bum. I'll never forgive him for that.'

'Let's face it, hen. That's what I was then.'

'He's your twin brother. It wasn't natural for him not to help you.'

'We've been through all this before, Caroline. I've told you, nobody could help me. I had to help myself in the end. I had to *want* to help myself. But all this had nothing to do with what I'm trying to tell you about Bernard just now.'

'What then?'

'There was a woman in the car with him. And it wasn't his wife. It might have been embarrassing for him, to say the least, if I'd gone forward to speak to him.'

Caroline was immediately intrigued and excited.

'See him, I always knew he was up to no good. I just knew it!'

Already Michael was wishing he hadn't mentioned the subject.

'Here, hen, this better be confidential. Just between you and me and Martha.'

Up to this point Martha had been too busy demolishing the plate of biscuits, chomping away with false teeth that had become loose with the years. He'd told her that it was time she got a new tighter-fitting pair but she always maintained, 'These teeth'll see me out.'

Now she said, 'Who was it?'

'Who?'

'The woman, of course. Who do you think?'

He hesitated.

'I don't know. Although, mind you, she did look vaguely familiar.'

'You've had that bullit head of yours punched once too often. It's affected your brain. You've got a memory like a bloody sieve.'

'Mammy! You know what I keep telling you about swearing.'

'Och, what are you worrying about? The weans are dead to the world.'

'I know, but it's a bad habit you've got.'

'What about flat-face here? He f's and c's.'

Caroline gasped.

'Oh, you're awful, Mammy. He does not.'

'He works on a building site, girl. Do you think fellas like that say gosh and golly?'

Michael said, 'I wish I'd never opened my mouth now.'

Caroline looked intrigued again.

'Fancy Bernard having another woman!'

'Now wait a minute, hen. There could be a perfectly innocent explanation for this. She could be a pal of his wife's and Bernard was giving her a lift home.'

'Away out there?'

'She could live out there. Some folk do. And anyway, Caroline. What Bernard gets up to is none of our business. We've got enough problems of our own with ould greedy-guts here.'

'You watch it,' Martha warned. 'I've floored you once before and I can do it again.'

It was a slight exaggeration but she *had* once given him a stoater of a black eye.

'Och, stop it the pair of you,' Caroline murmured automatically. Her eyes had acquired a faraway expression.

Chapter Twenty-One

'You really worry me,' Bridie said. 'I'm worried all the time. Never a day passes – '

'What have I done this time?' Frank interrupted. 'You might as well tell me and get it over with.'

Of course he could guess. It would be about the short story he'd written and which had been adapted for television. All Bridie's criticism and nagging always stemmed from her hatred of his writing.

'That story you wrote.'

'What about it? It got great reviews.'

Therein lay the problem. She would never admit it was his success that worried her, any more than he would come right out and say, 'Your problem, Bridie, is you can't cope with my success.' His play about the disintegration of a marriage said it all. The script was now finished. He wasn't a hundred per cent satisfied with it though, and he'd delayed handing it over to the television company. Instead he'd given them the short story.

'It was terrible, Frank, just terrible.'

'Didn't you read the reviews?'

'Oh, the reviews *would* butter you up. And of course the TV people are coining it. But it gave a terrible picture of Glasgow, Fıank. There were gangsters in it. When have we ever met or ever set eyes on a gangster in Glasgow? We've known nothing but nice folk in the working-class areas you depict. Nice, kind, generous, friendly folk. You ought to be ashamed of yourself. I'm ashamed of you. Your poor ma and da – God rest their souls – would turn in their graves if they knew.'

'Bridie, were you and I watching the same play? There were typical Glasgow folk in the story of the kind you're talking about. Their wonderful sense of humour was there too.'

'The play was about gangsters, Frank. And of course I know where you got that idea from, and no doubt the awful characters as well. It was from your Bernard. But, knowing you, you would neither have warned Bernard, or even mentioned a word to him, about how you were using him. Well, maybe you've gone too far this time, Frank. That's what worries me. Maybe this time you've used the wrong one.'

For a moment he succumbed to the infection of her fear. Then he pulled himself together. Bernard worked nights and was away a lot as well. He probably never watched television. And, damn it all, as a writer, people were his raw material and he had to get his ideas from real life. Another thing, Bernard was successful in his own field. He was nothing like Bridie, who saw everything he wrote as a personal threat. Bernard was not so easily threatened. It really was becoming a serious problem the way Bridie kept trying to worry him and undermine his self-confidence.

'Bridie, I do research. How many times must I tell you? Whether you like it or not, there *is* a twilight world that Bernard talks about. It *does* exist and there's nothing to stop me writing about that side of the city.'

'Oh no? We'll maybe see about that.'

He sighed.

'Bridie, if you're trying to hint that a posse of gangsters will arrive at our door to threaten me, forget it. They're more likely to be chuffed, flattered by the media attention. It was a piece of entertainment, a good story. If any of them have seen it, and if the reviewers are anything to go by, they'll have enjoyed it.'

'It was just terrible,' Bridie repeated as if he'd never spoken. 'I tremble to think of what you're capable of stooping to next. You used to have high ideals, Frank. You used to be a decent, hard-working man.'

It smacked of the attitude he'd been used to all his life from family and friends. If you didn't sweat and work at something physical like humping bricks, or digging roads, or emptying bins, or working in the bookie's, you were no use. What you did wasn't work at all. Even when he was in Goldmayers he was dismissed by family and friends as a 'pen pusher'. Bernard was admired because his work was physical, albeit in a different way, with his karate and his well-known speed at using his fists, as well as his high kicks. Bernard could knock somebody unconscious with his feet.

While he was writing his 'Twilight World' story, he'd tracked Robert Anderson down to ask his advice about the karate scenes. He'd tried to contact Bernard first of course, but somebody in his office said he was away on a job. Then he'd remembered that Bernard's teacher and mentor had been Robert Anderson. He'd contacted Bernard's old school but was told there that Anderson had been promoted to head of the art department at Sinnieglen School. They wouldn't give his home address. Frank had a vague idea that it was somewhere near Glasgow Green. Bridie's sister Doris was friendly with Anderson's wife and used to often visit her, but instead of contacting Doris and asking her he decided just to phone Anderson direct at Sinnieglen School. There had been no problem. Anderson had even invited him to his club to watch all the lads in action. It had made the karate scenes in his story and the drama adaptation a hundred per cent authentic.

The day after Bridie had spoken to him about the play, Bernard phoned.

'Hi Frank.'

'Bernard? Long time no see.'

'Yeah. I saw your play the other night.'

'Oh?' Frank made a determined effort to sound nonchalant. 'What did you think of it?'

'It wasn't bad. Beats me how you do it, Frank. I always think of you leading such a sheltered life.'

'I do research.'

'Well, if you're doing anything set in my territory again, ask me what you need to know. The ordinary punter maybe wouldn't spot where you went wrong, Frank. But I know a few who did.'

Frank was nearly bowled over by a rush of joy.

'Here, Bernard, do you mean that? You'd help me?'

'Sure. Be glad to.'

'Great, Bernard! I appreciate that. You've been around so much more than me.' (The truth was Frank hadn't been around at all.)

'You could say that, Frank.'

146

'How are you doing these days?'

'No bad, as they say.'

'We must get together, Bernard. You and your wife could come over here for dinner one night. Or I could throw a party if you'd like to meet some television people. Maybe you could meet somebody who'd be able to help you with your work. Sometimes they get stars and pop groups over from America. You do bodyguarding and that sort of thing, don't you?'

Bernard laughed.

'Still the same old Frank.'

'How about it?'

'I'll let you know when I'll be in Glasgow for a spell. Then we can fix a firm date. But I don't need any help with my work. I do OK.'

'Great, Bernard. Just great.' Frank was shouting with happiness. 'I'll look forward to it.'

Before he hung up he could hear Bernard's deep rumble of laughter again.

He could hardly wait to tell Bridie. He raced through to the kitchen, face alight with joy.

'Bridie, that was Bernard on the phone. He liked the play but said he could have helped me make it better and I've to ask him in the future. My God, Bridie, what a bit of luck. There's so much he can tell me about people I'd never normally meet. There's the chance here for me to create really marvellous authentic characters. I said we'd throw a party one night and to bring his wife along . . .'

Frank's enthusiasm wilted under the venom of Bridie's stare.'

'You said what?'

In his excitement he'd forgotten about Doris, and Bridie's attitude to Bernard.

'Now look, Bridie, he's my brother and let's face it, he hasn't done either of us any harm. All right, your sister's marriage to Bernard didn't work out, but that's well in the past now and it never was any of our business. What's more, there's always two sides to what goes wrong in a marriage. Even your mother says Doris was partly to blame.'

'Trust you, any excuse for a party. Any excuse to fill this place with that obnoxious shower you call your friends.'

'Bridie, it saddens me when you talk like that, when you get so bitter. Surely my friends and colleagues aren't so hard to take? Some of them are just struggling actors and actresses, trying to make a living, worrying about where their next job's coming from, in a profession where there's an unemployment rate of at least ninety-nine per cent.'

'Really? And where do the women get all the money for their expensive-looking make-up and trendy clothes? Sleep with the producer, do they? Or the writer?'

Anger flashed across his brain with such force he was within seconds of striking her. Instead he fished a can of beer from the fridge, tugged it open and took a swig. Then he said, 'Are you accusing me of being unfaithful to you, Bridie? Is that what you really think?'

'No.' The word was delivered with an impatient agitation of her head as if she thought he was just being stupid.

'What the hell are you saying, then?'

'It's just the thought of you inviting Bernard and Jane without first discussing it with me.'

'Well, OK, I'm sorry. But it's just how it worked out with him phoning like that. One thing led to another. I said we should get together some time. I hardly ever see any of the family now, especially since Da died. It seemed a natural thing to say. Then I suddenly thought of a party as a way of repaying him for his offer to help me. I could introduce him to some people from the studios who might prove useful to him. He was all for us getting together.'

'So you're really two of a kind then?'

'What's that supposed to mean?'

Ignoring his question, she said, 'It's a different story when I offer to help you.'

'It's research, Bridie. Research! He moves in a different world from us. He's my key, or my window if you like, into that world. A contact like that's invaluable.'

'I see.'

All at once she looked defeated. Her eyes behind her glasses acquired a helpless, confused expression.

'Och, Bridie,' he said. 'I'm sorry I've upset you about

inviting Bernard. Maybe we could just meet somewhere else. I could take him out to dinner or something.'

'No, it's all right. We'll have the party.'

'Are you sure?'

'Yes, I'm sure.'

The flame of Frank's enthusiasm was beginning to flicker into life again.

'I'll come with you to the supermarket to buy everything we'll need. Or better still, Marks and Spencer's. They've got all sorts of hors-d'oeuvres and really interesting stuff. Remember that smoked salmon we got there the last time? Superb, it was. They've every kind of food we could wish for. There'll be no need for you to cook, or to do anything, Bridie.'

'I didn't think there would be,' Bridie said flatly. 'There never is.'

Chapter Twenty-Two

'Derek, you didn't get into such a state when the nurse in the hospital had to take you to the toilet, did you?'

Laura realised only too well what a humiliation it was for Derek to have her perform such an intimate task for him. But it had to be done. He couldn't walk. He could only stand for a few seconds with her support or if he was hanging on to something.

'That . . . was . . . different.' It was such a struggle for him to force words out she suffered the stress along with him. To listen to Derek trying to talk, to witness the dreadful contortion of his face was an exhausting ordeal. As often as not she tried not to look at him.

'Come on, darling. It's all right. I'm your wife. I care about you more than any nurse.'

'And . . . I . . . care . . . about . . . you. That's . . . why . . . I . . . don't . . . want . . . I . . . can't . . . bear . . . you . . . to . . . see . . . me . . .'

'It's all right. Honestly, darling. When you love somebody it's all right. Try to think of me as just another part of yourself.'

She pushed his wheelchair towards the bathroom, then inched it through the door. The chair made it without a centimetre to spare. She stopped it as near to the lavatory seat as she could and braced herself for the weight of Derek clutching on to her. With difficulty, she managed to take down his trousers, turn him round, lower him on to the seat.

'I'll go and make us a cup of tea. Just give me a shout when you're ready.'

He nodded, shoulders hunched, eyes furtive with shame. She could have wept for him. Often she did. But in secret. She wept for Robert too. She needed him and missed him so much.

She'd had to give up her job. There was no way she could

leave Derek alone all day while she went out to work. Occasionally she was still forced to call on Mr Pritchett to help but she struggled with every last ounce of strength in her body in her attempts to avoid this. Derek worked himself into such a state if he thought anyone else was going to see him nowadays. Then Sophie McPherson had appeared unexpectedly on the doorstep. So attuned was Laura to Derek's needs and feelings now, she sensed his panic filling the whole house at the sound of Sophie's voice, even though he was through in the kitchen.

She'd invited Sophie to come into the sitting-room. Back in the kitchen she explained to an agitated Derek she couldn't very well keep the woman standing at the door.

'But don't worry,' she told him as she hastily set a cup for herself and one for Sophie on to a tray, 'I won't bring her through here.'

It proved the measure of her unhappiness and isolation, she thought later, when she'd actually been grateful for Sophie McPherson's company for half an hour. Sophie (she'd asked Laura to call her that) wasn't relaxing company. However, she seemed genuinely concerned about Laura's predicament and eager to help.

'I appreciate your kindness,' Laura said, handing the older woman a cup of tea. 'I really do. But I'm the only one who can see to my husband. He won't let anyone else near him. I'll just have to carry on . . . Keep going somehow.'

Sophie hadn't responded. With a restless, piercing stare she took in the dusty neglected sitting-room. Laura had little time or energy for housework. In the silence she felt words that she'd tried not to think, swelling up and spilling out.

'The terrible thing is, there's no end to this. I mean, it's not like a short-term illness when you know there's a light at the end of the tunnel. It's not as if you know if you just hang on and do your best, you'll get there eventually and everything will be all right. Derek will never get better. It's not even an illness at all. That's what I was told. It's just that the stroke has left him with a disability. Derek could live for another forty years. Forty years!' she repeated as if she could barely credit her own words.

'You'll have to be firm with him,' Sophie said. 'Or somebody will.'

'Oh, Sophie.' Laura shook her head. 'The poor man. If you just saw him. If you knew the hurt, the humiliation, the frustration he's suffering.'

'You need to get a break. Get out and about,' Sophie insisted. 'A bit of freedom. You don't look fit to cope for forty days, never mind forty years. You look as if a breath of wind would blow you away. Are you eating properly?'

Now that Laura came to think of it, she was hardly eating at all. To watch Derek eat, to try to help him and to clean up the mess he made of himself took away all her desire for food.

'I don't suppose I am.'

'It's time you did then. There's not a pick of flesh on you.'

Laura couldn't help smiling then.

'You're a fine one to talk.'

'Oh, I've always been like this. It's natural for me. But you've lost weight since I last saw you. A lot of weight. I'll bring some home-made soup along tomorrow. You see that you eat it!'

Laura was embarrassed, vaguely insulted even. She had always lived in Bearsden where one kept to oneself in troubled times, put a brave face on things. Unlike Sophie, who had come from the tenements where everybody knew of and shared in everybody else's troubles. Such gestures of help and comfort were commonplace there. Laura felt annoyed and ashamed of herself for blurting out her secret fears.

'Oh no, please. I'm perfectly all right.' She gathered some dignity, straightened her back, was careful not to allow her hand to tremble when she lifted her teacup.

'You don't look it.'

'I just get a bit tired, that's all.'

'You should insist on a nurse coming in a few times a week to let you off the hook.'

'I'm afraid that's not possible. I only wish it was.'

'I wonder if my husband could do anything about that.'

'How do you mean?'

'Well, he's a councillor. He knows so many influential people. Maybe he knows somebody in the health department or the hospital or wherever, who could pull a few strings . . .'

A variety of expressions jostled for supremacy in Laura's face. Hope, hopelessness, wistfulness, despair.

'No, I understand from the hospital that the caring is entirely up to me. The only alternative was for Derek to be institutionalised. I couldn't do that to him. And even if it were possible to get nurses here, Derek would never agree. He was upset enough with nurses having to do things for him when he was in hospital.'

'I wasn't thinking of him,' Sophie said dismissively, 'I was thinking of you.'

Laura hung on to the thought that Sophie meant well and was trying to be kind. Nevertheless she sensed a hardness, a kind of desperate ruthlessness that strengthened her protectiveness towards Derek.

'Somebody's got to think of him. And I am his wife. I'm sure you'd do the very same for your husband, Sophie.'

Although in fact she wasn't all that sure.

'Are you kept busy these days?' she said, changing the subject. 'Tell me all the local news.' She really wanted to know. It was as if she'd been imprisoned with Derek on another planet. He'd be working himself up into a temper through in the kitchen. She knew the fits of anger he was taking more and more often now were just part of the results of his stroke. She had been warned at the hospital that a complete personality change was quite common. And Derek's personality certainly had changed. Sometimes she wished he'd died, because that way she would only remember him as he had been before this terrible disability had ruined both their lives.

Sophie said, 'There's a concert at the church next Monday night. The Church of Jesus. My daughter is singing solo at it. You'll not have heard Andrina sing.'

'No.'

'Try to come to the concert. It doesn't matter that you're not a member of our church. It's a public event and you'd enjoy it. It would do you good to hear her.'

Laura doubted it but such was her loneliness she would have

gone if she could. No doubt Andrina wouldn't be the only performer at the concert.

'I wish I could. Honestly, Sophie. I'm not trying to be awkward. I know what Derek is like. It's simply not possible for me to leave him.'

'What about that man next door? I've seen him along at the shops. I asked about you. If he'd seen you. He told me about you never getting over the door and how he was having to get your messages now. I asked him if he'd be willing to look after your husband if need be, and he said he would. I wasn't thinking of the concert at the time but now that I have . . . Mind you, I don't like the look of that man. But desperate times need desperate measures.'

Laura felt a needle of resentment. The woman had no right to interfere like this. She began to understand Sophie's reputation of getting things done at all sorts of committees and in the church where all else and all others had failed. Her determination was almost frightening. Like an express train hurtling, unstoppable, towards its destination.

'I really don't think – '

'Nonsense. It's just ten or fifteen minutes away by car and it would only be for a couple of hours. My husband and I have to be there early. We've both been involved in organising the event. It's for a good cause. The RSPCC. I could get Robert to collect you and bring you back. He's got his own car now. Haven't you seen him recently?'

Laura shook her head.

'But,' Sophie's voice was like a machine rattling bullets out, 'you know he left St Francis.'

'Yes. We gave him a little farewell tea in the staffroom.'

For a horrible moment she thought the memory was going to bring a gush of tears to her eyes. Panic stopped them.

'Trust Robert,' Sophie said. 'Instead of changing to a better district he just moves up the road to Sinnieglen. An even worse place, my husband tells me.'

'It's difficult to get teachers to go to schools like St Francis and Sinnieglen.'

'I'm not surprised,' Sophie said. 'Why you? I said to him. Why you?'

'He's a very good teacher, Sophie. Most of the children there are deprived. Often neglected and abused. The teachers are the only stability in most of their lives. Their only decent role model. I admire Robert for what he does. He's a good man as well as a good teacher.'

'Oh, I know, I know. He's a decent Christian man. I wouldn't have allowed my Andrina to marry him if I hadn't thought that. It's just such a pity – for his family's sake if not for his own – that he's got no ambition. He has a wife and a child of his own flesh and blood to consider. It's doing them no good living in a place like Monteith Row.'

'It's got a nice outlook, being so close to the Green.'

'Huh! There's all sorts of wickedness goes on there now. You only need to read the papers. One of those awful murders was committed not far from there. And the buildings are degenerating into a slum. It's just his stubborn pride that's keeping Robert in that place. He won't accept any help. Won't allow my husband to lift a finger on his behalf. Won't accept a penny from us. Of course we try to make up for it by being as good and as generous as we can to Andrina.'

I'll bet, Laura thought. She looks a right spoiled brat.

'And to our granddaughter, of course. You know Jennifer, don't you?'

'Yes, she's a lovely little girl.'

'Not a bit like her mother.'

Laura stared at Sophie in some puzzlement. Was she comparing the child with Andrina in a detrimental way? Or was she glad that Jennifer was not like Andrina? There had been an odd ring of satisfaction in Sophie's voice.

'Well, that's settled then,' Sophie announced suddenly, as she rose and tidied down her skirt. 'You're going to tell that neighbour of yours that you need him to come in here next Monday night because you're going to the church concert. I'll tell Robert he's to call for you.'

'Oh, I don't think . . . I mean, I never . . .' Laura rose, sweating with distress.

'My goodness, look at the time,' Sophie said. 'I've got to run. I've another sick visit to make and then I'm chairing a guild meeting. I'll see myself out.'

Laura was left bracing herself, not only for the scene she was about to face with Derek, but also for the ordeal of asking for Mr Pritchett's help.

Chapter Twenty-Three

As usual, Neily Duffy was waiting for Robert the moment he got out of his car.

'Hallo, sir.' Neily was tall with thin, knobbly wrists and a protruding Adam's apple.

'Good morning, Neily.' Automatically Robert handed the boy his briefcase and a key. One or two of the other teachers thought he was about as mad as Neily in trusting the boy. There had been a time when Robert thought the same himself. On the first occasion it had happened, Neily had wriggled up to him as he had done in the classroom, wanting to be near him. A sort of cross between a snake and a dog.

'I'll carry your case up to the class for you, sir, and put it in your desk.'

He'd taken the chance though already he had come to the conclusion that Neily should be in a special school. Or having psychiatric treatment somewhere. He had come up from primary school with severe learning difficulties as well as behavioural problems. Indeed most of the time he made it impossible to teach the rest of the class in which he was a pupil. He seemed to be an uncontrollable exhibitionist. He would do anything, anything at all, to get attention. It was nerve-stretching, mind-bending, top-level frustrating stuff in the classroom. Every teacher in the school at some time or other (some all of the time) harboured thoughts of murder towards Neily.

Robert had had his share of run-ins with him, had been driven to bawl at him, belt him, bang him down in his seat so hard he feared he'd fractured his bum. Yet, despite all this, the boy seemed to like him. It was the only explanation Robert had for Neily gyrating and twisting about towards him every morning, and making all kinds of strange noises. Neily had never once stolen anything from his briefcase or his desk and was always to be found standing grinning in triumph when Robert reached the classroom.

'Thanks, Neily,' Robert said and gave him a pat on the back.

That was always the end of Neily's good behaviour for the day. He went from teacher to teacher leaving a trail of fury and disruption and, in the case of some of the women teachers, tears and even hysterics.

This morning Robert had Neily's class for the first period. Not a good way to start Monday morning. Especially this particular Monday when he was so confused about this invitation to the concert in Bearsden. Not to mention Sophie's request that he collect Laura and, after the concert, take her home. Andrina was staying at Sophie's overnight with Jennifer, and Sophie had arranged for a neighbour to babysit while they were all at the concert.

'There's no point in Jennifer being up so late and dragged across town to Monteith Row when there's a bed for her here,' she said. 'You'd be welcome too, Robert, but I know you've got to be at the school in the morning.'

So had Jennifer, but he was so distracted with thoughts of Laura he omitted to point this out. Andrina decided that she would stay too. Any excuse to be away from her own home, as usual. She was hardly ever in the place nowadays. Not that he cared any more. If that was what she wanted and what kept her happy, fair enough.

It was Laura he was worried about. She was trapped for ever with Derek in his tragic state. There was no escape for her. Sophie no doubt had nagged at her to go to the concert, probably even made the arrangement with Mr Pritchett. He couldn't imagine Laura asking the man for any favours unless in an absolute emergency. He wondered if, like him, the deciding factor had been the idea of being alone together for even a few minutes when he collected her and later took her back home in the car.

But oh, what a torment the idea was too. He so longed to help and comfort her. He ached to hold her close and stroke her hair and tell her he loved her, and was going to take care of her and keep her safe.

A verse of a poem by Robert Burns came into his mind.

Oh, wert thou in the cauld blast,
　　On yonder lea, on yonder lea;
My plaidie to the angry airt –
　　I'd shelter thee, I'd shelter thee.
Or did misfortune's bitter storms
　　Around thee blaw, around thee blaw,
The bield should be my bosom,
　　To share it a', to share it a'.

In a way he dreaded seeing her. He dreamed of taking her away, starting a new life together. But he knew that neither of them could run away from reality. He wanted to make love to her. Love as it should be, the ultimate giving of oneself, of being as physically close as possible, of expressing in the most intimate way the depth of his feelings for her. But neither of them could cheat on a man who had suffered more than enough already.

For weeks he hadn't been able to sleep properly, and that had never bothered him before. At one time he'd been out for the count the moment his head hit the pillow. Not getting a proper refreshing sleep was making the stresses of his work more difficult to cope with. There could be no taking it easy with any of the classes in Sinnieglen, even with the better-behaved classes. You had always to be in charge and be seen to be in charge. An endless supply of energy was needed, something he was becoming short of. Especially emotional energy. He did not feel at all able to put up with the exhibitionist behaviour of Neily Duffy today.

Neily had chosen to pick on the girls in the class. He was poncing about mimicking how Tina Agnew spoke and walked. The poor girl was bandy-legged and was cursed with a bit of a lisp into the bargain.

'Neily, sit down at once,' Robert roared.

Neily sniggered and said, 'Thorry, thir, I thought it was my turn to path out the penthils. Or ith it painths today, thir?'

'Sit down and be quiet, boy.'

'Ohi, ohi.' Neily began bouncing up and down, then leapt into the aisle between the seats, clutching his groin and gyrating about. 'I need to go, sir.'

This time he was trying to make a fool of another boy, Geordie Black, who had a bladder problem and had to make frequent visits to the lavatory. Geordie, however, never behaved in this manner. With a white anxious, apologetic face, he would just quietly raise his hand and get a nod of permission from the teacher to leave the room.

Geordie had never been a problem. Neily was the problem.

Robert began taking the register in as loud and as authoritative a voice as he could muster.

'Scott.'

'Here, sir.'

'O'Hara.'

'Here, sir.'

'Weir.'

'Here, sir.'

From the corner of his eye, he could see Neily tugging Mae Turner's hair. Mae tried to push him away and Neily called her a fuckin' wee cow. Robert could feel the anger grow and thump like a sledgehammer inside his head.

'Sweeney.'

'Here, sir.'

'Donovan.'

'Here, sir.'

Another girl was telling Neily to shut up and get back to his seat.

'Fuckin' wee cow,' Neily said again and made a rude gesture at her.

Robert's anger exploded. He strode rapidly towards the grinning Neily.

'I will not tolerate that language or that behaviour in my class.'

He got a grip of Neily by the back of the neck, rushed him over to his seat and slammed him into it with such force that the boy's head clattered down on to the desk. Neily squinted up, bloody-nosed.

'I'll bring my da up to you,' he warned, still cheeky, still showing off.

'I don't care a damn about you or your da,' Robert shouted. 'I hope the pair of you end up under a bus!'

This unexpectedly deflated Neily. He looked hurt and confused. Oh God, Robert thought, he's believed, despite our regular run-ins, that I genuinely care about his welfare.

'Here, son.' Robert took a hankie from his pocket. 'Wipe your nose with this.'

Neily appeared slightly mollified but still deeply wounded. Unusually silent too. Robert thought, Perhaps I'll be able to get on with some lessons before he recovers. He'd spent many hours in preparation and he'd no intention of wasting all his efforts.

There were enough difficulties without Neily. The attention span of most of the children was minimal; some were just not there at all. Others, who'd obviously been up too late the night before, were floating on the edge of sleep.

Over and above the actual teaching now it was his responsibility to run the department. He had to make sure that all the necessary resources were available. The money to spend on equipment and everything needed was never enough, and he'd to fight for every penny. He also had to set up tests and examinations, just a few of the extra jobs which he had to do in his so-called free time – mostly at home.

He didn't know, at the end of the working day, how he'd got through that Monday. Laura was the ghost at his elbow every long tortuous hour. Sometimes he thought he was going mad. He asked himself what he was doing with his life. What use was it? What could he achieve with these children?

The last class of the day confirmed this view. Later, he made Laura laugh about an incident that occurred in this class. Underneath the laughter, however, the sad hopelessness was there. They both felt it.

The incident had concerned Greta McGrinchy who had been off school for ages. Laura knew as well as he did that when pupils were off for a long time, they forgot how to behave in a classroom; even Greta, who had been quite reasonably behaved before, was no exception.

Robert had been writing on the board and she said to him, 'Your heid's in the way.'

In the last throes of an awful day he had snapped, 'What do you expect me to do – cut it off?'

She had replied, 'Ye can dae what ye like wi' the fuckin' thing!'

It was good to see Laura laugh. They were sitting in the car *en route* to the concert. But the laughter soon faded and they were left in the silence of their shared unhappiness.

'Never a day passes,' he told her eventually, 'that I don't think of you, and long for us to be together.'

She was silent, so he went on, 'I know it's not possible and yet I *will* it to be possible. I *pray* for it to be possible.'

'Oh, Robert.'

'Not that I wish Derek any harm,' he said. 'I don't. He's suffered enough already.' He kept repeating silently, desperately, to himself.

I don't. I don't.

Chapter Twenty-Four

Andrina was wearing a white shirt with silver buttons, a white skirt and dainty silver shoes. Against her luxurious auburn crown of hair, white looked startling. The dark bloom of her nipples clearly showed through the shirt, and the skirt hugged her hips and thighs, accentuating the long shapeliness of her legs. It was the kind of outfit she kept only for Bernard.

Since the supper at Pollokshields, he'd phoned and persuaded her that they must meet on their own and talk. He had only existed without her. His life had been on a back burner, only flaring into life when he'd been in her company. Andrina had felt exactly the same. Life had no interest without him. Her whole existence had been on hold. He lit the spark that brought fierce passion and vitality careering through her veins. He brought her to the peak of life.

The inhibiting fear of her mother was swamped by their sexual reunion in the Monteith Row flat in the bed she shared with Robert. The impression of Robert's head was still on the pillow, the imprint of his body on the mattress. It was morning, the blinds were still drawn, hazing the room with amber light. In wordless, witless rapture she and Bernard came together. Groans and grunts and wails of complete abandonment shattered the muffled silence of the room. Afterwards they talked and shared their despair at having been parted.

Then suddenly she heard footsteps on the outside stairs and all the fears about her mother rushed back. Her throat constricted in panic as she waited for the doorbell to ring. Bernard had to forcibly pin her down on the bed to prevent her running from the room.

It was only the postman. She heard the letterbox creak open and shut.

'Calm down,' Bernard commanded. 'Even if it had been your mother – so what? You could just ignore her until she'd gone away. Or, better still – let her in and face her with me, as I've always said we should. I've told you a thousand times, Andrina, there's nothing to fear from anyone.'

He held her in his arms and she clung to him like a distressed child.

'As long as you've got me, you're safe. You're safe, do you hear? Although what you have to fear from your mother, I've yet to understand.'

'I'm sorry.' She struggled up, swung her legs over the side of the bed and began smoothing down her skirt. This outfit alone was enough to damn her in her mother's eyes. Andrina could vividly imagine Sophie's horror at the sight of it. It was as if Sophie was already staring at her.

'I'd better change,' she announced suddenly.

'You look wild and wicked and sexually abandoned. Absolutely wonderful.'

But Andrina's attention had strayed away from him.

'She sometimes comes this early. To do shopping in town, she tells me, but I know it's just to check on me. She never rings before she comes. She just suddenly appears on the doorstep.'

'I wish your mother would drop dead.' Bernard leaned back on the pillow, his arms cradling his head. 'Then we could celebrate.'

'After the funeral,' Andrina said.

'Oh yes.' Bernard's eyes narrowed and glimmered. 'We'd have to do the decent thing. I'd buy you the smartest, most expensive black outfit I could find in Glasgow. In London, if you liked.'

'And a wide-brimmed black hat?'

'Sure. Sure. And long black gloves. And high-heeled black shoes.'

She giggled, unable to control herself.

'You're a wicked man.'

'I know. And you're a wicked woman.'

'I suppose I am. At least in some people's eyes. Because after Mummy's funeral, Bernard, I'd walk away and come straight to you. I wouldn't care about Robert or anybody. But let's face it, Mummy's a fit and active woman. She's probably got another twenty or thirty years in her yet.'

'Darling Andrina.' Bernard shut his eyes as if trying to lock in his exasperation. 'Are you saying there's no hope of us getting together permanently for another twenty or thirty years?'

'As long as my mother walks the face of this earth, Bernard, I couldn't cause any scandal like that – especially when it involves you. I'm so sorry, I know you don't understand. I hardly understand myself. I don't even want to. I can't bear to think about it.'

She got up, tore off the flimsy blouse and tight skirt, and began searching through the wardrobe for something else to put on.

'Wear your green wool suit – I love the way it clings to you. And the colour looks so beautiful against your hair.'

She had bought the outfit for a special occasion in the church in Bearsden. She'd never worn it since.

'Were you there?' she asked incredulously. 'In Bearsden?' It had been the wedding of Samantha Pemberton, the daughter of Sophie's next-door neighbour.

'I knew we'd be together again,' Bernard said. 'It's always just a matter of watching and waiting.'

Her heart jumped.

'Mummy might have seen you!'

He shook his head.

'I was across the other side of the road and in my car. Anyway your mother's as blind as a bat.'

'Nonsense!' She was genuinely astonished. 'Mummy has to wear glasses but – '

'Haven't you noticed the way she peers at everything? Bends forward and peers all the time?'

'That's just a nervous habit.'

Andrina felt anxious, remembering. Anxiety and apprehension had been the strongest influences of her life. They were the iron bars of her prison. She kept trying to break out, and succeeded in breaking out to be with Bernard, but it was never anything but a temporary freedom. It was never any more than a reckless flight of passion before the bars closed in on her again.

'You'd better go,' she said.

'What's the hurry? Robert's away all day. So is Jennifer.'

But he knew that it wasn't Robert and Jennifer who had taken over her mind. 'Look, darling,' he said gently. 'Remember the wonderful times we had when I had a place of my own?'

She sighed.

'Sauchiehall Mansions.'

'How would it be if I bought another place – unknown to anyone? Just you and I. How about a place in the country but near enough Glasgow for both of us to get to without too much time or trouble?'

Her face relaxed, brightened. Her eyes sparkled.

'Do you think you could?'

'Some place out past Bearsden so that you could leave Jennifer off there and it would be just a case of a bit further on.'

'Oh, Bernard.'

'My business is doing well. There's no question about the money side of it. Let's start looking around. Let's start right now.'

He bounded from the bed and swung her around in a wild dance.

She squealed with laughter and delight and sang out, 'A place of our very own. A love nest in the country. And it's springtime. What could be better?'

Instinctively she knew he was going to say, 'Being married to each other.' She put her finger to his mouth, silencing him.

'Let's go. We've hours and hours. Don't let's waste one precious minute.'

'No time is wasted with you, Andrina.'

He drove a red Porsche and she felt pampered and surrounded by luxury as they set off. She always felt that way with Bernard. He knew how to treat a woman and he had the means with which to do it properly. She admired the aggressive self-confidence that success gave him. He knew how to savour and enjoy the things that money could buy, and so did she. She lay back, eyes closing for a few moments relishing the smell of the expensive red leather, feeling the smooth plumpness of the seat against her thighs.

They visited an estate agent's office in town first and after looking at brochures they asked for the keys of several promising-looking cottages. They set off – and soon had left Glasgow behind. As they winged along the tree-lined country road, Andrina looked back and caught a glimpse of the city nestling in the Clyde valley.

'This is beautiful,' she sighed, returning her gaze to the road in front of them. Trees on either side were bending over, dappling the ground with golden light. To one side the forest was brightened by pools of yellow daffodils. Bernard pulled in and stopped the car.

'Come on.' He got out and dragged her after him.

'There's none of the cottages here, is there?' she protested.

She had noticed a few steadings dotted about as they'd been driving along, but on this stretch of road could see nothing but the trees on one side, and green and golden handkerchiefs of fields on the other. The air was still and warm.

As Bernard carried her over and laid her down on the carpet of daffodils, her laughter didn't echo. It was contained, muffled, enclosed in a secret, golden world.

His shadow spread over her.

'You've never looked more beautiful,' he said. 'I wish I'd brought a camera. I'd love to have a picture of you, just as you look at this moment, with the creamy alabaster of your skin against the green grass, the auburn of your hair spread out against the yellow daffodils. Beautiful. Beautiful.'

He gazed down at her for a long time. She felt hypnotised by his stare, by the warm stillness and earthy smells. A deep longing grew until she had to close her eyes to contain it. She had to wait, as always, until he was ready. Often when he asked her to parade before him, she enjoyed showing herself off. Like a peacock, she preened and posed and pouted, pushed up her hair and ran it through her fingers, and spread it out.

But lying underneath him, feeling the heat emanate from his body, she felt her breathing quicken until she could not bear it any longer. Moaning, she began plucking and pulling at him, willing him to come down hard on top of her.

But he took his time undressing her. They were in full view of the road. It was narrow and winding, hardly broad enough for two cars to pass each other. At the moment only the

Porsche was tucked in at the side on a grassy verge. Not even a tractor was in sight. It wouldn't have mattered if a sudden stream of traffic appeared: Bernard and Andrina were beyond caring about anyone but themselves. Caught in the vice of a passion that was a kind of madness, they defied all logic, all decency.

At least for a time. Then, passion spent, Andrina suddenly realised that she was naked for all to see. As she scrambled for her clothes, Bernard lay back, his laughter disturbing some wildlife high in the trees. A rustling and squawking rent the air.

Andrina laughed too. For there was no one there except themselves.

They returned to the car and swooped away. The road became bumpy, a succession of miniature hills building up to the wall of the Campsie Hills in the distance. They were on a rollercoaster – speeding up, flying from the ground, floating madly in the air for a second before bumping back down and racing onwards again. They yelled and screeched with laughter and became breathless like a couple of children at the fair.

Then they saw the cottage. The first one. The only one. A sparkling white gem. The hills reared up at the back like a green wall. To the front across the road was the forest. The white-painted cottage could be seen from the road but at the back was a small, sheltered garden bounded by mature trees and a high hedge.

This was their private world. Their secret garden. Here, no one would ever know.

Chapter Twenty-Five

Bridie felt torn. She loved Frank. She loved the decent, vulnerable, childishly excitable, daydreaming, impractical Frank who still existed underneath the sophisticated veneer, the outward self-confidence.

She had never been a good mixer. Not even in the Gorbals. She had never gone to the dancing like Doris, never had any boyfriends before Frank. When she'd worked in Murphy's second-hand bookshop she'd kept in the back as much as she could. In those early days in her mother's house, she'd always hidden away with a book or in any quiet corner. A quiet corner was almost impossible to find in the house she'd once shared with her mother and father and their enormous brood. Once she'd spent hours in a cupboard in the room just to get away from them all.

She had always been a loner and had believed Frank was the same. Poor Frank, she used to think, poor Frank and his poems that made him the butt of sneers and jeers, contempt and downright hostility because he couldn't be 'one of the boys'. He tried. When he was a lad, he'd run about and kicked a ball with the rest of them. But he was never very good at it. Football was never the be-all and end-all of his life that it was to his contemporaries. It was the same when he'd got older. She remembered him telling her, 'There's a surprising amount of political talk among the older men but with the younger ones, it's nothing but sex and football.' It wasn't said in a complaining or derogatory way. He was interested, intrigued. *That* was how he was different, and his contemporaries sensed it. It was *them* he was intrigued with. *They* were his hobby. They sensed it and they resented it. Just as she did now.

He wasn't a loner like her at all, though he was different from everyone they knew in the Gorbals all right. He had never been one of them. He had chosen to be on the outside looking in, watching them and how they lived their lives. He had been biding his time until he could join the people with whom he *did* belong.

In a way, he was like his brother Bernard after all. A watcher. A predator.

He didn't need to be. If he got his priorities right. If he used a bit of self-discipline But the only self-discipline he ever used was to shut himself away to write. She was not supposed to interrupt those sacrosanct hours. Even to take him a cup of coffee into his writing sanctum was met with barely concealed irritation or outright anger.

'How many times must I tell you, Bridie?' he'd shout at her. 'You ruin my concentration when you keep interrupting me like this.'

'We never used to quarrel like this when you had a decent respectable job in Goldmayers. We were perfectly happy then.'

'Oh God,' Frank groaned. 'I'm getting so sick of hearing about when I worked in Goldmayers. I was bored out of my skull in that musty wee office, Bridie, working the same boring hours every boring day. I would have gone mad if I'd thought I was going to spend the rest of my life there. The only way I survived was by being determined that I was *not* going to spend the rest of my life there. So, once and for all, will you stop nagging on at me about bloody Goldmayers!'

'We were perfectly happy then,' Bridie repeated, a mist of tears blurring her eyes.

'For God's sake, Bridie. Why do you do this?'

'Do what?'

'Try to spoil everything for me. We've the party tonight and my brother and his wife as guests. I was really looking forward to it.'

'Everythings ready for the party. You've seen to that,' she added bitterly.

'Well.' Frank flung down his pen. 'I guess there's no use me trying to write any more today. Satisfied? But I'll tell you one thing, Bridie, if you're going to be in this nasty mood tonight, it would be better if you were somewhere else, anywhere else but here.'

'Ashamed of me, are you? Not glamorous or smart enough for your television hangers-on?'

'Bridie, you keep talking about how I've changed. Well, take it from me, you've changed almost beyond recognition. And I don't mean in looks. I don't care about looks. I never have. It's what goes on behind the outward mask that's always interested me . . .'

'Oh, God,' Bridie said, 'here we go again with the high-falutin writer's talk. You talked about boredom, Frank. Well, no boredom you ever felt at Goldmayers could match the boredom I suffer day in, day out, with you. All you ever talk about is your boring writing. Boring, boring, Frank!'

She could see she'd hurt him. He looked away from her but didn't know where else to look. He became awkward; suddenly he was the old gawky, vulnerable Frank that she had always known and loved.

'Oh, Frank.' She put out her arm to comfort him as she'd done so often in the past. 'I'm sorry. I didn't mean it. I'll be fine at the party. Everything will be fine, I promise.'

'It's not the party I'm worried about,' he said, then glanced at his watch. 'But I might as well go and have a bath and get ready for it.

He brushed past her, ignoring her outstretched arms. Now she felt furious as well as hurt. He needn't try to come the big-shot television star with her. She wasn't going to put up with any of his Hollywood-type tantrums. Who did he think he was? She knew who he was. He was Frank O'Maley from the Gorbals – son of Patrick, the robber of trains. Brother of idiot Republican, Tony. Brother of Michael, the one-eyed ex-drunk ex-boxer. Brother of Bernard, the gangsters' friend.

As she stood fuming with bitterness and hatred, she noticed Frank's keyring still dangling with its bunch of keys in one of the drawers of his desk. Outside the silence of the room she could hear the water running in the bathroom across the hall. The writing-room door was open and she would be in full view if Frank suddenly emerged into the hall. Nevertheless, she was consumed with curiosity. Frank was so secretive about his work. For some considerable time now he'd kept his desk locked. Indeed, if he was going out of the house to the TV studios – or anywhere at all – he even locked the door of the writing room. He couldn't have just been writing one short story in all this time. What had happened to the play he'd been commissioned to write? Plays were his 'thing'. He definitely had been writing one. He kept saying he hadn't finished it yet, and his shiftiness hadn't escaped her. He felt guilty about something. He was holding the play back for this reason. This meant it must be something truly terrible. For the first time a thought struck her.

Maybe it was about her. Maybe it was about them. About their most intimate relationship. She went cold with hatred. He was so capable of doing this. She had never hated him so much.

She opened the first drawer. It contained only one sheet of paper. It was a poem called 'Let Us Not Lose . . .' She read it as if the words were hypnotising her:

> Let us not lose the instinctive caring
> That has bound us through the years,
> Let us not lose the joy of sharing,
> Nor exchange our smiles for tears.
>
> For I have seen a frequent dread
> Cloud your loving eyes,
> And heard beneath the words you've said
> A hint of bitter sighs.
>
> My scene has changed, I face new faces,
> You feel I've drawn apart,
> But if I walk in different places –
> It's only me, and not my heart.
>
> Let us not sink in this changing tide
> And leave our light above,
> But stay in sunshine, side by side:
> Let us not lose our love.

She replaced the page and shut the drawer. Then she went through to the bedroom, flung herself on to the bed, and buried her face in the pillow.

Chapter Twenty-Six

'I told you Derek would be all right, didn't I?' Sophie insisted. 'A pity you had to get that neighbour of yours, though. Sleekit kind of character. Shifty eyes. And he's well into his fifties, and never been married. There's something strange about that.'

Laura couldn't help smiling.

'Oh, I don't think we should hold that against Mr Pritchett. He's probably just not met the right woman. I wouldn't be here enjoying a cup of tea in your house just now if it wasn't for him sitting with Derek. And I wouldn't have managed to get to your church concert or to that exhibition in town – oh, I did enjoy that, Sophie. I'm glad you forced me to go. I'd never been in the Art Galleries for ages. It's a lovely building.'

'We used to live just across the road from it.' Sophie fussed over with a plate of home-made banana bread liberally spread with butter.

'You haven't had a piece of this yet.'

'I don't think I could . . .'

'Nonsense. You've neglected yourself long enough. You're needing building up.'

'You're very kind,' Laura mumbled, accepting a slice. Indeed Sophie had turned out to be a far nicer person than she appeared on the surface. Laura had come to the conclusion that the poor woman, no doubt because of her background, was a nervous wreck. But she had courage. She was continuously fighting to hold herself together. Laura believed that busying herself with other people's problems kept Sophie's mind off herself and her own problems. Helped keep her sane. She had as good as admitted this to Laura.

Gradually, an unlikely friendship had developed. Sophie needed to be needed. She needed someone she could trust. Once it had been her husband but since she'd discovered he had been on friendly terms with Bernard O'Maley behind her back, and that he met him regularly, did business with him, her unquestioning trust had shrunk into wariness, uncertainty, suspicion.

Laura had a gentle and patient nature and she was a good listener. Sophie felt drawn to her. There was nothing to worry about with Laura. There was no evil sexual devil in Laura to contaminate her. Laura never flaunted herself in front of men. Laura always wore modest clothes and only a discreet touch of make-up. Laura only wore a few pieces of good Victorian jewellery that she said she had inherited from her mother.

A good-living respectable girl, and so peaceful to be with, Sophie thought. If only Andrina could be more like her. Sophie's feverish attention honed in on her new friend. She was determined to help Laura Cairns, whether Laura liked it or not.

As far as Laura was concerned Sophie had become her only friend. People that she and Derek had known as a couple had all too soon faded from their social scene. In truth, she and Derek, as a couple, no longer had any social scene. She didn't blame their married friends. Derek had behaved in a painfully anti-social way on the few occasions that anyone had come to visit them since his first stroke. Since his second, he simply refused to see anyone. Mr Pritchett was an exception, and Robert had come a couple of times but both Derek and herself had been in agony. For different reasons, of course.

Poor Derek! She felt unbearably upset for him every time she remembered Robert's visits. The first time Derek had hidden away in order to avoid Robert seeing him. There was a deep broom cupboard in the kitchen and Derek had managed to back his wheelchair into it and jam the door shut. Robert tried to plead with him to come out, to assure him that they were still the same two men that they had always been and that nothing had happened to change their friendship.

But all they could hear in response were small childlike sounds chewed into a garble that defied understanding. Except for the heart-breaking emotion behind it. She had to tell Robert to go. He had returned just once. That time his visit had been unexpected and Derek had been caught in the sitting-room. His distress had been so terrible that Robert left hurriedly of his own accord.

'It's all right, it's all right, Derek! I'll go and I won't come back. I'm far too fond of you to upset you like this. But if you ever need me or want me to come, just let me know.'

Laura had run after him. In the hall, both of them had been close to tears. They could hear Derek's hysterical moans and squeals from the sitting-room and could still visualise his pathetic struggles to hide his contorted face and body from Robert's gaze.

'Oh God,' Robert groaned. 'Poor sod. I didn't mean to cause him any distress. I'm so sorry, Laura. Tell him I'm so sorry.'

She nodded, unable to speak.

He turned at the door. 'How can you stand it? It's so bloody painful. Just those few minutes . . . I feel gutted. I wish I could help you. I wish I could help you both.'

She shut the door after he went out and leaned against it for support. It was a few minutes before she could summon the courage, and the calmness, to return to the sitting-room.

Sophie had not reacted in the same way as Robert. When Sophie had called unexpectedly she had been brusque and dismissive:

'Now, now, let's have none of this childish carry-on. You're a grown man. Control yourself.'

Then she'd ignored him and started telling Laura about an exhibition of Turner paintings in the Art Galleries.

'It's not my cup of tea,' she said, 'but I thought with you being an art teacher, you'd enjoy it. You're looking far too thin and pale. You're going to take a stroke or something worse yourself if you're not careful.'

'It's very kind of you to think about me, Sophie, but . . .' She'd stopped in vague harassment.

'No buts. Just go! Get that man in from next door. I'd come to sit with Derek myself but I've a WI meeting tomorrow night. Here you are, my husband got this ticket to the private viewing. It's a first-night thing with wine and everything. You'll enjoy it,' she repeated.

Derek had been so angry about Sophie even thinking that

she could come and sit with him he forgot to make any objection to Laura going to the exhibition.

'No . . . way . . . that . . . awful . . . woman . . . Mr . . . Prit . . . chett . . . bad enough . . . but . . . better . . . No way . . . that mad . . . old . . . You . . . get . . . Mr Prit . . . chett. Do . . . you . . . hear . . . me?'

'Yes, dear,' she'd said and immediately phoned Mr Pritchett before Derek could change his mind. Mr Pritchett's bungalow was only a few steps away, but she never went to his door if she could avoid it. For one thing, the sour smell emanating from the place as soon as the door opened put her off.

'In a way, he reminds me of what you've told me about Neily Duffy,' Laura once remarked to Robert.

Robert had raised an eyebrow.

'In what way?'

'Well, he's such a harmless little man. Yet he annoys me. I know I'm probably being unfair but even when he speaks to me, I feel he stands too close – invading my space. Oh, I don't know, he just gives me the creeps.'

Sophie had agreed with her but, in her usual extreme way, had gone further.

'There's something wrong with that man. I feel it. We'll have to find some way to get rid of him.'

'That's going a bit far,' Laura laughed. 'Poor Mr Pritchett. I've really no reason to dislike him.'

'Instinct is a good enough reason. You know my daughter?'

Laura's voice in reply became wary.

'Yes.'

'A good girl but she needs a tight rein. I know instinctively that she's in constant danger of succumbing to the wicked lusts of the flesh. She's cursed by bad blood from Agnes Noble. *Noble!*' Sophie's thin lip gave an ugly twist. 'Noble she was not.'

'Was that . . . ?'

'Yes, Andrina's maternal grandmother. Strictly between you and me, Laura, the grandfather was just as bad. Wicked pair. Everybody in Bearsden thought I mourned. But I rejoiced when I heard they were dead. Rejoiced!'

'Oh, Sophie.'

'Shocked you, have I?'

'No. I've worked too long in tough Glasgow schools to be shocked at anything anybody says or does. I just feel sad for you.'

'Another thing about Andrina – I instinctively knew that a man who was after her years ago was no good for her. She needed protecting against him. A wicked lustful man.'

Laura was curious.

'What happened?'

'I sent him packing. But . . .' Sophie hesitated. 'Now I find my husband has been doing business with him. Friendly as you like behind my back. I don't like it, Laura. He'll do no good for my husband either. Bernard O'Maley mixes with all sorts of underworld people. People my husband – a bailie of the City of Glasgow – should have nothing to do with. No good will come of such an association. I told my husband but will he listen? No, he will not.'

'Bernard O'Maley?' Laura echoed thoughtfully. 'That rings a bell. I've heard that name somewhere.'

'Oh, it'll have been from Robert, no doubt. He used to be one of Robert's pupils. He went to Robert's karate club too. He might still do, for all I know. Nothing surprises me any more, Laura. Nothing.'

'Bernard O'Maley must have left St Francis by the time I arrived there to teach. At least, I never had him as a pupil. But now that you mention it, I have heard Robert talk about him. If I remember correctly, Robert seemed rather proud of how well Bernard O'Maley had done. Had his own business, employed a lot of men now, he said.'

'Trust Robert not to see through somebody like that. Robert thinks more of his horrors of pupils and spends more time with them than he does with his own family. Honestly, Laura, at times I don't know what to make of Robert. He never goes to church now, you know. Only occasionally to help his mother get there. Or, even less often, when they spend the weekend with us and I persuade him to accompany us, as a family . . .'

'He's a good man,' Laura murmured defensively.

'Oh, I know. I know.' Sophie felt uncontrollably impatient any time she thought of her son-in-law.

Suddenly changing the subject, she said, 'What you need is somebody to come in regularly to give you a break. A bit of freedom. Not that man from next door. Don't worry, I'll put a stop to him.'

'But I can't afford to pay for anybody. Especially now when I haven't a wage coming in. Anyway, even if I could, Derek wouldn't hear of it.'

'A nurse.' Sophie's mind was already busy working everything out. 'Somebody both professional and a friend, so to speak.'

'But I don't know anybody like that.'

'I do. In fact, there's more than one ex-nurse in the WI. I'm sure they'd do it if I asked them. After all, I've done plenty of charitable acts on behalf of the WI. They could take turns. You could have an afternoon or a morning off one day. And an evening off another time. At least two breaks for you every week. That's what you need. If necessary, I could take a turn as well.'

'Oh, Sophie!' It all seemed so impossible, so ridiculous, Laura couldn't help laughing. 'If only it could be that simple.'

'Leave it to me. Leave everything to me.'

'But I can't. For one thing, I don't want to be unkind to poor Mr Pritchett. Then there's Derek's feelings to consider. He can't bear anyone to see him the way he is.'

'He'll get used to folk if he has to. It'll do him good to have some different company. You'll have to be firm with him, Laura. For his own good, as well as yours. You're far too soft. As for that man next door – let him concentrate on looking after his cats.'

'Oh, Sophie,' Laura repeated helplessly.

Chapter Twenty-Seven

One of the outings Laura chose was to go with some of the Sinnieglen and St Francis teachers on their Saturday trek to the Campsies. She took her sketchbook and her watercolours.

'Perfect,' Sophie enthused. 'The fresh air will do you good. That bungalow of yours is like an oven. It's suffocating.'

'I know. But Derek likes it that way. He feels the cold with sitting all the time. His circulation – '

'Tuts!' Sophie waved a dismissive hand. 'He needs to exercise himself.'

'But he can't.'

'Yes, he can. He's not completely paralysed. I'll find out what kind of exercises he could do.'

'From the hospital?'

'If necessary. If not, my husband and I are friendly with a couple of medical men in Bearsden, I could ask one of them. Or his own doctor. Or the WI nurses. Don't you worry about it. Leave everything to me. You just go and enjoy your day out. I've told Robert to keep an eye on you.'

It had been decided (or, more accurately, Sophie had decided) that a whole day at a time away from Derek would be of far more benefit than a few hours in a morning or afternoon. That was when Laura tentatively had mentioned that she used to enjoy the outings to the hills that Robert and one or two of the other teachers used to organise. She had done some quite good watercolours there and she told Sophie how soothing and relaxing it was sitting in the sun with her head protected by her straw hat, just concentrating on the peaceful scene she was painting.

If it was a group of girl pupils (especially one of the better-behaved classes) who had been taken along, the chances were they would be sitting and painting and sketching too. If it was a mixed group of boys and girls, or just boys alone, things could be hectic with children roving and screeching and climbing on top of boulders and trees like monkeys. But she refrained from mentioning that to Sophie.

Derek was furious: not so much at her getting away for the day but at Sophie interfering so much in their lives. Especially for her organising the two buxom WI ex-nurses. Mrs Tunnicliff was to come in on Saturdays and Mrs Houston-Jones on Wednesdays. As it turned out, the women weren't just ex-nurses. Mrs Tunnicliff had been matron of an old folks home before her marriage to the successful (now deceased) defence lawyer, George Tunnicliff. Mrs Houston-Jones had been matron of one of the largest infirmaries in Scotland before her marriage to Hector Houston-Jones (also deceased), who had been much respected in merchant banking in Glasgow. Time had been lying heavy on the hands of both widows and they were delighted to have something worthwhile and useful to do.

Derek hated them both on sight and made no effort to conceal his hatred. On the contrary, he embarrassed Laura by being rude to Mrs Tunnicliff on the first Saturday morning as soon as she arrived. Mrs Tunnicliff wasn't in the least perturbed.

'Off you go, my dear,' she told Laura. 'I've had years of practice at dealing with difficult patients. Rest assured your Derek and I are going to get along just fine.' And she began rolling up her sleeves in what Laura worriedly took as a somewhat ominous gesture.

Reluctantly she had left a growling Derek. He had never looked more helpless and pathetic. He was like a deformed child, but held back by his deformities from being able to express, not only his anger, but his grief.

She'd told Robert afterwards. They hadn't had too much opportunity to talk because of the other teachers and the children. They both believed, however, that this was the best and only way possible for them to keep in touch.

'Hopefully he'll get used to them,' Robert said. 'It might even help him and do him good in the long run to get used to other people. This might be an important first step for him.'

'He didn't want to take it. That's what makes me feel guilty. You can imagine how upset he was this morning when I left.'

'But shutting himself away for the rest of his life in that claustrophobic atmosphere with you isn't going to do either of you any good. He'll begin to hate you as well as himself.'

'The person he hates most at the moment is Sophie. He blames her for everything. So does Mr Pritchett. He was in the other evening and I heard them talking about her. Or at least Mr Pritchett was talking and Derek was making noises of agreement, when Sophie unexpectedly arrived. You know how she can see our house from her front window? She must have been sitting there watching.'

Robert shook his head. 'Oh, I don't think she'd do that on purpose. She's always liked sitting there knitting or sewing and watching the world of Bearsden pass by. She loves that house, because it's in the middle of "the village", as she calls it.'

'I know but that was the second time it happened. She'd seen Mr Pritchett come in, and along she came. She was so rude and dismissive to the man, I was embarrassed. In fact, I was beginning to get quite angry. She has no right to behave like that to another guest in my house.'

'Not exactly a welcome guest.'

'No, but still . . .'

'How was she rude exactly? I know she can be over-zealous and she's definitely neurotic but I don't think I've ever heard her being rude or deliberately unkind to anyone. Quite the contrary.'

'It was just that she came right out with the fact it would be better if he left Derek to people who knew best how to look after him properly.'

'Well, she has a point there . . .'

Laura grimaced.

'I know. But she went on to say that it would fit him better to see to himself. "That shirt you're wearing is a disgrace," she told him. "If you don't start seeing to yourself and your own place instead of coming in here bothering folk, I'll report you to the sanitary department. They'll see to you all right!" '

'I can just hear her,' Robert groaned. 'But you know, she's right, Laura. You told me you don't like the man.'

'I know. But I felt sorry for him. He went away without

saying a word. He must have been terribly hurt. I went to the door with him and apologised for Sophie's rudeness. It really was awful of her.'

'True enough, but let's face it. You'd never have been able to get rid of him on your own.'

'At least when you spoke to him you were more diplomatic.'

'Maybe we're both too soft, Laura. Maybe that's our trouble.'

Laura smiled and surreptitiously touched his hand.

'I'll tell you one thing straight out – I'd prefer you any day to Sophie.'

She had hastily withdrawn as Lachlan McKenzie, another teacher, passed with two of the girls looking for a more suitable place to start sketching.

'She means well,' Robert said. 'It's just that she always goes to such extremes. She does the same with Andrina and Jennifer. She's so possessive with both of them. She absolutely dotes on Jennifer. And yet . . .' He shrugged. 'I wish I didn't worry about them all so much. Even at work . . . Well, to be honest, especially at work, I'm beginning to feel the strain. Maybe it's old age creeping on. I'm definitely not the man I used to be.'

'Oh Robert . . .'

Laura wanted to reach out and comfort him but it was impossible. Other pupils had decided that where they were sitting afforded the best view of the gully where a waterfall bounced and gurgled over the rocks below. Everyone was gathering round, squatting down, opening up sketchbooks, chattering.

'I'm sorry,' Robert said. 'You've a lot more than me to worry you.' He turned his attention to the children and said, 'It's time I was seeing how some of this lot are doing.' He moved away and it was the last contact they had that day.

She had taken her own car at Sophie's suggestion.

'I know Robert could easily pick you up on the way with the rest of them in that awful school van they use. But you need a bit of comfort and also some time on your own. Just to be yourself.'

She was right as usual. It was what Laura needed.

'And don't come back with them,' Sophie instructed. 'You make straight for the city centre. The shops will still be open. Park your car and have a wander round. Treat yourself to something – even if it's only a cup of tea and a cake somewhere.' Then another thought occurred to her. 'Next time, make a late afternoon hair appointment. Andrina always says that makes her feel good.'

Laura shook her head, laughing. She just couldn't be angry at Sophie any more. As Robert said, she meant well. She just kept pushing herself and everyone else too far, that was all.

'I've never heard you wasting your time or your money going to a hairdresser's, Sophie.'

'I'm old enough to be your mother. What does it matter about me? Anyway, you're the one under all the strain and needing to be good to yourself. Not me.'

She drove home after saying goodbye to Robert along with all her other goodbyes to Lachlan McKenzie and the children. She could have wept with the empty ache at not being able to have any time alone with Robert. Yet she was glad that at least they could keep in touch. The day out in the country, and away from having to struggle with Derek had made her feel more relaxed, better able to cope.

Big-bosomed, muscly-armed Mrs Tunnicliff met her in the hall, aglow with sweat and triumph.

'Everything's under control, m'dear. I've given him his bath. He didn't like it but I insisted. A slip of a girl like you isn't able for such a task. I told him, your poor wife's just not strong enough.'

Laura was too aghast to speak but Mrs Tunnicliff didn't seem to notice. She rolled down her sleeves and retrieved her coat.

'Now, I've left the table all set and ready for your tea. I'll see you next Saturday at the same time. Mrs Houston-Jones and I are going to meet at my place each Thursday to compare case notes.' She hitched on her coat, pulled on her hat and secured her large handbag over one arm. 'Everything's under control.'

And off she sailed, happiness vibrating from every inch of her ample flesh.

Laura's legs began to tremble. It was only with much difficulty that she made her way into the sitting-room where Derek was watching television. He turned to look at her when she entered the room. The look in his eyes broke her heart. His physical appearance was heart-breaking enough. It wasn't just his tense, contorted face and body. To some degree at least, she'd become accustomed to the sight of that. She'd become disciplined to ignore the worst of his appearance and concentrate instead on the shock of blond hair which, like his moustache, had remained as luxurious as it had ever been, a kind of flag of defiance in a way. Now she was shocked to see how dark and plastered down his hair was. His moustache looked a joke, painted on to a tight, glossy skin. He looked like a scrubbed clean child. Only his eyes betrayed the man, the man who remembered what he'd once been, and what he now was.

Chapter Twenty-Eight

'Shit!' Bernard said under his breath. Down in the shadowy basement of the Merchant City Club in Virginia Street, John Morgan, a real gangster type, was sitting at one of the corner tables with two of his colleagues. They were all men in their thirties. That, in Glasgow, meant they were tough; they were a serious bit of business because they'd survived.

Rod MacGowan greeted Bernard as soon as his big frame had manoeuvred a path through the dense crowds who were dancing to the music of a guitarist, a pianist and a girl singer.

'I thought I'd better phone you. The new owner, a young guy, still wet behind the ears – Willie Slattery his name is – has been in and out of the bog ever since I mentioned I'd spotted Morgan.'

'He seems quiet enough.'

'I know. I've been trying to tell Willie that he's just having a quiet drink. But he won't listen. Apparently he's spent his last penny doing this place up and he's terrified Morgan's going to smash it to bits.'

'Willie's obviously been watching too many Westerns.'

Just then a white-faced Slattery appeared and MacGowan said, 'Willie, this is my boss.'

'Get that gangster out of here,' Slattery hissed at Bernard.

'Why?'

'What do you mean, why? I don't want any trouble.'

'Neither do I.'

'Well?'

'Well, if he causes any trouble, I'll put him out. Meantime, everything's OK. He's just enjoying a quiet drink with a couple of pals. I see it's their usual champagne. Just you look at them as good paying customers, Willie.' He grinned at Slattery and gave him a wink. 'Relax. Hang loose. The cavalry's here.'

Slattery managed a smile in return.

'Aye, OK, boys. I'm not used to this game yet. I just had a wee village pub before. But I was left a bit of cash and this place came on the market. I wasn't all that sure at first but then as the wife said . . .'

Bernard was listening, but the sharp end of his attention was hooked on to the three men still sitting at one of the tables over in the corner. He kept getting glimpses of them through the crowd of dancers and the smoke-filled gloom. Cellar clubs, dark corners and strobe lighting had become trendy and popular. But it could make life more difficult in his line of business.

'Not a bad group, eh?' Slattery was saying now. 'The girl singer's really something, eh?'

'Aye,' Bernard agreed. 'You've got good taste, Willie.'

The trouble was, gangsters like Morgan were real schizophrenic types. You never knew what was coming out of their heads and they always carried weapons. You never knew if it was a knife or a gun or what they had. They could be sitting laughing and talking and drinking champagne, as they were now, and somebody could accidentally bump against them or in some innocent way interrupt their conversation or their enjoyment and suddenly they could turn ugly. They could cut somebody's throat or shoot them in the head at the slightest annoyance. They were totally unpredictable. Bernard watched Morgan get up and crush his way over to the lavatory near the door. Soon afterwards, Bernard became aware of trouble at the entrance. Not with Morgan, who hadn't yet re-emerged. One of his security men was obviously trying to stop trouble from getting in. Bernard nudged MacGowan and they both pushed their way rapidly through the crowd.

Outside the door they discerned two brothers, paper gangsters, petty villains that Bernard knew well, with about four of their troops ranged on the stairs above them. The bigger of the two brothers – and, Bernard always felt, the stupider – liked to be known as King Kong. He was at least six foot seven, and eighteen stone.

Danny McEndrick knew them and quite rightly was refusing them admittance. They'd already been barred from every other decent club in Glasgow for causing mindless mayhem and spoiling all the ordinary punters' enjoyment.

Bernard told McEndrick and MacGowan to step aside; it was too much for them to deal with. 'Lock the door behind me,' he ordered and stepped outside under the amber lantern-shaped globe that lit the small well at the foot of the stairs.

The big ape shouted, 'Get out of the way, we're going inside!'

'No, you're barred. The door's shut and it doesn't matter what you do to me – you can't get inside.'

'See you, you've been asking for it for a long time. I'm just about up to here with you.'

The smaller brother had barely enough room in the space between the door and the stairs.

'Wait, Eddy. They could phone for the police from inside. Wait till he's on his way home. See you, we're going to carve you up until even your mammy won't recognise you.'

'Aye, OK,' Bernard said. 'But meantime, fuck off.'

He tapped on the door and MacGowan unlocked it and opened it to allow him in. Immediately the big ape barged the door wide, knocking Bernard off balance. MacGowan whacked him before Bernard had the chance to. The blow only caused a grunt but just at that point, when the other brother and their troops were beginning to crowd around the entrance like grinning gargoyles behind their leader, the big ape noticed Morgan emerging from the lavatory and passing near the door.

'Hey, Morgan,' he shouted at the gangster. 'Look, you and me have done business together. Why don't we get together now and wipe these guys off the streets?'

MacGowan looked at Bernard. They both knew they were in trouble. Morgan and his men were very difficult to deal with. But for some reason known only to himself, Morgan glanced round in passing and said, 'No, this is your problem. You can get on with it.'

But before Bernard, MacGowan and Davy McEndrick had a chance to do much more than warn the intruders off again, Morgan came striding back with his men. Morgan said to Bernard,

'You guys step aside. We've got an argument with this lot.'

'This lot' hastily decided to escape back up the outside stairs but were caught in violence that was swift and lethal.

Knives flashed and sent blood spurting up to speckle the amber lamp and make scarlet patterns on the door. The small space at the entrance was filled with grunts and snarls. As the fight boiled up the narrow stairway, iron railings clanged and clattered, bodies smashed against them and men screamed as they were impaled on the iron spikes.

Bernard shut the door and went to phone the police and the ambulance, but as usual, by the time the police arrived, the violence was over and all but the seriously wounded or dead had disappeared. Anybody who was left alive would insist they didn't know what happened.

'All right,' the police sergeant said, getting his eye on Bernard. 'What happened this time?'

'Anybody would think,' MacGowan complained afterwards, 'that it was all our fault.'

Bernard shrugged.

'The poor sods don't get paid as much as us. Maybe that's what bugs them. Don't let them get to you.'

To the sergeant he said, 'Some guys were enjoying a wee night out and a crowd of these other guys came and spoilt it.'

'Come on. There must have been more to it than that.'

'No. Not a goddam thing.'

'Don't get smart with me, O'Maley.'

'Listen, sergeant, my men and I have to deal with this kind of situation day in, day out. It's any excuse to start trouble. Any petty excuse to start a fight with anybody – any ordinary punter just out having a drink, or any of us. I don't know about you and your lot, but we've to be quick on our feet and quick with our hands or we've had it.'

'It's funny that you and your lot are never the ones that end up in the hospital or the mortuary though.'

Bernard grinned. 'You ought to take a leaf out of our book and have a go at karate.'

'Aye, OK, smartass.'

'God,' MacGowan said afterwards. 'I'll put out the flag the day they compliment us for doing a good job or for helping them do their job.'

'Stop dreaming,' Bernard laughed. 'Come on. You too, Danny. I'll buy the pair of you a drink.'

He was in no hurry to go home. He wouldn't have cared if he never went home. At least, not to Jane. He cursed himself for marrying her in the first place. It hadn't been fair to either of them. He tried to be decent to her, to give her a good time, never grudged her anything (except himself). The trouble was all she wanted was him. Him sitting safely opposite her by the fireside. Chained there. Safe there. For her, and her alone. Her eyes told him that was all she wanted. Her eyes continuously devoured him, pleaded with him.

He could have smacked her. She seemed to be just asking for it. But he knew that was not the way to get free of her. Far from it. He always turned away, distancing himself more and more from her all the time – in spirit, if not all the time in person.

Once she'd said to him, 'Bernard, you're here with me, and yet I still feel you're miles away.'

There was nothing he could do about that. He longed to be with Andrina now that they had that beautiful love nest where they could indulge in every fantasy of love, every wild indulgence.

The last time they'd been there together he'd said to her, 'Andrina, we could be here together always.' He'd tightened his arms around her, pinning her to him, trying to prevent her usual escape into panic. Trying to ignore the fact that anything he did only made her worse.

'Darling, we could. What's to prevent us? And don't, for God's sake, don't say your mother. It's so bloody ridiculous. All you need to do is stay here. Don't go back to Robert. Forget about your mother. Both Robert and your mother will revel in looking after Jennifer. They obviously both dote on her. But if it's leaving Jennifer that's worrying you – bring her here. She'd love the cottage and the garden and . . .'

'You know perfectly well how I feel. Why do you keep tormenting me?' She began to weep and her tears were like daggers, twisting in his gut.

'Darling, don't cry, please. I love you. I only want you to be happy.'

'Then stop asking me to do the impossible.'

'God, I could kill your fuckin' mother.'

'Bernard!'

'I'm sorry for the language, Andrina, but not the sentiment.'

'Please don't mention Mummy again. Please, Bernard, don't spoil our happiness.'

He felt bitter about that. *Him* spoil their happiness?

He could kill that mad, interfering old witch, kill her with his bare hands.

Chapter Twenty-Nine

Sophie felt happy. Her life was skimming rapidly along on its usual surface level, yet there was now more to it than that. She had never been a person to indulge in any demonstration of affection. The ladies of Bearsden had got to know and accept Sophie's shrinking from such intimate contact. The ladies of Bearsden kissed when greeting each other or when saying goodbye after coffee mornings or soirées or church meetings, but they no longer attempted to include Sophie in these outward gestures, although they all had a considerable affection for her.

They knew she'd had a heavy cross to bear in her past life, and concluded (after much compassionate and enjoyable discussion) that poor Sophie had been so hurt in intimate relationships and so let down, she was now quite terrified to risk being in the slightest way vulnerable again.

So they no longer thought it strange that she tightened into herself, shrank away fron the warmth of normal bodily contact. Even a handshake was quick and unnatural, an ordeal – like touching something red-hot and dangerous. They no longer remarked on how Sophie and her husband always walked separately, never arm in arm like every other happily married couple they knew. They could even remain perfectly relaxed in Sophie's company now, completely ignoring her restless, agitated movements. She was always jumping up to see if anyone needed more coffee or slipping out to her own kitchen, or to the church hall kitchen, to check that everything was under control. When a visiting speaker to the Bearsden Literary Club had once blithely remarked, 'That woman is a right neurotic' he had been frozen out by every lady within hearing distance and he was never invited again. The good ladies of Bearsden were loyal to their own, and Sophie was one of them. They accepted her, neurosis and all.

Sophie knew this, and to say she was grateful was an

understatement. No words could ever express her heartfelt gratitude for being accepted.

This wasn't the only reason for her happiness, however. There was a new balance of a sort in her life. She was still anxious and alert about Andrina but the girl seemed to be more respectably settled these days and Robert at least had got himself promoted and was bringing home a bit more money. They even had a car of sorts. As well as Andrina, she now had the concern about Laura. Laura siphoned off some of the anxiety from Andrina – spread it over a wider area. Poor Laura, who was imprisoned in such a tragedy. Poor Derek. It seemed to Sophie that God had given her a special mission to help Laura and her disabled husband.

Sophie had done, and was still doing, her very best to carry out His work in many ways, but somehow she was finding more satisfaction in doing good work for people nearer home than by helping, for instance, raise money for missionary work in Africa. She was being rewarded. Not that she ever looked for reward. Yet small but deep pools of happiness had begun to soothe her. Every now and again she'd experience no longer a superficial feeling, but a deep, quiet, God-given stillness. And, astonished, she'd gasp to herself.

'I'm happy!'

It helped of course to have the pleasure of looking after Jennifer so often. Such a quiet, well-behaved child – everybody said so.

'Your family is a real credit to you, Sophie,' everybody said. 'A lovely daughter who is a committed Christian and such a dear, well brought-up grandchild.'

'I thank God for them,' Sophie replied. And she did. Fervently. And often. She prayed that God would continue to protect Andrina from the lusts of the flesh, and to cleanse her of any evil blood remaining in her veins from Duncan and Agnes Noble. In her prayers every night, she thanked God too for allowing her to be the instrument of helping Laura and Derek.

In a way, they had reminded her of her own youthful helplessness of so long ago when she had been sinking in confusion and grief. She had not been made outwardly ugly like Derek. She had been made ugly inside. Inside her body. Inside her heart. Inside her head.

The terrible thing was – nobody had come to her rescue. She had only been dragged further down into the pit. She still cringed inside, not knowing where to hide, when she thought of the 'home' in which she'd been placed, in so-called 'care'.

How long ago it was now. Long, long ago. Yet, how strange that it was as real now as it had ever been. She was still that ugly, terrified little girl inside.

Identifying with Laura and Derek's predicament and doing something positive about their misery, had somehow helped relieve her own. She felt a strange calm, yet exciting feeling. It was something she had never experienced before and it made her try all the harder to help Laura and Derek. She was eagle-eyed and conscientious in every way on their behalf. For instance, when she bumped into Mr Pritchett along at the shops, she'd said,

'I hope it's only your own messages you've been doing. I told you that either I would get whatever Mr and Mrs Cairns needed, or I'd stay with Mr Cairns to let his wife out to the shops.'

The man had become so furtive she'd suspected that he'd been up to something. She jerked open his shopper and peered inside. To her relief it only contained some packets of cigarettes and a lurid tabloid newspaper. Not the respectable *Herald* which Derek always read.

'No wonder you've got that horrible catarrh and cough,' she told the man. 'Smoking all these cigarettes. And look at those disgusting yellow stains on your fingers. Goodness knows what colour your lungs are.'

'I'll smoke if I like,' he'd muttered.

'Oh well,' Sophie said, moving off. 'It's your life you're putting at risk, not mine.'

She'd been on her way to visit Mrs Tunnicliff, who lived past the shops in a very nice villa not far from the station. Mrs Houston-Jones was going to be there too. They were all looking forward to having afternoon tea together. Later, after having supper at home with her husband, Sophie had to attend a meeting of the flower-arranging club in Kilmardinny House.

'You seem happy tonight,' McPherson remarked.

'Do I?' Sophie bustled about spooning bread and butter pudding on to their plates.

'Well, it's not often I hear you singing as you work.'

'Singing? Tuts, I was nothing of the kind.'

McPherson laughed.

'You were singing – under your breath – but singing all the same. Don't worry, I'm not complaining. You've rather a sweet singing voice.'

'Tuts, eat your pudding and don't be silly.'

But she said it in as near a good-humoured tone as she'd ever managed. Especially since she'd found out about his association with Bernard O'Maley.

'Where are you off to tonight?' he asked.

'The flower-arranging club.'

'The flowers in the church have improved recently.'

Sophie almost beamed.

'You noticed!'

'Was it you who did them?'

'This past couple of weeks. I told you. But you never listen.'

'Of course I listen. Well, most of the time anyway. Sometimes I've a lot on my mind. And you do go on quite a bit at times, Sophie.'

'I suppose I do.'

He could hardly believe his ears, not so much at what she said, but at the amiable silence that followed her words.

It was he who broke the silence eventually.

'That pudding was good. I've said it before and I'll say it again, Sophie. There isn't a chef in Glasgow who can match you at cooking.'

'Could you manage some more?'

McPherson leaned back and patted his wide and protruding girth.

'No. I know when I've had enough. So, where's your club?'

'Kilmardinny House.'

'You'll want a lift then?'

'No, it's a nice evening. I feel like a walk. You just relax and enjoy your programme on television.'

'Are you sure? What about coming back? It'll be dark and that's a long, quiet road.'

'Oh, there'll be plenty of other ladies there if I want a lift. But we're not in Drumchapel now, remember. I'd enjoy the walk back as well. The fresh air helps me to sleep.'

'Whatever you say, dear.'

He'd been looking forward to relaxing in front of the television. He was in even more committees than Sophie, but his involved much more serious matters than Sophie's. Then often when he came home, there would be the bridge club or the golf club or some other local social event to attend. Not that he was complaining about that. He enjoyed the Bearsden social scene. Sometimes, although not very often, he and Sophie would be alone together for an evening. It was always more difficult to unwind then. Sophie could never sit at peace. If she did sit down, her hands had to be busy. Usually it was her knitting needles click-clacking away at the same time as her tongue.

Tonight he could relax to his heart's content.

She scurried about clearing the table and washing the dishes and ferreting about looking for any crumbs that might have dropped on the dining-room carpet. Then, satisfied that all was perfection again, she donned her navy coat (Mrs Pemberton had persuaded only to wear her black for funerals) and navy velour hat. Tucked inside the collar of her coat was the little navy and pale blue and white silk scarf he'd given her for her birthday. He lit his pipe and gazed at her with quiet satisfaction through a haze of fragrant smoke. She had turned sixty-one and although she had a tense, stooping posture, she was as slim and sprightly as a young girl. Her skin was smooth and clear as a girl's too, and without the help of powder or paint.

She jerked and smoothed on her leather gloves. (Mrs Pemberton had told her that a lady never set foot out of doors without first putting on her gloves.)

'I'll away then.'

He nodded. Then she was gone.

Outside it was still light and Sophie walked at her usual brisk pace along Drymen Road, nodding occasionally at a familiar face.

She turned right at the other end of the terrace into the deserted Manse Road. Lush trees on either side of the road, heavy with greenery, made the evening suddenly darker. But the dark bower only added to Sophie's secret pool of blessed comfort and joy. She was almost smiling as she hurried along.

Up the hill of Kilmardinny Avenue now, the large mansion houses still far back from the road and still hidden by trees. Past the houses she could just see Kilmardinny Loch over on one side, glittering through the foliage.

Set back in a gentle curve in the Avenue stood the imposing Georgian mansion of Kilmardinny House. At the local history club of which Sophie was also a member (indeed she had served on the committee), they had tried but couldn't find the exact age of the house. The building had changed hands on many occasions and had undergone several major alterations over the years. But the house, the Avenue, the loch, and the surrounding parkland with its beautiful mature trees and shrubs, had once been part of the magnificent Kilmardinny Estate. The name Kilmardinny went back to ancient times and at the local history club everyone, especially Sophie, enjoyed delving into the fascinating history of the place. It made her feel part of something important. It gave her roots. She felt she belonged to this area so securely, it was as if she'd never lived or ever been part of anywhere else.

Some years ago, in 1965, the Bearsden town council purchased Kilmardinny, and over the years Kilmardinny House had been developed as an arts centre for the district. A beautiful place it was. Sophie attended many meetings there and loved the view of the loch, as well as the pillared grandeur of the house.

The flower-arranging club wasn't her favourite interest and at first she had been impatient with the whole procedure. She had also been somewhat clumsy. However, she had persevered. As Mrs Pemberton said, it was a most useful accomplishment for any lady. A 'must', in fact. Sophie still never bothered with flowers in the house, but she could now take her turn in decorating the church. She'd even been asked to be one of the flower ladies at the golf club's annual dinner. The Lord Provost had been there, and the Lady Provost had remarked on how artistic the floral arrangements looked. 'Works of art' were her very words. All the flower ladies, including Sophie, had felt pleased and proud.

At Kilmardinny House, chatting over a cup of tea, Sophie and some of the others relived the golf club dinner triumph and vowed, with the other enthusiasts, to strive towards even greater heights.

Afterwards, as people began to make for home, Sophie volunteered to clear up.

'Oh, you did it last week, Mrs McPherson,' Mrs Maitland protested. 'It was supposed to be your neighbour, Mrs Pemberton, tonight.'

'I know, but she developed a bit of a migraine and couldn't come.'

'Let me help you, dear.'

'No, no. Off you go. Your husband's hovering at the door, waiting for you. I know what men are like.'

Mrs Maitland rolled her eyes.

'Never any patience. You're sure, now?'

'Of course.'

If the truth were told, Sophie preferred the clearing up to the actual flower arranging. She got rid of leaves and twigs and petals and bits of fern that were left scattered about. Then a quick wipe round with a damp cloth, a smart but thorough sweep at the floor, and after a keen inspection of the place, and finding it to her satisfaction, she clicked out the light. On the way down Kilmardinny Avenue, she made up on a group of three of the flower-club ladies and was welcomed into their conversation. Soon they had to separate, however, as Sophie hurried off into Manse Road.

She became aware that it was very dark and quiet. Not another soul about. Nor did one person have a light on in any of the houses. She could discern no distant glimmer through the dense wall of trees. Of course, it was getting late. At least, by Bearsden standards. Decent people kept decent hours.

Sophie thought she heard footsteps behind her and turned, glad to have the company of one of her friends. But there was no one there. Strange. Every instinct alerted her to a physical presence. She quickened her steps, at the same time telling herself not to be silly. She was such a nervous person, so easily panicked. Always had been. Even as a child. Although, of course, she'd never shown it: everything she'd ever thought or felt had always been tightly locked inside her.

Once more she thought she heard something. Was it only the whispering of leafy branches? Or perhaps even the stealthy movements of a cat? She tried to reassure herself, to keep calm. But all calmness, all comfort, all her new-found happiness, had deserted her. Her flesh prickled with the sensation of somebody coming nearer. Panic scattered her wits. Choking for breath, she began to run.

Foolish woman, she bitterly chastised herself. Imagining she heard running footsteps behind her she thought,

'Foolish, foolish woman!'

Chapter Thirty

'You must be joking,' Robert said to the eager young man. They were at a dinner party at Jane and Bernard's place. The young man, Freddie Hancock, was a cousin of Jane's, and he had recently finished a teacher training couse in Inverness. Freddie had been expostulating at some length not only on the best and most effective teaching methods, but on what was wrong with the teaching methods currently used. Jane, Bernard and Andrina had long since become bored with the subject and were carrying on a different conversation.

'No, I'm not joking, Robert. The way I see it – indeed, I'm convinced of this – the response a teacher gets from children in terms both of learning and behaviour is totally related to the amount of work the teacher puts in.' He leaned forward to earnestly study Robert's face.

'Surely you know the problems there are with children in school, and out of it.'

'Indeed I do, Freddie. Indeed I do.'

'The children are violently punished, belted, shouted at, and all to no good effect. Quite the reverse. And it proves my point. Violence begets violence. It's surely time we tried another way. Give the children not only a better example but create bonds with them. If a teacher relates to a child, the child will relate back to him.'

'Where did you say you did your teaching practice?' Robert asked.

'In the Inverness area.'

'A beautiful place to live. And a different teaching situation there to the teaching situation in Glasgow.'

'I don't think so.'

'Oh, come on, Freddie . . .'

'I know there's more poverty and hardship in urban areas like this. Children are more deprived and tougher. They have to be to survive.'

'True.'

'But no child, anywhere, is evil or bad or stupid. They have only learning difficulties. Once you expose them to the light of reason, they'll respond.'

For a few minutes, Robert felt so tired, so hopeless, so lost for words, he just stared helplessly at the young man. Had he once been like this himself? He tried to remember with what high ideals he had started his teaching career. He was still convinced that it was worth while. Children were worth while. Yes, even the McNallys and the Neilys. But facts had to be faced. Life, either in or out of teaching, was not as simple and straightforward as Freddie was so confidently making out. For one thing, it didn't matter how much work a teacher put in, if the pupil had horrific problems at home, even if they were simply undernourished, or overtired, their response to education would, to put it mildly, be limited.

As far as relating to the teacher was concerned, Robert shuddered to think how gleefully some of the kids he knew would relate to anyone with a name like Hancock. Cock, needless to say, would be the operative part. Poor old Freddie would be off to a definite disadvantage in Sinnieglen.

But coming from a wealthy family he'd be far more likely to end up in Bearsden Academy.

'Don't you agree?' Freddie queried.

Robert sighed.

'I'm afraid you wouldn't survive very long at Sinnieglen, Freddie.'

'We'll see about that.'

Horror dealt Robert an unexpected body blow.

'You don't mean . . .'

'Yes, I've applied and been accepted by the languages department. I'll be teaching French and German.'

'Not in Sinnieglen?'

Freddie grinned.

'Why not? I'm looking forward to it.'

'God!'

Robert closed his eyes. He could no longer bear the sight of Freddie's bright, innocent face, so full of hope, high ideals and happy plans.

'I was very lucky that there was a vacancy,' Freddie went on. Obviously he was not aware that the vacancy had been created by Albert Melville having to take early retirement and treatment for a nervous breakdown at the outpatients' department of the local psychiatric hospital.

It was bad enough trying to teach English in Sinnieglen. Trying to teach foreign languages was a waste of time. It was almost as difficult as trying to teach art.

'Freddie . . .' Robert began. But what would he say? Teaching, like life, had to be learned the hard way, by practical experience. 'I wish you luck,' he managed at last. 'When are you supposed to start?'

'Right away. This coming Monday.'

Robert nodded, remembering now the staffroom gossip about the new lamb about to be led to the slaughter in the languages department.

'Well, if there's ever anything I can do to help or advise, don't hesitate to ask. Although, of course, Hamish McKendrick is head of languages.'

He had been going to add, 'He'll be able to help you better than me,' then realised what a stupid remark it would be. It was as much as old Hamish could do to help himself. He was nearing his legitimate retiral age and was hanging on by his fingernails to reach it safely. He'd only been saved from cracking up in the same way as Albert Melville by the fact that he avoided teaching as much as possible. For the most part, Hamish retreated into the windowless cupboard which he called his office and directed the department from there.

Hamish was, to use a typical Glasgow compliment, a gentleman and a scholar. Too gentlemanly by far for Sinnieglen. He had originated from the Isle of Skye and he still retained the gentle lilting accent of the Highlands.

'Thanks, Robert, but I expect I'll manage all right.'

After the dinner party, on the way home to Monteith Row, Robert said to Andrina, 'I really feel sorry for that poor bloke.'

Andrina raised an eyebrow but, as usual, he only had her vague attention. Her mind was elsewhere.

'What poor bloke?'

'Freddie.'

201

'Oh?'

She didn't ask why he felt sorry for Freddie but so strong were Robert's feelings for the young man's impending doom that he felt compelled to tell her.

'He's starting in Sinnieglen on Monday. In the languages department, of all places.'

'Oh!'

'They'll make mincemeat of him, especially with a name like Hancock. It'll be cock this and cock that . . .'

'Don't be coarse, Robert. At times you can be quite disgusting.'

His stomach knotted against her dislike of him. Her feelings were never strong enough, never passionate enough for hatred. Her attitude isolated him, emasculated him.

More than once, he'd made up his mind to say, 'To hell with you!' and move out. Even if he couldn't have Laura, he'd still made up his mind to leave Andrina. Then he'd see Jennifer's sensitive, vulnerable face, he'd detect the child's fear and insecurity, and he'd be unable to make the move.

Recently he'd tried to have a serious, exploratory talk with Jennifer to try to get to the root of her obvious unhappiness. At one point, she'd said, 'You won't leave me, Daddy.' Then, eyes wide and apprehensive, she'd added, 'Will you?'

'Of course not,' he'd comforted. 'Both Mummy and I love you very much and we'd never leave you. What's put such a thought into your head?'

But Jennifer didn't answer. The trouble was, Andrina left the child far too often with Sophie. He determined to speak to Andrina about that again. No, not just speak to her – really put his foot down. If necessary, he'd also lay the law down to Sophie. He'd never been happy about Sophie's influence on the child. Sophie was far too anxious and neurotic and that sort of thing, he believed, was as infectious as measles and even more harmful.

But now, going home in the car, wasn't the best of times to start an argument about Jennifer, or Sophie.

After he'd got home though, and had a generous slug of whisky, his resentment of Andrina's attitude surfaced again. Not only that, but the whole unsatisfactoriness of what was going on. She was definitely neglecting Jennifer. She was shifting her responsibility for the child to Sophie, and it had gone on long enough.

'Look,' he told her, 'sit down. I want to talk to you.'

She raised her usual cool eyebrow.

'This isn't your school, Robert. And I'm not one of your pupils.'

'We've got to talk.'

'It's nearly midnight and I'm going to bed.'

He barred the kitchen doorway.

'Not until we've had this out.'

This time she looked wary.

'Had what out?'

'Been honest with each other about what's been happening. I'm not blind, Andrina. I know what you've been doing.'

The colour drained from her face. He watched her go shakily over to one of the kitchen chairs, supporting herself with one hand on the table. She didn't just sit on the chair, she collapsed down on to it as if her legs had given way. She looked so scared it was obvious she'd been doing a lot more than leaving Jennifer with her mother.

Suddenly it all clicked into place. All the times she was supposed to be at God knows how many classes and meetings. He remembered how old Granny McPherson had insisted that Andrina was lying when she kept saying she'd been to visit her.

At the time he'd accepted Andrina's explanation (as did her mother and father) that poor old Granny McPherson was losing her marbles. After all, she was forgetful about other things. And of course, he hadn't been all that interested in where Andrina was, especially in recent months, she could have been to hell and back for all he cared.

He stared incredulously at her round baby face and wide eyes, usually full of innocence but now brimming with fear.

'You're having a bloody affair!'

'No, no, Robert! What on earth has put that into your head?'

She wasn't indignant. She wasn't offended. She wasn't angry. *He* was angry.

Infidelity was the last thing he wanted to talk about. He was no longer in love with her. She had been whittling away at his manhood for years and he wanted to be free of her. But he was so angry, he could have killed her with one vicious blow. Instead, he forced himself to go over and sit on the chair opposite her.

'I'm not stupid, Andrina.'

'I know that, Robert, but you've been under a lot of strain. That awful school. All your extra responsibility. Darling, please don't take it out on me. It's been a long day and we're both tired.'

She made to come over to him, arms outstretched.

'Sit down,' he rapped out in the same tone he used to his karate class. Except that to her it was spiked with hatred. 'You two-faced lying little bitch. All I'm concerned about is Jennifer. She's the only one I care about. It's Jennifer I want to talk about.'

A look of surprise glazed over the fear in Andrina's eyes.

'Jennifer? She's all right.'

'No, she's not all right.'

'What do you mean? What's wrong with Jennifer?'

'You tell me.'

'But . . .' She looked genuinely perplexed. 'I don't understand. Anyone can see how well fed, well dressed, well cared for she is.'

'Appearances aren't everything. The child is insecure, introverted and unhappy. Why should that be?'

'I don't know.'

Anger was beginning to surface in her. 'I don't believe what you're saying is true, and even if it was true, why should you take for granted that it's all my fault? Why should you start accusing me of all sorts of things, including adultery. Me – who's been a good-living Christian all my life.' She rose, in a fury now. 'Have you gone out of your mind or something?'

He looked away from her in disgust. But he knew that there had been times recently when he had asked himself the same question.

Chapter Thirty-One

It took Andrina a few days to get over the fright of Robert's accusation. She literally collapsed with anxiety and apprehension in case he'd repeat the shocking words to her mother. She was barely able to get Jennifer to school. Indeed, for a few days she did not get Jennifer to school. Jennifer had to dress herself, make her own breakfast, then find her own way to Green Street. Of course the child could dress herself perfectly well, and breakfast was just a matter of standing on a stool to reach the cornflake packet in the kitchen cupboard, and open the fridge to find a bottle of milk.

Robert insisted that she always take Jennifer to school and call for her, because of the main road. If he hadn't had to leave for Sinnieglen before it was time for Jennifer to get up he would have taken her to school himself, he said. Green Street was barely five minutes away and Andrina had trained Jennifer conscientiously on her kerb drill so she was sure the child would be perfectly all right. Anyway Jennifer had already proved, unknown to Robert, that she could safely cross the road. She'd done it on her own before.

Andrina always felt both upset and annoyed when she remembered the first time it had happened. She'd had a lovely time with Bernard and she'd been a few minutes late (no more than fifteen or twenty) in arriving to collect Jennifer at the school gates. Jennifer had waited for a while and then decided to make her own way home. (And why not? She wasn't a baby any more. She had to be allowed to grow up some time.) She'd just crossed the road, perfectly safely, when Miss Chisolm had seen her on her own and run after her. Miss Chisolm had been standing at the close, hand in hand with Jennifer, when Andrina had come breathlessly running down Monteith Row. The teacher had been very cool, even after she'd explained how she'd been out at Bearsden seeing her mother who wasn't keeping well and the traffic had been so terrible on the way back. She hadn't wanted to be late. She had been perfectly truthful about that.

Since then, she had only been late a few times and Jennifer had waited at the school gate. She always tried very hard to get back in time despite the fact that it was so much further to travel from the cottage. Bernard wanted to give her a lift to the school or to Monteith Row but she would never allow him to. Instead, she either got a bus from the nearest village or Bernard dropped her off at a bus stop in town.

After the awful night of Robert's accusation, she lay in bed unable to function, in an agony of suspense. She couldn't talk about it – not even to Bernard. She made some excuse about having flu and being unable to see him before he went off to Ireland bodyguarding some politician or other. She was in such a state she couldn't even worry about his safety. He'd once told her that it was with politicians and industrialists that he and his men really laid their lives on the line. They had to wear bulletproof vests and carry side arms. She'd chilled with the danger of it, but now, gripped by a more intimate danger herself, there was no place for Bernard in her mind. No place for anyone or anything except her feverish prayers for her own safety.

But the days of agony passed. Robert did not repeat his terrible words to Sophie. Nor did he broach the subject with her again. Life, their life, slowly returned to normal. They chatted to Jennifer but paid very little attention to each other. They visited her mother as usual. They were even on normal visiting terms with Jane and Bernard. It became obvious that Robert did not suspect Bernard. Why should he? He had known Bernard since Bernard was a schoolboy. According to Bernard, Robert had helped him to survive his youthful days in Blackhill. Robert trusted Bernard. He would be the last person on earth Robert would suspect.

Gradually Andrina relaxed with relief. She felt safe again. She went back to the cottage more and more often, and she and Bernard lived there as man and wife as much as they could. They had their own Christmas there two or three days before the official date. He gave her money to buy a tree and decorations; she bought a turkey and he provided the champagne. With his money she bought a lovely velvet and taffeta gown in aquamarine, a shade deeper than her eyes. She slipped her feet into high-heeled black shoes to match the glamorous black basque she wore underneath the dress. The diamanté earrings and necklace Bernard had given her reflected the sparkle in her eyes. Bernard wore a dinner suit and winged collar.

It was a perfect day. They pulled down all the blinds and closed the curtains. They lit the whole place with candles for their Christmas dinner and champagne. Afterwards they played their favourite Nat King Cole records and danced cheek to cheek. They gave each other their parcels. Then they made wonderful love. It was one of the happiest days of Andrina's life.

She didn't even have to hurry home for Jennifer, because she was on holiday from school and Robert was taking her to see a Disney film. Andrina had told Robert she needed to be on her own to do Christmas shopping.

'I'll just make a day of it and have lunch in town,' she'd said. 'The shops are mobbed at this time of the year. I'll never manage to find everything I want in the morning and it would be a bit of a nuisance rushing back here and then back to town again.'

'There's no need,' Robert said. 'Jennifer and I will have a special lunch. Just the two of us. Would you like that, Jennifer?'

Jennifer had nodded but her eyes were worried and uncertain.

'It's all right,' Robert assured the child. 'Mummy will be back in time for tea. You and I will go to the cinema and when we come back home, Mummy will be here.'

Andrina didn't mention that she'd heard there were long queues for the new Disney film every day, which meant they would be later getting into the cinema than Robert reckoned. Therefore they would be later getting back. But Robert and Jennifer would be perfectly happy in each other's company and she would be free to have a whole wonderful day with Bernard.

Christmas day at her mother's never lived up to Andrina's

Christmas with Bernard, but this year it was even worse than usual. On the surface everything seemed fine. The meal was excellent. Sophie's cooking was always enjoyable. Crackers were pulled. Wine was drunk. Presents were exchanged. Her father and Robert chatted amiably. Jennifer played happily with her new toys and Robert's mother smiled good-naturedly at the family scene. Jean Anderson's arthritis prevented her from helping Sophie to clear the table or go through with her to the kitchen to wash the dishes, although she did offer.

'Nonsense,' Sophie said. 'You just sit there and relax. Andrina and I between us will soon have everything shipshape. I'll bring through a cup of tea after we've cleared up.'

'You're very kind, Sophie. What a lot of work you've had. That was an absolutely wonderful meal.'

'I enjoyed cooking it,' Sophie assured her.

However, Andrina could see that her mother was under some strain: there was quite a haunted look about her.

In the kitchen Andrina said,

'Are you feeling all right, Mummy?'

'Yes. Why do you ask?' Sophie replied sharply, suspiciously. This was normal for her mother, so Andrina would usually have thought no more about it. She would just have felt her usual irritation at the neurotic response to a simple query. This time, however, she felt curious.

'You don't look very happy.'

Her mother never looked happy in fact.

'I'm all right,' Sophie said, then hesitated before going on. 'It's probably just my imagination.'

'What is?'

'A couple of times recently when I've been out at night – even just along the road to the church – I feel as if somebody is following me.'

'Following you?' Andrina echoed.

'And watching me. Sometimes, even when I'm in the house, I feel as if I'm being watched.'

'That's ridiculous . . .'

'Or the house is being watched.'

'Have you seen anybody following you or hanging about outside the house?'

'No.'

'Well then . . .'

Sophie gave herself a determined shake.

'As I said, it could be my imagination.'

'Of course it is. Why should anybody follow you about? What reason could there be?'

'None. None.'

'Well then.'

'And the phone calls could be a coincidence.'

'What phone calls?'

'The phone rings. Nothing's said. There's just silence. I keep saying "Who is it? Who's there?" but there's just silence.'

Andrina rolled her eyes.

'A heavy breather. That happens to lots of people, Mummy. Usually it's children doing it for a lark. Ages ago I got a couple of those calls and Robert said it would be children. Next time the phone went Robert answered and I couldn't repeat to you what he said, Mummy. He used very strong language and said he knew who it was and he'd sort them out if it ever happened again. It never did happen again so he must have been right.'

Sophie nodded, then fussed about putting dishes away.

'Andrew's always telling me it's time I pulled myself together.'

Suddenly it occurred to Andrina that her mother's pre-occupation with herself was the reason that Sophie had not been on the phone pestering her so often recently.

She experienced a wave of relief, and a sensation of freedom that was pure joy. She was glad her mother's back was to her and that she did not witness the light that had, for a few seconds, shone like a beacon in her eyes. Her gaze was lowered when her mother turned round.

'I'm glad I mentioned it to you. Your daddy's very good in many ways. But . . .'

'But what?' Andrina looked up, her round eyes blank and innocent.

'Well, he has his own life . . .'

'Goodness, Mummy, I've never seen a couple who do more together. You and Daddy are a right Darby and Joan.'

'In Bearsden, yes. But he has a different life away from here, away from me. He mixes with . . . with a different kind of people.'

Sophie looked furtive, her eyes flicking away from her daughter, then back again for a second. 'We'd better get back through to the room.'

Andrina thought, Has she turned her attention and suspicion on Daddy, I wonder? Again she felt freed.

'I'll make the tea, Mummy.'

'Oh, I forgot. My memory is awful these days, what with one thing and another.'

'Don't worry, you go and sit down. I'll bring it through.'

'Thank you, Andrina. You're a good girl.'

Andrina couldn't believe her ears. Good girl? Well, that's a turn-up for the book, she thought. Long may her imaginings about a ghostly watcher last!

Chapter Thirty-Two

To Frank's surprise, Bridie was very welcoming, to everyone who came to the party. She was even quite pleasant to Bernard and Jane. In fact, he could not have wished for a more sweet and gentle Bridie as a hostess.

He had always accepted and respected the fact that shyness was part of her nature and that perhaps he'd overdone the social scene in their flat when they'd first come to live in Botanic Crescent. It wasn't overdone in his terms: he'd thoroughly enjoyed every minute of every gathering. He'd hoped at that early stage that Bridie would get over her shyness and enjoy their social life too. In other words, he'd wanted her to change. Looking back, he felt guilty; he could be a selfish sod at times. Poor wee Bridie. Now here she was, her own dear self, trying her best, for his sake, to mix with and be nice to his friends. And when he thought of how she must feel about Bernard, seeing him with Jane while her poor sister . . .

He had never despised himself so much, or loved Bridie so much. He'd no right to subject her to such an ordeal.

Later, in bed, cradling her in his arms, he apologised for having the party.

'It's all right,' Bridie said.

'No, it's not all right. I did it for Bernard. I was thinking of him instead of you. God, Bridie, I can be so stupid.'

'No, Frank,' Bridie said quietly. 'You're not stupid.'

She sounded tired, defeated.

'I'll never have another party again. Never. I'll never have any of my BBC friends here again. I'll never have Bernard and his wife here again.'

'Oh, Frank.' She gave a helpless little laugh. 'You always go to such extremes.'

It was true. He was either up in seventh heaven with enthusiasm about something (usually his latest piece of writing) or he was plunged into the depths of despair (usually about his latest piece of writing).

'I'd go to any extreme for you, pet,' he said, 'because I love you. You mean everything to me.'

He sensed the almost imperceptible turning away from him. Not in body, but in spirit.

'I mean it,' he cried out. 'I've loved you from the moment I first saw you, Bridie, and I'll love you to the day I die.'

'Yes, dear,' she said. Then, 'It's terribly late. We've both had a long and busy day. I think it's time we said goodnight.'

He didn't want her to drift away and be lost in sleep, but he struggled with his selfishness and kissed her proffered cheek.

'Goodnight, pet. And thank you for . . . for being so nice to everyone at the party. I mean, for being such a good hostess. You know, for . . .'

'Goodnight, Frank,' Bridie said, and turned away.

I want to say too much, Frank berated himself again. I think too much. I talk too much. I write too much. Although, as it happened, the powers that be in television were complaining he wasn't writing enough. He'd offered to come up with another short story – a series of short stories, if they liked – that could be adapted into half-hour plays. He could first of all sell them to newspapers or magazines. He was getting a bit short of cash, and even selling to magazines and then doing an adaptation wasn't the best way to make the most money.

But the truth was, the television bosses didn't want short stories, adapted or not. He needed, they said, to go back to writing full-length plays that gave him room to develop a strong and memorable theme. There was a chance that a film company (even a Hollywood film company) would pick up the story and make a big film of it. He'd discussed with the Beeb the play about the disintegration of a marriage and they were eager (and growing very impatient) to get their hands on it. He knew himself, without anyone pointing it out to him, that he stood a better chance of making the really big time with that one than any of his others. They had made headlines in Scotland but, as far as he knew, nowhere else. It could be argued that a Glasgow bailie was peculiar to Glasgow, and even a priest in the Gorbals was peculiar to that specific area.

But the disintegration of a marriage could happen anywhere. There were no boundaries to emotions.

He read the play again as soon as he got back to his desk then carefully locked it away in the bottom right-hand drawer. He knew it was good. No – more than that. It was the best thing he'd ever done. And it *was* done, finished, polished, revised, checked and rechecked. There was absolutely nothing more he could do to it. He seemed to have been slogging away at it for years. He could no longer put off submitting it to television. For financial reasons, as much as any other. For the millionth time he went over in his mind what Bridie's reaction might be. He had disguised the people in it as much as possible. In actual fact, he had created new people. Neither he nor Bridie was in the play. It was not about a woman who couldn't cope with her husband's success; it was about a man who couldn't cope with his wife's success. Only the emotional truth was there, and it was there straight from his heart.

He made up his mind that it was a perfectly legitimate exploration of a modern phenomenon. Or one that was beginning to develop in modern society. His hand was actually on the phone to tell Scott Wallace, the producer, that he'd come along to the Beeb with the play right now when a needle of guilt and unease held him back.

He knew the play was a general exploration of a marriage disintegrating, and no longer anything to do with Frank and Bridie O'Maley. It was definitely and truly about Sol and Amy Slater. Frank and Bridie O'Maley were OK. They loved each other. Their marriage was as solid as a rock. They'd had their problems, their differences, their ups and down, but they'd both tried and succeeded in overcoming the difficulties. It occurred to him then that because he loved Bridie, he should trust her. Looking back, he saw he had been shutting her out – just as she'd accused him of doing. He'd become very paranoiac about his work, secreting it away from her in locked drawers.

Despite all this, Bridie had continued to make every effort to please him and to fit in with his selfish lifestyle. It was time he tried to please her for a change. It was time he trusted her. She had gone to spend the afternoon shopping with Doris and then the pair of them were going to the pictures. She wouldn't be back until late so there was no point in saying anything or doing anything until tomorrow. But tomorrow he'd ask Bridie if she'd like to read his new play and tell him what she thought of it.

Happy now, in a trembling kind of way, Frank lifted the phone, got through to Scott Wallace and told him he could deliver the play in a couple of days. That would give Bridie plenty of time to read it and give it the OK. He was certain – after all the painstaking work he'd done on it – that she wouldn't see any need for rewriting.

A celebratory lunch was arranged.

'No, dear boy, not at the Club.' The producer who had long since discussed the play with Frank in some detail, was obviously delighted. 'This one deserves the Buttery.'

'Great! Great!' Frank enthused. He was excited, yet paralysed. He couldn't settle down to write. He couldn't think of one word to put on the blank page in front of him. If only Bridie had been at home and he could have rushed to give her the play. They could have returned to the closeness of the old days without wasting another precious minute.

He gave up trying to strain over the blank page, paced the room for a time, then roamed through the flat before stopping in the kitchen to make a cup of tea. He wished he possessed some tranquillising tablets; he would have taken a few to try to calm himself. He drank a mugful of tea standing up, then went back to sit at his desk but adrenalin, or nervous electricity or something equally strange and unbearable, made sitting for more than a few seconds impossible. He decided to go for a brisk trot through the Botanic Gardens. That was his whole trouble, he decided. He didn't get enough fresh air and exercise. He was far too healthy and energetic to sit crouched over a desk all day and every day. When this sort of nervous energy became bottled up it was bound to cause problems. He forced himself round and round the park until he was choking for breath, lashed with sweat and fearful he was about to add a heart attack to his other anxieties. He was barely able to totter back up the stairs to the flat. It was ages, his long bony frame spreadeagled on the bed, before he felt any way normal again.

A stiff whisky helped. After that he fell sound asleep in front of the TV. Hours later, Bridie shook him awake and told him it was time for bed.

'It was a really good film,' she told him in the bedroom as he struggled to gather his wits together. His legs were aching and he still felt half-asleep.

'Doris and I enjoyed it. It was a bit of a weepie, of course. Poor old Doris went through my hankie as well as her own. But we managed a bit of a laugh about it before we said goodnight. As I told her, it was only a made-up story after all. The sort of thing that you make up any day of the week.'

What a bit of luck, Frank thought. The perfect lead-in to her reading the play.

'That reminds me,' he said. 'I've finished my play at long last. I'd appreciate it if you'd read it, pet, and let me know what you think of it.'

She looked surprised, startled even. He wasn't sure if she looked pleased.

'I'll give it to you first thing tomorrow morning. OK?'

'Yes, all right.'

First thing next morning he was up and ready. He gulped down a cup of coffee and some cornflakes without thinking, he was so eager and excited about handing over his play to Bridie to read.

Bridie smiled at him and shook her head.

'For goodness sake, Frank, calm down. I won't be able to concentrate on reading it if you're agitating about at my elbow. Why don't you take a walk down to Byres Road and get something for our lunch? I meant to go to the shops myself but if I've to have enough time to read all this . . .'

'OK, OK. I'll go.' Frank felt so grateful to her he would have raced to the shops at the other end of Glasgow if need be.

He tried to stay away as long as possible. After doing the shopping he walked the whole length of Byres Road and back again, forcing himself to go at an agonising snail's pace. He even went along part of Great Western Road before returning via Queen Margaret Drive to Botanic Crescent.

His hand was shaking as he turned the key in the front door of the flat. The play, this particular play, meant so much to him. He had put his heart and soul into it. It was so important that Bridie should share his deep feeling about it, his pride in it. In a way it was the open-sesame to their former loving partnership. He longed for that closeness again. He wanted to share everything with her. As well as giving her everything else, he wanted to give her himself.

'Bridie,' he called through his writing-room door. 'Have you finished with it? Can I come in?'

'Yes, come in, Frank,' Bridie called back loud and clear.

Smiling in anticipation Frank opened the door. Bridie was tearing up his manuscript.

He panicked. He rushed towards her, lunged at her, knocked her aside, grabbed what was left of his precious papers and yelled,

'You stupid, malicious cow! I'll never forgive you for this. Years of work. Years! Get out of my sight before I kill you. I'll kill you, you jealous, narrow-minded, ignorant cow!' He felt gutted. Destroyed. He didn't know how he'd ever recover.

Chapter Thirty-Three

Theresa had bought a budgie. She hadn't gone out with that intention. She needed some messages. She was always having to trail to the shops because Tony had an appetite like a Hoover. Her arms were being stretched to gorilla length with carrying so many heavy shopping bags. Sugar, tea, bread, milk, cakes, flour, potatoes . . . She could never stock up enough of anything. It all went.

Then there was wee Bobby. Not so wee now and getting more like his daddy every day. Hoover junior. Even when he'd been on the breast he'd nearly sucked the life's blood out of her. Marion was no better. Now of course she had always to lug wee Bobby and the wean to the shops. Already some of their older friends and relations (like big Martha Stoddart) were calling the wean Murn (the olds Scots version of Marion). Not that Theresa cared any more. She was too constantly tired nowadays to care about anything. And of course Tony had just given one of his big horsy laughs and said, 'Never mind, hen, there's nothing wrong with a good Scots tongue, eh?'

Then he'd begun to call the wean Murn as well.

She thought she was pregnant again. Tony wouldn't care about that either. He'd still fool about, go out with the boys for a game of pool, or a few drinks (more than a few sometimes), or to the dog track, or a football match. Tony, she realised now, had a mindless way of enjoying himself and no idea (and certainly no intentions) of facing up to responsibility.

He was never nasty to her, never lifted his hand to her, even when he was drunk. He just took his pleasure whenever and as often as he could. *Especially* when he was drunk. She had come to dread the crushing, breath-snatching weight of him and the merciless, never-ending thump thump of his body on top of hers.

She marvelled at how she'd once thought of him as manly and attractive. Not handsome exactly; even when she'd had a veil of love over her eyes she'd known that he wasn't handsome. But he was broad-shouldered and powerful-looking like all the O'Maley brothers, except perhaps Frank.

Tony had buck teeth but that had never worried her. They were lovely strong white teeth, she'd thought. He laughed a great deal and she'd admired that. So good-humoured and easy-going, she'd thought. He was easy-going all right. He was just another child for her to look after, to be trachled with, exhausted with. (He was worse than that, of course – much worse.) She had no one to help and protect her. No one to talk to. The once decent neighbours who'd lived up the close had either died or escaped to some other districts since Maureen and Patrick, her mother-in-law and father-in-law's time. Now some of the houses in the close were boarded up. Others had people in them that were either out working (some as prostitutes) or men on holiday from Barlinnie. In one there were a couple of old winos, probably squatters. Often their empty bottles were left lying about the stairs and the close. At night (and often during the day as well) Theresa would cower inside the house with her hands over her ears as gang fights or drunken brawls raged in the street below. She often marvelled at how the children slept through it all. She'd pray for Tony to come home from wherever he happened to be. But she knew he'd just laugh.

His brothers were more of a help and comfort to her than he'd ever been, even though she didn't see them very often. Occasionally Bernard called in and she was always glad when Michael and Caroline dropped by for a visit. Sometimes they brought big Martha and the children, or Caroline came on her own. One day Caroline had been full of gossip about Bernard having a 'fancy woman'. It had worried and upset Theresa. Right from the start Bernard had been good to her. He was the only one who spoke up for her to Tony and tried to make him see sense. She could have wept when Bernard came because he was so good to her. Several times over the years, he'd surprised her with presents – a box of chocolates, a bottle of wine. She would never forget the time he'd brought a lovely cake, and a bottle of perfume, on her birthday. Nobody else had remembered. Sometimes he even slipped her a fiver. Once, despite her protests, he gave her a ten-pound note.

'Go and see if some hairdresser can tame that God-awful frizz of yours,' he'd said. She hadn't, of course. The money had had gone on clothes for the weans.

She wished to God it was Bernard she'd married and not his brother. Not that Bernard looked on her, or had ever looked on her, with anything except pity. Nor did she have enough energy, emotional or otherwise, left in her body to feel anything for Bernard except gratitude. But she could see what a good catch he was for any female. Not only was he generous, not only did he know how to treat a woman, but he oozed sexuality. It was forever glimmering in his eyes. Tony was as randy as a bull. But there was a difference. Many's the time Theresa sighed and cried for the difference. The last time Bernard visited she'd thought she'd better warn him about the gossip.

'I don't care if you've got a dozen fancy women, Bernard,' she'd assured him. 'You're a good man and I'll have nobody say any different. I'm only telling you because I thought you ought to know.'

He'd thanked her. And that was all. So she was none the wiser whether he had a fancy woman or not. That was all right. That was Bernard's way. Quite the opposite from his big-mouthed, reckless, fun-loving idiot of a brother. If she'd had enough energy she would have hated Tony. But already she felt defeated and without hope. She could see her life stretching out before her, year after exhausting year, one long painful pregnancy. She longed for love, gentleness, sensitivity, tenderness – all the things she now knew beyond all doubt that her husband would never be able to give her.

As she trailed along yet again to the shops, trundling the old pram in front of her, she happened to stop for a rest and a breather at a pet shop doorway. Hanging in a cage was a wee green budgie.

'Hello there,' it greeted her.

Theresa smiled.

'Hello.'

It looked so pretty, so delicate with its little velvety chest and bright innocent eyes. Clever too.

'Hello,' she repeated.

'Hello there,' the budgie said, then added, 'ma name's Erchie.'

Theresa couldn't help laughing. It was the first time she'd laughed for months.

The pet shop man emerged from the shadowy cover of the shop.

'Clever wee thing, eh?'

'Clever wee thing,' the budgie echoed.

'He's the best speaker I've ever had in here. An' that's countin' your average Glaswegian.' He laughed uproariously.

The budgie bounced and flapped and fluttered, showing off before Theresa's admiring eyes.

Theresa laughed again. 'The wee soul,' she said with genuine affection. So cheeky yet so vulnerable.

'Ma name's Erchie.'

A surge of recklessness came over Theresa.

'How much is it?'

It turned out the cage was dearer than the budgie. Theresa trembled at such extravagance but thought, To hell, why shouldn't I treat myself to something. Tony spends whatever he wants on himself.

She bought the budgie (much to wee Bobby's excitement) and balanced the cage on top of the pram with firm exhortations to both Bobby and the wean not to touch.

This was her budgie. Her very own wee pet. She remembered to buy food for it and even a bell for it to play with.

Tony took the addition to the household with typical good humour.

'Ah like yer green jersey, son. You know what foot to kick wi', eh? Come here till ah shake yer claw.'

'Don't you dare touch him.' Theresa had sprung like a tiger to Erchie's defence. Tony was so thoughtlessly rough he would be sure to do wee Erchie an injury. She'd suffered all too often at Tony's hands herself.

'OK. OK, hen,' Tony had immediately conceded. 'I was only tryin' tae be friendly.'

'He's my budgie and nobody else has to go near him. Do you hear?'

'Aye. Aye. OK.'

It was such a relaxation to talk to wee Erchie and she talked to him all the time when Tony wasn't in. She told him all her troubles, including what she thought of Tony. Very soon however (but to her secret amusement – no, secret hilarity) she realised she'd have to be more careful about what she said because Erchie was too clever for his own good.

Once he'd actually said when Tony came in,

'The idiot's arrived!'

'What did he say?' Tony roared. (He'd had a few drinks at the time.)

'Something he heard on the wireless,' Theresa hastily explained. 'Some comedian keeps saying it. It's his – you know – what do you call it, like a signature tune . . .'

Actually it was what she said every time she heard Tony's key in the door. Fortunately (and because he was an idiot) Tony believed her excuse. He laughed uproariously.

'He's an awfu' wee bird, that!'

She and Erchie had become such pals and so fond of each other he would allow her to hold him carefully and very, very gently stroke his chest. Often he'd perch on her shoulder or nestle into her neck. She didn't tell anybody how she felt because she knew only too well how silly it would sound. Nobody, not even Bernard, would understand. Wee Erchie represented the only gentleness she'd ever experienced in her life.

Bernard was quite tickled with Erchie, and on a recent visit he'd amused himself teaching Erchie some new words and phrases. When Theresa heard what they were, she nearly had a fit, although she couldn't help laughing as well.

Erchie was happily chirping out,

'Up the 'Gers' and 'Three cheers for Willie Waddell!'

'Bernard, stop it,' Theresa pleaded, wiping the tears of hilarity from her eyes. 'You know what Tony's like.'

'Knuckle-headed bigot,' Bernard said.

'I know. That's why . . .'

'It's just a joke. I only wish I could be here to see his face but

221

I'll have to go. I just wanted to call in before I fly off to Brazil. I'll be there for a week or two. My first important job abroad!'

'Good for you, Bernard. You certainly get around. I've never been out of Scotland. Now that I come to think of it, I've hardly ever been out of Glasgow.'

Bernard shook his head.

'There's no bloody reason why Tony can't take you and the kids for a good holiday. I'll have another word with him when I get back.'

'Thanks, Bernard.'

She saw him to the door, then gave him a wave from the front-room window. She could hear Erchie enjoying the new addition to his repertoire: 'Up the 'Gers. Three cheers for Willie Waddell. Up the 'Gers . . .'

She ran back through to the kitchen.

'Shh, shh.' She put her finger to her mouth. 'Forget that, Erchie. It's like waving a red rag to a bull to mention that team or any Rangers players past, present or future, to Tony O'Maley.'

Erchie bounced and fluttered happily about, obviously having misunderstood.

'Up the 'Gers. Three cheers for Willie Waddell. Up the 'Gers. Three cheers for Willie Waddell.'

'No, you mustn't! Erchie, will you be quiet.'

'Up the 'Gers . . .'

'Little Miss Muffet . . .' Theresa desperately tried to draw Erchie out with the poem she'd successfully taught him only the other day. 'Sat on a tuffet . . .'

'Three cheers for Willie Waddell.'

'Oh God,' Theresa groaned. She decided that maybe if she ignored Erchie for a time he'd forget the offending words, so she turned away to see to Bobby and the wean. After they were put to bed she washed the supper dishes and tidied the kitchen without as much as a look in Erchie's direction. Her strategy seemed to work. Erchie fell silent.

Poor wee thing, Theresa thought, I hope he isn't offended. I hope he doesn't feel hurt because I'm ignoring him. He won't understand that I'm doing it for his own good. Erchie couldn't know that it was Saturday night. Even though he would have heard – as she had – on the wireless that Celtic had been beaten by Rangers in a football match that very afternoon, he wouldn't understand what a tragedy that would be to Tony. How was Erchie to know that Tony would be doing the round of pubs at this very moment drowning his sorrows and getting smashed out of his empty skull.

Much as Theresa had been grateful to Bernard in the past, it now occurred to her that he was an O'Maley after all. It had been a joke, he said. Well, she didn't think it was all that funny. To say the least, it was thoughtless of Bernard.

Suddenly Erchie broke through her reverie,

'The idiot's arrived. Up the 'Gers!' It was an absolute screech. 'Three cheers for Willie Waddell!'

'Be quiet,' Theresa hissed. 'For God's sake, Erchie, shut your beak!'

Tony burst into the kitchen, ashen-faced with fury.

'Whit was that he said the now?'

Erchie immediately obliged by repeating it.

'Up the 'Gers. Three cheers for Willie Waddell.'

Tony lunged at the cage and Theresa raced to claw at his back in a desperate attempt to pull him away. But Tony was too strong for her. He jerked the door open, shoved his big hand in and grabbed Erchie.

Theresa screamed, 'Don't you hurt him. Give him to me, do you hear? Don't you dare, don't you dare . . .'

But despite her pulling and pushing and screaming, Tony took Erchie to the cooker, turned on the gas and held him over the gas ring. In a matter of seconds, Erchie went limp.

So did Theresa. It was as if she'd died too.

Chapter Thirty-Four

'I saw Theresa today,' Caroline told Michael as she dished him a plate of steaming Scotch broth thick with parsley and peas and lumps of lamb. 'She looked an even worse mess than usual. I wish she'd at least get that mop of hers cut. Real frowsy, she looked. And pregnant again, of course. Twins, by the look of her. Twins fairly gallop in your family . . .'

'I blame the Pope,' Martha said, making Michael laugh.

'For getting Theresa pregnant?'

'You know what I mean. He wants all you Green Grapes to multiply and take over the whole place. And never mind how many poor women he drags down and kills with carrying too many weans.'

'Aye, OK, Ma.' Michael had been working like a galley slave since early morning and felt far too tired to argue.

Caroline said, 'It's not so much that. I mean, if a woman has a good man it's all right. Poor Theresa's lumbered with Tony. I know he's your brother, Michael, and I'm sorry if – '

'Oh, don't worry, hen. I know what he's like. I've spoken to him about having a wee bit more consideration for his wife – spend a bit more time with her – help with the weans. Even Bernard's tried. We might as well have talked to the budgie for all the good it did.'

'Here,' Caroline suddenly remembered. 'You'll never guess what happened to the budgie.'

'What?'

'Tony gassed it.'

'What?' Michael's voice leapt up an octave with disbelief.

Martha grimaced. 'He should be locked up and the key thrown away.'

'It's hardly a case for the High Court, Ma.'

Caroline said, 'I wonder what possessed him to do such a thing? Theresa refused to talk about it. I asked her where the budgie was and she just said, "Tony gassed it" and then shut up.'

'Cruel Papish bastard,' Martha said.

'Mammy! How many times have I to tell you not to swear in front of the children?'

Martha's whiskery jowls hardened into a huff.

'They're all the same.'

'No, they are not.' Caroline had become quite firm, even cheeky to her mother at times. 'You're just a silly old blether.'

'I'm not as daft as I look. I never came up the Clyde in a banana boat. You're carrying another wean!'

Caroline flushed with annoyance and embarrassment.

'For goodness sake, Mammy. Have a bit of decency. Even walls have ears.'

'Who's bein' silly now?' Martha sneered. 'They're weans, not walls. And they're not as daft as they look either.'

'I haven't had a chance to tell Michael.'

'Well, I've saved you the trouble.'

Michael was nearly sleeping over his soup. The job he was on at the moment was a new scheme away out near the Campsies which meant a hell of a lot of travelling to and from work. Then there was all the pushing and pulling at Big Martha's wheelchair after work. It was knocking the shit out of him. He and Martha had been out nearly every night for the past week at Co-op Guild meetings, pensioners' meetings, club meetings and Tenants' Association meetings. They had become leading lights in the Tenants' Association, had fought and were still fighting the good fight and getting quite a few much-needed improvements in the area.

But he wasn't getting any younger. Every time he sat down at home now, he found himself nodding off.

Caroline said, 'I'm right sorry about this, Michael.'

'Eh?'

'The new baby.'

'What new baby?'

'See him,' said Martha, 'he's getting as stupid as his buck-toothed brother.'

'Oh, be quiet, Mammy. I don't know how Michael puts up with you.'

The twins and Maureen began chanting, 'Please may we leave the table?'

They'd had their soup in the middle of the day and now had just enjoyed a plate of stovies (potatoes and onions cooked in butter) each.

'Yes, off you go. But don't stay out long. Remember you've homework to do.'

Caroline watched lovingly as the three children skipped away. She was proud of their good manners. Theresa's children were a disgrace. Wee Bobby's table manners were non-existent. There was no excuse for him behaving like a pig, except of course that his daddy behaved exactly the same. Theresa just sat there among all the mess of the house not doing a thing or saying a word about it.

'What new baby?' Michael repeated.

'I was going to tell you, dear. I'm expecting another happy event.'

Michael nearly said, 'Oh God!' but stopped himself in time.

Caroline said, 'Aren't you glad?'

'If you're happy, hen, I'm happy.'

This was true. Only another wean meant another mouth to feed and yet more work. He was beginning to feel over-whelmed. He was beginning to wonder how much longer he could cope.

Apart from everything else, money was tight. They couldn't afford another wean. The house looked faded and shabby and it was far too cramped since they'd had to move the twins and wee Maureen out of their bedroom and into the bigger one he and Caroline used to share. The dampness in the smaller room was a dangerous disgrace. He was still fighting for something to be done to treat all the houses in the building to rid them of the ugly fungi and the stench from it that clung to bed and clothes and hair and skin. You always knew somebody who lived in a damp house. You could smell them a mile off. He could smell it off himself and no amount of bathing and changing of clothes could get rid of it.

He and Caroline now had to make do with the bed settee in the living-room. There was some dampness in Martha's room and they'd moved her bed as far as they could from the affected wall.

Where they'd put a new wean he hadn't a clue. He was amazed that Caroline didn't look the least bit worried. 'A happy event', she'd called it.

With an effort he finished his soup, then the plate of stovies that Caroline placed before him. His fatigue, plus the comforting heat of the rich hot broth and filling potatoes, acted like a drug. Every part of him weighed a ton, dragged him down.

'Have you seen Bernard lately?' Caroline asked in a light, bright voice. Usually she either never mentioned Bernard, or spoke of him in a sarcastic or detrimental tone.

'Curiosity killed the cat,' he replied in as light and jocular a tone as he could manage.

'What's that supposed to mean?' Martha said.

Michael sighed.

'It means that you're both still curious about Bernard's socalled fancy woman. And I've told you before, the chances are it's perfectly innocent.'

'Huh! Bernard innocent?' Caroline said, reverting to her more normal 'Bernard' tone.

'He sometimes visits Theresa.'

'So she told me,' Caroline said. 'I'd love to know what he's up to.'

'If you ask me he'll be far too busy with his job to be up to anything. Anyway, Caroline, what on earth would he want another woman for? He's got a lovely wife, and a good home. What more could any man want?'

Caroline stopped *en route* to the kitchen with a pile of dirty plates. She leaned over and gave him a kiss.

'Not every man is as decent as you, Michael O'Maley. I'm a lucky woman and I know it.'

It always amazed Michael how Caroline continued to love and admire him. Through thick and thin, even during the worst of his drinking, her attitude towards him never changed, never wavered. He loved her with all his heart and soul and it was for her, and her alone, that he put up with big Martha.

'You're a funny pair, you and Bernard,' Martha said.

'How's that, Ma?'

'You're supposed to be twins and you're as different as chalk and cheese.'

'Thank God!' Caroline called from the kitchen.

'He's been good to Theresa.'

Caroline came back to clear the rest of the table.

'Don't be daft, Michael. He only sees her about two or three times a year. He can't see his own wife much more than that, judging by the times he's away from home. Theresa was saying he's away in Brazil just now.'

'A great life, eh?' Michael sighed.

'What? For him or his wife?'

'I could be wrong, though,' Michael said. 'It's not as if he just goes for a rest and a bit of sunbathing.'

'Oh, I expect he'll manage that as well. He looked pretty fit to me, the last I saw of him.'

'Aye,' Michael said. 'That's true. I wish I felt as good as he looks.'

Immediately he regretted his words. Caroline and, surprisingly enough, Martha, looked anxious.

'Are you all right, Michael?' Caroline asked. 'There's nothing wrong, is there?'

'No, no,' he reassured her. 'It was only a joke. I'm as fit as a fiddle.'

'Tough as ugly old boots, him,' Martha said.

'Aye, like you, ould yin,' Michael said.

'I hope you're remembering,' Martha said, 'that it's the special meeting of the Tenants' Association tonight?'

Oh God, he thought. No matter how good the cause, he was in no mood to fight it tonight. He felt knackered. He could have slithered off his chair on to the floor. Given up the ghost.

'About this dampness, we'll have to keep on at the Corporation or it's going to be the death of all of us. This special meeting's supposed to . . .'

'Aye, aye, Ma. I know.'

'Well then, don't just sit there like an accident looking for somewhere to happen.'

'One of these days,' he said, dragging himself up, 'you're

228

going to have an accident. That wheelchair of yours is going to shoot under a bus.'

'That'll be the day.'

'Aye,' Michael sighed. 'That'll be the day!'

Chapter Thirty-Five

Robert didn't know whether Andrina was having an affair or not. Nor did he care. Even her innocent protestations and her righteous anger cut no ice with him any more. At first, of course, he had been furious at the mere idea of her two-timing him. He wanted to know for certain if there *was* another man. And if so, who was he? But then what? A punch-up? A lethal karate chop? And then what?

He couldn't be bothered. If it meant getting a divorce and marrying Laura, he'd be bothered all right. He'd move heaven and earth to get a divorce. But as things were with Laura – what was the use?

He'd discussed it with Laura all the same. He'd phoned her up and pleaded with her to meet him on one of the days someone came in to look after Derek. He needed to talk, he said. They both drove their own cars out to the little hotel in which they'd met some time previously.

Over cups of coffee, he said, 'You know I've never really talked about Andrina before. I've always had a sense of loyalty to her because – despite no longer being in love with her – she is still my wife.'

Laura cupped her palms around her coffee cup and said nothing.

'But now,' he went on, 'I don't care about that any more. I see now she's not even the person I always thought she was. She's no innocent, for a start. I don't know for certain, because she denied it, but I think she's been having an affair. I suddenly feel overwhelmed by lies. I think the sly little cow's been lying to me for years.'

'What are you going to do?'

'That's what I wanted to talk to you about. I could go for a divorce. I suppose I could put a detective on her and catch her out if she's up to something. Then divorce her for adultery.'

'Oh dear,' Laura murmured worriedly. 'A scandal like that

would kill her mother. Poor Sophie has had so much to contend with already. And she's not been keeping too well recently. She says she's all right but she's so jumpy and nervous.'

'Sophie's always been a bit like that but now that you mention it, I did think she looked far from happy the last time I saw her. Kind of absent-minded too – as if she wasn't altogether with us.'

'She used to annoy me at first – always interfering, I thought. But in fact, she's been a wonderful help to me, Robert. I honestly don't know how I would have survived without her making sure I got away from the house for a few hours every week. And she's so proud of Andrina. I wouldn't like to see the poor woman devastated by a scandal involving her daughter.'

Robert sighed.

'I know. But I can't allow my life to be dictated by consideration for my mother-in-law. If you could get a divorce from Derek, I wouldn't hesitate to go all out for a divorce from Andrina.'

'You know that's impossible, Robert.'

For a long minute, Robert leaned his elbows on the table and supported his lowered head in his hands.

Laura said, 'Oh, darling, I'm sorry. I just couldn't. And you know in your heart, you wouldn't want me to.'

He straightened up again.

'Sorry. You're right. I don't know why I brought the subject up. I'm under increasing stress at school. Maybe that's loosening my tongue.'

'Talk about that. That's something we can both understand. Perhaps even do something about.'

'Not really. It's no longer just the kids, you see. It's the extra responsibility of being head of department. But over and above the discipline of the department there's the worry about getting enough resources, and all the setting up of tests and exams. But I don't want to bore you with all this.'

'You're not boring me.'

He shook his head, remembering something.

'Poor old Freddie . . .'

'The young man you told me about, that you met at Bernard and Jane's house?'

'Yes, the great idealist. I've about as much bother with him as with any of the kids. He keeps losing his calm. He hasn't any control at all, either with his pupils or himself. You can hear him screaming at them a mile off and his class is always complete bedlam. If he goes on like this, he may as well pack it in right now and forget the rest of his two years' probation, and his parchment.'

'Oh dear . . .'

'In an amazingly short time he's come to absolutely hate the children. He makes no bones about it. I'll have to do something about him. Yet I hesitate to be the means of a young man losing his job.'

'Have you spoken to him?'

'Several times. It's hard to get more than a half-dozen words in with him. When I do, he doesn't listen. He's in a constant uncontrollable rage against what he calls, to put it mildly, "that bloody gang of stupid idiots and criminals". If he's not careful he'll be having a heart attack or a stroke.'

The mention of a stroke made them both think of Derek and they were silent for a minute or two.

'How is Derek?' Robert asked eventually.

'Very depressed. I think he's really accepted now that he'll never get any better. I'm so sorry for him, Robert. It's awful to see him so defeated. But what can I do?'

'You're doing the best you can. You can't do any more.'

'I've felt so guilty about these two ex-nurses coming in. It was bad enough when it used to be Mr Pritchett.'

'You had to get out for a break. You said yourself you wouldn't survive if you didn't. What's Pritchett doing these days?'

'I saw him the other day nursing one of his cats and another two weaving about his feet. I can't help feeling sorry for him as well. I suppose he's been terribly lonely since his mother died, even though by all accounts she was a bit of a tyrant. Coming to see Derek gave him a bit of company and made him feel needed. Now he's only got his cats.'

'That was another favour Sophie did you.'

'I know. But still . . .'

'Be honest – you never liked him.'

'I know. But he's a poor soul all the same.'

'I've told you before. You're too soft for your own good, Laura.'

For the first time Laura smiled.

'Look who's talking. The man who's sorry for Freddie, the hopelessly bad teacher.'

'*Touché.*'

There was another companionable silence as they sipped at their coffee.

'So it's back to square one,' Robert said at last.

'Us, do you mean?'

'What's the point of me trying to get a divorce if you can't get a divorce and we can't marry each other?'

'There's your daughter to consider too, Robert. You know how you feel about her.'

'In the circumstances, if adultery on Andrina's part was proved, I would apply for custody.'

Laura looked uncertain.

'Oh, I don't know about that. Don't the courts always give preference to the mother?'

'Not necessarily. It would be worth a try anyway. And I'd certainly try my damndest for Jennifer's sake.'

Laura hesitated, then said, 'Perhaps if we could just continue to be patient, Robert. Jennifer would be older and more able to weather the storm of the break-up. And . . . and . . . I know it's an awful thing to even think, far less say, but Derek won't live for ever. It would be a mercy for the poor man and I know he longs for death now . . .'

'Oh, Laura . . .'

'I know. I'm sorry. Poor Derek. It's dreadful of me but sometimes I even long for his death myself.' She bit her lips and struggled unsuccessfully to control the tears welling up and spilling down her face. Looking away she hastily searched in her pockets for a handkerchief. 'I'm so sorry.'

'Don't feel guilty. It's only natural for you to feel like that.'

'Sometimes I think how cruelly unfair life is. There's that awful murderer going about Glasgow. Innocent women who are leading useful lives in decent jobs, or being good wives and mothers have had their lives cut short for no reason and somebody like Derek lives on and on . . . Oh God, don't let me talk like this.'

'It's understandable, Laura. And I know you. You don't want to see Derek continue to suffer as he's doing. That's all.'

She sighed and mopped at her face.

'I suppose you're right. It's absolute agony to see the poor man suffer the way he's doing. When I think of how he used to be . . .'

'I know. He was a great guy.'

'I came to listen to you. And when it's come to the bit, I've done most of the talking.'

'Oh, I suppose I was just making an excuse to see you, Laura. I knew neither of us could think about a divorce just now. There's no point.'

Eventually they left the hotel lounge arm in arm. Then in a quiet corner of the foyer, they kissed and held one another in silent loving unison.

Alone in his car, Robert drove towards Bearsden feeling so bereft he could have wept. He had to take deep controlled breaths in order to regain a firm grip on himself. It was Saturday and Sophie had invited himself and Andrina and Jennifer to lunch. Needless to say, Andrina had earlier deposited Jennifer with her mother on some pretext or another. Of course – he couldn't help thinking – he needn't sneer about any pretext she might be making today. Hadn't he lied about where he was going himself?

To hell with it. To hell with her. Arriving at Sophie's he was taken aback at the way she answered his knock. There was an unusual rattling of locks and chains and then Sophie's white anxious face peered through the shadow of a crack.

'Oh, it's you, Robert.'

She unhooked another chain and opened the door but gave a furtive glance outside before allowing him in.

'Who did you think it was?' Robert laughed but quickly realised it wasn't a laughing matter. Sophie looked positively ill. He'd never seen such a sickly colour.

'I don't like being in the house by myself.'

'It never used to bother you.'

She nodded, and he asked, 'McPherson not in?'

'He said he'd to meet a client or somebody. He's always going off to do something or meet somebody nowadays. Even on a Saturday. But he said he'd be back in time for lunch.'

'Where's Jennifer?'

'At the church hall. Andrina dropped her off there this morning. There's gymnastics. Andrina says it's good for Jennifer. Maybe she's right.'

'I'd better go along and collect her.'

'No, don't go.' The urgency of Sophie's plea worried him. The poor woman was in a state of fear. 'Andrina's going to collect her. Andrina said she'd collect her.'

'All right, Sophie. All right,' he soothed. 'Now, I want you to sit down here with me and tell me what's wrong.'

'Wrong?'

'What is it you're so afraid of? Now don't deny it,' he added firmly, 'just tell me. Talk to me.'

'It's funny how things work out,' Sophie said.

'How do you mean?'

'You. I've never thought much of you.'

Robert couldn't help smiling.

'Well, that's an honest enough start.'

'You'll think I'm just a silly old woman. You'll just say it's my imagination. That's what McPherson and Andrina say.'

'I'm not McPherson. And I'm not Andrina. I've got a mind of my own.'

Sophie nodded.

'You're a good man.'

'Never mind about me. What is it that's making you feel so afraid?'

'For some time now I've felt as if I'm being watched and followed.' She began to tremble and Robert leaned over and gripped her hands firmly in his.

'Go on.'

'It's all right for a time. Then it starts again. I hear footsteps behind me. When I quicken mine, the other feet quicken too. Sometimes when I look round, I see a shadow. It's not just my imagination, Robert. Maybe sometimes, but not all the time. I *have* heard the footsteps. I *know* there have been times when somebody is there.'

'All right,' Robert said. 'Now, there's two things we can do. First of all, we can get your doctor to give you something to steady your nerves and calm you down. Secondly, we can report the matter to the police.'

'Oh no!' Sophie cried out in anguish. 'It was bad enough when my father and mother died. The police were here. I was ashamed and upset enough then. But to have them involved with me again. What would people think?'

'Never mind what people would think.' He nearly added, After all, there have been five unsolved murders in the city. That means there's a nutter on the loose. Not that he believed for a minute that a nutter or anybody else was stalking Sophie. But if he mentioned the murderer poor Sophie might have gone right over the top and had hysterics.

'I can't help it, Robert. I do mind. Oh, please, no police.'

Robert thought for a minute.

'I tell you what. Why don't you come back home with us tonight and stay at Monteith Row for a few days? Longer, if you like. You'd have company all the time and you could get something calming from our doctor. You've been very good to us and given us lots of hospitality. It's high time we did something for you.'

'Oh, Robert.' Sophie burst into tears. This really knocked him sideways. He'd always thought she was so uptight she was incapable of such emotion. She had never even wept after her parents' suicide. He remembered thinking how callous her behaviour had been. 'Oh, Robert,' she repeated, as he sat, stunned into silence. 'I'm so very grateful. God bless you and always keep you safe.'

'You mean you'll come?'

'Yes. Oh yes. Thank you.'

'Right. Get yourself organised then. Go and pack a bag. I'll explain to McPherson and Andrina. We'll take you back with us after lunch.'

Like a child anxious to please, she hastened away to do what he'd told her. But at the room door, she turned.

'You do believe me?' she asked.

'Yes. I believe you,' Robert reassured her. But, knowing what a nervous wreck Sophie had always been, in his heart of hearts he was far from sure.

Chapter Thirty-six

'He what?' Bernard's voice was incredulous.

Andrina shifted the phone to her other hand and sent a furtive look towards the kitchen door.

'I'm telling you, she's in the kitchen right now making Sunday lunch. Robert took us all to church this morning. He's out for his usual sprint through the park at the moment. He always brings back the Sunday papers. Today he's bringing back Mummy's favourite paper as well. I think he's gone off his head.'

'He's actually invited your old witch of a mother to *stay*?'

'I can hardly credit it myself. Just when everything was going so well. She was so busy being paranoiac about somebody watching her, she was giving me a bit of peace. It was wonderful. Now she's actually here. Morning, noon and night. Why on earth did he do it?'

There was silence at the other end of the line.

'Bernard, are you still there?'

'Yes.'

'What am I going to do?'

'Look at it this way. You've now got a built-in babysitter.'

'I thought of that but having her here all the time is a high price to pay. And it sounds as if Robert wants me to babysit her, can you believe? Her nerves are bad, he says. As if I didn't know she's been a raving neurotic for years. If I go out, according to him, I've to take her with me. It's ridiculous.'

Another silence.

'Bernard? Don't you think that's ridiculous?'

'Yes.'

'Well, then . . .'

'You can't do that.'

'I know. It means I'd never see you if I did. I see you little enough as it is with you disappearing so often.'

'Disappearing?'

'You know what I mean. What's wrong with you? You sound strange.'

'I'm trying to think.'

'I couldn't sleep last night trying to think. I don't remember ever actually hating Robert before. But I hate him now.'

'Hating Robert won't do either of us any good. How long is she supposed to be staying?'

'Just a few days. A week maybe.'

'Well.'

'Well what?'

'That's not so long. Have patience. I have.'

'She upsets me so. She always has.'

'I know. But to get back to the reason that Robert did this. Is she ill? He surely must think she is. Robert has known your mother for years. He's never done anything like this before. What did he say exactly?'

'He never says very much to me about anything and that suits me fine.'

'He must have said something.'

'I told you. Her nerves are bad. He told me to take her to our doctor. I'm supposed to take her to the surgery first thing tomorrow. What our doctor is supposed to do that her own doctor hasn't done already, I haven't a clue. She seems to have convinced Robert with this ridiculous story about her being stalked by some ghostly presence. It looks like Mummy isn't the only one who's gone mad.'

'No, Robert's probably right about her not being safe to be left on her own. She does need locking up, but in an asylum. I'd have a private word with the doctor, if I were you.'

Another silence hung between them until Andrina said,

'For her own good, you mean?'

'Yes.'

'Poor Mummy. I can't help thinking about what happened to her mother and father. They were obviously unhinged. Poor Mummy does need watching.'

'Yes.'

'I'll have a serious talk with the doctor.'

'You do that.'

'Meantime, I won't be able to see you. Unless I think of some way. If I do, I'll let you know.

'Relax. Be patient.'

'All right. I'll try. I love you.'

She hung up when she saw the kitchen door open.

'You've been a long time on the phone.'

'Just chatting to a friend, Mummy.'

'Somebody from the church?'

'What's Jennifer doing?' Sophie turned back into the kitchen and Andrina followed.

'She's been helping her nanna bake some biscuits for our tea. Lunch is all ready. I won't be a minute in cleaning the flour off the table and setting it.'

'I'll do that, Mummy.'

'No, just you sit down. I like to keep busy.'

Andrina secretly fumed with irritation.

'What time did Daddy say he was coming?'

'He'll be here in half an hour or so. I thought at first he wasn't going to come at all. He was so put out at the idea of me staying here like this.'

I'm not surprised, Andrina thought.

'Can you tell me a story, Mummy?' Jennifer asked.

The phrase reminded Andrina of how she used to ask Sophie the very same question when she was a child. That was after her mother was saved, of course. Andrina experienced a tinge of bitterness, thinking the times before her mother found religion. Terrible times that normally she shut from her mind.

'Mummy,' Jennifer repeated, 'would you tell me a story please?'

'Jennifer, you can read perfectly well yourself now.' Sophie tutted.

'There's no need to talk to the child like that. She likes to be read to. There's no harm in that.'

But by God, there was plenty of harm in what you did to me, Andrina thought. How dare you think you're entitled to tell me how I should treat a child. Any child.

That woman, Andrina thought, as she stared at the busy, bustling figure, that woman used to leave me alone without food, without even a drink of water, in a cold, dark room for God knows how long.

Andrina suddenly saw quite clearly that the overriding emotion her mother had always engendered in her was fear. Her mother didn't love her any more than she loved her mother. The only emotion that bound them together was fear. But knowing this did nothing to free her. She was a prisoner, snatching illusions of freedom, pleasure and love where and when she could.

For the first time, she could look at her mother and think 'I hate you'. For the first time she realised that she'd always hated her. She'd hated her every fearful moment as a young child. She'd hated her as an adolescent and the way she'd tormented her by her silences and her emotional withdrawals. She'd hated her for never recognising or accepting her for the woman she was, not a perfect clone of Sophie McPherson. Not the perfect person Sophie McPherson wanted her to be so that she could bathe in her daughter's glory.

But simply Andrina, a woman in her own right, a passionate woman, who knew how to love a man and relished being loved in return.

'Why are you staring at me like that?' Sophie asked.

'I was just thinking.'

'Thinking what?'

Questions. Questions. She hated the millions of questions there had been through the years.

'That's the door,' Andrina said. 'I'll get it.'

'Hello, Daddy.' She greeted her father. He was looking portly and prosperous in his black homburg hat, Crombie coat and leather gloves.

'I don't know what to make of this, do you?' he asked in the hall as he unbuttoned his coat and gave it and his hat and gloves to Andrina.

'Mummy coming to stay?'

'What else?'

'Robert says it's just for a few days to give her a rest.'

'Rest? You know your mother. She won't rest here any more than she'd rest at home. I'm always pleading with her to rest. I've tried everything to get her to relax. But it's just not in her nature.'

'Have you noticed that she's been worse recently? Much worse.'

'I still can't see what coming here's going to do for her.'

'I'm going to take her to our doctor tomorrow. Get him to give her a proper going over.'

'Thank you, Andrina. I admit she has been getting worse recently. She's a poor soul. I can only pray that something can be done.'

Andrina was praying too.

Chapter Thirty-Seven

The fact that John Stuart Mill's housekeeper had torn up and lit the fire with Carlyle's manuscript of *The History of the French Revolution* – two years of solid work – was of no comfort to Frank. This knowledge, acquired many years ago, had awakened in him an anguish that had not diminished with time. The fact that Carlyle immediately sat down and started to write the book again increased Frank's pity for the man. He knew exactly how Carlyle felt, and if he could have got his hands on that housekeeper he would have throttled her on Carlyle's behalf. He would definitely have committed murder. He would have believed absolutely that he was meeting out justice by wiping that woman off the face of the earth. Stupid, ignorant cow.

His play might not be important in literary or academic terms like *The History of the French Revolution*. But it was every bit as important to him personally. In a different way, his play could have an even higher value because it was about ordinary people, about their relationships, about their human dilemmas.

But what hurt most about losing it was the fact that it was part of him.

He moved the settee from the sitting-room into his writing room so that he could just fall on to it after the continuous hours of writing he would now need to do.

At first, after finding Bridie tearing at his precious pages, he'd bawled at her to get out before he killed her. He believed if she'd stayed he really would have strangled her. She left the room without a word. He'd locked the door, still shouting at her to get out. Get back to the bloody Garngad where she belonged. He never wanted to see her stupid, ignorant face again as long as he lived.

He'd locked the door to prevent her return, and collapsed over his paper-strewn desk weeping with rage and grief. It was hours before he felt capable of emerging. He went through the silent hall to the kitchen and made himself a cup of tea. The house was empty and, not knowing for certain if Bridie would return in the evening, he dragged the settee through to his writing room. He couldn't bear the thought of lying beside her in their double bed. It would have been making a mockery of love. There was no love between them any more. It was time he faced that fact. Time to stop clutching at straws. Time to stop deceiving himself.

In between gulps of tea, he tried to piece together the bits of paper like a jigsaw puzzle. It was no use. Apart from the last three or four pages, which she hadn't had time to get round to, Bridie had done the job of an efficient shredder. There was nothing else for it. Like Carlyle, he would just have to start all over again. He groaned as he picked up his pen and sat staring at a blank sheet of paper.

At least, he thought eventually, he now had a good ending. His mind immediately rejected the word 'good' and replaced it with 'dramatic'. He'd never been all that sure of the play's ending. He'd written and rewritten the last scene until he felt he had to stop even though it didn't sound as perfect or as satisfactory in dramatic terms as he'd like. Or as convincing in terms of character development.

But now he had a perfect last scene for the play in which Sol, in a jealous rage, tears Amy's new and most important fashion collection only hours before the fashion show. Frank could see Sol's eyes, wild with hate, and the silver flash of the knife glittering through the delicate rainbow colours of the clothes.

He saw Amy's heartbroken face. He heard her scream at Sol, 'Get out! You jealous, ignorant bastard. Get out before I kill you. I don't want to see you again, you stupid bastard, as long as I live!'

He wrote this scene and felt comforted by how well it worked. Then he forced himself back to the beginning again. That was where the pain was now. When Sol and Amy first met and fell in love and dreamed their dreams together. He wept as he wrote of the beginning of their love and how it gradually, tragically, went wrong.

He was well into the rewrite and had long since drawn the

curtains and switched on his desk light when he heard Bridie's key rasp in the front door. Then her feet, muffled by the hall carpet, crossed the hall. He was glad he was locked in his writing room surrounded by soft shadows, softly illuminated by the amber pool of light from the desk lamp. He was relaxed here, happy here. He belonged here. He was protected from the harshness and ugliness of reality. He could write about it realistically but he didn't want to live it. Not now. He knew how to put his play right. But not his life. He wished he could stay there for ever in the quiet dark peace of the room. He could hear, outside of this quiet, doors opening and shutting and the gush of the bathroom cistern. He went over to the window and pulled the curtain aside so that he could gaze down at the trees of the Crescent and at the Botanic Gardens beyond.

He could see the sparkle of the moon on the glass on the Victorian greenhouses. He and Bridie had explored their tropical interior and admired the thick jungle of ferns and orchids and giant palm trees. They had sat close together, arm in arm on one of the slatted wooden seats, until suddenly a wee mouse had run out from under the seat. Bridie had jumped up and agitated him away from the place. She'd refused to ever set foot in the greenhouses again. She had not been keen to visit them in the first place. As usual, he had been the one with the curiosity, the eagerness to see what things were like. She just tagged along. But less and less often, he realised now.

He allowed the curtains to drop shut. He was overtired and becoming uncertain. His anger had fizzled out and sadness was taking its place. He longed to be close to Bridie again, to hold her in his arms, be one with her. Yet the Bridie he had once known had gone. He sat at his desk again and tried to continue with his work but his head kept sinking down on to his arms. He fell asleep like that, hunched forward on his desk, and awoke at five in the morning, feeling as if his shoulders were fractured. It took him a minute or two before he could sit up and move his arms without stiffness and pain. He wondered if it was worth transferring to the sofa and settling to sleep there for a couple of hours, then decided against it. Instead, he quietly unlocked the door and went through to the bathroom to relieve his bladder and have a wash and shave. After that, a cup of strong tea cleared away the last dregs of sleep. He returned to his desk with another steaming cup and hunk of bread liberally spread with butter and orange marmalade.

He had completed nearly three hours' solid work when he heard the bedroom door open and Bridie go into the bathroom, then the kitchen. After a while she opened the writing room door and stood looking at him with hard, blank eyes.

'What do you want for breakfast?'

'I've had something, thanks. I was up early.'

'I'll make lunch early then – about 11.30.'

'All right. Thanks.'

She left, closing the door carefully behind her.

It was terrible being so stiff and formal as if they were strangers. He felt sick. It took him a long time to return to the play. His mind and his heart dragged so heavy inside him.

At 11.30 he went through to the kitchen carrying his dirty breakfast cup and plate. The kitchen table was set, and as soon as Bridie saw him she began dishing soup into bowls. Frank cut some slices of bread. In the middle of eating the soup, Bridie said, 'So you're going ahead with it then?'

His mind, paralysed with misery, didn't latch on to what she meant at first.

'What?'

'The play.'

'Of course. Why shouldn't I?'

He forced himself to keep spooning soup into his mouth.

'You know perfectly well why you shouldn't.'

He put down his spoon.

'No, Bridie, I don't. If I've told you the obvious once, I've told you dozens of times. But I'll repeat it yet again. Writing is my living. To make a living with writing means writing plays. Get this into your head once and for all. The nice little love poems you like me to write wouldn't keep you in tights.'

'You made a living in Goldmayers.'

'Oh God,' he groaned, 'what's the use?'

'You deny it now because you've forgotten but we *were* happy when you worked at Goldmayers.'

He said nothing. He lifted his plate and spoon and took it over to deposit it in the sink. Then he came back and sat down. Bridie dished some stew and potatoes. His appetite had gone but he speared a piece of meat with his fork and pushed it into his mouth.

'If it's money you're worried about, I could get my job back in Murphy's.'

'And we could go back to live in the Gorbals,' Frank said.

'Yes.' Bridie's voice quickened with eagerness.

Frank fixed her with a steady stare.

'That's obviously what you want to do, Bridie. Perhaps you should.'

'I meant together.'

'We stopped being together a long time ago. Now we don't even know one another. You certainly don't know me.'

'That's a stupid thing to say. We're man and wife. I've known you since you were a boy.'

'You maybe thought you knew me – like I thought I knew you. But we've both been mistaken. The woman who maliciously destroyed two years of my work isn't the person I thought I knew when we were boy and girl.'

'Don't you talk to me about being malicious or destructive.'

He looked away from the ugliness of her expression and made another attempt to eat.

'I'm not stupid,' she went on. 'I know what that play was about.'

'It was about Sol and Amy . . .'

'Was it fuck,' Bridie sneered. She suddenly reminded him of her father in one of his worst alcoholic excesses.

'Don't swear,' he said, 'it doesn't suit you.'

'It doesn't suit you,' she mimicked. He had never seen, far less experienced, such hatred. He put down his fork.

'Look, Bridie, this can't go on. There's no point. I think we should call it a day.'

'Oh really?' she said. 'Well, I've a surprise for you. I'm not Doris to be cast aside when an O'Maley wants to be rid of her. You'll never get a divorce from me.'

Chapter Thirty-Eight

Sophie was glad of the long summer's nights. She began to feel safer. The tranquillisers that Andrina's doctor prescribed helped enormously, although she'd been upset to learn that Andrina had tried to persuade the doctor to have her examined by a psychiatrist in Hawkhead Asylum. Oh, it was called 'Hospital' now but it was still an asylum. McPherson tried to get her to have the visit arranged through her own doctor. Apparently Andrina's doctor had said that was the right way to do it as she was only planning to be at Monteith Row for a few days.

After a week at Andrina's and religiously taking the tranquillisers, she didn't mind returning home. That was the first she'd heard about the psychiatrist idea – after she'd arrived home. It had shaken her faith in Andrina again. The girl had sneaked behind her back and tried to make out she was mad. McPherson had said, 'No, no, it wasn't like that.' But of course it was. He had known. He had been all for it. She felt isolated, vulnerable, with no one to turn to. Yet she felt calmer than she had been before. She marvelled at the power of modern drugs. She'd even managed to confide in Mrs Pemberton and the other ladies over afternoon tea – not about what Andrina and McPherson had tried to do but about being watched and followed.

The ladies had been thrilled. Mrs Jones claimed (at some length) to have had the very same experience. But everyone took that with a pinch of salt. Mrs Jones was the leading light in the drama society and never missed the opportunity of playing a dramatic part. But Mrs McPherson – a different type altogether – was definitely to be believed.

'Just think,' Mrs Jones still clung to the limelight, 'it could have been the Glasgow murderer, Mrs McPherson. Watching and following us both.'

Mrs Pemberston cut in with a gentle 'Remember, this is Bearsden, dear.'

Mrs Dinwoodie, the minister's wife, said, 'Wickedness knows no boundaries. Mrs McPherson, you poor soul! When the dark nights come in again you must be careful never to walk anywhere alone.'

'Nor must I,' Mrs Jones said. 'Have you noticed it has been ladies like us – women in the prime of thier lives – who have been his victims? Never young girls.'

'Such a pity if we're not going to be able to walk at night,' Mrs Hawthorn, the banker's wife, said. 'I often prefer a walk on a crisp winter evening to taking the car.'

Sophie agreed.

'Yes, I often say to my husband, "Don't bother taking me or picking me up, I'll enjoy the walk." But I'll probably think twice about it after this. Such a pity though, as you say.'

'Bearsden is so beautiful and peaceful in the evening, I always think,' Mrs Pemberton said. Then she added firmly, 'And one mustn't get too carried away. I'm sure nothing could possibly happen in main roads or well-lighted streets. Indeed I still find it hard to believe that this dreadful murderer person would dare to come to Bearsden.'

'But there *was* somebody,' Sophie said. 'I *know* there was.'

'I'm not doubting you for a moment, dear, but surely there are other possibilities. It could for instance be somebody who had got some sort of grudge against you and who's perhaps just trying to frighten you.'

Sophie had never thought of that.

'Anyway,' Mrs Pemberton said, 'there hasn't been another murder for ages.'

'But why should such a man,' Mrs Jones said darkly, 'stop at five victims? He'll be biding his time until the winter nights creep in again. You mark my words!'

All the ladies shivered. But by the time they had enjoyed another cup of Lapsang Souchong and sampled Mrs Pemberton's home-made French cakes and coconut fingers, they, including Sophie, felt comforted. They even managed to change the subject.

Afterwards, however, the thought did return to Sophie's mind that someone might bear a grudge against her. That seemed to tie in with the phone calls. She'd forgotten to mention the phone calls to the ladies. But still she felt amazingly calm. She treasured the tranquillisers like pieces of gold. She'd had tranquillisers before from her own doctor but they had not worked magic like this.

'You certainly seem much better,' McPherson conceded.

'Oh? Do I?' She raised a cool brow. She talked to him like a polite stranger now. Well or unwell, she would never trust him again as long as she lived. Not trust the way she had before the O'Maley incident. Now she had also to protect herself against any recurrence of his collusion with their daughter to put her in an asylum. She had to be careful to *appear* well, whether she felt it or not.

'But I still think,' he said, 'it wouldn't have done any harm to have had a talk with that man at Hawkhead. Robert said it wouldn't do any harm.'

Even Robert. She couldn't even trust Robert.

'The psychiatrist, you mean?'

'He's a doctor who specialises – '

'In the mentally ill.'

'No, not necessarily, Sophie. As far as I understand . . .'

'Which isn't very far. Not nearly far enough. Now would you prefer apple or rhubarb tart for pudding tonight?'

He sighed.

'Apple, I suppose.'

'Then apple it shall be.'

She avoided going out with him when she could now, preferring her ladies' clubs and meetings.

Some of these evening events were held in the church hall which could be reached by going along Drymen Road. Unfortunately, many others were held in Kilmardinny House. This meant either a walk along quiet tree-shaded roads or getting a lift from McPherson. In their new cool relationship, Sophie resented being obliged to or dependent on McPherson for anything. But it was not just resentment she felt towards him. It was a determination to tighten her armour of self-defence, not to betray any vulnerability or need. She didn't dare be dependent on him for anything.

It was the same with Andrina. For a short time when her nerves had been at their worst she had trusted Andrina to help her. She had, in her need and gratitude for any crumbs of help and understanding, come nearer to loving the girl than she'd ever done before.

But look what it had got her. She would never make that mistake again. Her first assessment of the girl had been the right one: she was exactly the same as Agnes Noble. Voluptuous, shameless, devious, sly, and shockingly, cruelly wicked.

Even now, in her sixties, Sophie could be felled by memories of how her mother (and her father) had betrayed her. She would be doing some normal job like dusting. Perhaps she'd have forgotten to switch on the wireless or the television and the house would be still and quiet. Then suddenly, out of the silence, would come the terrible, unendurable pain. Down through the years, she'd hear her anguished cry –

'Why did you do this to me?'

She'd be forced to sit down for a minute to nurse herself, rock herself back and forwards. Then she'd pounce on the wireless or the television, and fill the house and her mind with noise. Drown out memory.

She had trusted Duncan and Agnes Noble. Trusted them and loved them. Oh, but never again. Never, never again.

Occasionally she asked Mrs Pemberton for a lift if the Pembertons happened to be going to the same class in Kilmardinny House. But it was a worry; there had always to be some convoluted excuse in case Mrs Pemberton wondered why she couldn't get her own husband to chauffeur her. What if Mrs Pemberton got suspicious – began asking if there was something wrong between her and McPherson? One had to be so careful about gossip. Best to be discreet. Independent.

She had walked home alone from Kilmardinny several times during the summer months and had even begun to enjoy the experience again. Once the nights began to draw in, however, the walk had once more become an ordeal. But she'd managed it successfully. Indeed she'd felt secretly proud of her courage. Admittedly it had still been light. Well, not quite daylight, more twilight. The road and the loch had looked beautiful in their soft veil and the trees were still lush with leaves. She'd passed two or three other walkers, which had been comforting. The Glasgow murderer and the dramatic resolution of never walking at night again had obviously been forgotten or never even thought of by some. She had seen Mrs Hawthorn strolling along one evening and they'd chatted together for the rest of the way with the trees whispering gently all around them. There was never a mention of followers or watchers or any danger whatsoever. It became, in fact, almost as if it had all been a dream.

There had been a problem about the tranquillisers, though. When she'd gone to her own doctor to ask for more he'd given her a prescription for the ones she'd originally had from him.

She'd told him (perhaps somewhat tactlessly, she realised now, but it had been so urgently important to her) that they were no use – not nearly as good as the ones she'd had from the doctor in Glasgow. He'd been quite abrupt. He'd said the prescription the other doctor had given her were far too strong to take regularly over a long period. They had just been a short course for that temporary emergency. He knew what was best for her, he said, and jabbed the buzzer on his desk to summon his next patient.

Being without the good medicine frightened Sophie. Suddenly she found herself bereft of her crutch, her safety net, her comfort blanket.

She was on her own again. She struggled determinedly on, keeping herself busy, telling herself there were plenty of people worse off than herself. Poor Laura Cairns across in the bungalows, for instance. But she'd got Laura pretty well organised. There was nothing much more she could do for her. The two ex-nurses never missed a stint of duty and Laura was grateful for getting out of the house for a few hours twice a week. Nevertheless, she was a poor soul. There was such a sad, defeated look about her. And no wonder, having to return each time to such a wreck of a man and have to lift and lug him, and do such intimate tasks for him. Mrs Tunnicliff told her that sometimes Derek didn't ask for the toilet or didn't ask in time.

'Oh, the ghastly stinking mess!' Mrs Tunnicliff had said. 'It's not as if he was a baby. Nevertheless, I'm used to cleaning up grown men and women. Did it for years. It's poor Mrs Cairns I'm sorry for. She's got him all the rest of the time and she's such a delicate little thing.'

That reminded Sophie of something she could do. She'd go along with one of her bowls of soup. Very nourishing her soup was, and Laura had enjoyed it before. Probably Derek did too. She decided to pack a picnic basket that very night with the soup and an egg custard she had in the fridge.

She busied herself quite happily packing the basket, adding a few of her home-made fruit slices for good measure. No doubt Laura never got the chance to bake nowadays. Even if that poor woman had any spare time, she'd probably just flop down on to a chair or collapse into bed.

The bungalows were along at the quieter end of Drymen Road, at the opposite end from the shops. And they were set back from the road, not bang on the pavement (or near enough) like the terrace houses.

'Where are you off to tonight?' McPherson asked.

'Along to visit Laura Cairns.'

'Are you remembering that I'm going out?'

'Does it matter?'

'It would matter if you didn't take your key.'

'I've got my key.'

'That's all right then. I've some business to do and I might be late.'

'Business? At this time of night?'

'It's only eight o'clock.'

'You know what I mean. You could be seeing another woman, for all I know.' She knew it was a ridiculous idea. She'd just felt the need to be sarcastic.

He gave a genuine guffaw.

'Chance would be a fine thing!'

'I'm away.'

Once out the front door she happened to glance round to the left towards the shops and it was then, in the side street of Kirk Road, that she saw the car. It was parked across from her side window and facing towards the main road. It was dark, and powerful-looking and she knew it didn't belong to anyone in the Terrace. Anyway, everyone had garages at the back. In that first glance she had experienced momentary curiosity. But curiosity immediately turned to shock when she noticed the man sitting at the wheel.

Dark and powerful like the car, he stared back at her. When she'd last seen him with her husband, he'd shown a modicum of politeness by rising and giving a faint smile. There was no polite smile now. Only a steady stare of hatred.

Sophie longed to run back into the house but daren't allow McPherson to see her in a state of nervous collapse. By some miracle her legs began to move. Sweat poured down her face and body as she made her way, still clutching the basket, along Drymen Road.

She kept thinking, 'Oh God, oh God, please help me!'

Chapter Thirty-Nine

1972 was not the best of years for teachers, especially teachers in schools like Sinnieglen. At the beginning of September the school-leaving age had been raised to sixteen. Idealistically speaking, this might seem a good thing. But there were few idealists left in teaching, at least in schools like Sinnieglen. Poor Freddie Hancock had already, after only a few months in the place, thrown most of his high ideals (and hopes) out of the window.

In a better school, perhaps, the idea of giving pupils another year's education would be all to the good. In places like Kelvinside and Bearsden, parents could afford to keep their children not only for another year at school, but also for several years at college or university. Another year gave the pupils a better chance to be prepared for moving on to such temples of knowledge and excellence.

It was all part of a process of building a good career, acquiring qualifications, getting a better job. It was a worthwhile path for pupils with caring, optimistic, hopeful (and financially solvent) parents.

If, however, you came from Provan, Garngad, Riddrie or Blackhill, and your parents had no hope, it was a different story. If your father was unemployed, your mother had struggled to bring up nine or ten of you and had now thrown in the towel and escaped to the bingo or worse, what was there to be optimistic about?

As far as the teachers were concerned, children had always been unteachable on Fridays. They were too restless, and impatient to be shot of the place. The raising of the school leaving age meant a whole year of solid end-to-end Fridays. In fact, it was much worse. There was anger, resentment, downright revolt in the air.

Robert was beleaguered by teachers in his department in the last resort marching pupils into his office room and dumping them there for him to deal with. As if that wasn't enough, he suspected Freddie Hancock was developing, or had already developed, a drink problem. Not that he drank on duty but more and more often he was taking time off on one pretext or another. Old Hamish McKendrick, head of the languages department, was being driven demented by him, even being drawn back into the classroom.

An agreement with the powers that be in Education, and the unions, meant staff had to cover for the first three days of any absence. After that, a supply teacher would be sent out. Advance warning had to be given, however. It was never possible to do this with Freddie.

He'd be off on Monday, saying he was coming in on Tuesday. Then he'd be off on Tuesday saying he was coming in on Wednesday. On Wednesday he wouldn't turn up and it was by now urgent to send in a request for a supply teacher. But old McKendrick would be assured by every means except carrier pigeon that Freddie would be back on Thursday. Sometimes he did turn up on the Thursday. More and more often he didn't, and the rest of the languages department, which apart from Freddie consisted of Jeff Barclay and old McKendrick, both of whom had been valiantly taking Freddie's classes, were now up the creek without a paddle for the rest of the week.

At school, Freddie was fighting a losing battle to contain his stress. He would begin by speaking very quietly when giving a pupil a row, then slowly his voice would rise until it went over the top into near-hysteria.

Robert could hear him now, and see over the glass partition. Apparently, he had been inspecting the state of books the class had been allowed to take home. Allowing pupils to do this had always been a risky business because of the appalling state they were likely to be in when returned. Freddie had taken Effie McGill out into the corridor to speak to her in so-called privacy. Her book was dog-eared and dirty. The cat had slept on it. The dog had peed on it. The baby had torn pages out of it. It was an absolute disaster of a book.

Freddie showed it to Effie and said quietly, 'Would you mind telling me to which pupil I'm supposed to give this book next year?'

There was no answer to that. He didn't know the answer. No one knew the answer. So of course Effie's reaction was to shrug her shoulders.

'You impertinent girl,' Freddie said (slightly louder). 'Answer me. Which one!'

'How should I know,' Effie said in obvious desperation.

'Which one?' Freddie's voice grew louder still.

Robert thought he was going to go back into the class and get a class list so that Effie could point out who was to be the unfortunate recipient of the wretched book. Eventually, Robert went out to the corridor and said, 'Would you like me to have a word, Mr Hancock? Effie has been a pupil of mine for several years.' This was a slight exaggeration but Freddie was too grateful to be rescued to worry about accuracy.

In French, he said to Robert, 'You can have a fuck with the little toe-rag for all I care. As long as you get her out of my sight.'

'Come on, Effie,' Robert gestured to the girl. 'Into my class just now.'

Old McKendrick didn't know what to do about Freddie. He didn't want to rock the boat; he needed a smooth passage towards his retirement. As far as Jeff Barclay was concerned, he was a decent bloke who didn't want to blow the whistle on a colleague. So both men were working all their so-called spare time to cover for Freddie.

Finally they'd pleaded with Robert to visit Freddie at home and see what the situation was. Maybe he had a family problem that could be sorted out.

'Why me?' Robert had protested.

'Well, you know him personally. Outside work.'

'I only met him at a friend's house and that was ages ago.'

'Didn't you once say he was a relative of somebody you knew?'

'The cousin of a friend's wife.'

'Well then . . .'

He was about to argue further but he sympathised too much with their predicament. They had sacrificed enough time for Freddie within school hours. It was little enough for him to do to pay Freddie a visit.

'OK. I'll go and see him.'

So after work he made his way over to the West End where Freddie had a flat. It was up a tiled close in Roxburgh Street, a very respectable-looking place. Peering at all the name plates, Robert knocked at the door that said, in brass, F. HANCOCK. There was no reply. Robert knocked louder, then clattered the letter box. Freddie had been off work for two weeks – supposedly on this occasion with a bad dose of flu. From somewhere in the nether regions of the hall a slurred voice shouted,

'There's nobody in.'

'Freddie, it's me, Robert. Open the door. I'm not budging from here until you do. I'll batter at it non-stop for hours if I have to.'

'OK. OK.'

The door opened at last, and Freddie shuffled back into the house. Robert followed him into a large kitchen. The place was in a dreadful state. He'd obviously been drinking for a fortnight. The kitchen floor was littered with empty vodka bottles. The whole flat was a filthy mess. Freddie was unkempt, unshaven and unwashed. He was dehydrated and his eyes were suppurating.

'For God's sake, Freddie. Why didn't you ask for help? From Jane, from any of us?'

'OK. I'm asking for your help, Robert. I've got money. So if I give you some, will you go down to Byres Road and buy me a bottle of vodka?' He fumbled with a wallet. 'Better still, two bottles.'

Robert kicked aside some rubbish and went over to the sink to fill the kettle.

'The first thing I'm going to do is make you a cup of coffee.'

He put the kettle on the cooker. 'Meantime, you should drink a tumbler or two of water.'

'God forbid!'

'Does Jane know about this?'

'Haven't seen her for months. She's got enough problems of her own, I suspect.'

'She's family. She'd want to help you.'

'Anyway, I've got my pride.'

'Pride?' Robert scoffed. 'What kind of pride is it that allows you to do this to yourself? You need help.'

While Freddie was drinking the coffee Robert went through to the hall and phoned Pollokshields. It was Bernard who answered.

'Hello, Bernard.'

'Robert?'

'Is Jane there? It's about Freddie.'

'Something wrong? He's not dead, is he?'

'No, but if he goes on hitting the bottle like he's doing, he soon will be.'

'I see. Where is he?'

'At his flat. That's where I'm speaking from.'

'I'll drive Jane over there right now.'

'Will you tell her then?'

'Don't worry.'

'Thanks, Bernard.'

You could always depend on Bernard. Steady as a rock.

He waited until they arrived before he left for Monteith Row. It was getting late. Exhaustion deflated him. It had been a long day and he'd had nothing to eat except a sandwich at lunch time.

Suddenly he remembered that this was one of his karate club nights. He'd have to go back to Sinnieglen. He felt as if he was drowning in the hopeless dregs of humanity. They were relentlessly dragging him down.

Oh, a long, long day.

Chapter Forty

The dark nights had returned, and with them, Sophie's terror. She kept thinking, 'I might have known it was him. I might have known.'

Her instincts had warned her right from the start that he was dangerous. From the very first moment she had set eyes on him all those years ago she had known, and been afraid. And for all these years no one had listened to her. Who would listen now? Now it was a case of cry wolf. They had called her mad for less. But she had seen him with her own eyes. He was the one. Bernard O'Maley. He had been terrorising her all this time, watching, waiting, phoning. Trying to drive her into a madness of no return.

Then another, even more terrifying thought occurred to her. What if it wasn't what Mrs Pemberton said? What if it wasn't someone just trying to frighten her. What if Bernard O'Maley was more than just a patient tormentor with a special grudge against her.

What if Bernard O'Maley was the Glasgow murderer? Hadn't he always moved in the underworld, mixed with gangsters and criminals?

She collapsed inside. Her thoughts, her nerves, the very blood in her veins, scattered in panic. She was too distressed for tears. She wanted to blot everything out of her mind as she usually did, busying herself scrubbing, polishing, hoovering. This time, however, she didn't know where to start. She wandered about the house, bumping into things, knocking things over. She shrank away from the windows. She kept chastising herself, telling herself not to be ridiculous. Why should Bernard O'Maley go around killing strangers? There had been five victims. She must not allow herself to imagine things. She had not imagined him watching her but as far as anything worse was concerned . . . When the doorbell suddenly rang, she cried out in anguish. It rang again. Then a voice called through the letterbox,

'Coo-ee. It's only me.'

Trembling with relief, Sophie hastened to open the door. She knew Mrs Jones must have some urgent reason for this uninvited call. It wasn't the done thing simply to knock at someone's door.

'Mrs Jones. Do come in.'

'My dear, what's wrong?' Mrs Jones peered at Sophie once they'd reached the sitting-room. Sophie realised that sweat was trickling down her face. She felt weak.

'Please sit down, Mrs Jones. I was just going to have a cup of tea. Do join me. And forgive me for sweating like this. I've been dashing about doing far too much today.'

Mrs Jones smiled as she seated herself comfortably.

'You know what they say, Mrs McPherson. Horses sweat. Men perspire. Ladies glow.'

Sophie tried to return her smile as she mopped at her face with a handkerchief.

'Well, I'm certainly glowing.'

'Actually, why I called,' Mrs Jones's eyes widened dramatically, 'was to tell you that poor Mr Hawthorn has died.'

'The Hawthorns at the end of the Terrace?' Sophie's mind was still in chaos.

'Yes. Our dear friend's husband.'

'But I saw him only yesterday.'

'I know.' Mrs Jones's voice lowered as if she was afraid of being overheard. 'That's why I thought I'd better warn you right away. In case you phoned Mrs Hawthorn for some innocent reason or met her and made an unfortunate *faux pas*. Asked if Mr Hawthorn was coming to the whist drive tonight, something like that.'

'He looked so well.'

'Yes, it just goes to prove that death can strike any of us at any unexpected moment.'

Sophie began to sweat again.

'What on earth happened?'

'His heart. He dropped in the bank. Right there in front of a customer. Can you imagine the shock?'

'I spoke to him. He said the long dark nights were drawing in.' (Mr Hawthorn had never been a cheerful man.)

'Little did he know,' Mrs Jones was obviously enjoying the drama of the occasion, 'that his nights were numbered.'

'My husband will be shocked. They were good friends.'

'I know.'

'It makes you wonder who'll be next.'

Sophie's eyes flew wide.

'What do you mean?'

'Well, none of us are getting any younger. Especially the men. Did you know that most married men die before their wives? I read that somewhere. But you've only to look around. There's widows everywhere. Just think of the number of widows in our church alone. Mr Hawthorn was overweight. That's always a bad sign. You'd better keep an eye on Mr McPherson. He tends to be rather portly, doesn't he? A fine figure of a man, of course. But then, so was Mr Hawthorn.'

'I'll go and fetch the tea.'

'Oh, don't bother on my account, my dear. I've still to tell Mrs Pemberton the sad news. This was her afternoon at the sewing bee but she should be back by now.'

'Are you sure?'

Mrs Jones rose.

'I didn't phone anyone in the Terrace. I thought it kinder to call personally. Soften the blow. He was such a good friend and adviser to us all.'

'Yes, he was.'

Sophie followed Mrs Jones to the door.

'Who would have thought,' Mrs Jones looked quite carried away by her own moving performance, 'the grim reaper would scythe down someone like Mr Hawthorn. He was in his prime. And playing such a wonderful part in the community. But, as I said . . .' she gave Sophie a last, lingering, meaningful look, 'he was very overweight.'

Turning back into the house, Sophie felt quite disorientated. The shock of learning about the unexpected death of a neighbour, mixed with her previous terrors, removed all logical thought. She made the tea automatically, her mind on hold.

She took two tranquillisers with the steaming brew, and gradually began to feel a bit better. She was only supposed to take one but one had no longer any effect. Her worry now was what would happen when the doctor queried them finishing quicker than they were supposed to. What if he refused to supply her with any more? They were absolutely essential. She would beg, weep, go through any humiliation to get them.

Although, when it came to it, she couldn't weep. She found herself fixing the doctor with a desperate dagger of a stare and demanding another prescription. He refused. She insisted. She needed them, she told him. She couldn't live without them. She depended on them.

That was the problem, he explained. She had been taking them for too long and had become addicted. She needed help of another sort. She was distracted. He too wanted her to go to Hawkhead.

'It's just another outpatients clinic,' he assured her but she didn't believe him. 'It's just to have a talk with one of the specialists there.' Why didn't he just say psychiatrist? 'You've obviously an underlying problem that's causing you to be overstressed.' Why didn't he just say mad? She knew that's what he was thinking.

She had never felt so alone, so betrayed, so trapped, so much in danger. There was not one soul in the world she could trust. She realised now, there never had been.

By some miracle of endurance, she continued with her normal life. If it could still be called normal. Each day, each meeting, each social event, each dutiful call, was preceded and overshadowed by anxieties about whether she would have someone, anyone, to walk the roads with or to get a lift with. McPherson was out so often on his own in the evenings now. But her pride prevented her from asking for the safety of company. Only occasionally, and with studied casualness, did she enquire if a neighbour or friend happened to be going in her direction, when she was expected to attend her usual busy round of meetings, clubs, social functions and mercy visits to the sick and needy among the church members. The need was rarely a financial one (or at least not a financial one that was admitted to), but perhaps one caused by sickness or disability; perhaps a helping hand was required with shopping or filling in forms of collecting and delivering prescriptions. Or more long-term practical help was needed, as in the case of Laura Cairns.

She hadn't been along to check on Laura Cairns since the terrible night when she'd seen Bernard O'Maley watching her. Now she felt obliged to make another visit and was glad of something with which to occupy her time. It was still light when she hurried along the road, and she comforted herself by telling herself that she wouldn't be long. Anyway, as Mrs Pemberton said, what could possibly happen in main, well-lit roads? And that's what Drymen Road was.

It took her a great deal longer than the usual five minutes or so to reach the Cairns bungalow: several people stopped her to discuss in shocked tones the tragic death of Mr Hawthorn. She almost turned back because already daylight was softening into dusk. The street lights flickered and burnished the golden carpet of autumn leaves. They rustled and crackled under Sophie's hurrying feet.

She kept darting glances behind her and started nervously every time she saw a car approach. But no sinister dark car appeared to be following her.

Just as she reached Laura's gate, she saw Mr Pritchett in Laura's front patch of garden. The garden was unattended and had a wild, neglected look with ragged, overgrown bushes and knee-length grass. As Mrs Pemberton's friend had complained, 'I can sympathise with the poor woman's predicament. I know she won't have time to keep the garden decent but surely she could employ a gardener for a few hours a week. It's really lowering the whole tone of the place. It's bad enough with that Pritchett man and all his cats. But at least he cuts his grass.'

'What are you doing here?' Sophie snapped at Mr Pritchett. She hadn't meant to sound harsh but her nerves were in such a state. In truth, the man looked in a bit of a state himself and for the first time, she felt a stab of pity for him.

'I've lost Fluffy. I thought he might have wandered in here.'

He was wearing a baggy old cardigan, drooping at the elbows and frayed at the sleeves. His shirt looked like crumpled tissue paper and his black tie was stained. His faded, wispy hair needed cut, his skin was a sickly putty colour, and a sandy stubble was clearly visible on the lower part of his face. It occurred to Sophie that he might be the next candidate for a heart attack.

'Well, you know how cats upset Mr Cairns, so you'd better be careful in future. There it is!' She pointed at a big grey Persian who'd suddenly emerged from the undergrowth.

Mr Pritchett grabbed the cat up into his arms. She noticed that he was trembling.

'Insteads of all these animals, what you need is a home help, or somebody to clean that house of yours,' she told him 'Those windows are a disgrace.'

Suddenly, breathlessly, he took to his heels and scuttled away. She watched him disappear into his bungalow.

What a peculiar man, she thought. Then she stabbed at Laura's doorbell. She was not so bound by convention and what was or was not 'the done thing' as some of her Bearsden friends. Her tenement upbringing always won the day when it came to someone in need.

'Oh, Sophie. Come in!'

Laura looked genuinely pleased to see her. It did Sophie's heart good the way the younger woman's eyes lit up with surprise and pleasure. 'I haven't seen you around for a wee while.' Laura was long past caring about 'the done thing'.

'You need stronger light bulbs in here,' Sophie remarked as she followed Laura through the shadowy hall.

'Do you mind just coming into the kitchen? Derek's watching television in the sitting-room.'

'Fine. Fine. How is Derek?' Sophie accepted a seat at the kitchen table. Laura carefully closed the door.

'He just sits there as if he's made of wood. I think he's terribly depressed but what can I do? The doctor says it's a miracle he's still alive.'

'It would have been a mercy if that last stroke had taken him away.'

'Oh, Sophie!'

'For him, as well as for you. It's no life for either of you.'

'A cup of tea? Or would you rather have coffee?'

'Tea will do fine. Here, I've brought you one of my fruit cakes. It should last you and your man all week.'

'You're very kind. What with one thing and another, I shudder to think what I would have done without you these past months. I don't believe I would have survived.'

'Talk about shuddering, I spoke to that Pritchett man as I was coming in. Him and his awful cats. One of them had come into your garden.'

'I've to watch the doors and windows all the time. Derek gets into such a state if one of them manages to slip in. They jump up on him, and he feels so helpless.'

'I sent him packing. Well, in actual fact, all I said was that he needed somebody to clean his house and he scuttled off as if I'd said I was going to kill the cat.'

Laura laughed.

'Maybe he was afraid you'd fix him up with a couple of buxom ex-nurses. Or even go in and sort him out yourself.'

'Maybe that's not such a bad idea. But what on earth will the place be like inside? I wonder if he has cat litter for those animals. Or does he just let them roam about?'

'I mostly see them sitting on his windowledges staring out. God knows how many he's got. But now that I come to think of it – any time I've had to go to his door, the smell emanating from inside is pretty awful. I wouldn't venture in there if I were you.'

'We'll see. We'll see,' Sophie said. 'But I must confess, I'm a bit like Derek in that respect. I don't feel easy around cats.'

Laura settled opposite Sophie at the kitchen table. 'What's been going on in the village? Tell me all the news.'

'Mr Hawthorn, the bank manager dropped dead!'

'No!' Laura gasped.

'Right in front of a customer in the bank.'

'How awful!'

'Yes, but as I always say,' Sophie went on. 'It's a quick way to go and he wouldn't have known anything about it. It's poor Mrs Hawthorn I'm sorry for.'

She enjoyed the tea and the gossip with Laura and, for a time at least, all thoughts of murder and Bernard O'Maley's dark watchful eyes, were banished from her mind.

Chapter Forty-One

'A what?' Theresa said.

'A greyhound.'

'You've bought a greyhound?'

'That's what I said. I'm going to collect it now. It's got a great pedigree, this one.'

'More than what you've got.'

Tony laughed. He never took offence unless he was drunk and that just happened every Saturday night. He'd never been an alcoholic like his brother, Michael. As Tony always said, 'I can take it or leave it.' Theresa wished he would leave it. He could be very nasty on Saturday nights.

'Why?' Theresa said helplessly. 'Have I not got enough to see to with this house and you and four weans?' (The last pregnancy had produced premature twins). 'Why add a greyhound to my problems?'

'I'll look after it. I'll take it for walks. And I'll feed it. All you need to do is buy in its food. You having a pet made me think of having one. Remember wee Erchie?' Tony added with his usual lack of sensitivity.

She'd never, as long as she lived, forgive him for gassing her budgie.

'This'll be even better than an ordinary pet. It'll make us money. But of course I can't just feed it scraps from Herraty's. It needs a special diet. It's a racing dog and has to be kept thin and full of beans. Well, not real beans, if you know what I mean.' He guffawed at his own joke. 'Full of energy. He's just to have things like white of eggs and chicken jelly – especially before a race. We could make our fortune, hen.' He rubbed his hands at the thought. 'I've seen him run. He's like a flash of lightning. A real winner, so he is.'

'Whites of eggs and chicken jelly?' Theresa echoed in disbelief.

'Oh aye.' Tony turned very earnest. 'He couldn't run on a

full stomach, hen. No, it's got to be nourishing but without any bulk. The man told me.'

'What man?'

'The one that sold me it. He's emigrating and couldn't take the dog with him. A real winner it is. I've seen it streaking round that course. You get plenty of eggs and chicken in, and I'll away and collect Light of my Life.'

'Eh?'

'That's his name. Light of my Life.'

Theresa hadn't the energy to stamp and weep and shout and batter Tony's skull in. She just slumped in a shapeless heap in her chair with children wrecking the room around her and seethed quietly.

How dare he say scraps weren't good enough for the dog when scraps from Herraty had to be good enough for her and the weans? How dare he bring a dog into the house and feed it with whites of eggs and chicken jelly when he'd gassed a poor wee budgie who had been perfectly content with a few pecks of dried seed?

The dog arrived. It was honey coloured, narrow-faced and long-legged. Theresa glared at it resentfully. It went sniffing and padding about the house not caring the slightest what she thought of it. It was obvious that as far as the dog was concerned, Tony was the boss, the one who fed and took it out and about. It ignored everybody else, including the children.

It turned out that whites of eggs and chicken certainly wasn't the only light nourishment it got. It was costing her a fortune. Admittedly it had already won several races, but Tony had drunk the winnings or spent it on other personal pleasures. Neither she nor the children enjoyed any benefit whatsoever.

To make matters worse, Tony got bored with having to take Light of my Life out for walks, and she was given the job. During the day she'd have to struggle with hanging on to a pramful of weans and the dog's leash, while it tried to run a race down Acrehill Road. It paid absolutely no attention to her screams of 'Stop' or 'Heel' or 'I'll murder you, you stupid bastard!'

Even last thing at night, she'd be ordered or wheedled – 'I've been slaving all day in that butcher's shop, hen. I'm knackered' – to go out with the thoroughly detested animal. At least, she detested it. Tony was reaping and enjoying the rewards of several wins and often said, 'That dog really is the Light of my Life.' Tony was leading the life of Riley. He wouldn't have cared if the Glasgow murderer had got her one dark night, as long as the dog returned safe and sound.

Next he wriggled out of feeding it. Either he wouldn't be in to do the job or he'd lie back with his feet up and say, 'Just you give it its wee bit nourishment before you take it out, hen. It won't take you a minute. I'm watching the news.'

She'd 'wee bit nourishment' him. The bloomin' dog cost more to feed than her and the weans.

'Right,' she told the animal before its next race, 'see you, I'm going to put a spoke in your wheel.'

She fed it with a big bowl of bread (a whole loaf actually) liberally soaked with Bovril. Light of my Life gulped down every crumb, licked its lips and looked up at her with new respect and interest.

It lost the race that night. Tony was furious. He kicked it up the backside as soon as he came in the door. The same thing happened at the next race after Light of my Life had enjoyed a large suet pudding.

'See that bloody dog,' Tony shouted. 'If it doesn't win tonight, it's had it.'

She fed it on a whole pot of potatoes with a tasty Bovril gravy. Then spotted dick for afters. She'd never seen man or beast relish anything so much.

It not only lost the race that night. It came in last. So Tony told her. He came home, disgusted, drunk and minus the dog. He never told her if Light of my Life had been snuffed out or if it had just been sold to someone else. She never asked.

The relief of not having to cope with the extra work of the dog was intense. She was getting less and less able to cope with anything. Then she found she was pregnant again. Had she not believed it was a mortal sin to have an abortion, she would have had one. She prayed for a miscarriage, then prayed for forgiveness for the first prayer.

She drank tumblerfuls of gin and deceived herself into

thinking she was just 'enjoying a wee refreshment'. Or just trying to buck herself up. Another set of twins would finish her and twins didn't just run in the O'Maley family, they galloped. Then one night she took ill. Pain tore across her abdomen, making her moan and groan and eventually cry out for help.

Tony was watching *Dixon of Dock Green* on the telly. 'Aye, just a minute, hen.' His eyes remained glued to the screen.

Doubled up on the living-room settee, she felt something begin to soak between her legs. She struggled up, hanging on to the table and chairs, anything for support. She had to get to the bathroom. Then she saw a rivulet of blood flowing down her leg.

'Tony, for God's sake, phone for the doctor.'

'Aye, in a minute, hen.'

In the bathroom, in a nightmare struggle, she managed to strip off her pants and examine herself. She hunched on the lavatory pan in mental as well as physical agony. She had caused this. By her own wickedness. Now God was punishing her with pain far worse than in normal childbirth.

She tried to clean herself but the blood kept coming. Not knowing what else to do, and with a towel punched against herself, she crept along the cold lobby, feet scuffling on the linoleum. In the bedroom she collapsed into the bed and hid herself under the blankets. She didn't feel so faint when she was lying down.

After a while, Tony appeared.

'How about a cup of tea before I pop out to the pub, hen?'

He would expect her to make it.

'Go and phone the doctor,' she managed. 'I'm bleeding. If you don't get the doctor, I'll die along with the wean.'

He stood staring at her, his mouth hanging open, buck teeth showing in a stupid half-smile. He wasn't used to getting his Saturday routine interrupted.

'Please, Tony.'

'How'll I phone? There's never a phone working within miles of here.' He suddenly brightened. 'There's one in the pub though. I could phone from there.'

She managed to pull the blankets aside and show him the

bloody mess she was in. She nearly said to go and knock on a neighbour's door. Fetch somebody, anybody, to help me. But he was stupid enough to knock on the door of the old winos. She just closed her eyes and prayed for the doctor.

'Christ!' Tony backed away from the bed and then ran from the house.

Let him find a phone, she kept thinking. Please let there be one phone that's not vandalised.

She didn't know if she'd fainted or what, but the next time she opened her eyes there was the doctor standing just a few yards from the bed. He looked very posh, dressed in an evening suit, black bow-tie and white silk scarf. She couldn't imagine anyone looking more out of place in her shabby, untidy box of a bedroom. She didn't blame him for not coming nearer. He could have ruined his lovely suit. But even from where he stood, she could smell the whisky. He'd obviously been called away from some important do. She felt she ought to apologise but hadn't the strength.

'You'll have to go to hospital,' he said. 'I'll arrange for an ambulance.'

Then his voice faded away with the vision of him. There had been something in his voice that made her feel sad. A class distance, a disapproval, a disgust. Maybe he was only annoyed at being dragged from his important dinner, or whatever it was, to a dump like Blackhill. Maybe in her distressed state she'd imagined his lack of common humanity. If only, she thought as she drifted away again, somebody had held her hand.

She didn't hear the wail of the ambulance, or see the huddle of people on the windswept pavement outside watching her being carried into the ambulance on a stretcher.

She was reported dead on arrival at the hospital.

Tony phoned all his brothers and asked,

'What am I to do with the weans?'

At Botanic Crescent, it was Bridie who answered the phone.

'Bring them over here,' she said on an impulse. Although it could have been at the back of her mind that the noise of children in the house would distract Frank from his writing.

Afterwards, she certainly experienced a deep sense of achievement and satisfaction.

Chapter Forty-Two

Robert had seen the day when he would have made a fuss, had an investigation about the disappearance of ink-markers. Inkmarkers were stolen more often than anything else. Children loved anything messy. Now he couldn't face the hassle. He had more important and more personal problems to think about than the disappearance of ink-markers. Or paint. Paint vanished too; more often than not it was used by the boys to squirt at the girls or smear on their faces. Now a new problem was being brought to his attention. All sorts of odd things were going missing – chairs, crockery, cutlery, even a rug from the headmaster's office. The janitor locked and barred every gate and outside door, yet still things went missing. Milk and biscuits from the staffroom. A thermos flask. A blanket from the nurse's room.

Mr McDowall, the headmaster, demanded a solution to the mystery.

'Even if I have to get to the bottom of it myself,' he'd boomed at all and sundry, 'I shall do so!'

He began rooting round after school hours like a giant bloodhound, sniffing into every corner, every cupboard, for clues. He billowed along corridors, through classrooms, followed by a breathless but equally determined janitor. The janitor was responsible for the school's security and he was both enraged and offended that his efficiency was being challenged.

'Nobody could have got in here after school hours,' he insisted. 'Anyway, the place was still locked. No locks have been tampered with. It must be a bloody ghost.'

'I do not believe in ghosts,' Mr McDowall replied. 'Bloody or otherwise.'

Then a discovery was made – no, pounced upon, with an ear-splitting roar of triumph. Oh, of course, Robert silently groaned, it had to be in his art room. Mr McDowall spotted loose floorboards, prised them up and there underneath was a tunnel with a couple of boxes positioned as steps down.

'Anderson, you come along with me,' Mr McDowall commanded, as he began lowering himself downwards.

'Sir,' Robert protested. 'Don't you think it would be better for the janitor and I to go on our own?'

'I do not. I am your commander-in-chief. I am your leader and I shall lead the way.'

Robert groaned to himself again. The headmaster was a very large man. He wasn't built for underground tunnels, even though this one was floored and beamed with good strong-looking wood. They discovered there were pipes too. Maybe something to do with their ancient central heating.

'Bring a torch, Anderson, in case we've to separate down here. It looks as if there's a rabbit warren of passages.'

True enough, underneath the school there was more than one dark passageway. The three men crouched forward, flashing their torches around. 'I must check to see if all this is recorded in the plans of the school,' Mr McDowall said. And then, 'What on earth is this?' He tugged aside a piece of curtain (previously missed from the domestic science room) and shuffled inside the hidden area to investigate.

'Bugger!' The word exploded around. 'This has been used as a shit-house. I've got it all over me. Somebody is going to be sorry for this. You mark my words, gentlemen!'

The stench was now unmistakable. It was then they heard scampering feet. 'This way!' Mr McDowall shouted to the janitor and Robert. Then he added for the benefit of whoever was further along the passageway, 'I'll have you, you rascals. There's no escape for you. Retribution will be mine.'

The passageway suddenly narrowed and lowered, and Mr McDowall's huge bulk became firmly wedged. It took the janitor and Robert some time and struggle to push him through. Then they found at the end of the passageway a wider area in which sat two chairs and a little table (from the woodwork class). A rug lay on the floor, and various other articles including a paraffin lamp and two sleeping bags added to the effect of a lived-in room.

'Would you believe it?' asked Mr McDowall, now purple-faced with his exertions and a filthy caricature of his dignified and well-dressed self. He'd lost his hat and his gown had become torn in the earlier struggle to extricate him.

'Two rascals have been living here in my school. Actually sleeping in my school overnight.'

'Well, at least,' the janitor said with some satisfaction, 'we know they didn't break in. They just never went out.'

Mr McDowall was now shining his torch and looking for an escape route because the room obviously held no 'rascals' and he had not met them in the passageway. The route was soon found – not by Mr McDowall's torch but by the screams of Miss Winnie Purdie from domestic science, who'd stayed late to clear up the usual mess created by a lesson on pastry-making. She tackled the flour and fat on the floor while the janitor would climb up the ladder to remove pastry bombs from the ceiling.

The screams were coming from above Mr McDowall's head. His torch picked out an open trapdoor with box steps underneath it. Clambering through the trapdoor, the three men found themselves in the ladies' lavatory with a dishevelled and now hysterical Miss Purdie cowering in a corner.

'Calm yourself, dear lady,' Mr McDowall commanded. 'We are in pursuit of the rascals and we will catch them, never fear.'

Robert stayed behind to try to soothe the distraught woman and revive her with a glass of water. Mr McDowall and the janitor pressed on and caught, Robert heard a few minutes later, a boy and a girl in his class that he knew well. Both had mothers who were separated or divorced from their husbands and who had brought a boyfriend into the house.

It was easy enough to guess what had happened. They'd run away from home and nobody had even bothered to report them missing. In a way, they hadn't been. They had continued to turn up for classes each day.

Mr McDowall sent for the police and in the end both children were taken into care. Their effort at making a home together was the talk of the staffroom for a while, until it was replaced by other disasters.

'Well, at least they'd be comparatively warm and dry and safe there,' Robert said. 'Not like wee Ina Nolan who used to sleep in shop doorways. Remember her?'

They had all shaken their heads over the fate of wee Ina. She too had managed to come to school every day. Later she'd been raped and beaten up. At first they'd thought it was the work of some local gang of thugs, but it turned out to be a married man who'd been kerb-crawling. Old enough to be the child's father. Grandfather, even. They had all felt sick at the time. And Robert, like the other teachers, had thought, how can one educate a traumatised child like that? Indeed, what did education matter in such circumstances? Ina Nolan needed so many other more important things.

It made him realise that Jennifer was really a very fortunate little girl. At least she was loved and had a good home and Andrina, despite all her faults, would never purposely harm the child. He had convinced himself of this. He could now envisage a scenario in which, if he and Andrina divorced and even if she obtained custody (but of course he'd fight this tooth and nail), he could still see the child. He could make certain she was all right. He would assure her that he continued to care about her and love her. Love was the important thing.

Granted it was usually better for a child if the parents didn't split up. But some things were inevitable. In an imperfect world with imperfect people, some things happened and had to be faced. More and more he was beginning to feel that whether or not Laura could leave Derek and come to him, he would have to leave Andrina. He was living a lie. As indeed, he believed, she was. He and Andrina had nothing between them any more. Not even friendship. They ate together, visited friends together, slept together – to all appearances they were like any other normal married couple. Yet they were stranger than strangers.

He tried to keep up a picture of normality in front of his mother, in front of her mother, in front of friends and especially in front of Jennifer. But it was getting more and more difficult. He had already left Andrina in mind, in heart and in spirit.

He'd told Laura this. They met fairly regularly now, either

for a coffee on Saturday mornings or for a cup of tea on Saturday afternoons. They purposely met in busy public places, restaurants in town rather than their favourite country hotel. It was heart-breaking. At the same time, it meant they could keep in touch but not be able to do anything they'd later regret.

Laura had tried to persuade Derek to let Robert come and visit them both at the bungalow as he used to but Derek always refused. Eventually she'd told Derek that it made her sad losing touch with such a good friend (because, truthfully, they were good friends) who, apart from anything else, kept her up to date with all the news from the school. She asked Derek if it would be all right with him if she met Robert occasionally for a cup of tea and a chat. Derek had nodded his agreement. Every time when she got home now, if they'd met, she told Derek all Robert's news. The funny stories and the sad stories from the school. She even touched on his problems with Andrina.

It seemed to give Derek a link with the outside world. And Robert. In a way, they were back to their *ménage à trois* friendship: they were enjoying each other's company at a distance.

Robert collected paperbacks of war stories and gave them to Laura to pass on to Derek. Derek loved these books and read them over and over again. Robert felt happy for Derek every time he found anything about RAF pilots, and could hardly wait to give the books to Laura. Once when he'd been visiting the McPhersons he decided to walk along with a couple of 'finds' for Derek. Both were about the adventures of a Spitfire pilot.

As soon as Laura opened the door, he said, 'Don't worry, I won't come in.' Then, before he left, he shouted into the house, 'Derek, I've just handed in a couple of great stories about Spitfire pilots. Hope you enjoy them.'

He felt quite light-hearted as he walked back along Drymen Road, but once back in his mother-in-law's house he was plunged into an atmosphere of tension and unhappiness. Sophie was as bad as ever again. She'd been so much better and calmer during that time she'd stayed in Monteith Row.

Apparently her doctor had stopped her supply of tranquillisers. She'd even gone back to plead for a supply from the doctor she'd seen while she was staying at Monteith Row, but he too had refused her. Robert thought it a bit harsh, although of course he realised that she would develop, possibly had already developed, a serious addiction.

Still, just to cut them off like that . . . She was obviously suffering from withdrawal symptoms on top of everything else. Andrina, it seemed to him, was surprisingly lacking in understanding. He'd always thought that she and her mother were so close. Too close at times. Now, although she spoke pleasantly enough to Sophie, he detected a hardness in Andrina's eyes. He had more compassion for Sophie than Andrina had. He was beginning to think that he even liked his mother-in-law better than his wife.

Chapter Forty-Three

'If you don't shut up,' Bernard hissed at Tony, 'I'll shut you up with this.' He showed Tony a clenched fist. Tony continued to fill the crematorium with noisy howls and sobs, drowning out the priest's words.

'. . . our dear sister Theresa who has gone beyond the veil . . .'

Jane put a hand on Bernard's arm and whispered, 'Try to ignore him. The service is nearly over.'

Bernard said, 'Obviously Rod hasn't got my message. He had to be at the other end of the globe at a time like this. I feel hell of a bad about it. His only sister.'

'You weren't to know about Theresa when you sent him on that job. He'll understand.'

'I've always felt bad enough with that idiot being my brother and him treating Theresa the way he did.'

'Rod has never blamed you for what Tony was like. He knows you've tried to make it up to Theresa. She thought the world of you. And Rod knows it. You paid more attention to Theresa than he did.'

The service was over. The coffin had disappeared, to ear-splitting howls of Tony until a vicious dig in the ribs from Bernard winded and silenced him.

'Now, I'm warning you,' Bernard hissed at the gasping Tony as the family began to lead the mourners out. 'Next time I'll knock you unconscious. Stand there and shake hands with everyone as they come out and keep your big mouth shut.'

They all retired to a nearby hotel for the funeral meal. At one of the round tables Jane happend to sit next to Michael's wife, Caroline. Bernard was at another table still keeping an eye on Tony.

'Poor Theresa,' Caroline murmured.

'Yes,' Jane sighed. 'Tony's obviously going to miss her.'

'It was kind of Bridie to take the children, wasn't it?'

'Yes. She certainly has a big heart, taking on four of them. I know I should have volunteered. I've a bigger house than Bridie but honestly, Caroline, I just couldn't face it.'

'Well, not to worry,' Caroline said. 'I'm sure everyone understands you have plenty of problems without that.'

Jane hesitated, a puzzled expression creasing her face.

Then Caroline added in a quieter, more confidential tone, 'Well, to be honest, maybe everyone doesn't know. I'm not one for gossip and neither is Michael.'

'What do you mean?'

'About Bernard.'

'What about Bernard?'

'And his love nest out Strathblane way.'

Jane's face drained of colour.

'Love nest?'

'Michael saw him a couple of times. Once with a woman in his car. And another time disappearing into a cottage. Michael had a job out there for a while, building a nice little private estate. Lovely, he said it was. All surrounded by trees and the Campsie Hills at the back. Oh, here,' Caroline's hand flew to her mouth, 'I thought you knew. For goodness sake, don't let on to Michael that I've told you. He'd never forgive me. I shouldn't have said. I'm sorry, Jane, I really am. I shouldn't have taken that second whisky. Drink always loosens my tongue. I'm just not used to it.'

'That's perfectly all right,' Jane said politely. Then she turned to speak to the priest, who was tucking into steak pie and potatoes.

Caroline had to admire Jane's self-control when later she watched her leave arm in arm with Bernard, on the surface at least, with her usual pride in herself and in him. They made a very handsome couple.

Caroline felt no guilt in upsetting their comfortable and affluent apple-cart. Bernard O'Maley had been rotten to Michael. He had kicked his own brother when he was down. She had never forgotten that, never forgiven Bernard. Now she had the satisfaction of revenge. Now she could banish that painful episode once and for all from her mind. She felt relieved and skittish with happiness, although she tried to hide this behind a solemn face. It was, after all, poor Theresa's funeral. But secretly, every now and again, she couldn't help relishing the thought of the hell Jane would be giving Bernard the minute she got him home.

In fact Bernard noticed no difference in Jane's attitude towards him and, dropping her off at the villa, he went on to check on some of the clubs.

The next day Jane got in touch with a private detective. She told him she wanted to find out if her husband had a cottage in the country in which he entertained another woman. The detective took only a couple of days to deliver his report. It made it perfectly clear that yes, her husband had a cottage just outside Strathblane. He had met a woman there who had alighted from a Glasgow bus. He had taken her in his car to this cottage. He had pulled down all the blinds and spent several hours there with the woman before emerging with her, getting back into his car, and returning with her to Strathblane, where the woman boarded a bus for Glasgow.

Immediately Jane gathered up all Bernard's clothes, shoes and shaving gear. She went racing, stumbling through the house, grabbing at all his belongings, everything, and throwing them from the upstairs window. She raided his desk and sent papers and files and letters flying through the air. Clothes landed on trees, on bushes, on the gravel driveway. Papers were littered everywhere, right out on to the street.

She had a man come and change the locks on the doors and windows.

She wept. But they were tears of anger and wounded pride as much as of grief. Her initial feeling was that she had been made a fool of. She wanted nothing more to do with him. She wanted to cut him out of her life as if he'd never existed. The next few hours she spent in a punishing workout in her gym until she was too exhausted to feel anything.

It rained for a couple of hours before Bernard arrived and found his expensive designer clothes scattered around in sodden abandonment. He didn't bother to try the door. Gathering up as much as he could, he flung everything into the car and drove away. He dumped the clothes at the cleaners and then booked into a city centre hotel. From there he phoned Andrina.

'Are you alone?' he asked. 'Are you free to talk?'

'Not really.'

'This is important. I'm at the Central Hotel. Meet me here right away.'

'What happened?'

'I don't think we should discuss this over the phone.'

'Where did you say?'

'The Central Hotel. You'd better come. And quick.'

He hung up.

Andrina felt worried, unsettled, uneasy. That morning, they had been at the cottage and had such an idyllic time. She couldn't imagine what could possibly have changed his mood. There had been a hardness, an anger in his voice, not his usual deep and passionate tone. He hadn't talked as he usually did, unashamedly, of what he was going to do to her when they met again. This time he had issued curt and impatient commands. She felt confused, yet excited, suspecting this was yet another way Bernard had decided on to stir her passions. She was slightly nervous, but only because she'd heard that some lovers enjoyed aggression and violence: she'd once seen a film where a woman was handcuffed by her lover to a bed. She and Bernard had acted out many fantasies in the past but they had never resorted to anything that gave physical pain. Surely Bernard must know that she wouldn't like that. Firmly she banished any tremors of nerves. Bernard would never hurt her on any pretext.

Robert was sitting at the kitchen table marking school work from an exam, despite the fact that it was Saturday. It was always work, work, work with him.

She made an excuse about having to run into town for an hour or two to do some shopping, and could he collect Jennifer from the children's party? It was one of her classmates' birthdays and she had been invited to the celebration. Robert gave her a cold, critical stare. He looked so schoolteacherish when he wore his reading glasses. She expected him to say, 'I thought you were supposed to be shopping in town this morning when Jennifer was at gymnastics', but he said nothing.

Taking his silence to mean he would collect Jennifer, she

freshened up her make-up and brushed out her long hair until it was like an auburn cloud framing her creamy-skinned face. She widened innocent eyes at herself in the mirror, fluttered long lashes, pouted full lips, turned this way and that to admire her curvaceous body.

She felt pleased and happy at what the mirror revealed.

It was a cold, wet day and the trees of the Green were swaying in the wind and splattering rain on the narrow Monteith Row. Water cascaded along gutters. Andrina wished now that she had worn boots instead of high heels. In a matter of minutes her feet were soaked and her coat and skirt were clinging to her like a second skin. Even the frilly umbrella that Bernard had once given her was not much use. In desperation she hailed a taxi. There was no real need to worry about the expense: Bernard would reimburse her. Bernard was extremely generous with money.

In the taxi she used her powder compact mirror (the gold compact was another of Bernard's presents) to rearrange her hair and check her make-up. By the time the taxi reached Central Station she was well satisfied with herself again.

Bernard was waiting in the foyer. Without a word he led her into the lift and upstairs to his bedroom. As soon as they were inside, Bernard said, 'She knows.'

Strength immediately drained from Andrina's legs. She sat down on the bed.

'Who knows – what . . . ?'

'Jane. I don't know how much – but enough to throw all my clothes and belongings out the window. First you destroy my flat and all my stuff, and now Jane does this.'

'Oh my God. She doesn't know it's me, does she?'

'I hope to Christ she does. Enough is enough. I'm damned if I'm going to put up with any more of it.'

'Why are you getting angry with me?' Andrina cried out. 'It's Jane you should be angry with. It's her fault this has happened.'

'No, damn it.' For the first time Bernard shouted at her. 'It is not Jane's fault this has happened. It's yours, Andrina . . .'

'Mine?' Andrina was not only distressed and panic-stricken, but astounded. 'My fault?'

'Yes, yours. You could have left Robert years ago – before I ever met Jane. We could have been together, probably married by now. But no – you had to keep me dangling on like a fool for years – years!'

She began to cry. This wasn't the Bernard she knew at all. This was hard-faced, glittery-eyed fury.

'Now, watch my lips . . .' he went on. 'I've had enough of it. No more. No more, do you hear? I've told you I love you and I want to marry you. And I still do. But it's getting a bloody humiliation. I'm sick of this hole-in-the-corner, off and on, meeting occasionally just when it suits you affair. I've had more than enough of it.'

'You know the reason for the way it's been. It's not my fault – '

'I'm telling you, it *is!* Now, it's time to make a choice. Either me or your mother. It's a simple as that.'

'It's not simple at all. I can't – ' she wailed.

'OK. That's it then. Fuck off.'

He made the door in a few fast strides. 'You can try giving me a ring when you grow up but I doubt if I'll be able to wait that long.'

Andrina couldn't believe what was happening. She was too confused by the speed of events to take them in. She wandered from the room, along the corridor, into the lift and then out into the rain-lashed Glasgow street.

Chapter Forty-Four

Glasgow looked unusually beautiful in its Christmas white and the Salvation Army band made a joyous sound as it rang out carols in Argyle Street. Girls in blue uniforms and bonnets tied under their chins were singing 'God rest ye merry gentlemen' as Bernard gloomily plodded through the crisp glittery snow loaded with parcels. He felt obliged to at least get a few things for Tony's kids.

Just over a month had passed since his wife's funeral and he was acting as if he'd never been married. Before any of his brothers had time to find out and stop him, he'd given up the house in Blackhill and gone back into digs. He'd even bought himself a motorbike. Next thing he'd be saying he'd no money to buy anything for the kids. He was completely irresponsible. Poor Frank was now lumbered with them. Frank had invited Bernard to spend Christmas Day with him and Bridie and the children. Apparently Bridie's mother and father and Doris had gone down to Newcastle to spend Christmas with one of their sons who'd recently got married to a Newcastle girl. They hadn't managed to get to the wedding, but were celebrating Christmas with the newly-weds at the home of the bride's parents.

Bernard wasn't looking forward to Christmas at Frank's but it would be better than being stuck in the cottage on his own. He could of course work non-stop in the clubs and pubs.

Alternatively he could have left Rod in charge and gone off abroad somewhere, but he knew he'd miss Andrina just as much in America or Spain or France as he did in Glasgow.

In one way, he regretted losing his temper with her. In another way, he was glad he'd brought things to a head at last. There was a limit to what any man could take from any woman. After she'd gone and his anger had cooled down, he realised that she wouldn't be able to speak to her mother. Then suddenly a thought occurred to him. Why shouldn't he speak to her? Why shouldn't he bring everything out into the open? Once it was a *fait accompli*, Andrina would have no excuse.

'Now your mother knows,' he could say, 'there's no need for any more arsing about' (or words to that effect).

He remembered Andrina's panic when he'd suggested taking the initiative. But once it was done it was done. No matter what the result was as far as he and Andrina were concerned, he would feel the better for it. It would be worth it just to see Sophie McPherson's face: it would be the Christmas present she deserved. Although it would be after Christmas before he could manage to get out to Bearsden.

He collected the car and went to the West End to deliver the parcels. He'd got the shop assistants to gift-wrap them and they looked very Christmassy and attractive in their gold, silver and red paper and fancy bows. Snow had blanketed silence over the Crescent. The only sound to be heard as he got out of the car was the occasional creak and drip of the trees.

Bridie welcomed him quite warmly, which was something of a change. Not that he was all that surprised. Tony's kids were enough to get anybody's problems into proportion and change even the most spoiled of characters. He'd always thought Frank spoiled Bridie. He'd doted on her for years. Of course, he wryly chastised himself, he was a fine one to talk. But at least Andrina was beautiful. Any man could be forgiven for doting on her and spoiling her.

Bridie was a walking disaster. Especially now, since she'd to struggle with four undisciplined little horrors. When he arrived, they were racing and yelling about the house: he could hear the racket as he was coming up the stairs before he ever reached their door. An unwelcome contrast to the peace outside. When they saw the parcels they pounced on them and would have torn them open right there and then if he hadn't given the four of them a smart clip on the ear and told them if they dared to touch the parcels again, he'd tell Santa Claus not to come to them this Christmas.

He deposited the parcels under the tree to the accompaniment of howls and sobs and Bridie's desperate attempts to pacify them. A harassed-looking Frank appeared and asked, 'What the hell's wrong now?'

'I gave them a clip on the ear.'

'Good for you,' Frank said. 'I wish you'd kicked them up the backside as well.'

'Go through and play in your room,' Bridie told the children and then, to Bernard and Frank, 'You ought to be ashamed. You're grown men. They're motherless children.'

'But they're not fatherless,' Frank said. 'At least not yet. If I get my hands on him, I'll kill him. He's gone over the score this time. Did you know he gave up the house, Bernard?'

'Just found out the other day.'

'Could you beat it? I mean, I didn't mind helping him out by taking the kids off his hands for a few days' – although in fact he had minded – 'but he's obviously dumped them on me.'

'I don't know what you've got to complain about,' Bridie said. 'It's me who's got to look after them.'

Frank gave her a dismissive glance.

'You know perfectly well what I've got to complain about. And you needn't act hard done to. You've brought this on yourself.'

So Frank's marriage wasn't made in heaven after all, Bernard thought. Frank had obviously found Bridie's clay feet.

'Anyway, thanks for the presents, Bernard,' Bridie said. 'Are you staying for dinner?'

'No, thanks all the same.'

'You can't go away out to Strathblane on a night like this,' Bridie said. 'Why you bought a place away out there, I don't know.'

'I think I do,' Frank said. 'To get a bit of peace and quiet. How about if we change places, Bernard?'

Bernard laughed.

'I'm not sure if I'll keep it on. I'm finding it a bit too quiet for me.'

This was the truth. It was one thing having an isolated love nest in the summer in which to enjoy passionate hours. It was quite another to live there in the dead of winter on one's own.

He was a city man: he liked to be where the action was. And, among other things, that meant people.

'I've some more presents in the car for Michael and Caroline's kids. I don't fancy going out to Castlemilk on a night like this either, but I promised Michael. I'm sorry for that guy. Talk about being lumbered, Frank. Think yourself lucky you didn't get somebody like Big Martha dumped on you. Apparently she eats like a herd of horses. Michael never has a penny to his name, what with keeping her and Caroline and the kids.'

'I know,' Frank said. 'Can you not give him a job, Bernard? He gets peanuts as a brickie.'

Bernard sighed. 'A one-eyed man isn't much use in my line of business, Frank. He'd be a danger to himself and to the others. He's maybe fit enough, but I doubt it. And he's had no experience of the martial arts. That's something that's essential. I've thought about some job in the office – maybe answering the phone – but I thought that kind of sedentary job might insult the poor guy.' He shrugged. 'Anyway, I doubt if Caroline would allow him to work for me. I've never been her favourite person. Although recently for some reason she's seemed more affable. Almost friendly.'

It must be the Christmas spirit affecting his sisters-in-law, he thought. Or maybe they were just taking pity on him because his marriage had broken up. To be on your own at the festive season wasn't the choicest of situations.

He could, of course, pick up a woman at one of the clubs. He'd never been short of opportunities or offers. He might still do that if nothing happened with Andrina. He was not made to live a monkish existence.

'At least stay and have a cup of tea,' Frank said.

'No, I'd better get going.'

'Well, don't forget, you're here for Christmas lunch tomorrow.'

'I won't.'

Bridie saw him to the door.

'Somebody had to take the children,' she whispered. 'I couldn't see them landing in an institution. That's what Tony would have done with them.'

'I know. It was very good of you, Bridie.'

'I mean, what would it have looked like? His own brother's children.'

'You did the right thing. I obviously couldn't have taken them, and Michael's got more than enough on his plate.'

'Frank thinks I did it just to spite him. Just to prevent him from writing.'

'You ought to know what Frank's like by now. He's writing daft. Don't worry about it.'

She nodded, her eyes vague. He winked at her.

'Stay cool.'

'Aye, OK. Cheerio, Bernard. See you tomorrow.'

Well, he thought, it was a strange old world when Bridie was confiding in him as if he was a close friend. All it needed was for Caroline to invite him for Christmas. They weren't coming over to Frank and Bridie's. The children were recovering from measles and Caroline didn't want to take them out in the cold.

It was a nightmare drive through a blizzard of snow and slippy ice to Castlemilk. Even the snow couldn't hide the bleakness of the place. It was a vast wilderness, the biggest housing estate in Europe, he'd heard. However, according to Michael, there was some sort of community spirit – at least in his part of Castlemilk. He and his mother-in-law had become leading lights in the fight to improve living conditions. Without much success, as far as his own building was concerned. The dampness was disgusting. You could smell it even before the door was opened. No wonder Caroline and her mother and the kids didn't enjoy the best of health. Even Michael didn't look good. Especially Michael, in fact.

A thought suddenly occurred to him. A cottage in the country might solve all Michael's problems – and it would be too good for even Caroline to resist. If he'd been absolutely certain that Andrina was not going to come to him, he would have offered the place in Strathblane to Michael for a nominal rent right there and then. The cottage was of no interest whatsoever to him without Andrina to share it.

But first he must confront Sophie McPherson. He'd see what happened after that. Andrina might come running to him as she'd once promised she would the moment her mother was dead and buried.

Well, it didn't look as if there was going to be any funeral just yet. But Sophie was going to have one hell of a shock.

Chapter Forty-Five

'I knew it!' Frank shouted. 'Why didn't you tell him to phone back? Or take his number so that I could phone him. Or ask for a forwarding address. Anything!'

'He hung up on me before I could say anything. He just told me he was going back on the road with his drums. He's joined some band or other.'

'He's forty years of age. Who'd want a middle-aged drummer?'

'He's probably lied about his age. You know he doesn't look anything near forty.'

'He doesn't act like it either. I'll kill him if I ever get my hands on him. I'll kill him. How could he just up and off like that and leave his children? And on Christmas Day of all days.'

'I haven't told the children. It's just too cruel. Oh, Frank, try to be nice to them. It's not their fault that Tony's the way he is.'

'When have I not been nice to them? Didn't I take them over to the park this morning to let you get on with making the lunch?'

'Well, yes . . .'

'But I must make this clear, Bridie. Somebody's got to discipline them for their own good. Nobody likes noisy, spoiled, bad-mannered pests. They've got to be taught how to behave.'

'That's easier said than done.'

'You should have thought about that before you told Tony to bring them here in the first place.'

'I thought it would only be for a few days. You've acted on impulse before now. And without discussing things with me first.'

'All right, all right. I'll do what I can to help while I'm here.'

Bridie looked startled.

'What do you mean – while you're here?'

'I'll have to find an office or a room somewhere to work in. I can't work here any more. Not with the racket they make.'

'Bobby and Marion will soon be back to school. And I'll get the twins into a nursery school. Then after the summer holidays they'll be starting the primary school.'

'Oh God,' Frank groaned. 'The summer holidays. And before that the Easter holidays. No, it'll have to be an office room, somewhere I can work regular hours in peace.'

Just then the children came crowding into the kitchen.

'We've seen Uncle Bernard from the window. Getting out a red car. Can I open the door for him?' Bobby shouted excitedly.

'Please,' said Frank, 'Can I *please* open the door.'

'No,' Bobby glowered. '*I* want to open the door.'

Bridie couldn't help laughing but she managed to say, 'Bobby, what Uncle Frank meant was that you should always say please when you ask for something. You should say, Please can I open the door?'

'OK.' Bobby was jumping about with impatience. 'Can I?'

'Say please!' Frank shouted.

'Please.'

'Right. Now go and open the damn thing.' There was a stampede through the hall.

'Frank,' Bridie said. 'That didn't sound like you. You were making as much noise as the children there. Keep your voice down when you speak to them. Don't get like Tony, for pity's sake.'

'Don't you dare compare me with that selfish idiot,' Frank said. 'If I don't sound like myself, it's because you've messed me up good and proper. My mind's in a bloody turmoil. And I know you did it on purpose, Bridie. You don't fool me one little bit. But you didn't succeed in destroying me when you tore up my manuscript, and you won't succeed with this ploy.'

'Is this a private fight,' Bernard said, dwarfing the kitchen with his big frame, 'or can I join in too?'

'Sorry, Bernard,' Frank put out a hand. 'Merry Christmas.'

'I've set lunch in the dining-room today,' Bridie told him.

'The kitchen would have been OK for me.'

'No, no. Christmas lunch is special. The children have helped me put all the crackers out.'

The children were jumping up and down with excitement.

'We helped Uncle Frank and Aunty Bridie with the decorations too. And the balloons.'

'It was me who saw to the balloons,' Frank said. 'I've hardly a puff left in me. I need a drink. Come on through to the sitting-room for a minute, Bernard.'

'Maybe Bridie needs a hand.'

'No, on you go. I'll give you a shout after I dish the soup.'

'Can we open our presents now, Uncle Frank? Please,' Bobby added.

Frank laughed.

'Immediately after lunch we'll all open our parcels. It won't be long now. Be a good boy and away and play with the ones Santa brought last night.'

'OK,' Bobby said, and off he skipped with Marion and the twins, Daisy and Danny, following close behind.

In the sitting-room Frank poured two glasses of whisky and handed one to Bernard.

'Sorry about that when you arrived. I've had a lot of problems even before the children came on the scene. Bridie can't stand my writing.'

'She used to be OK about it.'

'I know. But that was before I became successful.'

'Oh, I get you.'

'I wouldn't say this to anyone else, Bernard, but I've been on the verge of throwing in the towel.'

'Leaving Bridie?' Bernard knew Frank well enough to realise he didn't mean giving up his writing.

'Yes. She made it plain she'd never give me a divorce. And I just thought – Oh, to hell . . .'

'God, what next?' Bernard said. 'You and Bridie always seemed . . .'

'I know. I know. Then this happened.' He flung a hand in the direction of the sound of children's squeals and laughter. 'She did it purposely. I know she did. Anything to put me off my work. Although, of course, she doesn't see it as work. She would be perfectly happy if I was back at Goldmayers. Or even a brickie like Michael. I think she'd settle for anything now as long as it had nothing to do with writing.' He brushed a hand through his hair. 'I'm sorry, Bernard. I shouldn't be telling you all this. It's not like me to blab out my troubles. Nothing's like me. I feel I've lost myself. I don't know who I am any more.'

'You're a damned good writer. That's who you are. More power to your elbow, Frank.' Bernard raised his glass. Frank raised his in response.

'As if you haven't got enough problems of your own at the moment. Has Jane been in touch at all?'

'Just a letter from her lawyer.'

'Divorce?'

'That'll be my second. I wonder what's wrong with me, Frank.'

'You're too randy?'

Bernard grinned.

'Could be.'

'Who's the other woman? Or shouldn't I ask?' Bernard was silent and Frank answered himself, 'I shouldn't ask.'

Bridie called then.

'Soup's out.'

As the two men rose, Bernard said, 'If I can help with cash, Frank . . . There's no reason why you should bear the full burden of the kids and I'm not short of a bob or two.'

'It's not the money. But if you happen to meet up with Tony, give me a chance to land one on him. Don't hog him all to yourself.'

Bernard laughed.

'Don't worry. Michael wants a go at him as well. So he'll have the three of us to reckon with.'

'How is Michael, and his lot, these days? We did invite them, you know. But there was something wrong with his kids . . .'

'Measles, I think. But they're OK. At least, as OK as they can be in that dump of a place.'

'Has he tried to get a move?'

'Him and a few thousand others. But once you're out there you're stuck out there.'

'It's a miracle he hasn't gone back to the booze.'

'I admire the poor sod for that. I didn't think he'd be able to hold out.'

'He looked as if he needed a drink last time I saw him.'

'Who did?' Bridie asked as they entered the dining-room and took their seats.

'Michael,' Frank told her.

'They should never have gone out to Castlemilk. Fancy leaving our lovely wee house in the Gorbals.'

'To hear Bridie nowadays,' Frank couldn't hide the bitterness in his voice, 'anybody would think the Gorbals was some sort of utopia.'

'We were happy there.'

'I wish you'd change the record,' Frank said.

Bernard lifted a cracker and held it out to Bobby.

'Stop the bickering, you two. It's Christmas.'

After that they made a real effort. They pulled the crackers with shouts of hilarity. They put on paper hats. They smacked their lips over the meal that Bridie fussed back and forth from the kitchen to produce.

'That was great, Bridie,' Bernard congratulated her afterwards.

'Oh, I'm not much of a cook, really. Not for anything fancy, at least. I'm no use at anything that Frank's fancy friends are used to.'

'Look,' Bernard said, 'before you return fire, Frank, let's open the parcels. Even during the Great War they had a Christmas Day truce.'

Frank grinned.

'OK. OK.'

There was a good-natured rush for the sparkling tree and the rainbow of presents underneath it. But suddenly amidst the childish laugher and the excitement, Bernard felt sad.

He thought of so many wasted years. He and Andrina could have been married and had children together. He tried to tell himself that once their relationship was out in the open, she would come to him and they would, at long last, be able to make a permanent commitment to each other.

But still depression weighed heavy on him.

Chapter Forty-Six

Freddie Hancock had been persuaded to go to Alcoholics Anonymous. He'd also gone to stay permanently with his cousin, Jane, at Pollokshields until he got straightened out. He did get straightened out and, after Jane had arranged for someone to clean up his flat in the West End, he returned to it. He also returned to Sinnieglen. Before he did, however, the languages department, in desperation, had taken on a foreign assistant.

It very soon became obvious that this German had been brought up in a very selective school for brighter children and he'd never seen an area like Blackhill in his life. He'd especially never been faced with a class like 2F. Most of them could neither read nor write. They'd never seen a book in their homes. Not even a newspaper. Even by Blackhill standards, it was a dreadful class.

Müller was his name, and Hamish McKendrick had suggested he told the class something about the Second World War.

'They like hearing about the war. And speak to them about yourself.'

'But,' Müller said, 'I cannot tell them about the war until I first explained to them the fall of the Weimar Republic.'

When Jeff Barclay got to this part of the story in the staffroom, there were loud groans.

'I told him,' Jeff said, 'there was no point in that. He'd be better just to talk about personal things like his home and family and so on.'

Jeff had to go and see the headmaster about something and when he got back and looked in to see how Müller was doing, he found the classroom practically wrecked. The board was, like in a Junior Honours history class, filled with stuff about the Weimar Republic. When Jeff asked if he'd managed to get any of it over Müller replied, 'The noise was considerable and teaching was impossible.'

Later Jeff said, 'Miss Purdie was next door and I asked her what happened. She said that as soon as Müller began talking to the children, they started singing at the pitch of their voices, 'Go home you Hun' and kept it up the whole period.'

It was just as well that Freddie returned fit and well. Müller didn't last long: even the female pupils could chew him up and spit him out. Pupils like Lexie Brown whose family stole coal from the gasworks and went around selling it in Blackhill. They kept a horse and cart to transport the coal around the houses. They sold dung for gardens and it was said that they kept the horse in the bathroom. Robert didn't believe this but Lachlan McKenzie swore that he'd visited the place and had actually seen the horse. Admittedly, it was a small horse. But it was in the bathroom.

Robert had seen them selling chips from a window of their council flat. They were an enterprising family and were one crowd that could, with a bit of luck, end up by making a fortune. But my God, they were tough. Lexie Brown in particular. But Lexie had recently fallen pregnant. A friend of Miss Purdie's, who had been in the hospital at the same time, said Lexie was in the bed on one side of her and another young unmarried girl was on the other. No boy came up to see either girl. It seemed to be a case of momentary pleasure, perhaps somebody they'd just met that night. They live that kind of animalistic life, Miss Purdie told the staffroom. 'Totally irresponsible.'

These developments put somewhat of a dampener on Freddie's mood of defiant optimism on his return to duty. He lasted a few months, during which he gradually sank into the abyss again. When Robert went to see him he found him (and the flat) in an even worse state. As well as a sea of vodka bottles, cigarettes were scattered all over – whole cigarettes and half-smoked butts. Freddie had never smoked before. Robert phoned the AA, only to be told that there was nothing they could do because Freddie didn't want to stop drinking. As long as he was under stress, he'd drink to escape it. He needed a psychiatrist to help him cope, or he needed to get away from the stressful situation.

'Don't we all?' was the staffroom cry.

Robert and the others coped or didn't cope in different ways. None of them used the bottle as a crutch.

Robert hauled Freddie out of the flat, stuffed him into his car and drove him over to Jane's house. Jane promised to organise the psychiatrist and after they managed to half carry Freddie upstairs and deposit him on a bed, Jane asked if Robert would like a cup of coffee.

'Thanks.' He followed her back downstairs and into the sitting-room, where she pressed a bell at the side of the fireplace.

'I've got a live-in housekeeper now. Bernard was against me having one before. I used to wonder why. Now I know.'

A neat little woman with finger-waved grey hair looked into the room and Jane asked her to bring coffee and biscuits.

After the housekeeper withdrew, Robert said, 'How do you mean?'

'He must have wanted to clear his pitch. Keep the place free for him and his other woman. No doubt he phoned her every time he knew I was going out. It makes me sick every time I think of it.'

'Now, you don't know that . . .'

'What other reason could he have? He knew I could afford a whole houseful of staff if I wanted them. Now that I look back – there were lots of things. Signs I ought to have recognised. Maybe I just didn't want to. Sometimes the bed looked as if it had been remade. It looked different. He had a woman in our bed, Robert. I know it.'

'I'm so sorry, Jane. I wish I could do something to help. What the hell's wrong with the guy? You're a beautiful woman. He had a luxurious home here. You obviously loved him. He must be crazy.'

'I loved him all right. Now I just feel so humiliated and betrayed.'

'Do you think it would do any good if I spoke to him? I haven't seen him around for a while but I could easily get in touch with him through his office, or one of his brothers.'

There was a silence as the housekeeper entered with a tray and placed it on a small table beside Jane's chair. She smiled at the woman.

'Thank you, Mrs Craig. I'll see to it.'

She poured the coffee.

'Had we just quarrelled about something – anything – Robert, I would have said yes. I would have been grateful for your help. But when I think of him having this woman here . . . When I think how deceitful he's been – telling me he's going to work every day or every night, when in fact he's been living with her at Strathblane. Even when he was on so-called duty, he was with her. He would never take me or allow me to go to a night club or any place where he was in charge of security. He made the excuse that it was for my own safety. Or that he needed all his concentration on the job.' She shook her head. 'When I think of it now, Robert, I actually saw him with the woman. I got Freddie to take me to the Locarno Casino one night and I saw Bernard talking to and laughing with this Spanish-type woman. Beautiful, she was. Dark-eyed with glossy black hair drawn back. I could tell the way he was looking at her . . . You know that sexy way his eyes can narrow and glimmer . . .' She blinked back tears, then went on, 'He actually bought that place in Strathblane and I never knew a thing about it.'

Robert looked perplexed.

'I don't understand him. He's a great guy in so many ways . . .'

'Oh yes,' Jane gave a helpless half-laugh. 'He's a great guy all right.'

'No, I mean it. It says a lot for him, coming from his background, that he's built up that business. And he's helped me out a lot in the past with the boys at the club – even given some of them jobs and a decent start in life. He just doesn't seem to be able to settle into a committed relationship. I knew his first wife. Poor wee Doris never got over it when their marriage broke up.'

'I hadn't anything to do with that, Robert. He was separated from her before we started going out together.'

'I'm quite sure it was nothing to do with you. Doris and Bernard were never right for one another. But I really believed that you and him were hitting it off. I thought you were so perfect together.'

'So did I. We used to work out together in the gym. We used to sweat together, and laugh together . . .'

She looked away, obviously fighting for control.

'That woman looked different from me altogether.'

'Didn't you ask him about her at the time?'

'I asked who she was. But you know he talks sometimes. "Just a punter," he said and then clammed up. At home afterwards though, he was furious at me for turning up like that. Now I understand why.'

'Are you going for a divorce?'

'I suppose so. I've been so shocked and upset I haven't thought about what I'm going to do. But he's never contacted me to persuade me otherwise. Never said he was sorry. Nothing. God, it hurts, Robert. He obviously just doesn't care, you see.'

'I take it you've got firm evidence. How did you find out? Did you put a detective on him?'

'Yes. But I suppose I'd have to employ him again to find out who the woman is. I'd have to name her as co-respondent.'

'Well, as I say, if there's anything I can do, just let me know. And do feel welcome to come over and visit at Monteith Row at any time. Don't wait for an invitation. There's no need to stand on ceremony. If you feel lonely or need someone to talk to, just get into your car and drive over. You'll always be made welcome.'

'Thanks, Robert. You and Andrina have been good friends. I appreciate it. I always feel better after I've spoken to Andrina. Now it's the same with you.'

Afterwards, although he seldom held any conversation with Andrina these days other than was absolutely necessary, he thought he'd better relay what Jane had been telling him so that Andrina would be prepared for a sudden visit and, he hoped, be sympathetic and comforting.

Personally he had come to believe that Andrina was a selfish bitch who had no sympathy or understanding for anyone (not even her own child) but herself. But Jane seemed to regard Andrina as her best friend, and a paragon of all virtues.

'You might be getting a visit from Jane,' he said.

'Poor Jane,' Andrina murmured. She was preparing their

301

evening meal and moving about the kitchen with a sexy movement of her hips that once would have quickened his pulse.

'You know, of course, that she chucked Bernard out?'

'It must have been awful for Bernard too. Daddy was saying that one of the councillors was visiting someone in the street and saw Bernard gathering up all his things. Some of the clothes and papers had blown right out into the road. What a humiliation!'

'At least hearing about it would make your mother's day.'

'Oh, Daddy didn't tell me in front of Mummy. He never mentions Bernard's name in front of Mummy.'

'I'd to take Freddie over to Jane's place today and we had a talk.'

'Oh?'

'Andrina had her back to him as she peeled potatoes at the sink. The water was splashing noisily and she was clattering pots about. He raised his voice.

'Apparently she knows who the other woman is.'

'Oh?'

'At least, she's seen him with her but doesn't know her name. She's going to put a detective on him again.'

'Where did she see them together?'

'In one of the clubs he works in. He claims of course she was only one of the punters – to use his term. But Jane thinks not. Anyway, she'll be dropping in to see you for tea and comfort. Try not to let her down.'

'Why should you say that?' She turned to face him with eyes stretched wide like a child, vulnerable, innocent.

'Because I know, even if she doesn't, you're not as angelic as you always try to make out.'

She turned away from him again and continued preparing the meal. He opened his newspaper and shut her out.

Chapter Forty-Seven

The withdrawal symptoms had been so bad that at one point Sophie had been literally tearing her hair. By some miracle she prepared McPherson's breakfast each morning. She had always prided herself on her routines in dealing with all household jobs. Perfect organisation was the reason that she could keep the house looking shining and spotless. She could cook and bake and entertain and attend innumerable committee meetings and social events. Now she seemed to be sinking into chaos, desperately floundering, wandering about, or paralysed into complete inactivity. Often she felt like climbing the walls. She could have screamed as millions of insects seemed to scurry and clamber over every nerve.

At last the doctor had taken pity on her and given her, not more tranquillisers, but a prescription for sleeping tablets to ensure that she had a good night's sleep. She dreaded finishing the tablets in case he would refuse to give her any more. Not that they made too much difference to how she felt during the day. But they did help her over Christmas. She determinedly tried to think things out and make plans beforehand. She made lists and took notes, then lost the pieces of paper she'd written on. Laboriously struggling to break through the paralysis of her mind, she'd gone over the whole process again. At least it had enabled her to organise the Christmas food. She could only pray that Andrina and Robert and Robert's mother wouldn't notice that the house wasn't up to its usual immaculate standard. She could have wept at the mess the place was in. It shamed her.

Nevertheless, Christmas was somehow got through. It was good to see Jennifer's eyes fill with wonder and joy when she opened the big box from her Grandpa and Granny McPherson. Inside was a doll's house with doors and windows that could open.

'Later on, I'll make curtains for the windows,' she'd told the child. 'I just haven't had time recently. But you tell me what colour of curtains you'd like and I'll make them.'

She'd spoken to Robert's mother on the telephone and told her about the doll's house and Jean had volunteered to buy miniature furniture. Each parcel that Jennifer opened contained yet another small chair, or sideboard, or table. Sophie had never seen Jennifer so happy. It helped soothe Sophie's overstretched nerves. Her racing pulse slowed down and she was able to sink into a chair and rest for a while. Leaning back on the cushions it struck her how fatigued she was.

Still, the family had enjoyed the good meal, that was the main thing. She looked over at Andrina and Robert. They seemed on the surface to be just the same as usual. Yet she detected something . . . a coolness perhaps? She got the feeling that each was acting as if the other wasn't there. Maybe it was her oversensitive nerves but she even imagined a different atmosphere towards her. Not from Robert but from Andrina. Again, on the surface, Andrina appeared the same. Earlier she'd looked as angelic as usual as she sang her Christmas Day solo in the church. Now, there was something in the steady way Sophie caught Andrina looking back at her. She would quickly turn to find Andrina staring at her. The aquamarine eyes would quickly slide away, the head would lower in that apparently shy manner she had at times. Although, of course, Andrina had never been in the slightest shy or backward in coming forward.

Something in Andrina's eyes made Sophie uneasy. Despite her unease, however, she almost nodded off to sleep in her chair, until she heard Jean say, 'Andrina, your poor mother's exhausted. Could you wash up, dear? Robert will give you a hand, I'm sure. I'd do the dishes myself but I'm so crippled with this nuisance of arthritis. I can't stand for any length of time.'

Before Andrina could answer, Robert said, 'I think it's time the men did the clearing up for a change. Andrew,' he called over to McPherson, 'do you want to wash or dry?'

Sophie roused herself and gave a half-laugh.

'He's never either washed or dried a dish in his life. Sit down, Robert. I'll do them.'

'No, you stay where you are, and that's an order.' Robert used his authoritative schoolroom voice. 'It's time McPherson learned how to give you a hand.'

McPherson heaved his heavy body from the easy chair, where he'd been enjoying a cigar.

'All right. All right. I'll come quietly.'

Sophie tutted.

'I was going to make us all a cup of tea.'

'That's OK,' Robert soothed. 'I'll make the tea. Just you relax.'

Through in the kitchen, he said to McPherson, 'Sophie isn't looking so good.'

McPherson sighed.

'She's a constant worry these days. I don't know what to do about her. I know it looks bad that I've never helped her in the house, but the truth is, she would never allow me to. She's always obsessively house-proud, and even if someone does the dishes she'd just do them all over again. She never trusts anyone to do anything right. Never up to her standards.'

'She looks as if she's worn herself out. Once the better weather comes in, you should take her away for a holiday.'

'Good idea. Mind you, I doubt if she'd agree to go.'

'Make her go. Buy the tickets. Book the hotel. Insist.'

'A good idea,' McPherson repeated.

Between them they cleared the kitchen table, then took tea and Christmas cake back through to the sitting-room. Andrina was down on her knees with Jennifer playing with the doll's house. Jean and Sophie were chatting away about people they'd known in the past at the Rose Street church. It looked a cosy family scene and the room was more lived-in and homely than usual. Over at the window, the tree winked and sparkled with coloured lights and baubles. The fire glowed warmly. The carpet was strewn with Christmas wrapping and ribbons, and presents – boxes of chocolates and jars of boilings, scented soap and bath oil, silk scarves, and knitted sweaters and socks, aftershave lotion, books and toys. The spicy aroma of Christmas pudding and pies still lingered in the warm air.

'Oh thank you, Robert.' Sophie accepted a cup of tea with genuine gratitude. She felt she really needed the tea to give her the energy to get out of the chair.

Later she managed to see everybody to the door and wave them goodbye.

'I think I'll have an early night,' she told McPherson who'd switched on the television and was settling down to enjoy the rest of the evening's programmes. She was afraid to sit down in case she wouldn't be able to get up again.

'Fine,' he said, then, 'It all went well, as usual. Even better than usual, I'd say. That was a brainwave getting Jennifer the doll's house.'

'Yes.' She hovered at the sitting-room door, leaning against the lintel for support. 'It was good to see her so happy. I'll away upstairs then.'

'Aye. Goodnight, dear.'

'Goodnight.'

She climbed the stairs slowly, clinging to the banisters for support, undressed and fell into bed without folding her clothes and putting them neatly on a chair as she always did.

For the first time in months, she had a refreshing sleep. Even when she took the sleeping tablets she never felt refreshed the next day.

Boxing Day was quiet, just her and McPherson. After attending church, they had lunch then went for a walk up to Kilmardinny and round by the loch. It was a frosty day and everything – the roads, the pavements, the bushes and trees, the dark waters – was covered with a silvery veil. The world looked a beautiful place. It seemed like a dream that she'd experienced fear in this very road she now walked with McPherson. Maybe she had imagined it all. Yet she knew that was a pathetic hope. Bernard O'Maley had been watching her and following her and oh, with such hate in his eyes. She shuddered at the memory of his cold stare.

McPherson said, 'Are you cold?'

'Somebody must have walked over my grave.'

'I've always thought that was a daft saying. It doesn't make sense.'

She shrugged.

'I suppose not.'

It didn't make sense Bernard O'Maley watching her and following her. Or did it? Did he hate her so much that he was simply getting perverted pleasure from frightening her?

Although physically she was the better of her walk – her cheeks tingled and she felt invigorated – the memory the road to Kilmardinny evoked put her on edge. Her mind fevered with trying to sort out what she could do, how she could protect herself. After the holiday period her usual meetings would start up again and there might be the worry of getting safely to and fro along the quiet Bearsden streets.

She had another restless night that left her disorientated. But somehow she managed to make McPherson's breakfast and see him off to work as if nothing was wrong.

It wasn't long after he'd gone that she heard the doorbell give a long hard ring as she stood in the kitchen, her mind going round in circles, wondering what job she ought to start on first. She thought it must be McPherson back for something he'd forgotten. Then she remembered that McPherson had a key. He had left his key behind before, of course. She hastened through and opened the door.

Bernard O'Maley's big bulk filled the doorway, blocking out light. Black coat, black hair, eyes black with venom.

'I want to talk to you,' he said.

She banged the door shut before he even had time to jam it with his foot. She ran back to the kitchen, fists bunched against mouth to stifle the high-pitched animal squeals of terror.

The front door kept opening and shutting in her mind. Bernard O'Maley's big bulk blotting out light. Black coat, black hair, eyes black with venom.

She heard him shouting, 'I'm not going away until you open this bloody door.'

Opening and shutting, opening and shutting. Then she heard him bawl, 'Do you want me to shout through it and give all your neighbours a treat?'

Opening and shutting, opening and shutting.

'OK. If that's how it's to be. I wanted you to know that I've been fucking Andrina for years. For years, do you hear? She would have left Robert years ago – wouldn't have married him in the first place – if it hadn't been for you. It was me she wanted to marry but you, you interfering old witch, ruined her life and Robert's life, as well as mine.

'Andrina and I love each other. We always have. And we've been loving each other and fucking each other for years. I just wanted you to know.'

Chapter Forty-Eight

The last straw for Freddie was actually a globule of spit. One of many that he'd suffered.

'Filthy savages,' he screamed. 'Ignorant bastards!' Roars of laughter from pupils echoed up the well of the stairs to the roof in the howling crescendo of delight.

Lachlan McKenzie rushed out to the landing and Robert raced up the stairs, punching pupils aside, to reach Freddie and drag him into the nearest classroom.

'Shut up, Freddie,' Robert commanded. 'If McDowall hears you, you're out on your ear for good.'

'Sacked, you mean?' Freddie was half laughing, half crying. 'Lose my job? Christ, what a tragedy. I can't bear the thought.'

'Are you going to take him home?' McKenzie said. 'Or will I?'

'You get Jeff Barclay to cover for him. I haven't a class for the last period so I'll take him.'

'There's nothing wrong with me, you know.' Freddie was ashen-faced and violently trembling. 'It's these animals out there. Every day I'm covered in spit. I didn't work my way for years through university to get a degree and then for more years through Inverness Teacher Training College just to be spat on.'

'I know. You're not the only one, pal,' Robert assured him. 'But come on. We'll talk some more once you get home.'

The bell clanged and the laughter and the clatter of feet faded away.

'Let's go while the going's good.' Robert took Freddie's arm and levered him out and down the stairs. Before he got into the car, Freddie took off his jacket, folded it outside in and put it in the back seat.

'Do me a favour, Robert. Put that into the cleaners for me. There's one in Byres Road.'

'Sure.'

'I don't understand what I've done wrong. Why do they hate me so much?'

'They don't hate you. Getting spat on is one of the hazards of the profession. It's sport to them. Even the best of them. It's one in the eye – or in the school, one on the jacket – for authority. It's nothing personal.'

'It's revolting. It makes me sick to my soul.'

'The more they see that it gets to you, or that anything they do gets to you, Freddie, the more of a victory it seems to them and the more they'll do it.'

'I wanted so much to help them. I had such plans . . .'

'I know. But they live in a jungle, Freddie, and you've got to have some understanding of what it's like in order to be able to deal with them.'

'So it's just dog eat dog, after all. We've got to function on their level.'

'No, that's not what I meant. It's a matter of knowing what their background's really like, what their problems are, *why* they act as they do, and are as they are.'

'That cures them, does it? We wave our magic wand of understanding and – '

'No. It's not as simple as that and you know it as well as I do. For one thing, teachers are not magicians. Neither are they psychologists or social workers. Although I'll admit, too often people expect us to be all three – and at the same time don't give us credit for being anything. The attitude with most people – even most of the parents of these children – is that we've got a real cushy number.'

'God!' Freddie groaned. 'Let them try it. I've had enough.'

'No, don't despair, Freddie. You just picked the wrong place. My advice to you is to put in for a transfer. Pull strings. Get a doctor's letter. Do anything and everything you can to get into a school in some place like the West End or Bearsden. You'll make a good teacher in a good school. You were on a losing wicket right from the start trying to teach foreign languages in Sinnieglen. Everyone in the staffroom knew that before they even met you.'

'Do you really think I could still make a go of teaching?'

'Yes, I do. But remember, never let them get to you. Be in charge but keep calm. Hang on to any sense of humour you've got, too. That's important. But mainly, be self-disciplined so that you can keep them disciplined. And never expect too much from children, Freddie. Even children from posh schools. They can be little devils as well if they think they can get away with it. You know what they say – boys will be boys.'

As soon as they arrived in the flat, Freddie took a long swig at the nearest vodka bottle.

Robert prised the bottle from him.

'That's no answer.' He poured the rest of the contents down the sink. 'Promise me you'll go back to the psychiatrist and to AA. Self-discipline, old son, starts right here and now. The shrink ought to be able to help you with the school transfer application. You're going to be all right. Believe it. Perhaps, though, it might be a good idea to go back to stay with Jane until you get everything fixed about another school. It might not be for the best to be on your own just now. Remember she wanted you stay on. I think she needs a bit of company herself.'

Freddie hesitated.

'I suppose it does make sense. Poor old Jane's having a rough time as well. It was selfish of me to leave when she was pleading with me to stay a while longer. I'll give her a ring.'

'Do it right now.'

Freddie nodded and went through to the hall. After a few minutes he returned.

'She was as pleased as punch. It sounded as if I was doing her a favour instead of the other way around.'

'Throw a few things into a case and I'll run you over.'

'I'm so sorry about all this, Robert. It's getting a habit, isn't it? Rescuing me. I really appreciate it. You and the other members of staff. I think you all deserve a medal. Not just for putting up with me and standing by me as you've all done, but for putting up with that mob of young horrors day after day.'

'Oh, most of them aren't so bad once you get to know them. In fact, I often think it's a miracle that they're not a thousand times worse.'

'God forbid!'

On the way to Pollokshields, Robert said, 'It might help, once you feel a bit better, to find a karate club. There's bound to be one – if not in the Southside, at least in the centre of town. I know there's more than one in town.'

'Me? Karate?'

'Why not? There's nothing better for teaching you self-discipline and absolute control. It's part of the ethos. It would also build up your confidence. Think about it, Freddie. It's certainly made it possible for me to deal with and survive any problems I've ever encountered.'

'But look at you. You're as hard as nails. My body's a boneless jelly in comparison.'

'You'd harden up with training. Believe me. There's nothing to beat it. Not in my experience, anyway. Do me a favour. Think about it.'

'Later maybe. Right now I feel fit for nothing.'

When they arrived at the villa, Jane wanted Robert to come in but he said, 'No, I'd better get home. I've the karate club tonight.'

'I'll never know how he does it,' Freddie groaned. 'I feel a migraine coming on at the mere thought.'

Robert laughed. But more and more he didn't know himself how he was doing it. Freddie wasn't the only one that stress was getting to. It didn't make life any easier to come home to an impatient, unloving atmosphere in which he was barely tolerated. It took all his karate training in self-control not to blow up in Andrina's face and tell her how he felt and what he thought of her.

To his surprise, that night, after forcing himself to return to Sinnieglen for the karate club, he found Bernard there too.

'Long time no see,' Robert greeted him.

'Yes. I've missed my workouts. I thought it's time I took myself in hand and got myself together again.'

'You know you're welcome at any time, Bernard.'

'Do you mean that? I know you think a lot of Jane. I wouldn't blame you if – '

'Forget it. What happens between you and Jane is none of my business. We're old friends, right?'

'Right.'

'Well, don't say it with such a gloomy face. Friendship is something to cheer about. Especially a long-standing friendship like ours.'

'Don't think I don't appreciate it, Robert. No matter what happens, believe me, I've always appreciated our friendship. I've never wanted anything to spoil it.'

'My God, you don't just look depressed, Bernard, you sound it. Let's go for a drink after the session and we can both drown our sorrows.'

'You're on.'

Chapter Forty-Nine

God bless whoever invented the front-loading washing machine, Bridie thought. Before the children arrived, she'd hated the thing. Indeed, she'd despised the dishwashing machine and every labour-saving gadget Frank had ever bought her. Now she thanked God, the Pope, the Blessed Virgin, every member of the Holy Family, for everything in her kitchen.

No withdrawing for hours into a book now. No mulling over Frank's faults. No seething over injustices, imagined or otherwise. There just wasn't the time. As for Frank going away to his office room every day (he'd been allowed to use one in the BBC Club), she was only too thankful to get him out from under her feet. Frank was pretty useless really, except for his writing. He didn't know one end of a screwdriver from another. He could stir the occasional scrambled egg and brown a bit of toast but that was his stretch as far as cooking went. It could be said that he was good with the children, but that was only because he behaved like a child himself. He could get down to their level, make a fool of himself, have them laughing. But the sensible, practical side of the running of the house, and looking after the children, was left to her. Secretly she prided herself that she had become quite good at it. It was true what Frank said about the children needing discipline and having to be taught how to behave, but he was all mouth and no action. When it really came down to it, he was the one who ended up spoiling them. She had to tick him off as well as them.

Once lunch used to be eaten in silence. That seemed so long ago now. Frank would have a notebook beside his plate; she would be reading a book while she ate. Now it was all noise, shouting and laughing, and general chaos with her trying her best to bring order to the proceedings.

In the evening there was the kitchen to clear up again. The

children seemed to drop as much food on the floor as they put into their mouths. Then sewing and mending to do. She'd even taken up knitting because they couldn't afford to keep buying everything the children needed. She reckoned if she kept knitting jerseys for Bobby they would still be all right for Danny to wear when Bobby grew out of them. She had, she soon realised, not reckoned on Bobby's fascination with climbing trees in the park. On more than one occasion he'd got into difficulties. She'd nearly taken a heart attack when she'd discovered him up a tree, hanging from a high branch by his jersey. She'd had to run for the 'parkie', who brought a ladder and with much difficulty (and cursing), rescued Bobby. She had never believed in corporal punishment or any kind of violence. Her father, so she'd thought, had put her off violence for life. But she'd been so harassed and in such a state, she'd boxed Bobby's ears the moment his feet touched the ground.

Bobby had sobbed, 'I'll tell Uncle Frank on you.'

And she said, 'Oh, be quiet or I'll box Uncle Frank's ears as well. I bet it's him who's been encouraging you. I knew he'd been up to something, taking you all to the park so often.'

Frank of course defended Bobby when she'd tackled him about it.

'Boys have to be adventurous. It's what toughens them up. He wasn't doing any harm.'

'I'm warning you, Frank,' she said. 'I will not have him and Danny turning out to be a couple of wee toughs. Or monkeys either. I'd better not see Bobby climbing trees again. Or Danny. You know how he copies Bobby. And another thing, stop filling Marion and Daisy's head with nonsense. Especially rude nonsense.'

'Och, it was only a wee poem to make them laugh.'

'It didn't need to be rude, Frank.'

'OK. OK.'

She could have said, It would fit you better to help me with all the extra housework I've to cope with now. (The mountains of ironing alone took hours.) But she held her peace. He would have only got in her way and made a worse mess. At least he helped her bath the children and wash their hair. And she was glad of his help in settling them into bed with a story or two. It gave her a chance to clean up the mess in the bathroom and get their clothes sorted out for the next day.

As often as not she just tumbled into bed absolutely exhausted. Frank was back sleeping in their bedroom. The sofa in his writing room was murder on his back, he said. Sometimes they laughed together in bed about the children's antics or things they'd said that day. Sometimes they even made love, just as they used to.

She'd been so busy, she'd even forgotten to watch his play when it came on television. He'd never mentioned it. Now that she came to think of it, he'd never even switched the television on that night. Although, of course, there would be a TV set in the club. Somebody could have taped it for him. Be that as it may, she had more important things to think about and to occupy her time.

She'd said as much to Doris when she'd come to visit Botanic Crescent after the Christmas holidays. There had been all the news about the family's trip to Newcastle, of course, and how the wedding went. A great time had been had by one and all apparently. But then Doris got on to her usual moan about Bernard.

'Fancy you having him here for Christmas.'

'He's Frank's brother.'

'And you're my sister!'

'So?'

'So you should show a bit of loyalty.'

'If Bernard had said a word against you, I would have shown a bit of loyalty, Doris. But he never even mentioned your name.'

'But having him here. After how he treated me . . .'

'Oh, for goodness sake, Doris. Will you never give up? You're like a worn-out gramophone record. I'm sick and tired of hearing you talk about Bernard. Forgive and forget. That's what I say and it's high time you did too. Get on with your life.'

'Oh, well, if that's your attitude . . .' Doris rose on her dignity but to her astonishment Bridie pushed a pile of plates so roughly against her that they nearly knocked her off balance. She tottered backwards on her high heels.

'Shut up and set the table. Frank collects the children from school and they'll all be there in a minute, and I haven't even the kettle on. The trouble with you, Doris, is you haven't enough to trouble you.'

'Well!' Doris gasped. But she set the plates out and before she could think of anything else to do, there was a racket, a regular stampede, across the hall and Frank and four boisterous, rosy-cheeked children exploded into the kitchen. Scarves and woolly hats and coats were flung off, then retrieved again as Bridie shouted commands.

'Pick these up and take them through to your rooms. Nobody's getting anything to eat or drink until everything's tidied away and hands are thoroughly washed.'

Frank winked at Doris.

'She means me as well, you know. I haven't the life of a dog. A regular sergeant-major, you sister's become.'

'I can see that.'

'Doris,' Bridie said, 'don't just stand there. If you want to make yourself useful, finish setting the table. You know where everything's kept. Frank, away through and get them to watch children's TV until I'm ready. I'll give you a shout when it's time to let them through.'

'OK, pet.'

'Well!' Doris repeated. But soon, watching a harassed but obviously happy Bridie hare about the kitchen doing half a dozen jobs at once, she had to laugh.

'You seem to have taken to motherhood like a duck to water. Who would have thought?'

'They're good children really.'

'What a rat he is, though.'

'Frank?' Bridie cried out incredulously, angrily.

'Not Frank, you idiot. Tony.'

Bridie relaxed.

'Oh, him.'

'Haven't you heard anything?'

'No. And I don't want to. The children are far better without him. They're happy with me and Frank.'

'There's no telling what he might do though. What if he

does come back? You know how irresponsible he is. He could take it into his head for no reason at all to take them back.'

'You're always so cheerful, Doris. The life and soul of every party.'

'You never know with that family, Bridie. I never thought that Bernard – '

'Not that again, Doris, *please*!'

'Well, it's for your own good. What if he got married again? All the O'Maleys are randy. They're never without a woman for long. Tony could get married and set up home again and take the children back. By law he'd be entitled to. Haven't you thought of that?'

She hadn't.

Chapter Fifty

'Jane.' Andrina kept a blank face. 'Come in.'

'I should have phoned. But I was in town seeing my lawyer and I somehow couldn't face going home and being on my own.'

'That's all right. There's nobody in. I'm glad of the company too.'

Jane didn't know she was the other woman. If Jane had found out, she would have already dropped the bombshell on Robert. He'd been out at the villa only the other day. Nevertheless, Andrina felt compelled to be cautious.

Jane followed her through to the kitchen.

'You know, of course, what's happened?'

'Robert told me. I'm so sorry, Jane.'

'I think I would have gone completely mad if I hadn't had Freddie to see to. He's out this afternoon at his psychiatrist. Then he's going on to the AA.'

'Tea or coffee? Or could you take something stronger?'

'No, it's too early in the day for me. Coffee will be fine, thanks. Did Robert tell you about the cottage?'

'I think he mentioned it. Yes.'

'He bought the place and I knew nothing about it.'

Andrina concentrated intently on the coffee-pot.

Jane went on: 'When I think of the times I've been alone in the villa thinking he was at work and all the time he's been with this other woman . . .'

'How did you find out?'

'Caroline told me. At Theresa's funeral, of all places.'

'Michael O'Maley's wife?'

'Yes. Apparently, Michael had been working out near Strathblane and saw Bernard going into the cottage. He got a glimpse of the woman too. The lawyer says I'll have to find out who she is so that I can cite her as co-respondent.'

Andrina willed her hand not to shake as she poured the coffee.

'How will you do that?'

'Put a detective on him. Get photographs. These detective agencies have ways of finding out the necessary details.' Jane bit her lip. 'But it's all so . . . so sordid and awful. I keep wishing that I'll wake up and find it's been a bad dream and Bernard will be beside me and everything will be all right.'

Andrina bent her head over her coffee cup and tried to take comfort from it. Sweat was prickling all over her body and her heart was racing at such a pace she had a horror that she was going to crumple into unconsciousness. She felt sick.

Jane spoke of bad dreams. No nightmare could be worse than this. Yet, Andrina kept telling herself, she was safe. So far, no one knew her identity and now, far from being distressed at Bernard's cruel and dismissive treatment of her, she thanked God the break had happened when it did. Although deeper still than her gratitude for the escape was the sadness that this time their parting meant for ever. Every time in the past, when they'd fought, she had never truly accepted that their relationship was finished. But now, like it or not, it had to be over. Knowing him, he wouldn't feel as she did. Detectives wouldn't bother him. He'd go out and face them, tell them. Tell the world. That's what he had always wanted to do. Bernard thrived on confrontation and danger. That was his life.

It wasn't hers. To a certain degree it had been exciting and thrilling going along with Bernard's way of living on the edge, flouting danger. But she wasn't nearly as brave or as strong as him. During the times that they'd made love almost under Jane and Robert's noses (and they'd done the same when he was married to Doris), danger had spiced the thrill of the sex act. Danger had pushed them to witless, animal abandon. Never had there been any excitement like it.

Life on the dangerous edge. That was Bernard. Challenging fate. That was Bernard. Defiance. That was Bernard. She believed that Bernard didn't know what fear meant.

She'd never felt anything while she and Bernard made love except passion. But now, sitting opposite Jane, she was drowning in a morass of different emotions – Bernard had said it was her fault. But he had taken the initiative in the first place (a lifetime ago, it seemed now), as far as the sexual side of their relationship was concerned. He had practically raped her. She had struggled against him.

She remembered that very first encounter. He and Doris had stayed overnight at Monteith Row. Was it after a party? In the morning, Robert and Doris had gone off to work, then Bernard had brought her a cup of tea in bed. He had only been wearing a pair of shorts. Startlingly white they'd looked against his tanned, muscular body. Then before she knew what was happening, he was on top of her, and plunging inside her. She had struggled. Yes, she remembered. As well as the physical delights she had never experienced before, she had felt horror at the idea of committing adultery. She had expected God to punish her, to strike her dead right there and then.

She had fought with herself for quite a time after that, knowing it was wrong, knowing she had committed a sin. But all the time she was drawn deeper into a web of passion that was to last for years.

The more she thought about it, the more she saw Bernard as leaving a trail of unhappy women in his wake. Trembling inside, she longed for comfort. She wanted to confide in Jane. Ask if they could still be friends. She knew, of course, that this was impossible. Jane would be far more likely to spring on her and claw her eyes out. That's certainly what Doris would do if she ever found out.

Jane said, 'I keep thinking. Why should he do it? I look in the mirror and I try to tell myself, "You're as good-looking as that woman." What has she got that I haven't? I've even got money, Andrina. And as well as a lot of other things, Bernard and I had our interest in physical fitness in common. Have you seen our gym in the villa?'

'No.'

'I had it put in especially for him. We used to work out together every day when he was at home.'

'But didn't you tell me before that there was a problem?' Andrina ventured.

'Oh, the sex thing? Yes, I came to terms with that eventually. Or at least I thought I had. I thought that at times he was just too tired with overwork. Or stress at work. At other times, when we'd been abroad together for instance, our sex life was marvellous. Now I don't know what to think.'

'I'm sorry,' Andrina said. She didn't know what else to say.

'I shouldn't be burdening you with all this, Andrina. But I thought . . . because we're friends . . .'

'Of course. I'm glad you came.' Lies. Lies. Thousands of them over the years. A jungle of lies. Impossible to see her way out of them any more.

'Christmas was hell.'

'Oh Jane, I didn't realise. We were at my mother's for lunch, but you could have come over here in the evening.'

'It's just as well I didn't. I wouldn't have been very good company. Freddie said it was like being at a wake. Have you heard from him at all?'

'Freddie?'

'No, Bernard. I thought maybe Robert . . . Although the last time he was over, he never said.'

'He hasn't to me either.'

'I just wondered. With him and Robert being friends.'

Jane shrugged.

'What's the point? He's the one who should be asking about me. The least he could have done was phone up or even write and say he was sorry. Sorry for hurting me. Anything.'

'Would you take him back if he did?'

She shrugged again.

'I don't know. Maybe. If we talked things out. If he explained. If I understood.'

She stared unhappily at Andrina for a moment or two before adding, 'I still love him.'

'Maybe . . . I mean in that case, maybe you shouldn't rush into divorce proceedings, employing detectives, all that sort of thing. As you said yourself, it's so sordid and unpleasant. Maybe you should wait and try for some sort of reconciliation.'

Jane shook her head.

'Even if I don't go through with the divorce, I still want to know who the woman is. I want to confront her. Tell her what I think of her. I've always been honest and straightforward in my life, Andrina. And whatever else I've lacked, even Bernard could never claim I was short on courage. That woman will be sorry, I can tell you, once I get not only my tongue, but my hands, on her. Are you feeling alright, Andrina?'

'A bit sick. Coffee doesn't seem to agree with me these days. I shouldn't have taken it. I'd forgotten I felt sick yesterday morning as well.'

Jane smiled.

'Has it occurred to you there might be another reason?'

'What?'

'Morning sickness? Aversion to certain food and drink? I've never been pregnant myself but I'm told that's the sort of thing . . .'

'Pregnant?' Andrina echoed in horror.

'Would it be so terrible?' Jane raised an eyebrow. 'Probably Robert would be delighted. And I'm sure it would be lovely for Jennifer to have a little brother or sister.'

'Oh God!' Andrina couldn't contain the words.

'What's wrong? *Wouldn't* Robert be pleased?'

'It's not that. I've probably got some bug or other. There's a lot of tummy upsets going around at the moment. It's just a worry about passing anything on to Jennifer. She's such a delicate child.'

Oh God, she repeated the words to herself. Oh my God!

Chapter Fifty-One

'Sophie?'

Right away, McPherson knew there was something wrong. Every night when he came home the hall light was switched on to welcome him. Usually Sophie would come bustling through from the kitchen, an apron tied round her waist, a ladle or some other kitchen tool in her hand.

'I've poured your dram,' she'd say. 'Just go through and sit down. I won't be long.'

Always something like that. Regular as clockwork.

He'd go through to the sitting-room and sink back into his comfortable armchair for a minute. Then he'd untie his shoes and put on the slippers that Sophie had ready for him. His pipe would be on the ashtray on the coffee table beside his chair, next to it a crystal tumbler containing a generous measure of his favourite malt whisky.

He would relax back and savour both until Sophie announced that dinner was ready. Sometimes she came through and had a glass of sherry with him and told him all the Bearsden news and gossip while the steak pie was browning in the oven. Or whatever delicious dish they were having.

'Just another five minutes,' she'd say. She always had everything timed down to the last second.

Tonight the house was in darkness. There was no bustling appearance at the kitchen door. No warm welcoming cry (or at least warm for Sophie) of 'Oh, it's you!'

'Sophie?' he called again. He found the hall light switch.

He could see through the open sitting-room door that even the fire hadn't been lit. He felt worried and apprehensive. He'd never known Sophie to be out when he arrived home. He was certain that if she did have to go out, she would have let him know. They'd had disagreements, over Bernard for instance, so she was cooler towards him, more distant, but she never neglected him. Never neglected her wifely or housekeeping duties.

The kitchen too was icy cold and in darkness. He switched on the light and was startled to see Sophie crouched down in a corner, a tight ball of terror.

'Sophie, my dear, what on earth's happened?'

He went over and helped her to her feet. She strained back from him, her eyes darting behind him and towards the kitchen door. He'd never seen such fear. It upset him to such a degree his chest painfully tightened.

Sophie moaned, 'Is he with you?'

'Is who with me? Why should I have anybody with me? You know I'd never bring anyone home for a meal without asking you first, Sophie.'

'That wicked man.'

'What wicked man?' he asked, but a light was beginning to dawn. The only man Sophie had ever spoken about in such terms – apart from her father – was Bernard O'Maley. He was really worried now. Had Sophie gone over the top – gone beyond recall into insanity?

'Bernard O'Maley.'

'Sophie, why on earth would I bring Bernard into this house – your home as well as mine – when I know you dislike him so much? I'd never dream of it. Even though I believe your feelings and your opinion about him are quite unjustified. Believe me, Sophie, I would never dream of doing such a thing.'

'He's been following me and watching me. He's been the reason my nerves have been getting worse. He's been purposely trying to frighten me. He's been – '

'Now, wait a minute, Sophie. You must get a grip on yourself and not let your imagination run away with you. What possible reason have you, what evidence can you possibly have – '

'Someone *has* been following me and watching me. That has not been my imagination.'

'Even accepting that to be true, why should you think Bernard would be the one? The fact that you dislike him so much is no reason for you to make such an accusation.'

'I saw him. A few weeks back. I was going to visit Laura Cairns and just as I was coming out of the house, I happened to look round and I saw his car in Kirk Road and he was sitting in it.'

McPherson sighed and tutted and shook his head.

'Sophie, he was waiting for me. We had a business meeting in Milngavie and my car was in the garage getting the steering fixed. Remember? He was giving me a lift. I didn't mention it at the time because you get so terribly upset at the mere mention of his name.'

'He stared at me with such hatred.'

'Well, I could believe that. He has much more reason to hate you, Sophie, than you have to hate him. He has never, I repeat, *never*, done you any harm, but you denied him the woman he loved and wanted to marry. Even when he was only a young lad he told me he wanted to marry Andrina.'

Then an astonishing thing happened. Sophie began to cry. Never in all the time he'd known her had he seen her weep. It distressed him so much he didn't know what to do. Eventually, awkwardly, he put an arm around her shoulder and eased her tentatively against his chest. Never, except briefly in bed, had he ever been allowed to hold her in his arms. Now she leaned helplessly against him, her body heaving with broken-hearted sobs.

'Oh, Sophie, please don't. You acted in what you believed were Andrina's best interests at the time. And she did get a good husband in Robert. I know he's not as ambitious as we'd like but all the same – '

'He came to the door this afternoon.' Sophie wasn't listening to him. She was almost hysterical.

'Who?'

'Bernard O'Maley.'

'When?'

'Today.'

'Oh, Sophie . . .'

'He did. I'm not mad. Although I'm sure he's trying to drive me insane. Why else would he say such terrible things?'

'What terrible things?'

'Oh, Andrew, I couldn't repeat the foul, filthy language he

326

used, and shouting it out for all to hear. I'll never be able to face Mrs Pemberton again. Thank God we're at the end of the terrace and she's the only neighbour likely to have heard. Unless there was anyone passing on their way to the shops. And of course, if Mrs Pemberton did hear, she'll tell all the others, I'm sure. Everybody in Bearsden will know by now . . .'

'Now, just a minute, Sophie. Calm down.' He led her over to a chair beside the table and sat her down. 'I'm going to put the kettle on and make you a cup of hot, sweet tea. Have you got any of your tranquillisers left?'

'You never listen.' Sophie wiped at her eyes with the corner of her apron. 'I've never had any for ages. The doctor won't give me them any more. I told you.'

He plugged the kettle in.

'How about a wee dram then, while the kettle's coming to the boil? It'll maybe help steady you.'

'Anything. I don't care. What does it matter any more?'

He went through to the room to pour two glasses of whisky. He noticed his hands were shaking. He no longer knew what to make of the situation. It was beyond him.

'Drink this down,' he told Sophie when he returned to the kitchen. 'It'll warm you as well. This place is like an icebox.'

Sophie did as she was told. Then coughed and spluttered and wiped at her face with her apron again.

'I'm sorry I haven't the fire lit or your dinner ready.'

'Oh, don't worry about that.' He downed his own whisky, then made a pot of tea and poured two cups of the steaming, comforting liquid. 'All I care about is you, Sophie. I would have thought that after all these years of marriage you would have known that your welfare comes first with me.'

She curled both palms round her cup and gazed over the rim at him with tragic eyes.

'But you're friends with him. You do business with him.'

He took a deep sigh.

'Sophie, why shouldn't I? He has nothing to do with our marriage, our relationship. How many times must I tell you – you have a quite unjustified attitude to this man. It's come to be a phobia, an obsession. He's actually a very decent – '

'Decent?' She began to weep uncontrollably again. 'He's been defiling Andrina for years. He shouted it through the door at me. He used filthy language to tell me that he and Andrina . . . for years . . . For years, unknown to us, they've been . . .'

'Oh God,' McPherson groaned. This he could believe. Bernard had never been one to give up on anything. He'd seen this in the way he conducted his business. Bernard had a definite obsessive, determined streak. He never allowed anything or anyone to defeat him. 'Oh God,' he repeated, although in truth all that bothered him was the language Bernard had no doubt used and the fact that any of his Bearsden neighbours or friends might have heard him. It wasn't a nice thing to happen on one's doorstep.

'Look,' he said, after a minute or two's thought. 'I'll speak to Bernard about this. He had no right to come to our door and behave like that. I'll tell him in no uncertain terms. How dare he upset you like this? Don't worry, Sophie, I'll deal with him. He won't come near you again. I give you my word on it. As far as the Pembertons hearing anything – isn't today her sewing-bee day? And old Pemberton would be at the golf club. That I'm certain of.'

Sophie's sobs gradually quietened.

'I forgot about that. At least that's something. She wouldn't be in. Mrs Jones and Mrs Hawthorn go to the sewing-bee too.'

'There you are then. I'll tell you another thing you've forgotten. Most of the shops take a half-day today. It's usually as quiet as the grave in Drymen Road . . .'

'Of course. Of course. I was so frantic with distress, I couldn't think. I didn't know what day it was.'

'There you are then,' he repeated. 'And he'd be in the porch and you know how deep our porch is. It would muffle his voice, absorb it, especially if he was shouting close to the front door.'

She nodded. Her tears stopped. He could see her usual hard shell closing in on her again.

'It doesn't change what he said. The disgusting way he and Andrina have been behaving. She's no longer a daughter of mine. I never want to speak to her again. I never want to set eyes on her again. Never, as long as I live!'

'Now wait a minute, Sophie . . .'

'Tell her that.'

Chapter Fifty-Two

Andrina was taken aback to see her father at the door. She couldn't remember him ever coming on his own and un-invited like this.

'Daddy, what a surprise. Come in.' She glanced behind him. 'Isn't Mummy with you?'

'No.'

'Let me take your coat and hat,' she said. Then, 'On you go through to the sitting-room. Would you like a cup of tea?'

'I'd rather have a whisky.'

'Yes, of course. Sit down and I'll pour it. Is there something wrong with Mummy?'

'You could say that.'

Andrina's eyes widened.

'Is she ill? Is it serious?'

'She's very upset. Very upset indeed.'

'What's happened?'

'Bernard turned up on our doorstep.'

'Bernard?' Andrina echoed faintly and sat down.

'Your mother was there on her own and very frightened. You know how she's always been about him.'

'I know.' Andrina made a pathetic attempt at laughter. 'It's ridiculous.'

'Is it?'

'You know it is, Daddy. You've said so yourself.'

'I thought I knew a lot of things. I thought you were a good-living girl who was faithful to her husband.'

Andrina's face seemed to suck in, grow smaller and whiter and thinner. She aged before his eyes in a matter of seconds.

'What . . . what do you mean?'

'Bernard told your mother that you and him had been lovers for years. She shut the door in his face but he continued to shout obscenities through it.'

She looked as if she was going to faint but he didn't make a move to help her. Two-faced, scheming hussy, deceiving not only Robert but Sophie and himself. Who would have thought to look at her in the church? Or anywhere else, for that matter. The lies she must have told to cover her tracks. The way, for years, she must have kept Bernard dangling. She obviously wanted to have her cake and eat it. The security and respectability Robert could give her and the sexual excitement no doubt Bernard had supplied. And of course, all along, she had been the golden girl to everybody. The obedient daughter. The dutiful wife. The caring mother. The angel.

Although now he was beginning to see that she was not even such a caring mother as he'd once thought. Now he could see all the times she'd left Jennifer at Bearsden in a completely different light. She had just been using him and Sophie. She didn't care about Jennifer. All she cared about was herself and the pursuit of her own carnal pleasures. She was a disgrace. He felt ashamed of her. He believed in the sanctity of marriage and although, admittedly, he'd always thought that Bernard would have made a better match for her than Robert, once married, that was that as far as he was concerned. No way could he condone the breaking of one of God's commandments.

'It's been a terrible shock to both of us to learn that you've committed adultery. But even more so to your poor mother because you sinned with Bernard – a man rightly or wrongly she's always despised.'

'I . . . I . . . don't know why Bernard would say such a thing. Except that he's always had an obsession about me. Ever since I was a girl. He's watched me and followed me . . .'

'Are you saying that it's not true?'

'Of course it's not true,' she almost shouted, leaning forward, stiff, bug-eyed.

It made him wonder. That bit about watching and following . . . He felt confused. Could Sophie have been right after all? *Could* Bernard have been watching her and following her? Surely not. It would be too terrible to think that nobody believed her if in fact it was true and the poor woman was genuinely being tormented. By God, he'd speak to Bernard about this. He'd find out the truth, one way or another.

To Andrina he tried to keep his severe and admonitory tone.

'I find that hard to believe, Andrina. Why should Bernard say you and he were lovers if you were not?'

'I don't know. Wishful thinking maybe. He's obsessional. You must know that. You see him oftener than I do. You know him better then I do.'

It was then he remembered that Bernard and Robert were lifelong friends and that Robert and Andrina regularly visited Bernard and his wife and vice versa. He was appalled all over again.

'You're on regular visiting terms. You're friends with Bernard's wife.'

'That's surely not a sin, Daddy.'

'And Bernard is Robert's best friend.'

She began to cry. She looked so childish and helpless that it was hard to believe that she was capable of being so devious and wicked. He felt his chest tighten with distress.

'I'm sorry to have to tell you this, Andrina, but your mother says – ' he hesitated to utter the cruel words. He didn't want to say them but his first loyalty was to his wife – 'that you're no longer any daughter of hers. She says she never wants to speak to you again or ever set eyes on you again.'

'Oh, Daddy . . .'

He rose.

'I'm sorry, Andrina. Now I must go. I've still to see Bernard. I phoned his office and made an appointment through his secretary. He'll be waiting for me in town.'

'In his office?' she queried, rising and hastening anxiously after him. The question made him suspicious again. She obviously wanted to phone Bernard and warn him. Why else would she want to know?

'No, not in his office.' His voice was abrupt and he left without saying goodbye. He had to take the stairs slowly, holding on to the banisters. He wasn't able for all this worry and upset at his age: he felt as if the secure foundation of his world was dissolving into quicksand underneath him. He had always been a family man. Everything he'd ever done was for the benefit of his wife and daughter – to give them a good home and a Christian background. All right, he'd done himself a bit of good financially in the process but anything he'd got meant nothing without the security and happiness of his home and family. Money and the accumulation of money for its own sake did not interest him. It was what money could provide – that was the thing. He'd made a good home for Sophie with it, and many personal comforts. He'd gladly provided everything Andrina and Jennifer needed, and would have done much more had Robert allowed it.

Now as he drove towards the Central Hotel, where he'd arranged to meet Bernard, his mind was confused. Had he done enough for Sophie? Had he let her down by not believing her for all this time? Where had he gone wrong with Andrina? He remembered her as a beautiful affectionate little girl, sitting on his knee, her arms clinging round his neck. She had been innocent then.

And Bernard. What was he to make of him now? He had liked Bernard ever since he was a young lad – liked him, admired him, trusted him. Had he been so wrong?

He needed a drink and it was the first thing he insisted on before he broached the subject with Bernard. They found a quiet corner table in the hotel lounge and Bernard ordered a couple of double whiskies. McPherson took a mouthful of his. Bernard silently watched him. Then he said, 'OK, McPherson. Let's have it.'

'You came to my door yesterday.'

'Yes, I did.'

'And nearly frightened the life out of my wife – a woman in her sixties.'

'I didn't mean to frighten her. I'm sorry about that.'

'What the hell *did* you mean to do?'

'I simply wanted to have a talk with her, put her straight about how it was with Andrina and me. Andrina has always been so afraid of her mother that no matter how often I pleaded with her to tell Sophie, she just went into a panic. I realised eventually that she would never tell her, that we'd go on living a lie for the rest of our lives. I'd had more than enough of it, McPherson. It's been absolute hell deceiving everybody – especially Robert. Believe me, I'm not proud of myself for that.'

McPherson believed him. He groaned inside when he thought of Andrina again. How could she? For all these years? He felt like weeping with disappointment. He had been so proud of her.

'I'm sorry,' Bernard said. 'I didn't enjoy deceiving you either. But at least you knew right from the start that I genuinely loved Andrina and wanted to marry her. I still do.'

'Oh, what a mess,' McPherson said. He suddenly felt an old man. His shoulders sagged, his head drooped. A tremble was making if difficult for him to lift his glass. He didn't know how he was going to find the strength to go home.

Chapter Fifty-Three

Sure as guns, just as they had feared, Tony turned up and wanted the children.

There he stood on the doorstep, his usual big, grinning, swaggering self. Hanging on his arm was the cheapest gum-chewing tart Bridie had ever seen. Sadie's hair was peroxide blonde with dark, greasy roots. Her black eye make-up looked as if it had been plastered on with a trowel, the same trowel that had smeared scarlet paint across her mouth. She was wearing bibbed hot pants, a style more suitable for a slim teenager, which Sadie definitely was not. To give up Bobby, Marion, wee Daniel and Daisy to the care of such a woman was out of the question.

'You've got a smashin' house, hen. Must be worth a bob or two, eh?' All the time energetically chewing, Sadie strolled around the sitting-room peering at pictures, lifting up ornaments.

Tony, all horsy grin, said, 'Frank makes a bomb with his stories. Dead lucky, he's been. Haven't you, Frank?'

'Yes,' Frank said. 'And the harder I work, the luckier I get.'

'Would you like a cup of tea?' Bridie asked coolly, grudgingly.

'Christ, Tony,' Sadie gave a howl of laughter. 'Look at that drinks cabinet and she's offering us tea.'

Frank went over to the cabinet and elbowed Sadie aside.

'Whisky? Gin? Vodka?'

'Vodka for me and whisky for Tony.' Sadie lit up a cigarette. 'I've never read a storybook in my life.'

Frank looked over at Bridie.

Bridie nodded. She didn't usually bother about drink but on this occasion she felt the need of something. Sadie kept wandering around, touching things, until Frank said, 'Sadie, will you sit down. It's distracting with you prowling about like that.'

Sadie shrugged and, still chewing, came over, fag in one hand and her glass in the other, and sank deep into an easy chair. She crossed a vast expanse of leg. Bridie thought she looked obscene.

'Now,' said Frank, 'is this just a social visit or is there some other reason for it?'

'Where's the weans?' Tony asked.

'Across in the park with my sister, Doris,' Bridie answered. 'It's their Easter holidays from school.'

Tony grinned.

'We've come to collect them. Sadie and me've got married, so they'll have a mammy again.'

'You can't do that,' Bridie cried out.

Sadie's eyes narrowed.

'Why not, eh?'

Bridie turned desperately to Frank.

'Frank . . .'

'Look, Tony,' Frank said, 'think of the children. They've never seen you for ages. They've never clapped eyes on this woman at all . . .'

'Hey you,' Sadie's mouth took on an ugly twist, 'less of the "this woman". I'm as good as her – ' she cocked her head in Bridie's direction – 'any bloody day of the week.'

'I'm just trying to think what's best for the children,' Frank said, 'They know us. They're settled and happy here. I think for their sakes they should stay with us. You could see them as often as you like, of course.'

Sadie said, 'Huh, big of you, I'm sure. Ta very much.'

'Naw.' Tony shook his head. 'It's not right. They're my weans.'

Bridie gave a sarcastic laugh. 'You're a fine one to talk about what's right. Was it right of you to disappear and leave them in the first place? Your sudden desire for the children wouldn't have anything to do with collecting their family allowance, would it?'

'See you,' Sadie sneered. 'Think you're somebody. Well, you're not. We've come for the weans and it doesn't matter a shite what you say.'

Frank said, 'Tony, think of the children. Think of the shock

336

to them. Coming in as usual for their tea and then being suddenly snatched away.'

'But I'm their daddy and Sadie's their new mammy. They'll think it's great.'

'Don't be an idiot. And what about their school? Where are you going to live?'

Sadie said, 'Not that it's any of your business but we've got a place in Possilpark. They can go to school there.'

Oh God, Bridie thought. *Possilpark*. She had never believed that the Gorbals deserved the worldwide reputation it had gained as a result of a bestselling book about gang warfare and razor-slashing in the area. She had always loved the place and the warm-hearted people who lived in it.

But Possilpark? That was a different story. Impossible to allow the children to go anywhere with this woman, but totally unthinkable to allow them to go to a place like Possilpark. She couldn't believe that all this was happening.

Nobody in the world knew the children (or cared about them) as she did. Bobby was a bit noisy and energetic and more exhausting to look after than the other three put together. But he was such an open-hearted loving child. Not long after he'd come to Botanic Cresent he'd been sitting next to her at the breakfast table when unexpectedly he'd leaned his head against her arm and said, 'I wish I could stay here with you for ever and ever.'

Marion, Daisy and Daniel had often hugged and kissed her but Bobby had been the only one to say the words, 'I love you, Aunty Bridie.'

She loved him too. She loved them all. Marion, who was already quite the little housewife, the practical one – the bossy one, the other children called her – who enjoyed helping her in the kitchen. Her clothes protected by a big apron tied round her waist, she would stand on a stool at the kitchen table and busy herself with rolling out pastry or biscuit mix. In her enthusiasm she got as much flour on the floor as on the table. Nevertheless, she had mastered the art of making good little pies and biscuits. Then she would organise the others, her apron reaching the floor as she bustled about.

'You put out the plates, Bobby. Daisy and Daniel, go and wash your hands before you sit up at the table.'

'Bossy-boots,' the children would complain. But Bridie would sometimes catch Marion looking anxiously round at her, as if to say, 'Am I doing all right?'

Daisy and Daniel were still her babies with their innocent, trusting little faces. Uncharted maps. They needed protecting against the outside world. Their world was the comfortable flat in Botanic Crescent with her and Frank, surrounded by love, feeling safe and secure. They trusted her. She couldn't let them down.

'I cannot, I will not, allow you to take the children away to Possilpark, or anywhere else. They belong here.'

'See you,' Sadie's eyes became black slits. 'You'd better get off your arse and pack the weans' things. If you don't we'll take them without their stuff and then get the police on to you.'

Just then the doorbell rang. Bridie went to answer it and as the children skipped unsuspectingly past her into the house, she caught at Doris's arm and urgently whispered, 'Doris, Tony's through in the room with an awful woman he's got married to. They're trying to take the children away. They want me to pack their cases. Right now. Can you believe it?'

Doris caught a squeal of dismay with a palm against her mouth.

'I told you, didn't I? I warned you. Oh, the poor weans.'

'I'm not going to let her take them,' Bridie hissed. 'I'm not going to let her.'

She could hear the children's voices, chorusing 'Hello, Daddy.' Then silence as Tony said, 'This is your new mammy.'

Bridie and Doris hastened through to the room. The children were standing in an apprehensive cluster. Bobby piped up, 'We don't want a new mammy. We've got Aunty Bridie.'

'Well, you've got one whether you like it or not.' Tony rose. 'Where's their case? Like Sadie said, with or without their things, they're coming with us.'

Frank rose too.

'Now wait a minute, Tony. For God's sake, can't we talk about this? Arrange something to everybody's satisfaction. I could help you out with some cash. I know you're always short.'

They were all on their feet now.

'I'm doing OK,' Tony said. 'Sadie's a smashing singer. Really belts them out. The clubs go for her in a big way. We're doing OK, aren't we, hen?'

She was chewing gum again.

'Sure are.'

'Well, if you're doing so well, why do you want the children?' Frank said in desperation.

'They're my weans.' Tony looked indignant. 'I want my weans.'

The children began to wail in unison. Bridie put her arms around them. 'Well, you're not getting them.'

Frank said, 'Bridie, we can't use force. Leave it just now and I'll go to a solicitor and see what can be done.'

'They're not leaving this house with that awful woman.' Bridie's face was white and clenched.

'Oh, is that so.' Sadie stubbed out her cigarette and advanced on the children. 'Come on, Tony. We've wasted enough time with these toffee-nosed shites.'

Bridie clung to the small, trembling bodies. They began to cry, then scream.

'Bridie.' Frank grabbed her and shook her and shouted, 'Don't do this. You're only making it worse for them.'

The children were torn away from her.

Chapter Fifty-Four

Andrina was abandoned in the icy darkness of her babyhood. Helpless, not knowing what to do.

'Mummy.' She spoke close to the phone, clutching it against her mouth. 'Mummy, please don't hang up. It's not true. He's a wicked man whose had this terrible obsession about me. I told Daddy – ' But the phone had already gone dead.

Jennifer was on holiday from school and she came trailing into the hall like a shadow.

'Mummy, I'm hungry. Aren't we going to have any lunch today?'

Andrina ignored her as if she didn't exist. She stood with the receiver in one hand, her other wavering over the phone. She'd already dialled several times during the last few days and every time had been plunged into the same dark abandonment. Even when she wasn't making these desperate attempts to contact her mother, the terror remained, the paralysis of the mind, the helplessness.

They usually went to Bearsden at the weekends, especially if Robert was on an outing with his pupils. He wasn't going anywhere this weekend. At Bearsden on a Sunday, she sang in her mother's church. They had lunch at her mother's. What was going to happen this weekend? What could she say to Robert? What excuse could she give? She put the phone down.

She was trying to be nice to him. Trying to tempt him to sleep with her again. They did sleep together in the same bed, but had never made love for years. Tonight she must lie closer to him, touch him, make him want her. Then the baby could be his.

She hadn't been to the doctor but she was certain she was pregnant. Her mind tangled about, trying to sort out images and feelings. The shock of Bernard's hard glittering eyes when he told her to fuck off! The plummeting into a deep dark pit, not even knowing Bernard any more. The shock of her father's words danced like devils in her head. The horror of her mother knowing was unendurable.

She was an adulteress sinking alone in her own deceit, frantically casting about for a way, any way, to claw herself to safety. She was more than ready to believe that Bernard was an obsessive madman, who had been lying to her father and mother. Surely he *must* have been mad to have gone to Bearsden and shouted for all to hear like that. It didn't bear thinking about, it was so dreadful. Once she and Robert had made love, she could, without hesitation, swear to herself and everybody else that the baby was his.

Her thoughts flew to abortion, but she didn't know how to arrange it. Her mind cast about for anyone who might help her. Her neighbour Josie? But Josie had been so shocked at the sex in the wedding-dress episode, she'd been barely polite to her ever since. Doris? Dare she speak to Doris? Certainly she wouldn't give any hint to Doris about her love affair with Bernard. Doris, far from helping her, would be more likely to kill her with her bare hands. The same applied to Jane.

Yet she needed help so desperately. Again her thoughts turned to her mother. Her mother had always been at her best when looking after anyone who was ill or in trouble. She was marvellous at shouldering the load, making everything all right.

'Oh please, Mummy,' Andrina's mouth moved soundlessly as she stood gazing down at the telephone, 'please help me.'

Jennifer gently tugged at her sleeve.

'Please, Mummy, I'm awful hungry.'

'Oh, go and take an apple or a biscuit or something,' Andrina snapped impatiently. There was no mistaking whose child Jennifer was with her thin face, olive-shaped eyes and mousy brown hair. She felt a pang of guilt for speaking so sharply to the child who now trailed away again, shoulders sagging, head lowered. But she was distracted by many far more urgent things than making lunch. Robert was away getting something done to the car. It was a dreadful old banger. As if he couldn't have brought a decent car when he was at it. After all, there was such a thing as hire purchase.

Her mind floundered into murky waters again. Hadn't she heard or read somewhere about drinking gin and taking very hot baths? That could bring on an abortion. Right away she hastened through to the drinks cabinet and poured herself a tumblerful of gin. Shuddering at the taste, she gulped it down. Then she ran a hot bath. The bathroom misted with steam and made her sweat. Getting into the bath she squealed at the scalding heat. She lay in agony as long as she could, even topping up with boiling water from the tap as the bath began to feel more bearable. Afterwards her skin was so red and tender, she wept as she patted herself dry.

Oh God, she prayed, please have mercy on me. Save me. Don't let me be pregnant. If you do this for me I'll never have illicit sex with Bernard or any other man again. I promise. I'll be good. I swear I'll never sin, ever again. Oh please, please God, help me!

The gin was making her feel sick. The heat in the bathroom was intolerable. She retched over the washbasin.

There was a gentle tapping at the door.

'Mummy, can I take any of the ice-creams that are in the fridge?'

'Oh, do what you like,' Andrina shouted. 'I don't care. Just go away and leave me alone.'

Groaning, she leaned her brow on the cool edge of the basin. She wanted to die. In a continuing nightmare, she somehow managed to dress and escape from the room. Then she remembered that not long before Jennifer had been born, somebody (was it the nurse?) had told her to take a big dose of castor oil, 'to help her on the way'.

She forced herself back, found the bottle in the bathroom cabinet and took a large dose. It tasted foul and nearly made her sick again. With a struggle she managed to keep it down.

She tried to tell herself that it could be stress and anxiety that had made her late. Indeed, she used to be very irregular when she was younger and occasionally since – at least once that she could recall – she had been late. It could be a mixture of that and a stomach upset. There were a lot of bugs going about just now. The comfort she gave herself with these thoughts, however, was just a peripheral glimmer. It couldn't reach the black terror at the centre of her soul.

When Robert arrived home, she was sitting in the hall beside the telephone table lost in the jungle of her thoughts. She was oblivious to the fact that none of the house lights were switched on, the fire was out and there was no tea on the kitchen table. She had completely forgotten about Jennifer, who was also sitting motionless in the dark kitchen.

Robert switched on all the lights.

'What the . . .'

In the kitchen Jennifer blinked up at him as if she'd been asleep. He hoisted her into his arms and went back out to the hall.

'What's happened?' he asked Andrina. 'What on earth are you sitting like that for?'

Now was her chance. Make him feel sorry for her. Touch her, comfort her. She needed him as she'd never needed him before.

'I don't feel well.'

'I don't care how you feel. There's no excuse for leaving Jennifer sitting in a cold, dark room like that.' Then to Jennifer, 'When did you last eat, pet?'

'At breakfast, I think.'

Robert paled with anger. He sent a dagger of hatred towards Andrina.

'I'll speak to you later.' Then to Jennifer, 'Come on darling. Daddy'll light the fire and make you something nice to eat. Your wee hands and legs are frozen.' He rubbed at the child's skinny legs. 'Never mind, Daddy'll soon have you warm as pie.'

Andrina forced herself to get up and follow them through to the kitchen.

'If you do the fire, I'll make the tea. It's just a matter of heating spaghetti bolognaise. I prepared it earlier today.' She had actually had it in the fridge for a few days. 'I meant to have it for our lunch, but then I took this sick and dizzy turn – I had to sit down. But I feel not so bad now. Some sort of tummy bug, I suppose. There's a lot of it going about. I hope Jennifer doesn't get it.'

Robert ignored her. He didn't care about her any more. She realised that she'd known this for some considerable time. It hadn't mattered to her, but it did now. She felt childishly in need of being held and cuddled and told that she didn't need to worry. He would make everything all right. Just as he'd done with Jennifer.

She didn't want Bernard. He was not the dependable trustworthy type that made you feel safe. Bernard was for lust and excitement and danger. When you felt ill, these things were no longer important. Right now she needed her comfortable bed in her own comfortable house. She needed looking after by her own boring, dependable and normally kindly husband.

Or her mother. Tears spilled down Andrina's face and she longed for her mother to come back to her. Just as she'd done in another cold dark room, a long time ago.

Chapter Fifty-Five

It was obvious to Bernard that Andrina was not going to get in touch. He had forced the issue at last. She'd had to make a choice. Now she'd made it. He supposed he'd always known that was how it would be. Andrina had such a fixation about her mother. Nothing was going to change it. There was also her fear of scandal and he suspected it wasn't just for her mother's sake but for her own. Andrina couldn't give up the saintly Christian image people had of her.

He groaned when he thought of all the wasted years of his life. She'd kept him dangling for half a lifetime. He'd been such a bloody fool. She'd never had any intention of leaving Robert or telling her mother or doing anything that would deny her not only her good reputation but her good husband and her good home.

And yet . . . and yet, the years hadn't been totally wasted when he remembered the hours of passion he'd enjoyed with her. She was a beautiful, sexy woman. There would always be that powerful sexual chemistry between them until the day he died.

But, as he'd told her, as far as everything else was concerned, enough was enough. He'd done everything in his power to have her as his own. He could do no more except try to be a good loser. In a way he was relieved. Now at least he knew where he stood and he could get on with his life. He could also look Robert in the eye and know that he didn't need to behave like an ungrateful louse. It was only now, when the affair with Andrina was over, that it hit him – really caught him in the gut – what he'd been doing to a man who'd been his best friend and mentor for so many years.

He went to Robert's karate club at Sinnieglen as often as he could and worked so hard while he was there that Robert took him aside and spoke to him.

'Bernard, it's obvious to me that you're not a happy man.

OK, you can get some release by working your guts out. But don't forget, too, the karate ethic of control. That is far more likely to help you towards peace of mind. You can always talk to me about anything that's troubling you. We've been friends for a long time.'

'Yes,' Bernard agreed with a bitterness aimed solely at himself.

'I'm always here for you, remember,' Robert said.

Oh Christ, Bernard thought. Now I should tell him. But I can't. I didn't care a shit about telling Sophie McPherson but I can't tell him. No doubt Robert would find out soon enough when he visited his in-laws. And then what? He kept going to the karate club, willing Robert to tell him he was the lowest fucking shit that had ever crawled the earth. He wanted Robert to get it over with and beat the living daylights out of him. At other times, his mind was filled with work, or with what to do about the cottage.

He thought again about Michael and Caroline. That Castlemilk house was going to be the death of them if something wasn't done. He went to see them. Caroline answered the door.

'Oh, it's you, Bernard. Come away in.'

Recently he had noticed a subtle change in her attitude to him. Before, he'd detected a stiffness, a resentment. She'd barely been able to be civil. Now she was more relaxed in her greeting. She even seemed quite anxious to make him feel welcome and at home.

'We're just having a cup of tea. I'll fetch another cup. Away through to the room.'

'Thanks.'

Michael's battered face lit up with pleasure at the sight of him.

'Hi there, Bernard. What brings you out to the wilds of Castlemilk today?'

'Hello Martha.' Bernard nodded towards Michael's mother-in-law who seemed to fill half the room. Her whiskery jowls were chomping on a slab of cake.

She nodded to him in return.

'Must I have a reason to visit my brother and his family?'

346

'No, no.' Michael laughed. 'You know we're always pleased to see you. Sit down.'

Caroline poured him a cup of tea. Then she asked, 'Are you still staying with Frank? Or are you back at the cottage?'

'Actually, it's the cottage that I came about.'

'Oh?' Caroline sat down, her plump face puzzled.

'I've decided it's not convenient for me. I'd be better with a small flat in the city centre nearer my office. So I was wondering if you'd like to rent it from me. I wouldn't want as much as you pay here.'

There was a stunned silence. At last Bernard broke it.

'There's good fresh air out there. It would be the making of the children. How about if I take you and Caroline out to see it, Michael, and then you can talk about it between you and let me know what you think in a day or two? Or whenever you like. There's no hurry.'

Suddenly Caroline burst into tears and Michael rushed to put his arms around her and hug her plump body tightly against him.

'I feel awful,' Caroline wailed, and Bernard thought, what the hell's wrong with her? I'll never understand women. Out loud he said, 'Look, I didn't mean to upset you. Forget I spoke.'

'No, no,' Michael said. 'It's just . . . Well, you don't know what this means to us, Bernard. This place is killing us. We've got coughs and colds all the time and the kids' asthma is getting worse. Ma's arthritis is killing her and now she's getting chesty.'

Caroline's tear-stained face emerged from Michael's chest.

'I've to heat all the sheets and blankets every night in front of the fire and you should see the steam rising off them. Everything's rotten damp. Michael and Mammy's tried their best but they can't get the council to do anything about it.'

Big Martha spoke up then.

'Would you believe it – they told Michael it was caused by heavy breathing and he and his wife shouldn't make love so much. Or when they did, they should keep the window open. And we're supposed to keep all the windows open if we have a bath. If we don't die with the bloody damp, we'll freeze to death.'

'Mammy, don't swear,' Caroline sobbed. 'I keep telling you.

'Oh, shut up and stop your stupid blubbering. Tell the man you'll take the cottage.'

'You really mean it, Bernard?' Michael asked.

'Of course I mean it.' Bernard fished in his pocket and tossed a bundle of keys over to Michael. 'It's yours for half what you pay here.'

'Oh no,' Caroline's sobs became louder, 'we couldn't.'

'What do you mean, you fucking couldn't?' Martha shouted.

'Mammy! You don't understand. I feel awful.'

'You look awful as well. Just shut your stupid mouth or I'll come over and shut it for you.'

Michael said, 'Why do you feel awful, pet? It would be the saving of us.'

'I know, but it's too good of Bernard and at such a low rent.'

Bernard said, 'Forget it. I'm making more money than I can use. As far as I'm concerned, you can have it for nothing. You'd be doing me a favour to look after it for me.'

Caroline dabbed at her eyes with her apron.

'No, we must pay you rent, Bernard. And thank you most sincerely. This is very good of you. We all appreciate it. I'm sorry if at times in the past I haven't been all that nice to you – '

Bernard interrupted her.

'Just do as your mammy says and shut up. Now, do you want me to drive the pair of you out right now to see the place?'

Caroline was crimson with pleasure.

'Would you see to the weans, Mammy? I'll ask Mrs Dempsey to pick them up at the school with her lot. Then they can stay in and do their homework until we get back.'

'Away you go,' Martha said. 'The weans'll be fine.'

Bernard felt quite envious of Caroline and Michael's excitement, then sad at their raptures as he showed them round the cottage.

There seemed to be part of Andrina in every room and it was both painful and depressing to have the love nest he'd shared with her invaded, taken over, by other people. This, more than anything else, made the finality of their love affair become real to him.

The reality was Michael and Caroline dancing joyously through the cottage hugging their new and happy life to themselves. The passionate love scenes he'd experienced here with Andrina faded like a dream, and were gone.

Chapter Fifty-Six

'Should I tell him, then?' McPherson asked.

'Tell him what?'

McPherson sighed.

'Sophie, we can't keep putting them off every weekend without giving a reason.'

'She knows the reason.'

'I'm talking about Robert. What's he supposed to think?'

'Let her tell him.'

'You know perfectly well that she won't.'

'Yes, she'll lie till the end. To all of us. There's no limit to her lies.'

'We owe Robert an explanation. He's liable to arrive on our doorstep to try to find out what's gone wrong. He'll maybe think you're ill or something and don't want to worry Andrina.'

Sophie gave a sarcastic, humourless laugh.

'Well, don't you think,' McPherson persisted, 'we should at least be prepared? Something's bound to happen. Should we just say you and Andrina have fallen out and not go into any detail, I wonder? Would he be content with that, do you think?'

'I'm not going to lie to him.'

'You mean you'd tell him?'

'If he comes here, or he phones me and asks me what's wrong, I shall tell him the truth.'

McPherson chewed worriedly at the stem of his pipe.

'I've always found there are times when it pays to be diplomatic . . .'

'Oh yes. I can believe that.'

'The truth can be too painful. Why should we be the ones to cause Robert such pain? Wouldn't it be better to think of something else – a kind of half-truth, perhaps?'

'You're not in the City Chambers just now.'

'What's that supposed to mean?'

'This is family we're talking about.'

'So?'

'So I think we owe Robert the truth.'

'But Andrina's the one whose our own flesh and blood. She's our daughter.'

'She's no daughter of mine.'

'Och, Sophie . . .'

'How do you think I would feel? What do you think I should do? Would it do Andrina any favours if I covered up for her? Condoned her behaviour? Helped her continue with her wicked deceits? Would it do her any good? Would it do Robert any good?'

McPherson sighed.

'I suppose not. She's a grown woman. I doubt if she'll ever change now.'

'She's got away with everything for far too long. Let her now face the consequences of her own behaviour. I won't volunteer any information, nor should you. But if Robert asks us, I believe we should tell him the truth.'

'I suppose you're right. Otherwise we'd get all tangled up in lies and never know where we stood. Yes, you're quite right. But oh God, it's an awful situation.'

'The only person I'm really upset about is Jennifer.'

'I know. I'll miss the wee girl as well. We can't cut her out of our lives, Sophie. She needs us. I've always suspected she wasn't as happy as she ought to be. Now I can understand why.'

'Yes, only the good Lord knows what that child has been subjected to. What she has seen and heard.' Sophie put a palm across her eyes. 'It doesn't bear thinking about. I'll never forgive Andrina. Never!'

'Well, what can we do about Jennifer? She's our only grandchild.'

'Robert's her father. He'll have a say in what happens to the child. I don't think he'd deny us access to her. Why should he? We've always been good to her.'

'That's true.' He felt a bit easier. But not much. It was a dreadful predicament to be in. He wished there was some trip he had to go on for the council – as far away as possible – but there was nothing at the moment. He could only hope that if Robert did arrive on the doorstep, he would be at the City Chambers and Sophie would be the one to deal with the situation.

As it happened, of course, he was at home when Robert appeared. Sophie brought him through to the sitting-room where McPherson had been watching television and enjoying a pipe and a dram.

Robert said, 'I was along at the Cairnses delivering some books for Derek, so I thought I'd just drop in and see how you both were, while I was in the area.'

'Would you like a dram?' Sophie asked.

'I wouldn't mind a beer if you've got one.'

Sophie went through to the kitchen to fetch a beer and a glass. McPherson prayed she wouldn't take long. He could feel beads of sweat on his forehead and his chest was tightening, making him tip his face back to draw in breath.

'Are you all right?' Robert asked.

'No, he's not and neither am I,' Sophie said, handing Robert a glass and sitting down in a chair beside McPherson and facing Robert.

'Oh, what's wrong?' Robert took a swig of the beer, then looked over at them with some concern. 'I was wondering why we hadn't heard from you . . .'

'We're terribly upset, Robert.'

'What about?'

'Oh God,' McPherson groaned. 'Believe me, Robert, we feel terrible about this.'

'About what?' Robert repeated.

'About what Andrina's been doing. We didn't know a thing, Robert. For all these years – '

Sophie interrupted.

'She's been fornicating with that O'Maley creature. I always knew he was a wicked man and would do her no good. I tried to stop them years ago and I thought I had. I've tried, as God is my witness, to keep her on the path of righteousness, but I've obviously failed. We've just found out. I'm sorry, Robert. Truly sorry. And I hope and pray that you won't deny us having contact with Jennifer. I want nothing more to do with

Andrina. I've told her she's no longer a daughter of mine. But Jennifer will always be my grandchild.'

Robert's face was impassive. Even his eyes betrayed no expression. He finished his beer and gently placed his glass on the coffee table. A silence lay heavy on the room until eventually McPherson burst out in anguish: 'For God's sake, say something, man.'

'Yes, you can continue to see Jennifer.' Robert measured his words as if timing them was of the utmost importance. 'I'll arrange to bring her at regular intervals. We can talk about the details later.'

Sophie said, 'If need be, Robert, she can stay here. She can stay here as long as you want her to. She'd be more than welcome, wouldn't she, Andrew?'

'Oh, definitely,' McPherson agreed. 'We're really fond of Jennifer. She means a lot to both of us. Always has done.'

'I'll keep that in mind,' Robert said. He rose. 'I'll be in touch.'

McPherson said, 'We're sorry about all this, Robert. And ashamed. I really feel – '

'It's not your fault,' Robert interrupted. 'Just one thing before I go. How did you find out?'

Sophie rose, in readiness to see him to the door.

'That O'Maley creature. He came here and told us. Told me. Shouted it at me.' Her mouth tightened. 'I'll never forget it. It's him she'd always wanted to marry, he said – '

McPherson rose in distress.

'Sophie, that's enough.'

'He said I'd ruined their lives. He said they'd been . . . for years . . . He used horrible, filthy language . . .'

'Sophie!' McPherson put a hand on her arm but she shook it off and shrank away from him.

'Sophie, you're just getting yourself into a state again.'

'He blamed me. Me! And all I've been doing all these years is trying to protect her against him, against herself. But it's been no use. She's got the Noble bad blood, you see. She's the same as my filthy, perverted mother and father – '

'Sophie, be quiet!' McPherson was shouting now and becoming breathless and purple-faced. 'Control yourself.'

'Watch Jennifer,' Sophie said. 'Robert, don't let her do to Jennifer what my mother did to me. Her and that O'Maley man could do the same to Jennifer as my mother and father did to me. Please, oh please, protect your wee girl.'

'It's all right, Sophie,' Robert said quietly, 'I'll keep Jennifer safe.'

Sophie nodded, struggling to contain herself, pressing her thin lips tightly together. She followed him to the outside door. Then, without thinking, she returned to the window and waved him goodbye.

Chapter Fifty-Seven

Frank and Bridie were walking aimlessly through the Botanic Gardens, gazing around as if hoping to see the ghosts of the children.

Bridie said, 'I told you it was no use seeing the solicitor.'

'I had to try something.'

'God knows what's happening to them.'

'Try not to get upset, Bridie. You'll make yourself ill.'

'How can I avoid getting upset? I care about them.'

'So do I.'

'You've a funny way of showing it. You disappear every day as usual into that BBC Club . . .'

'That's enough, Bridie. You know perfectly well I go there to work. And we're surely not going down that road again.'

'What road?'

'You getting all bitter about my friends and colleagues. We've been through all that. Now I want us to be together on this one. We've got to see this through together.'

'But what can we do?'

'We can go and see them for a start.'

'The children?'

'And Tony and Sadie. She's had them for a few weeks now. You know how much work they are. Can you see that woman managing? Especially when she apparently goes singing as well.'

'Oh, Frank, I forgot about that. Surely she doesn't leave them on their own at night.'

'At least we can go and find out. And surely now that the dust has settled, so to speak, and with us being their aunty and uncle, they'll allow us to take the children out for a treat. We could take them to the zoo or to the cinema – wherever they like.'

'I long to see them again and I've been so worried.'

'What do you think I've been?'

'Oh, I know, Frank, I'm sorry.'

She linked her arm through his. 'We mustn't quarrel. You're right, the chances are that woman will soon have had more than enough of them. But oh, I daren't think how she might have been neglecting them, Frank.'

'And of course Tony won't be much use. He might fool about and play with them if the mood takes him but that'll be about it. I don't suppose he'd purposely do them any harm. He's just thoughtless and irresponsible.'

'Let's go right now,' Bridie said. 'We've wasted long enough.'

'OK. But keep it casual, Bridie. We don't want either of them to get up in arms. That won't serve any useful purpose. It's for the children's sake, remember. We want them to agree to let us have access.'

'It won't be easy but I'll try my best.'

Immediately they'd decided on positive action, they both felt cheered. Their spirits rose, their step quickened. The sight of Possilpark, however, pulled them down into gloom and depression again.

'What I'd like to know,' Frank said, as they walked along bleak, littered streets, 'is why they build such drab places nowadays. Why don't they build tenements as they used to in warm red sandstone like ours in Botanic Crescent? Something with designs that have stood the test of time and still look beautiful. Why this cold, uniform grey stuff, like rows of tombstones? Is it cheaper than the sandstone or what?'

'Think of the children being brought up here, Frank. They won't stand a chance.'

'Now keep calm. Here's their close. Be nice, remember. We've just popped in to say hello and ask how everybody's getting on. Don't, for God's sake, criticise Sadie or put her back up. If you do, we've had it.'

'All right. All right.'

They were both smiling on the doormat when Sadie opened the door.

'We just popped by,' Frank said, 'to ask how you're getting on.'

Sadie stood aside to allow them in. It was difficult to tell from her automatic, gum-chewing face what mood she was in, or what she was thinking. Her eyes were guarded.

'You'll be glad they're all at school,' Bridie said. 'It'll give you a wee bit of peace and quiet. I remember what a noisy handful they were when we had them. Frank had to rent a room at the BBC Club to work in. He just couldn't write in the house any more.'

'Well,' Frank said, 'it wasn't so bad normally. It was the summer holidays that were the killer. Where's Tony?'

The school holidays were only a few weeks away.

'God knows. He just disappears whenever and wherever the fancy takes him. I'm getting bloody sick of it.'

'Is there a local poolroom?' Frank asked. 'He used to play pool day and night when he was married to Theresa. He also, if I remember, spent a lot of time in the pub. I don't think poor Theresa saw very much of him, in fact.'

Sadie lit a cigarette.

'Well, I'm not fuckin' Theresa.'

'No,' Frank soothed. 'I'm sure you're more than capable of sorting Tony out.'

'He's not going to use me as a cook-cum-skivvy to dump her kids on either.'

'Well, Sadie – ' Bridie began, but Frank quickly cut in.

'Look, I think we've come at a bad time. You've obviously got enough on your plate, Sadie. Maybe we'd better go.'

Sadie shrugged.

'Suit yourself.'

Frank dragged Bridie away. Out on the street she turned on him furiously.

'All I was going to say was we'd be willing to take a turn with the children. Take them off her hands during the summer holidays . . .'

'Be patient, Bridie. I've a feeling things are working out just fine. The way things seem to be going it looks as if Sadie's had about enough of my big brother. If you ask me she's ready to pack him in.'

'Walk out on him, you mean?'

'Could be. She sees what he's like now and he's not going to

357

change. She's going to be left with his four children to look after without him lifting a finger to help.'

'Oh, Frank, do you really think so?'

'I know Tony, even if she doesn't. Keep your fingers crossed that at least Sadie's got a bit of sense. Or self-preservation or something.'

'I'll do more than that. I'll pray like I've never prayed before. And you should too. You've never been to Mass for ages.'

'OK. OK. We'll go together this week.'

In a few days, they did. Frank was surprised how taking Mass and kneeling side by side in the church and praying together deepened the bond between him and his wife. It felt as if they were reaffirming the sanctity of their marriage and the depth of their love for each other. They came out of the church holding hands. They'd never felt closer.

'Maybe,' Frank said, 'we gave Sadie a little push in the right direction by arriving like that the other day. Maybe we got her thinking some more.'

'If anything got her thinking it was you mentioning the summer holidays, Frank.'

'Well, she ought to think about that. It is a handful to have four children all day and every day. If she's not able or willing to take that on, now's the time she should face it. Now's the time she should do a runner.'

'Oh Frank,' Bridie laughed. 'Are we being awful?'

'I thought you said you'd do anything for the children.'

'I know. Yes, it's for their sake, isn't it.'

'Definitely.'

'You think she will? Before the holidays?'

Frank grinned and gave her a wink.

'I'm not an expert on character for nothing. What do you bet?'

Bridie laughed again.

'I might have known you'd bring your writing into it.'

'Well, pet, I am a writer and people are my raw material.'

'I know. I know. Oh, Frank, I hope you're right.'

Chapter Fifty-Eight

'You're getting as brown as a berry, Ma.' (More like brown as an old leather boot.) Michael was cutting Big Martha's hair outside. She liked to sit out in the back garden in her wheelchair.

'This is like another world to me.' She looked around as if she could not believe her eyes. The lush greenery, the peaceful hills.

'Keep your ould head still or I'll have an ear off you.'

'Would you believe, all my life, I've never been in the country.'

'Och, come on now, ould yin. Don't exaggerate the sob stuff.'

'Well, maybe a few days at Millport or Rothesay, when Caroline was wee.'

'Doon the watter, eh? And at the Glasgow Fair, I'll bet.'

'But that was the seaside, not like here. And I never was anywhere when I was wee. Never been out of Glasgow – hardly ever out of Garngad, even when I was a grown woman. A run in the tramcar – or sometimes I walked – into the city centre and that was a great treat and a great excitement. Looking at all the big shops and all the posh-dressed folk in Sauchiehall Street.'

She shook her head again. It was white now. So were her whiskers and, like the hair on her head, they had become softer, thinner, downier. It somehow gave her a more vulnerable and pathetic look, especially when Michael washed her hair and it clung inadequately to her head, revealing naked patches of scalp. Even when it was dry now, it was a poor cover. He tried to comb it so that it spread out and disguised the naked patches.

'You look posh yourself, Ma, when you're dressed up in your good fur coat.'

'God, that took a while to pay up, but it's been worth it. I've had years of good wear out of that coat. Where's our Caroline?'

He noted the 'our'. It was the first time she'd included him with her like this. The poor ould sod's whiskers weren't the only thing about her that was getting soft.

'She's taken the weans to Glasgow to buy them new shoes.'

'The cheaper rent here has made an awful difference as well.'

'You can say that again. I was thinking we might be able to afford a wee car. I'm earning good money, and what with that vegetable patch . . .'

'I've never tasted such good spuds.'

'It must have been the previous owner to Bernard that planted all the vegetables. He'd never have had the time. You could see by the weeds and how everything was overgrown he'd never even – '

'You shut your face,' Martha growled. 'I'll not have a word said against that brother of yours ever again.'

Michael had to laugh. He felt like saying, 'So it suddenly doesn't matter any more that he and I are both Green Grapes does it?', but he thought better of it.

'What are you laughing at?' Martha loudly wanted to know.

'Nothing, Ma, nothing. It's a smashing day. The sun's belting down on us. We're here in the best wee place on God's earth. I just feel happy, that's all.'

'Aye, well, just you watch it.'

'As I was saying about a car . . .'

'What the hell do you want a car for?'

'To get around, of course.'

'I'm perfectly happy here and so should you be. Why should we want to get around anywhere?'

'You selfish ould bisom,' he said. 'I'm having to waste a lot of time hanging around waiting for buses to get to my work and back for a start.'

'There's nothing wrong with buses. There were times when Caroline's da had to walk miles to get to his work and home again at night. Just you think yourself damn lucky.'

'Aye, OK, Ma.'

But he had already made up his mind to purchase a cheap,

second-hand car. Only the other day he'd had a word with a man in a garage in Strathblane.

Martha said, 'I never want to move from here. You can bury me in this garden if you want.'

He laughed again.

'God forbid! After me taking so much trouble with these vegetables. You'd poison the lot, ould yin. No, it's back to Glasgow for you.'

He finished her hair and dusted down her shoulders. Then he became aware of her silence.

'What's up?' he asked. (Surely she couldn't be *serious* about being planted in the garden.) 'You were born and bred in Glasgow and your man's buried there.'

She sighed.

'I suppose you're right. It wouldn't be very convenient.'

Convenient? he thought incredulously. The understatement of all time!

'And,' Martha went on, 'it's not that I've got anything against Glasgow . . .'

'I should think not. After all the great stories you've told me about it. You're a true Glaswegian – spunk and all. I'm even surprised that you took to living out here. I thought I was going to have a hell of a job convincing you. Getting you to make the move.'

'If I'd still been in my nice wee place in Garngad, it might have been different. But you've no idea what I suffered with that dampness in Castlemilk. A bloody disgrace, that house.'

'You feel a lot better here then? With your arthritis, I mean?'

'Of course I do. What a bloody stupid question. Another thing, when I was young – or even up till a few years back – I could walk the Glasgow streets – anybody could – and feel safe. Now there's gangsters and God knows what else. There's that murderer, for instance, killing decent women in their sixties and seventies. What reason can he possibly have for killing old women? According to the paper, it's not robbery or rape. Whatever reason could there be for killing an old woman?' she repeated.

Michael could think of a few, but all he said was, 'I think I hear Caroline and the weans at the front.'

'They know their way round the back.'

'Hello, dear. Hello, Mammy,' Caroline greeted them. 'I'm dying for a drink of tea. I'll just go in and dump these parcels and then I'll bring us all out a cup.'

The children had already pounced on the swing and see-saw that Michael had made for them at the foot of the garden. Creaking, bumping, squealing, and laughing echoed in the still, warm air.

Michael went in to replace the scissors in the dresser drawer. The kitchen was cooler and darker than outside with its low, beamed ceiling and rust-coloured flagstones.

'Here,' Caroline said. 'You'll never guess.'

'What?'

'I dropped in to see Frank and Bridie while I was in the area and they've got the children back.'

'Tony's dumped them on Frank *again*?'

'Yes, isn't it awful? Well, it is in one way. But in another it's great. Or so Bridie and Frank seem to think. They're happy as larks. But Michael, you'll never guess . . . oh, it's so like the thing . . .'

'OK, you tell me. What will I never guess?'

'Bridie's pregnant.'

'Good God, and her already lumbered with four weans.'

'And what do you bet she'll have twins? You know what your family's like for twins. But isn't it so like the thing? Bridie's been trying for years to get pregnant and now she's adopted four weans, and has given up even thinking about getting pregnant, that's exactly what happens. Did I tell you that Tony has agreed to let them adopt his children? He's signed papers and everything.'

'Poor wee Bridie.'

'No, she's over the moon about it. She'll be delighted, she says, if it's twins. Frank's as pleased as punch as well. Can you believe it?'

It wasn't easy but he supposed it must be true.

'How's he going to manage to write?'

'Oh, apparently he's got an office room somewhere. He goes out every morning and comes back every afternoon.'

Suddenly there was a foghorn voice from outside.

362

'Have you two gone to bloody China for that tea? I'm sitting here with my tongue hanging out.'

'Mammy!' Caroline shouted back, 'if you don't behave yourself, you won't get any tea.'

'Och, you're a hard bisom.' Michael gave Caroline's soft wobble of a bottom a hearty smack. 'Shouting at a pour ould woman like that.' Ignoring her cries of 'Here you, that was sore' and her return punch, he lifted the tray and carried it out to the white lace-patterned table in the garden.

'Nothing to eat?' Martha said. 'What do you think you're trying to do? Starve me or something?'

Strangely enough, Martha hadn't been eating nearly as much since she'd moved to the cottage. Her voracious appetite had gone. She enjoyed her food but didn't make a pig of herself any more. Sometimes Michael found himself trying to tempt her to eat.

'Come on, Ma,' he'd say. 'You always take second helpings. And this is your favourite, remember?'

'Stuff it in your own mouth, if you're that keen to get rid of it,' she'd say. 'I know when I've had enough.'

'Well,' he'd scratch his cropped head, 'I never thought I'd see the day . . .'

It wasn't only Martha who had changed of course. The whole family were more relaxed and content. He only wished he could do something for Bernard so that he too could have a bit of happiness in his life. He realised now that Bernard had always been the one who had helped out in any family crisis. Rock steady he'd always been. And tough. Even as a wee boy.

'You'll always be welcome here, Bernard' he kept telling him now. He tried to encourage his brother to confide whatever was troubling him, but Bernard had always been one to fight his own battles. Even though they were twins, Michael had never been able to get close to him.

'As different as chalk and cheese' Caroline used to say. Now, like her mother, she wouldn't hear a word against Bernard. Although she agreed that, despite his usual laid back, casual sense of humour, there was something about his eyes . . .

'I worry about Bernard now,' Caroline said.

Chapter Fifty-Nine

This time he was on his own. There were other men on the ground but he was the one glued to the principal, the one giving close protection.

This time he wasn't dealing with some local pop group or its fans. Basic crowd or spectator control was an ability on its own. It was intricate and he had to know how to apply his men and deal with the situation in the right way.

Bodyguarding was a whole different scene. For a start you had to be much tougher. He remembered the punishing training he'd got from the ex-SAS guys in Bodyguards Incorporated, way back in his teens. He'd lied about his age to do bouncer work at the time and Bodyguards Incorporated had picked him out while he was working at one of the clubs. They'd seen him as good material for their outfit. My God, did they give him the works. Up at 4.30 every morning to do a gruelling assault course. Then there was close protection techniques, firearms training. He'd already been well prepared on the martial arts side, thanks to Robert Anderson.

He'd never had all that much occasion to use violence, however. He could look after himself – violence was the last resort. He'd developed an instinct for knowing if something was going to happen. He was a believer in creating an aura around himself too. The aura was invisible but he knew people could sense it. They knew how far they could push him, and no further.

No aura, however powerful, could stop a bullet or a bomb, though, and that's what he had to think of when taking on a bodyguarding assignment. Bodyguarding meant laying your life on the line, without a doubt. The only thing that gave him the ability to do that part of the business was the fact that working on the streets had sharpened his instincts. That sharpness wasn't the result of training. It was learned. The SAS could teach you but if you were brought up and worked on the streets for many years (especially the Glasgow streets) your instincts grew naturally razor sharp.

With bodyguarding he had always to think ahead. The last thing he wanted to do was stand and fight. He had to extract the principal from danger. If someone pulled a gun, he had to block the bullet. Then, if possible, fire back. If it was an attacker with a knife, he had to disarm him, or keep him at arm's length, away from the principal. To take either a gun or a knife off an attacker took a lot of nerve and was something few of his men liked to contemplate. But he'd disarmed attackers before and would do it again if necessary.

The point was, bodyguarding meant defending. The principal had to be thought of first at all times; yourself second.

When he'd accepted this particular assignment, MacGowan had said he was mad. It was common knowledge that a suicide squad was after this principal.

'Don't worry,' he'd assured all his men. 'I've quantified the risks. I'm liaising with the anti-terrorist police, and the Special Branch.'

They knew of course that he'd be wearing a bullet-proof vest and carrying side arms. But they still told him he was crazy.

Maybe he was. He did feel fear. That was natural – and useful. If you were completely devoid of fear, you could be careless. Fear helped give a good shot of adrenalin and he knew how to channel the adrenalin into the right places. That's what made him tick. This time, though, there was a recklessness about him. He did everything by the book as usual: he was too well trained, too much of a professional, too alert and watchful to be careless or negligent in any way. He would defend the principal, all right. He would deal with any attacker. But if he was killed in the process – what the hell.

The problem with this principal was the fact that his enemies weren't just the suicide squad. No doubt the Special Branch had already sussed most of them out. Probably the squad had drawn straws and only one of them – who would have a better chance of quietly infiltrating a crowd – would be there to pull the trigger. What complicated this assignment was that the majority of people in any crowd who might be milling about the streets would hate this principal. They would all be likely to look aggressive and menacing. The danger points would be every time the principal hit the streets, out of the airport into the car, out of the car into the hotel, where he was conducting the business he'd come over for, then out again next day and into his car and back to the airport.

Bernard wasn't so worried about the overnight stay. One floor of the hotel had been taken over and there would be several anti-terrorist police posted along the corridor. The principal was in a two-bedroomed suite and Bernard was to stay in the next bedroom to him overnight.

So it was those few minutes each time they hit the street that he was most concerned about. First of all he arranged for a tarmac transfer, which meant that the principal didn't need to walk through the airport. Instead he got off the plane and into the limousine on the tarmac. Bernard sat in the front seat beside the chauffeur. He'd already vetted the chauffeur and thoroughly checked over every inch of the car.

The principal didn't speak – a dour-looking man with heavy jowls and hooded eyes, he sat back on the cushions staring fixedly ahead, looking neither left nor right for the whole of the journey. A hostile crowd was waiting outside the hotel. Bernard had already sussed out that people were also milling about the side lane and at the narrow back entrance. It was a safer and quicker bet to guide the principal straight in the front. He got out of the car first, and before opening the back door (and indeed all the time), his experienced eyes took in the scene. Too many people were booing and cat-calling and shaking fists. He couldn't accurately pick out the potential assassin. Shielding the principal with his big frame, he rushed him into the hotel.

So far, so good.

That night he hovered, fully dressed, on the edge of sleep, a light coverlet thrown over him. In the morning, the principal had a meeting with a couple of business types and a well-known titled man that Bernard had seen on television several times. All of them were indignant and insulted when Bernard insisted on searching them and their briefcases before allowing them access to the suite. The principal had also been angry and impatient.

'Don't be ridiculous,' he'd shouted at Bernard. 'I know these men. They are the people I've come to meet.'

Bernard ignored all the protests and satisfied himself that the men were 'clean' before allowing them over the threshold. He was not so easily impressed or put off as were the police who, in his opinion, ought to have made the search long before the men got near the door, or even the corridor.

But all was well. The meeting lasted all morning. Coffee was sent in, and lunch. On both occasions Bernard stopped the waiter, searched him and the trolley, went into the suite with him and accompanied him out again. The same procedure was gone through each time the waiter returned to collect the trolley. Bernard ordered a sandwich and ate it, standing by the big double doors of the suite.

Early afternoon, the three men emerged. They left. Now came the last leg: getting the principal into the limousine and back to the airport. But apparently the man was in no hurry. He ordered a whisky and soda. The waiter was good-humoured about yet another search.

'I think you enjoy doing this,' he told Bernard.

'Sorry, pal,' Bernard said. 'You're not my type.'

'You'd rather have something in skirts, eh?'

'That's right, and the shorter the better.'

The waiter laughed, then delivered the whisky.

Afterwards Bernard began to feel restless. He kept glancing at his watch. If the principal didn't come out soon, he'd have to go in and remind him about the time of his plane. When he did appear, Bernard's adrenalin began pumping. If anything was going to happen, now was the time. He walked close to the principal down the corridor, then into the wide, empty foyer. Empty, that is, except for some anti-terrorist guys and staff members who were on duty at the reception counter. Suddenly Bernard spotted a woman in hotel staff uniform come out from behind the reception counter, smiling and holding a bouquet of flowers.

A sudden insight flashed into Bernard's tense mind. In one

rapid movement he grabbed his principal by the collar and thrust the man behind him. He thudded against the wall.

Time seemed to slow down into individual movements as if filmed under strobe lights. Bernard felt himself looking into the barrel of the female's gun. There was a dull roaring in his ears. Round the corners of his vision, he saw police running in slow motion, hotel staff transfixed with slack jaws and staring eyes. Holding his left arm like a solid bar behind him, he leaned back, whipping his right hand out and up, the gun jerking spasmodically with sharp, snapping cracks. He saw the woman pitched back off her feet as if by some giant puppeteer. Simultaneously, he was aware of hot pulses and a surprising wetness at his neck. Dizziness swept over him as he slid slowly downwards.

Bloody women, he thought before he lost consciousness. They'd never brought him any luck.

Chapter Sixty

Andrina believed she was going to die. Bernard had told her that his sister-in-law, Theresa, had died of a miscarriage. She had forgotten about that until now. When the bleeding first started, she had felt exquisite relief. Over and over again she had thanked God. Then it had become frighteningly heavy. What looked like dark lumps of liver were slithering out with gushes of blood. Never before in her life had she been so terrified, so appalled. Alone in the bathroom, she sobbed in distress. She tried to calm herself. She kept pulling the chain and flushing everything away. A couple of times she fainted, then came to lying on the bathroom carpet. She struggled up again, cleaned herself again, wiped at stains on the carpet, felt faint again.

She could hear a tremble of a voice from outside the bathroom door.

'Mummy, what's wrong? Mummy, please come out . . .'

'Go away and leave me alone,' Andrina moaned.

Robert was away at Bearsden doing his usual good Samaritan act with the Cairns man. No doubt he'd pay her mother and father a visit while he was there. She hated him. She hated Bernard. She hated all men. They took their pleasures and left the woman to suffer.

It was always the woman who suffered. It was terrible being a woman. The nightmare in the bathroom lasted for hours. She fought to survive, willing herself not to die in this scandalous fashion for everyone to know and be shocked and disgusted at her. She couldn't bear anyone to know. Her mother must never find out. It was this last desperate thought that steeled her to survive. Sweating, she cleaned herself again. She repeated out loud over and over, 'I'm going to be all right. I'm going to be all right.'

She padded herself then crawled about cleaning every carpet stain. She wiped the lavatory bowl. Clinging on to the handle of the bathroom door, she heaved herself to her feet.

'Mummy, what's wrong?' Jennifer's white face and large frightened eyes had a luminous quality in the darkness of the hall.

'Help me get to bed, Jennifer.'

She leaned on the little girl and somehow between them they reached the bedroom. Andrina crawled between the sheets. 'Make Mummy a cup of tea, would you? That's a good girl. Mummy's just caught a nasty tummy bug. I'll be all right after a rest in bed and a cup of tea.'

She lay listening to Jennifer move about the kitchen, drag chairs across to stand on to reach cupboards, drop things. She was such a slow, clumsy child. When, at long last, she returned to the bedroom, she was carrying a tray with big-eyed, lip-biting concentration as if the cup and saucer and plate of biscuits might at any moment leap up and attack her.

'Nothing to eat, dear,' Andrina said. 'Just a cup of tea.' She lifted the cup from the tray and sipped gratefully at it. Normally she didn't take sugar and of course Jennifer had forgotten. On this occasion, however, she was glad of the hot sweet drink. It helped revive her. 'You eat the biscuits.'

'Are you going to be all right?'

'Of course. I told you. Away through and watch television until Daddy comes home. And switch on all the lights,' she added, remembering Robert's fury the last time he'd come home and found Jennifer sitting in darkness. 'And don't be telling Daddy you had nothing to eat all day and make him angry with Mummy. I can't cook when I'm not well. Before you watch television, you'd better have some supper. There's soup in the fridge. Heat that up and take bread and butter with it. Then some apple pie for pudding. That's in the fridge as well. Hurry up now, and for goodness sake, watch you don't burn yourself at the cooker.'

She finished her tea and lay back, weak and exhausted. She must have slept because when she opened her eyes, Jennifer was standing by the bed again.

'Have you had your supper?'

Jennifer nodded.

'And washed your dishes and put them away?'

Another silent nod.

'That's a good girl. You're a good help to Mummy. What time is it?' She glanced round at the clock on the bedside table. 'Goodness, I didn't realise it was that late. I must have gone into a deep sleep. Is Daddy not home yet?'

'No.'

'Well, you'd better get undressed and go to bed now, Jennifer.'

'Is Daddy all right?'

'Of course he's all right. He's out visiting in Bearsden.'

'Granny and Grandpa?'

'And a friend who lives near them.'

'Is he coming back to us?'

'Of course he's coming back to us, Jennifer. What a silly question. Why shouldn't he come back to us?'

'Betty McIvor's daddy went away and never came back.'

'Who's Betty McIvor?'

'A girl in my class at school.'

'And Alex Dill's mummy – '

'Oh, for goodness sake, Jennifer. Can't you see I'm not well. I'm not able for your silly talk. Just because these things happened to people at school doesn't mean they're going to happen to you. Now away to bed like a good girl.'

Andrina allowed herself to be kissed but finally had to disentangle Jennifer's clinging arms from around her neck.

'Jennifer, please, Mummy's not well. Goodnight, dear.'

Afterwards, she dozed. Then wakened again. It was very late. The house was silent. Robert definitely should have been home by now. Perhaps he was reading in the kitchen. Sometimes he sat reading until late, or working on school papers. She wanted to get up and look but hadn't the energy. Her weakness was all pervasive. She listened to the needs of her body, knowing with an animal instinct that in sleep it would be healed.

The lights were still switched on in the morning. She felt puzzled, then realised that Robert had not been in bed beside her. Cautiously, she eased herself out from between the covers. She still felt ill and weak but the flow of blood seemed at least to have diminished. She crept to the bathroom, washed and changed the padding. Then, still shuffling carefully along

371

like an old woman, she went through to the kitchen and made a pot of tea. The tea helped. She poured herself a second cup. Had Robert stayed overnight at her mother's? How dare he do that without letting her know? She wondered what she should do. If she phoned Bearsden, her mother would just hang up the moment she heard her voice. She decided to try, on the off-chance that her father might answer. She was lucky – or so she thought for the first second or two when she heard his voice. Then, before she could ask for Robert, her father said, 'I'm sorry, Andrina. I didn't want to say anything to Robert but your mother thought he deserved the truth and maybe she was right.'

'She told him . . . what Bernard said?' The blood drained from her head. The hall began to gently swim around.

'I thought you would know by now. Hasn't Robert – '

She replaced the receiver. She was still sitting in the hall when Jennifer came through from her bedroom.

'Mummy?'

'Go and get dressed.'

'But Mummy . . .'

'Do as you're told.'

She had to get dressed herself. She had to claw herself back to some sort of normality. Think. Decide what to do. The nightmare must stop some time. If she could just hold on, keep going . . . She took a long time dressing and putting on her make-up. She was sitting with Jennifer at the kitchen table when she heard Robert's key in the door. With an effort, she straightened her back, tipped up her chin. It was a comfort to know that even in sickness, she could look beautiful. Her pallor was striking against the warm tints of her hair, the vivid aquamarine of her eyes and her pink, pouting lips.

He looked as if he hadn't shaved and his eyes were dark and sunken. But he seemed perfectly calm and in control of himself. He smiled at Jennifer and bent to kiss the top of her head.

'Now that the schools are closed,' he told her, 'how would you like to go out to Granny and Grandpa's for a few days? While you're there that'll give me time to arrange a nice surprise place for us to go on holiday.'

372

'If it's to the seaside, can I have a pail and spade, Daddy?'

He winked at her.

'The best pail and spade we can find. And Daddy'll help you make the biggest and best sandcastle you've ever seen.'

He turned to Andrina then.

'Pack her case.'

'Now?'

'Right now.'

'Is Mummy coming to Granny's too?' Jennifer asked.

'No, not this time. You go to Granny's and that'll give Mummy and Daddy a chance to get everything arranged.'

With an effort Andrina got up and went through to Jennifer's bedroom. She packed her clothes while a now excited Jennifer collected her favourite dolls and teddy and put them in a bag. Andrina helped Jennifer on with her coat, automatically making sure her plaits were not caught inside.

As she knelt before the child, she felt her life's blood begin to seep from her again.

'Say goodbye to Mummy.' Robert spoke from the doorway.

'Bye bye, Mummy.' Jennifer kissed her.

Robert said, 'I'll speak to you when I get back.'

Chapter Sixty-One

'Why don't you stay here until you decide what you're going to do,' Sophie suggested to Robert. 'McPherson's leaving after lunch for a trip to London. He'll be away for nearly a week. I'd be glad of the company.'

This was only too true. Since her shock of opening the door and being confronted with Bernard O'Maley, she was terrified of being in the house by herself, especially at night. McPherson had gone no way in convincing her that it hadn't been O'Maley watching her and following her. Quite the reverse. Arriving on her doorstep like that to shout obscenities at her proved that Bernard O'Maley was the one determined literally to drive her mad or frighten her to death, or both. She tried to cling on to some shreds of normality by telling herself that what he was doing to her was something quite different, a separate issue entirely, from the accounts in the newspapers about the Glasgow murderer. She told herself firmly that it was just a coincidence that these other elderly ladies had been followed. Bernard O'Maley could not be a mass murderer. It was too bizarre. Why should he kill old ladies? She must put such a thing completely out of her mind or she would sink into the abyss. Yet even so, she was not totally convinced. Could such a coincidence happen? All the victims had previously complained of being followed, but nobody had believed them. She felt chilled at the thought. What helped was the fact that her drug withdrawal symptoms were gradually, very gradually, diminishing. If she could just keep her terror of Bernard O'Maley at bay . . . He would succeed in his purpose if she allowed such imaginings to get the better of her.

'Oh, I wouldn't want to put you to all that trouble,' Robert said. 'I'd be more or less under your feet all day.'

'I thought you said you kept your karate club going for most of the summer. It keeps the boys off the streets, you said.'

'Well, yes . . .'

'That's settled then.'

'Only for a few days, Sophie, until I get things sorted out.'

'Yes, of course. At least keep me and Jennifer company while McPherson's in London. That's him now. I'd better go and dish the lunch. He's leaving right afterwards.'

McPherson nodded to Robert and sank into a chair opposite him.

'How are you, Robert?'

Robert shrugged.

'All right.'

'What's happening? With you and Andrina, I mean?'

Robert shrugged again.

'I'm going back to Monteith Row later today to have a talk with her. But Sophie wants me to return here and stay wtih her until you get back from London. It might be a good idea. Give me a chance to work things out.'

'You'll not have had time to see Bernard?'

Sophie came into the room then.

'If he has any sense, he'll have no more to do with that man. I know you'll want to tell him what you think of him, Robert. Even want to give him a thrashing. It's understandable and he deserves it. But I don't want to risk you having to suffer any more trouble and grief. That man's done us all enough harm. I've always said – '

'Well, he's not in a position to do anyone any harm at the moment,' McPherson interrupted.

'What do you mean?' Sophie asked.

'He's been shot.'

'Shot?'

'He was supposed to come to the City Chambers to discuss something with me before I left for London. He didn't keep the appointment, which wasn't like him, so I phoned his office. He was on a bodyguarding job and some terrorist shot him.'

'Dead?' Sophie struggled not to sound indecently anxious for a positive reply.

'No. He was lucky. There were other security men there who managed to stop the bleeding until the ambulance arrived. But he's laid up in hospital. They expect him to be there for at least a few days.'

She would rather have had him dead. Only that would have given her permanent freedom from fear. But a few days was better than nothing. It was a blessed reprieve. It gave her a wonderful sense of relief; she could have wept tears of gratitude. It wasn't just in her mind either. Every muscle in her body was unexpectedly soothed. She relaxed as she never remembered relaxing before. It was sweetly intoxicating. She couldn't stop herself smiling.

'Come on through to the kitchen and have a bite of lunch. Jennifer's out in the garden. I'll call her in.'

She left the room with a song in her heart. Tonight she would make the most of her freedom. She would go to the meeting of the flower-arranging club in Kilmardinny. She would walk home alone in the dark knowing that she was perfectly safe. She loved a stroll on a lovely summer's evening. It seemed so long since she'd had the peace of mind to enjoy such a pleasure.

'Will you be back before evening, Robert?' she asked after lunch when he was leaving for Monteith Row. 'To babysit, I mean. I thought I might go to my flower-arranging club.'

'Yes, sure.' He stopped in the hallway and turned towards her. 'Sophie, what has happened between Andrina and me needn't affect your relationship with her. She's your daughter. Your first loyalty ought to be with her.'

Sophie's face hardened.

'She no daughter of mine.'

'That's nonsense and you know it. If McPherson can still keep in touch with her, so can you.'

'How can you condone – '

'I'm not condoning anything. I feel like . . . No, better not go into how I feel. The point is, she's your flesh and blood. You don't have to consider my feelings. I'll be OK.'

'No doubt she will too,' Sophie said bitterly. 'She's always managed to get what she wanted. And without a thought for anyone else. Don't ever mention her name to me again.'

He hesitated, then just said, 'See you later.'

The front door clicked behind him and it took her a few

minutes, standing alone in the hall, to recover from the mention of Andrina's name. Then slowly her feelings of safety and relaxation returned. She went through to the kitchen to chat to Jennifer. She cleared the table and washed the dishes. Then Jennifer taught her a song she'd learned at school before the holidays. They sang it together. After a while they both went along to the shops.

The line of terraced houses was quieter than usual. Mr and Mrs Pemberton were at St Andrews on holiday. In fact, nearly everyone was away either on business or on holiday this week. Mrs Hawthorn and herself were the only ones left at home. Again Sophie felt glad that Robert was going to be staying with her. Then she remembered that there was no need, not for a few days anyway, to feel nervous about being alone. Bernard O'Maley was confined to a hospital bed.

If only, she thought, she could feel like this all the time. It made her realise what stress she had been under and for how long. As soon as McPherson returned, she would have a serious talk with him. She would force him to do something, anything. An idea occurred to her – why couldn't he threaten O'Maley with cutting him off from whatever lucrative business he was obviously putting O'Maley's way, threaten him that if he didn't stop following and frightening his wife . . . One way or another, she would make McPherson do this. She had to. Taking a positive outlook like this cheered her. She allowed Jennifer to help set the table for an early dinner. Robert arrived laden with a suitcase, briefcase and sports bag.

'Just put them upstairs in your room and then come straight back down and get something to eat,' she told him.

Later, after the dishes were washed, the kitchen cleared and Jennifer was in bed, Sophie set off for Kilmardinny. She told Robert she'd be home by 10.30.

'I'll have the kettle boiling ready to make us a cup of tea,' he said. She smiled and waved him goodbye.

For all his faults, Robert was a good man, she thought as she made her way along Drymen Road. All right, he didn't believe her any more than McPherson did. That had become sadly obvious when he too had tried to persuade her to see a psychiatrist. Nevertheless, he always did his best to be kind.

Just before turning into Manse Road, she glanced across at the bungalows. There was no sign of life at the Cairns window but she detected a twitch of the curtains in the bungalow next door. Just then a car drove into Laura's driveway. It looked like the doctor's car. Had Derek taken a turn for the worse? she wondered. It would be a blessing if he would just slip away. She'd said that to Laura more than once. She would phone her the moment she returned from Kilmardinny to see what had happened and if she could do anything to help. At the club they were very short of people – so many members were on holiday – and it was important to have the flowers ready in baskets and vases to take round to the church first thing in the morning. In the afternoon, the television people would be arriving and setting up all their equipment. It was very exciting. There was going to be a special service and they had to get the floral arrangements done, even though they were much later than usual in finishing.

Sophie stayed on last to clear up and it was quite dark when she left Kilmardinnny House and began walking towards home. She felt peaceful and happy.

Suddenly she became aware of footsteps behind her. She turned just in time to see a shadow flick from the pavement to blend in with the blackness of the bushes. Someone was following her. She couldn't believe it. For a brief moment, her mind refused to accept it. She felt confused. Then blind terror took over. She began to run. Footsteps came after her, fast as the wind.

Chapter Sixty-Two

By a quarter past eleven, Robert had begun to worry. He felt he couldn't leave Jennifer alone in the house to go and look for Sophie. He stood on the pavement and peered along the street. The terrace was in darkness except for one lighted window at the other end. That, he knew, would be Mrs Hawthorn watching the late-night film. Sophie had told him that since she'd become a widow, Mrs Hawthorn suffered from insomnia.

'She just hates having to go to bed, poor woman.'

Indeed, one of the times he'd met Mrs Hawthorn she'd told him so herself. He decided to go along and ask her to stay with Jennifer until he walked up to Kilmardinny to see if he could find Sophie.

He called through Mrs Hawthorn's letterbox after ringing the bell, so that she would know who it was and not be frightened.

She opened the door at once.

'Robert, is something wrong?'

'Well, I'm hoping not. Sophie said she'd be back from the flower club by 10.30 at the latest. I'm beginning to feel worried.'

'Oh, my goodness, yes. She definitely should have been back long ago.'

'I wondered if you'd go along and sit in Sophie's – you could watch the film there. Jennifer's sound asleep but I don't want to leave her in case she wakes up and calls out or something . . .'

'Oh, certainly, Robert. I'll just get my keys and fling on a coat.'

As soon as he'd seen Mrs Hawthorn into the house, he retraced his steps along Drymen Road. It was not long after he turned into Manse Road that he heard the screams. He broke into a run, shouting as he did so when he saw struggling figures in the distance. Immediately his powerful voice exploded through the air, one of the figures melted away and disappeared. He reached a hysterical Sophie in a matter of minutes.

'It's me, Sophie. You're all right. You're safe.' He made to run past her into the trees on the other side of the road but Sophie caught him and clung to him. 'Don't leave me, Robert. Don't leave me. Oh please, please, don't leave me.'

Her voice had a strange rasping sound and she was beginning to choke and cough.

'All right. Don't try to say any more just now. I'll take you home and then I'll phone for the police.'

It wasn't until he got her back to the house that he saw the bruise marks on her neck. There was also a break in the skin in the shape of a fingernail and from it blood was trickling down to make scarlet patterns on her white chiffon scarf.

'Oh, Mrs McPherson.' Mrs Hawthorn ran to comfort the distraught Sophie and help her into a chair.

'Make her a cup of tea,' Robert said. 'I'll phone for the police and the doctor.'

'He was going to kill me.' Sophie was violently shivering.

'Don't try to talk just now, Sophie. Wait until you calm down a bit and then you can given the police a full description.'

'I didn't see his face. He grabbed me from behind. But I know who it was. I wasn't able to think at the time. But now I remember the smell.'

'The smell of what?'

'Of cats. And that sour horrible smell he always has.'

'You mean . . .' Robert stared at her for a minute. 'That guy that lives next door to Laura and Derek Cairns?'

He had a sudden pang of concern for Laura's safety.

'I know it was him. It's been him all the time, Robert, and I never once suspected. I was so certain it was Bernard O'Maley.'

A new urgency possessed Robert. Something had to be done about Pritchett. And fast.

'God knows what the police will make of what you've just said. Is smell considered a valid means of identification, I wonder?'

'It *was* him, Robert. I'm certain of it.'

'I know. I'm just hoping that the police will have enough to go on.'

'I was tearing at his hands, trying to get them off my neck. I'm sure he must have scratches. I clawed behind me at his face as well.' She shuddered. 'His face was close to my head. I could feel his breath on my skin. Smell it too.'

'Don't upset yourself any more. It's going to be all right. It's all over.'

He forced himself to wait until the police and the doctor came before escaping to go and check that Laura was all right. The murder victims had all been elderly women but still . . . He restlessly paced the room while Mrs Hawthorn and Sophie drank tea to calm themselves down.

'It's all over. You're going to be all right now', Robert repeated and Sophie smiled at him and nodded.

The doctor arrived, examined Sophie and put a dressing on her neck. Then he told her, 'I'm going to give you something to calm you, Mrs McPherson. Take one just now and another . . .'

Sophie took a deep breath.

'No thank you, doctor. I don't want tranquillisers any more. There was a time when I needed them but as Robert has said, it's all over now. I'll take one of my sleeping tablets to help me tonight, and that's all.'

'You were becoming seriously addicted, Mrs McPherson. I couldn't allow that. But tonight you need help.'

She shook her head thinking, I've needed it all my life but no one has ever succeeded in helping me. Tonight, certainly, she was grateful to Robert. Without doubt, he had saved her life from a maniac, a murderer, a devil incarnate. But there would be no last-minute rescue from the devil within herself. She would have to face that never-ending struggle alone. She knew that long, long ago her life had been destroyed. But she wondered, just for one hopeful moment, if the saving of her tonight could be a sign, a kind of rebirth, a chance to wipe the slate clean and start again. Then she smiled sarcastically to herself. She should be so lucky.

The doctor was speaking to Robert.

'You'll not have heard about Mr Cairns?'

Sophie said, 'I thought I saw your car at their door earlier on. I was going to phone Laura.'

'I think I'll go along and make sure that she's all right.' Robert rose but the doctor put a detaining hand on his arm.

'Leave it just now. I've given her a sedative. She was very upset. Her husband died earlier this evening.'

Sophie sighed. 'A blessed release for both of them. The poor man had no life at all.'

'I believe you've been very good to them, Mrs McPherson. Mrs Cairns told me. I remember she once said she'd be eternally grateful to you.'

'I must find out about the funeral.'

Sophie's mind was already making all the arrangements, compiling the menu for the funeral meal. She would do the catering, of course. There wouldn't be many guests. Poor Laura had no one except her, but some people in the church would want to pay their respects. She'd go along to the bungalow first thing tomorrow – or today, as it was now.

After midnight already and the police had still to arrive. She tutted impatiently and was just about to complain about their tardiness when there was a loud ring at the doorbell.

While Robert went to answer it, Mrs Hawthorn lowered her voice to try to hide the tremor of excitement.

'Just think, Mrs McPherson. You're the first one that's survived the Glasgow murderer. You'll be the means of actually catching him. What a relief it will be to everyone to know that, thanks to you, we can now all sleep safe in our beds – '

She stopped when the police entered the room.

Robert was surprised at how quickly Sophie seemed to have recovered. She was an amazing woman. He was impressed at how, despite her ordeal, obviously still in pain and having difficulty with her voice, she answered the police questions with thoughtfulness and clarity. She even offered them a cup of tea and sympathised with their anti-social working hours. But his thoughts were still with Laura. The doctor insisted she would be sound sleep by now. But still . . .

*

Laura felt numb. Earlier she'd wept. She'd still been weeping when the doctor arrived. But now she felt dazed. She looked at the tablets the doctor had given her. She supposed she'd better take one. Perhaps with a drink of hot milk. She wandered through to the kitchen and poured milk into a saucepan. Back in the sitting-room she was just about to take the tablet when she thought she heard something outside. It was very late and dark. At this time of night, Bearsden was usually silent and asleep.

Perhaps it was one of Mr Pritchett's cats. There were always some of the animals creeping around the place.

Peering out the side window she was startled to see by the faint light of one of the street lamps the shadowy form of Mr Pritchett. What a time of night to be out looking for one of his cats! Unexpectedly, a police car drew up. On seeing it, Mr Pritchett sped away, out of her line of vision. He was rapidly followed by two burly policemen. Laura was still standing, transfixed and confused, when a few minutes later the policemen returned with Mr Pritchett gripped between them and disappeared round the front of the bungalow.

For decency's sake Robert tried to quell the surge of hope in his heart after hearing about Derek's death. He decided not to risk phoning Laura in case his voice betrayed him so he sent a formal note of condolence with Sophie, who was toing and froing between the bungalow and the terrace organising the funeral. Mr Pritchett had been taken into custody. Further evidence had been found in his house, and of course Sophie had put up a good fight. He was covered in scratches. Amazing woman! She actually seemed in her element. She was the heroine of the hour. Even the minister had spoken about her courage and commitment, her never-failing service to her fellow human beings in their hour of need.

It was in all the papers. Robert wondered if Andrina would get in touch. But, as far as he knew, there had been no word. This puzzled him. After all, her mother had suffered a terrifying attack. But of course, as Sophie had once said, Andrina was totally selfish. She cared for no one but herself.

He doubted if she'd even got in touch with Bernard to see

how he was. Rapidly his mind switched off any thoughts of his one-time, so-called friend.

Probably Bernard and Andrina deserved one another. They could rot in hell together for all he cared.

Chapter Sixty-Three

Every room in the flat was oppressively quiet. Andrina wept in the silence after Robert had packed his bags and left. Not because she had lost him but because she was alone and frightened. The bleeding had stopped, but she still felt weak and in shock. She couldn't bear to be on her own.

Shaking with anger as well as fear, her mind searched for people to blame. She hated Bernard who had seduced her, taken years of pleasure from her and then blamed her when things began to go wrong for him. He all but physically threw her out of his life. Not even content with that, he'd blackened her character, shouted obscenities for all to hear. She'd never forgive him for that. Never trust him again as long as she lived.

She hated Robert. She hated the looks of disgust he'd given her, the obvious lack of caring in his eyes. When had he ever cared about her? He'd always spent more time and trouble with his precious pupils than his own wife and child. A right do-gooder, always searching for books for Derek Cairns, while her mother did her so-called Christian best for Laura Cairns.

Memories came crowding back to Andrina of other good works her mother had done, especially soon after she'd been 'saved'. When Andrina was still a child Sophie had filled the Dumbarton Road flat with people, including ironically enough any neglected or abused children of the neighbourhood. Tough, snotty-nosed little boys called her 'Aunty Sophie'. They were made a fuss of and sat up on the draining board beside the sink at the kitchen window. They had their noses blown, their faces scrubbed, their hands washed. They were told what good boys they were. They were given a bag of black-striped balls or jelly babies.

Andrina had been darkly jealous of them then and she looked back now with equally strong emotion. The boys were usually angelic in her mother's presence but outside the house, the language of even the youngest could be foul. One little boy, when they met on the stairs, used to spit on her. He was one of her mother's special favourites. But no matter how good Andrina tried to appear, it never merited the conscientious attention and concern that her mother gave to strangers.

Robert and her mother made a right pair. Thick as thieves they were. She hated her mother most of all. She wished the man who had attacked Sophie had succeeded. Where was the justice in life when such a man succeeded in killing five innocent elderly ladies in Glasgow, but failed with one woman in Bearsden, the only one who deserved to die? Her mother had ruined her life right back as far as she could remember and beyond. Andrina trembled with indignation and anger.

The newspapers said Sophie had put up a tremendous fight for her life. They kept talking about her fighting spirit. Well, she could have some fighting spirit too. She'd show them. She'd show them all. She'd find a job, start a new life. She'd once worked in one of the biggest and most fashionable stores in Glasgow and she could do it again. She could find new interests, make new friends.

Immediately the thought seized her, she felt excited by it. She stopped sniffling, blew her nose, and dried her eyes. Then she went through to the bathroom and showered and powdered and perfumed her body. She took extra care with her makeup and the brushing of her auburn cascade of hair. Then she dressed in a lacy bra, a ribbon of a suspender belt and lacetopped stockings, before wriggling into an emerald green suit that clung provocatively to her body. It made her eyes brighter and more sparkling green than emeralds. She stepped into high-heeled shoes, then gazed at herself in the mirror. She pouted her lips, fluttered her lashes, widened her eyes. She looked good. She would take strength from that.

Bernard had to get it over with, once and for all. His flesh wound had healed but his conscience still hurt. He determined to go to face Robert at the karate club, accept the punishment that he deserved. The bullet had failed to kill him – now

Robert was welcome to finish the job. His 'what the hell' attitude had never been stronger. Yet, as he approached the gloomy prison-like exterior of Sinnieglen School, he was steeling himself, hardening his muscles, clamping his jaws. He even walked with his usual aggressive, shoulder-hitching swagger.

He arrived as the junior class was drawing to a close and made his way across the back of the hall, aware of Robert's clear, alert eyes following him.

Bernard was never afraid of physical confrontations but he felt clammy sweat sheen his chest and stomach as guilt and self-loathing washed over him. He regretted nothing about his love for Andrina except that it had meant the betrayal of the one man who had stood by him, guided him, and helped him drag him from the gutter to success. With a final tug of his frayed black belt, he strode over to the dojo.

Robert watched as Bernard entered the hall and started a ferociously demanding warm-up routine. Finally, beaded with sweat, strong face flushed with effort and hair plastered to his skull, Bernard knelt at the side of the hall waiting for recognition. Robert studiously ignored him. He left him in isolation at the edge of the class for some minutes while he explained a particular technique to the others. Finally, with a peremptory nod of his head, he acknowledged Bernard's existence. Bernard bowed his head fully to the floor and then, with one explosive bound, leapt straight to his feet and ran to his place in the class.

For the rest of the session, Bernard drove himself unmercifully in his efforts to expunge his remorse and sadness, the plethora of emotions that swirled around him, the thoughts that kept hammering at him. He had lost the two people that he'd loved and respected. What price success and money if he didn't have love and friendship? Eventually, sheer exhaustion, the repetitive moves and the rhythmic staccato shouts in Japanese from Robert allowed his brain to switch off its turmoil, and find blankness. It was a sort of peace.

The class drew to a close and partners were called to finish, as usual, in sparring practice. Robert called over to Bernard and they bowed, ready for the fight. Bernard lauched himself forward in a suicidal attack, leaving glaring gaps through which Robert could punish him for his betrayal. Instead, Robert, with icy control, only touched him gently time and again. As they fought, Robert realised Bernard's guilt but did not respond to the bait. What good would it do? His state of control was in charge, helping him reason. But he also felt bereft of emotion, drained and empty. Not because of the adultery – he'd long ago got used to that. Anyway, Andrina had been a stranger to him for years. No, it was the loss of trust that affected him. The betrayal chipped away at his idealism. It shook the foundations that anchored him and allowed him to cope with the raucous children, the sullen insolence, boredom and arrogance that he was faced with every day of his teaching life. He had dozens of Bernards, or potential Bernards, here, in this very room.

Yet, despite everything, he still couldn't truly convince himself that they weren't worth it.

The fight finished. He and Bernard bowed and shook hands.

The funeral of Derek Cairns was well attended, mostly by friends who had known him before his disability. There was even an ex-pilot who had flown in a Spitfire with him during the war and had read of the death in the *Herald* obituary column. After the service in the church, and the burial, everyone went back to the bungalow for the buffet meal that Sophie had prepared; there were too many people to have accommodated a sit-down meal.

Laura was quietly dignified as she spoke to the attenders and thanked them for coming to pay their last respects. Hardly a word passed between her and Robert.

He felt sad, uncertain, worried. Yet, of course, what could be said? When at last everyone shook hands with her and murmured their last condolences it came to his turn and, just for a second, he held her soft hand in his. It was painful not being able to hold her in his arms. Laura withdrew her hand but just before closing the door she said gently, as she'd once said long ago, 'One day at a time, Robert.'

He nodded before turning away.

They'd always known that there was a time and a place for everything.